TROUBLE WILL FIND ME

A Max Strong Thriller

MIKE DONOHUE

ALSO BY MIKE DONOHUE

MAX STRONG/MICHAEL SULLIVAN PREQUELS

Sleeping Dogs

The Devil's Angel

MAX STRONG THRILLERS

Shaking the Tree

Bottom of the World

Hollow City

Trouble Will Find Me

Burn the Night

Crooked Prayers

SHORT STORIES

October Days

For my Dad –

If you hadn't said the first one was readable,
there wouldn't have been anymore.

CHAPTER ONE

The hammer banged against his hip as he walked up the neatly laid brick path. It hung differently from his belt than his normal tools. Given a choice, he was partial to a two-piece hammer with a hickory handle. For long days and big projects, he found it muted the vibrations and lessened fatigue. But this would not be a long day, so he'd made the lengthy trip to the big Home Depot in Charlottetown back in the spring and bought a cheap one-piece steel hammer. He was confident it would get the job done.

Later, he would wonder if he should have burned the house down. But, standing in the kitchen with the hammer, he'd felt the fury that he'd lived with for decades rise in him. Burning everything to ash would send a message, but it wasn't the one he needed to send.

She finally needed to be heard, too. That was the whole point. He wasn't even sure they saw his first attempt. It might have been too subtle. The rain might have washed it away. Or the incompetent police may have stepped on or obscured it. He almost laughed. Wouldn't that be ironic? They had all worked so hard for so many years to hide it and now, when he puts it out there for the world to see, it gets wiped out by accident.

No, he would make damn sure they wouldn't miss this one.

Burning it to cinders might be the smart way to save himself, but he knew that he wasn't playing a long game. He only had one actual goal left: to call those responsible to account. To pluck away their masks and reveal their true faces. Then let the true judgment come. Let the Lord weigh their hearts. There would be no more hiding.

He stepped up and knocked on the door.

He wiped the blood and strands of hair on his pants and slipped the hammer back into his belt. He would need it again. He stepped around the body. The man's leg twitched. He'd given him a good wallop, felt the skull pop like the skin of an overripe tomato, but he wasn't dead. He'd probably even survive if he received medical attention soon, but that wasn't going to happen. Pretty reached down and grabbed the man's collar and dragged him down the hall. The man gave a soft groan and a trickle of blood ran down one ear and smeared across the floor as Pretty pulled the body behind him.

Pretty hadn't been expecting the man to be home at this hour. He usually wasn't. He hadn't been the two previous times Pretty had been inside. Or the times Pretty had sneaked past the property in the last week. He'd always been away. Pretty assumed the man was at his office. The surprise must have shown on his face, too, because the man waved a hand when he first opened the door.

"Hello. Pretty, right? Don't mind me. Somehow, I picked

up a terrible head cold. Can you believe that? In the middle of summer? Nothing worse than having a fever in August. C'mon in. I'll stay out of your way." He turned and started back into the house. "So, what does she have you doing today, anyway? She didn't mention you were coming by."

Pretty glanced back over his shoulder. The sprawling house was isolated up on the bluff and he didn't spot anyone or anything moving nearby. This was unexpected, but it didn't change the plan. He stepped inside and raised the hammer.

The hardest part so far had been getting the man to stay still. He smiled briefly at the absurdity of trying to get an unconscious person to sit still. He pulled the man up onto a wooden kitchen chair only to have him slump back over and topple to the floor with a heavy thud anytime he let go to grab the rope. Eventually, Pretty had to move the chair, and the man, into a spot where the two parts of the granite kitchen counter came together in an L-shape. The countertops held the unconscious man upright. Pretty then secured the man's wrists and ankles to the chair spindles.

Finished with the last knot, Pretty stood back and considered the man. His eyes remained closed; he hadn't made a noise since Pretty had lugged him down the hall. His breathing was shallow but steady. Out of curiosity, Pretty reached a hand out to the man's neck and felt for a pulse. It was thin and thready. The blood that had trickled out of his ear had stopped and dried along his neck and jawline. Pretty felt nothing. The man was just a bag of bones. He left him slumped against the designer cabinets and went to explore the rest of the house. He still needed more information.

· · ·

The first name had shown up like a thunderbolt out of the blue. When he thought about it, and he thought about it a lot, it felt like the hand of God had reached down and slapped him across the face to wake him up and snap him out of his stupor.

He'd caught whispers and furtive glances for a time when he was growing up, but all that had stopped now that he was a grown man. He hadn't forgotten, though; at least he tried not to. But he worried he was losing her all over again. He had trouble remembering her face. He started doubting his memories. Was this real or was his mind filling in the gaps? It felt like one more cruelty on top of everything else.

For a long, long time he didn't know what to do about it. Didn't know if there was anything he could do. He didn't know how to start. It made him angry, and he felt like he might drown in the bubbling rage that roiled his guts. And then? God provided. He delivered a name. He gave him a place to start. Not all of it. But maybe enough. Pretty might not be the smartest man, but he was very stubborn. Give him a start and he would damn sure finish it.

He walked through the living room. One entire wall was floor-to-ceiling windows that looked out over the dark water of the Northumberland Strait. If he just wanted the bodies to disappear, it would be a simple thing to carry them to the edge of the bluff and drop them over. Unless he was unlucky with a trawling fishing or lobster boat, the odds were good they'd never be found.

He looked away from the windows and scanned the shelves full of framed photos and abstract art that hung on the walls. Pointless trinkets. He moved deeper into the house. It was unlikely he'd find anything helpful out on display. What he needed would be hidden. If it was here at all. He passed through a dining room and then a hallway that took him into an unfamiliar part of the house. The previous times he'd been inside, he'd largely stayed in the kitchen or the patio. He passed a bathroom, a guest room, then a home gym. He stopped in the gym's doorway, momentarily dumbstruck by the racks of weights, Nautilus machines, and cardio equipment all reflected twice in the wall-to-wall mirrors. Somehow this display of wealth struck him more than the custom kitchen or pricey views of the Strait. It all felt so wrong. An entire room purely for hubris.

The next room was a study. Unlike the rest of the house, with its expansive windows, blonde furniture, and colorful splashes of art, this room felt distinctly masculine and out of step with the rest of the house. There was a massive oak desk with dual computer monitors set up to the left and a multiline phone and various Lucite knick-knacks on the right. A short, pudgy filing cabinet sat next to the desk. Bookshelves lined one wall. Pretty walked over and examined the titles. Nothing he recognized, of course, but they didn't appear to be for show. The spines were cracked and worn from being read. A mix of business, technology, and biography titles. A large 50-gallon fish tank, an inlaid bar area, and a door were on the opposite wall. He pushed open the door with a knuckle. A small half-bath.

He took a pair of thin gloves from his pocket, pulled them on, and went about searching through the desk. He nudged the mouse that sat near the monitors and both screens lit up, but the computer was password protected. He dismissed it and focused his attention on the desk drawers. The search didn't take long. There was little paper. From what he could tell, the documents all related to the house: insurance, warranties, service contracts. The bottom drawer had some personal financial documents. Again, not his specialty, but he found the balances interesting. Not what he would have expected.

He knelt by the filing cabinet. It was locked. Nothing

heavy duty and probably only meant to keep out a child or the prying eyes of an assistant. He pulled his Leatherman tool off his belt. Using the small knife, he had it open in thirty seconds. Both drawers were stuffed with folders, papers, CDs, and a box of thumb drives. He picked out a few folders at random. Unlike the desk, these documents were all for the man's business. Pretty doubted there was anything that would help him, and it could take days or weeks to go through everything on the off chance he might find a name he could use. There were better uses of his time. He slid the drawers shut.

He left the office and walked to the end of the hallway into the master bedroom. A king-sized bed dominated one wall with matching nightstands on either side. A low modern dresser and an upright chest of drawers filled out the room. A door opened to the left, probably a closet. This felt right. If what he needed was in the house, he thought it would be in this room. People hid things they wanted to keep safe close to where they slept.

He started his search with the nightstands. He didn't find it in either one, but he did find it in the closet. She'd hidden it, but not all that well and not all that cleverly.

He went back into the kitchen and sat down to wait. He didn't think it would be long now.

He was right. The automatic garage door sounded ten minutes later, and the bright white headlights of her Mercedes swept across the room as she pulled up the drive.

A minute later the door rattled, and she called out, "Topher, are you awake? How are you feeling?"

Pretty thought the answers to those questions were likely *sort of* and *really crappy*. Christopher Arnsfeld, Topher to his friends, had briefly woken when Pretty had returned to the kitchen. The man's mouth moved, but no sounds came out. Pretty could see the pupil of his right eye was large and dilated, the sclera a bright red from burst blood vessels.

He'd dragged the bound man back over to the kitchen table and patted him genially on the shoulder. "Almost over."

Arnsfeld's head had turned, though his right eye drifted out of focus. This time he managed a scratchy sound. "Why?"

"That is a long story. You are only a short footnote." Pretty dropped the book on the table between them and took a seat himself. "Wrong place, wrong time. Terrible time to pick up a cold."

Arnsfeld stared at him for a long time. Pretty looked back. He could see death coming for Topher Arnsfeld even if Pretty wasn't there to help him along. Apparently, the man could feel it, too, or he read something in Pretty's face.

"Go to hell," he said before he passed out again.

"No need. Been living there a long time now."

The woman was carrying two brown paper shopping bags and didn't notice her husband or Pretty right away. She put the bags down on the counter and turned, about to call out again, and saw them. She gasped, one hand flying to her mouth. Then she rushed to her husband's side.

"Topher! Topher, are you okay? What happened?" Then she saw the rope, or her brain just caught up. She looked over at Pretty. "What did you do?"

"Hit him in the head with a hammer."

"What? Why? What's going on?"

She bent over her husband. Pretty could see he was still breathing. She didn't know what to do with her hands. They flitted around his face, wanting to comfort, but not wanting to do further damage.

Pretty stood. "I'm here about this." He pushed the small

black leather book a few inches across the table. He watched
her eyes recognize it and then her shoulders tighten up
before slumping, her entire body going loose. Was that resig-
nation? Acceptance? It was a long time to live with a lie.

Pretty slipped the hammer from his belt.

CHAPTER TWO

Max would remember two things about the day all the trouble on the island started: the weather and the foot.

The weather was perfect. It was already August, but Max was learning everything came to Canada slowly, even summer. From first light, the sky had been a deep cerulean where it became difficult to discern where the Atlantic water met the horizon. It was a day that made you want to use the word cerulean.

Working in short sleeves, hauling traps and setting bait with a salt-water kissed breeze on his skin, Max felt good. It felt like a day designed to keep away the demons. For the first time in weeks, since he'd made it over the border and onto the island, Max realized he felt different. No voices in his head. No ghosts pestering him. No second guesses. It took him a moment to pinpoint the emotion, but he realized he felt at peace.

Then, on the next line, he hauled up the foot.

. . .

He'd been a helmsman on The Miss Ashely for six weeks. The Miss Ashely was a 42-foot Nauset lobster boat docked out of Prince Creek that was pushing 25 years old but with a solid fiberglass hull and an engine that Archie claimed he'd rebuilt by hand the previous winter. Max didn't know if this was true or not; he'd learned in their short time together that Archie liked to talk and sometimes embellish his stories. Archie believed this prerogative came with a fishing license.

Max had been clueless at the start. Despite growing up within a mile of the ocean in Boston, he'd rarely been on any boat in his life, but Archie had been desperate. All the experienced deckhands had been signed for the season. Archie's previous guy had been with him for three years, finished his apprenticeship, and was waiting on his own license when he had a momentary lapse of concentration, stepped on a line while they were dropping pots, and went overboard. He'd survived but had broken his ankle and torn up the ligaments in his right knee. He was out of commission for at least six months.

There were two lobster seasons on Prince Edward Island, each lasting approximately 60 days. The first ran from May till the end of June, and the second from August until October. For the captains, it was a mad, frantic dash to make the bulk of their annual income in a handful of weeks. With the price of lobsters falling for a decade now, the margins were increasingly thin.

Archie and The Miss Ashely had been fishing the southeast quadrants for over 20 years but, as Archie was fond of telling him, there were no shortcuts. A good bit of luck, but no quick hacks. You baited your traps, laid your lines, and hoped for the best.

The work was tough and demanding. But Max found that he had decent sea legs, a strong stomach, and he had never minded hard physical labor. Actually, he now appreciated any work that left him so tired by the end of the day that he had no choice but to drop into a dreamless sleep.

By 6 a.m. that fine morning with the cerulean sky, Archie had The Miss Ashely out of port and zigzagging in and out of buoys to locate his traps.

While Archie navigated, Max prepped bait. As they hit the open waters of the Strait and veered south to hug the rocky shores near Eglinton and Bay Fortune, Max slid chunks of redfish and porgies onto a bait needle, which looked like large metal BBQ skewers with an eyelet at the end, and stacked them in an empty waterproof container.

Every time Archie found one of his lines, he reached over the side and grabbed the line with a hook and fed it through a winch. Then, one at a time, a hydraulic hauler would bring the traps up and out of the water. Max was learning the sea was fickle and indifferent. One day the traps would be brimming with lobsters, pushing the capacity of the boat's storage tank. Other days, they'd call it quits early as they barely scraped more than silt up from the depths.

Today was somewhere in the middle, Max thought, the bright sunshine fueling a rare bout of optimism. As Max emptied the traps and replaced the bait, Archie measured the lobsters with a special gauge to make sure they were legal.

In just a few weeks, Max had seen some weird things come up in the traps. Strange, prehistoric looking fish. Giant hermit crabs. A disconcerting amount of trash. So, the beat-up Nike sneaker didn't exactly catch him off guard until he saw that the foot was still attached.

He jerked his hand back. "Jesus Christ!"

Archie glanced back from his spot next to the hydraulic boom. "What? What's wrong?"

"There's a foot in the trap."

"Another one?"

"Another one? What do you mean another one?"

Archie hit a button to stop the lift. He showed no signs of surprise or being squeamish. He reached in and pulled it out like it was a 3-pound keeper. The flap of fabric that covered the toe box was gone. He held it out to Max. "What do you think? Does that look like six toes or the regular five?"

"What the hell is going on, Archie? How often does this happen?"

He considered the foot and the shoe for another moment and then tossed it into an empty container in the corner. "Not that often."

"Well, that's a relief."

"But more often than you'd probably guess. I think this makes 15 or 16 in the last 15 years."

"You're kidding?"

"Nope. I'm sure the number's higher. Fifteen is only the number that have washed ashore or got stuck in traps or nets and hauled up." He must have caught the look on Max's face. "Don't get any weird or grisly ideas. There's no serial killer lurking or mass grave of plane crash victims. It's much more mundane and scientific. Most of the poor souls are suicides or drownings. We got the Continental Bridge nearby and a well-populated coastal area. Add those facts to wind patterns and the way the currents work in the Strait and you get body parts." He waved a hand at the container. "Mostly feet."

Max rubbed a hand over his face. "Why feet?"

"More science, my boy." Archie was warming to the subject. "It turns out that in water, human bodies naturally come apart at the joints, so hands and feet often disconnect from the body after soaking in the sea. The sneakers usually keep them afloat. I bet," he paused and walked over to the foot. "Yup, this isn't a running shoe. Looks more like a fancy hiking sneaker. Heavier plastic. Maybe a steel plate in it to protect against rocks on the trails. Didn't float."

Max could only shake his head. "I just … I don't know. It's about the last thing I expected to be in a trap."

"Do this long enough and you see a bit of everything. I once brought up a guy's wallet, bills, credit cards, and ID still inside, 5 miles offshore. We'll let the chief know about the foot when we get back." He walked back to the lift. "Ready?"

Max nodded, and Archie hit the button to get back to work.

Archie said once he could make a year's pay in less than 6 months of fishing and lobstering. Those days were gone, but a life on the water is something that Archie swore he'd never give up. "This is my way of life and I love doing it. And I will keep on doing it until I can't do it anymore," he told Max when he explained the harsh economics on their first day.

Inside the shelter of the harbor's rocky jetty, Achie steered the boat to the floating dock where his lobster dealer did business. Max offloaded the catch from the tank onto pallets. One of the dealer's guys hauled the pallets over to the scales.

Despite the beautiful weather, it was not a great day. The catch was a little under 300 pounds. Not the worst day, but Archie looked a little deflated by the total. The day's price per pound was written on a nearby whiteboard: $2.74. Archie needed to catch at least 150 pounds each day just to cover gas and bait. Unlike the price of lobster, fuel and bait costs kept rising. Archie would probably clear about 200. A sternman's cut was twenty percent of the net, so Max's working day was worth forty bucks.

Still, finished with the dealer, back in their own berth, hosing off the deck and hanging up his waterproof bibs, Max felt good. His muscles ached, but in an agreeable, wrung out way.

Max moved the damp bibs aside, slotted his boots into the narrow locker, and closed the door. He was looking forward to a cold beer and a shower, maybe a game of chess with Mose, if he was around, as he climbed the short steps out of the hold to the deck and spotted the police car fishtail into the lot with full lights and siren.

Max felt his stomach roll over. His mouth suddenly felt like he'd been chewing on cotton. Max glanced up and down the dock but saw nothing out of the ordinary. No apparent emergency that would require this response. The police car straightened out and headed right for him.

Unless he was the emergency.

CHAPTER THREE

Max climbed out of the passenger seat of the truck and gave the side panel a light tap. Archie raised a hand as he backed down the worn, red dirt path until he hit the cracked pavement of the trailer park's cul-de-sac, then he turned the rusting truck all the way around and headed toward town with a quick bump of the horn.

Max normally would have walked back from the harbor, it wasn't far, just over a mile, but Archie had insisted. "I've got to fill up the truck so I'm going right past on my way to the station. Don't be an ass. Get in the truck."

Max walked the rest of the way down the path, between the two sugar maples and low scrub brush that set his trailer off from the rest of the park on Bishop Avenue, into the small clearing that held his own trailer.

At one point, the owner had lived back here, but he'd passed away last year. His son had inherited the place and found it easier to just write a check to a management company than find another live-in manager. The son lived off-island outside Fredericton and was happy to rent the places cheaply, keep them occupied, and pocket a little extra income. Angel Court was old, most of the dozen trailers dated back to the 1970s but were well maintained. The trailers had to be to last through the island winters. Max had been living here for a month, since answering an ad in *The Chronicle*, and moving out of his efficiency motel. He hadn't regretted the choice.

His trailer was a typical, prefab, single-wide with off-white siding and small blue shutters. It had been ferried over to the island as temporary housing when the oil and gas and fishing industries were booming. Forty years later, the aging trailers were the few remaining artifacts of those boom times in Prince Creek.

A six-by-six porch, really two wooden pallets painted and nailed together, sat out front next to the steps that led up to the front door. Two old beach chairs, maybe once a set, the woven fabric of each bleached white by the sun, the metal legs crusted and rust-pocked from spending all year outside, sat on the porch. A small camp stove sat on top of a big over-turned wooden spindle, that might have once held telephone wire or coaxial cable, filled out the outside decor.

A 1970 Chevy short-box pickup was slowly disintegrating to the left of the trailer. It had once been orange with white stripes down the side, but it was hard to tell for sure through the rust, dirt, and general neglect. It had come with the cabin. The owner said he was free to use it if he got it running. Max had looked it over when he'd first arrived and then asked around. None of the current residents had ever seen it move, and one couple had lived there since Reagan was in office. Max could change a tire, a battery, the oil, and swap out spark plugs, but rebuilding an engine was way beyond him.

But maybe not beyond Mose. Prince Creek was a very small town. Word had gotten around. Max had come home from the docks one day to find a tall, wiry man with a sharp, pointed nose and a long unkempt beard drinking a beer and banging at something under the Chevy's hood. He wore a long-sleeve light blue shirt and long dark pants despite the summer sun. Dark suspenders dangled from his hips. He offered Max a beer. There were worse ways to start a friendship.

Max would soon learn that Mose was part of the Amish community that had a large and growing settlement just outside the town proper. He had lost his wife in childbirth and hadn't yet remarried. He made Mission-style furniture for a living and had an interest and talent in learning how things were put together, whether it was a tongue-and-groove joint or the exhaust valves in a modern engine. His mild eccentricities were either ignored, tolerated, or accepted by his community. Max had never asked.

"Honey, I'm home," Max said. He could see Mose leaning over the Chevy's hood now, shoulders deep into the old pickup's 8-cylinder big block engine. His jacket hung from the side mirror and a sweating bottle of beer sat on the front bumper.

"The captain chauffeuring you around now, huh? Thought you were better than that."

"Thought you were better than freeloading another man's beer while he's off at work."

"Better your beer than your woman."

"I don't have a woman."

"I noticed. Also, you know what they say about assumptions." He walked over, wiping his hands on an oil-stained rag hanging from his waist, and pointed to a cooler that sat next to one of the beach chairs. "Not your beer." He glanced down at the melting ice. "At least not for another hour or however long it takes to drink the last three I picked up on the way over. Then you are on your own."

Max dropped into the other chair. "Three? Definitely not an hour then."

They sat and drank the beers, at one point Max went inside and replenished the cooler with a six-pack from the fridge, and Max told Mose about the foot and then about the police chief showing up at the harbor to get Archie.

"You didn't know Archie's brother was the chief?"

Max definitely didn't know about Archie's relationship with the Prince Creek police chief. If he had, he might not have gone after the sternman job. With his background, he didn't need to cozy up to law enforcement in any form. It could lead to awkward questions. "Nope. I had no idea. That man can talk but rarely says much that doesn't involve fishing or lobstering. Didn't know Jermane Roy was his brother or that Archie himself was a part-time deputy."

"Everyone's got two jobs up here. Hardly anyone can make ends meet with just one."

"How can Archie be a deputy and fish full-time?"

"There isn't much crime up here that goes beyond drunks and petty crap, that the chief and D'arcy Alford and a few deputies can handle. You run into D'arcy yet?"

"Nope. Not that I know of."

"You'd know it. D'arcy's Roy's corporal. Sort of second-in-command. Bit of an officious prick but, by all accounts, he knows what he's doing."

"Chief doesn't know which way's up?"

"Didn't say that. He's not the community's favorite person, but maybe he'll rise to the occasion if he's tested. He's still relatively new. He grew up around here but left for a bit. Worked at Shepton, that's the correctional center over in Summerside. Left that. Worked some private security, I hear, before coming back here and getting himself hired as the chief."

"How'd he manage that?"

Mose shrugged. "Don't know the ins and outs. He's good at the politics, the glad-handing. He got tight with the deputy mayor and some town councilors. Enough to get the job. Just had his contract renewed, if I remember right. That's the second time. He gets to a third and inertia will kick in and he'll probably stick around for a while. I'll admit nothing has gone terribly wrong since they elected him, but he hasn't had to deal with much either."

Mose grabbed another two beers. "Last call." He popped the tops with a church-key tied to the cooler's lid with twine. "Getting back to the original question. Other than Jermane and D'arcy, there are two other constables you'll likely come across. Henry Stratton is full-time and Travis Chravette is part-time. Archie is what I'd call more of a security guard. Jermane taps him and a couple of other guys when he needs extra hands. You know, things like the Christmas parade, Old Home Week, or crowd control for fires or water main breaks. Is that what happened today? Mrs. Jarrett finally fall asleep with one of her cigars?" He sat up suddenly, the chair screeching in protest. "There wasn't a buggy accident was there?"

Max waved him off. "Not a buggy accident but I think the chief is about to get that test."

CHAPTER FOUR

"You're kidding me? Why didn't you call me right away?" Thorne Taylor stood up and grabbed his windbreaker off the seat. It was summer, but the nights cooled off considerably if the winds were blowing back across the island.

The Rink was a narrow building situated a couple of blocks off Prince Creek's main drag. Painted bright blue on the outside, it was perpetually dim on the inside. It was mostly lit by free beer signs from distributors or the two televisions mounted over the bar. An old jukebox gave off a blue and pink glow in one corner. The only thing to distinguish it from any other neighborhood dive were the photographs lining the walls showing bowling, hockey, and Little League teams going back to the 1980s. Jerry, The Rink's owner and primary bartender, might not put much into the decor, but he was a soft touch for sports sponsorship.

There was a small stage at the far end for the occasional band. Booths covered in thick red plastic went down the right. The bar and kitchen were on the left. Billiards and darts were in the back. A motley assortment of loose tables and chairs, that could be moved for dancing if the band was any good, took up the rest.

Right now, the place was half full, a lull between what made up the dinner rush and the more serious drinkers digging in their heels. Patrons occupied only four of the dozen stools lining the bar. A man and his two boys were finishing up at a four-top near the juke. Max and his group sat in Thorne's preferred front corner booth.

"I had a feeling. Redd, didn't I tell you I had a feeling. Something in the air." Thorne Taylor looked less like a newspaperman and more like a regional bank vice president. He was tall, starting to stoop slightly, with thick gray hair neatly parted but bachelor shaggy on the sides. He patted his coat pockets, didn't find what he was looking for, and moved down to his pants. He pulled a small notebook free, then started the routine again.

"Ear," Charlie said, smiling.

The town's sole reporter reached up and grabbed the nub of pencil that was permanently stuck behind one of his ears, between his teeth, or in one of his pockets. "Thanks. Hey, I wonder why you haven't gotten a call, Redd."

"I believe Burke is up in the rotation," Redd Martin replied, taking a sip of his beer. Redd was thin and spindly, with large expressive eyes under an unruly thatch of wavy, dark brown hair. Along with Burke Mulvaney and Bridget Heathers, Redd was one of three doctors who served Prince Creek and the surrounding incorporated areas north to East Point, west to St. Peter's Bay, and then south to Cardigan. Along with Duncan's Funeral Home for pickup, they also covered any necessary medical examiner duties.

"My daughter had Lilly over to Dr. Heathers for that ear again and she mentioned Burke was limping around in a big knee brace. Supposedly tore it up golfing," Charlie said.

"Ah, Christ on a cracker." On queue, Redd's cell phone

started chirping from his pocket. He pulled it out and glanced at the screen. "Number's blocked. It's either a crafty Ukrainian telemarketer or Marline." He answered. "Uh-huh. Uh-huh. Okay. Yeah, I know where that is." He disconnected, put the phone away, and glanced wistfully at his remaining half pint, then pushed it away and stood up. "C'mon, Thorne, you might as well give me a ride. The Duncans can get me back."

"So, it's true?" Taylor replied.

"It's true that Burke tore some ligaments and is prepared to milk that fact to get out of ME duties for the next few months."

"C'mon, what did Marline say? Gimme a head start."

"A head start on what? You're the only game in town. Besides, she didn't say much. I've got an address and presumably a body to declare. You can find out the rest on your own."

"Oh, I plan to. Goodnight, gentlemen. Sorry to cut our evening short." He dropped some bills on the table. "Didn't I tell you, Redd ..." Max and Charlie could hear Thorne start up again as he followed Redd toward the door.

"You made his day," Charlie Gagnon said as he watched the pair exit by The Rink's side door that led to the narrow parking lot that the bar shared with the town's second-hand shop, creatively named Second Time Around.

"I feel bad. I wasn't sandbagging him. I'm still getting used to living in this fishbowl."

"The milkman rear-ending Mrs. Coates could be front-page news." Charlie waved Max's protest down. "Don't worry about it. As Redd said, it's not like Thorne has a lot of competition. If you'd tipped him earlier, he likely would have been standing around making a nuisance of himself. At least this way he got to eat dinner."

Charlie Gagnon ran the local bookstore, which doubled as a coffee shop. He was a short fireplug of a man with a brown and white goatee under rosy cheeks and curly hair that was slowly retreating from his forehead like an ebbing tide. Max had met Charlie on his third day after moving into Angel Court. He'd cleaned and scrubbed every inch of the trailer twice and needed something else to distract his mind. He'd walked the 3 blocks down to Main Street and found Poor Charlie's Artisan Bookshop at the tail end of a very modest business district. The bookstore was in a two-story weathered pine box of a building that looked like it belonged on a western movie set until you noticed the Chinese takeout place next door and a Robin's Donuts franchise across the street.

A small cafe took up the right half of the first floor when you walked in. There was a counter and three tables in the back corner along with an old couch stretched out under the window. A local girl helped out Friday through Sunday. Charlie handled the rest himself. Opposite the coffee, spread out on tables and shelves, were the fiction titles. Non-fiction and Charlie's small apartment were upstairs. Max bought three used paperbacks that first day and was back two days later for more. That had cemented their friendship. "A reader and a repeat customer. You now have a friend for life." He'd introduced Max to Redd and Thorne soon after. The group met up occasionally for drinks or dinner at The Rink. Max was reticent at first. He had never made friends easily and didn't like lying to people, but the men seemed happy not to pry and even more happy to have a new set of ears to listen to their well-worn stories.

"Hey, Charlie, you ever hear about feet washing up on shore around here?" Max asked now.

They batted that topic around for a while and drank another round.

A little before 8 p.m., Max noticed a steady uptick in the traffic, both foot and cars, going past the bar's dingy windows, all heading northeast out of town. Charlie, his back to the door, kept talking. Max was about to comment on it when Wally Backus, a dockworker Max knew in passing, poked his head inside the door on his way past. "You guys hear? The Arnsfelds were murdered." He didn't wait for any response, just ducked back out and kept walking.

Gagnon turned and took in the street now. "You didn't say it was the Arnsfelds."

"Didn't know," Max replied. "Sheriff just said double murder out on … um … Crane Road, maybe."

"Lee Crane Avenue. It's essentially a private road. The Arnsfelds have the only house on it. Looks like everyone is heading that way. Want to go?"

Max wasn't that interested at whatever waited on Lee Crane Avenue, he'd had his fill of violence for a lifetime, but he could tell Charlie was keen on the idea. Small town, big news.

"Sure, why not?"

CHAPTER FIVE

The sky was now a bruised purple and pink as the sun faded. They cracked open the cans of beer they'd grabbed from Jerry and joined the migration toward Lee Crane Avenue. It wasn't everyone from Prince Creek, but it felt like at least half of the town's residents had heard the news and headed out for a look.

As they passed Robin's Donuts, Max said, "Hold up a second. If we're doing this, not showing up empty-handed might help." He ran inside and bought a dozen of the almost day-old donuts. He doubted the cops would taste the difference. He let the kid behind the counter pick 'em and then jogged back to Charlie on the sidewalk.

"Donuts. Really?"

"It's a cliche because they taste good."

They walked on, more people coming up from the side streets and joining the ranks. More than a few were drinking. A strange feeling in the air persisted. Almost like a party. Or a celebration. It made Max uneasy.

"Why is the name Arnsfeld familiar to me?" Max asked.

"The Arnsfeld Association. You've probably seen the sign

or driven by their headquarters. Big steel and glass box up near the East Point light."

Max snapped his fingers. "That's it. Off Route 16, right? Near Mackimmons Point. You can see the building from the water."

"That's the one."

"What do they do?"

"That's a more complicated question. Right now, if you looked it up, you'd find The Arnsfeld Association is a nonprofit research organization working on solutions to sustain our natural resources."

"Why did you say 'right now'?"

"That wasn't always the plan. Christopher Arnsfeld made big money during the first dot-com boom. Or maybe it was the second. In the early aughts before the housing thing in the US almost destroyed the world. Or so they'd have you believe."

Max had heard some of Charlie's more esoteric theories over drinks at The Rink. He could quickly get wound up, and you'd find yourself sidetracked for a half-hour wondering where you took the wrong turn.

"How'd Arnsfeld make his initial stake? Website? E-commerce?" Max asked, hoping to cut off any conspiracy tangents.

"No. I don't know the exact details or the tech, but it was something with payments. He made it easier for websites to set up and take secure payments online. Sold it for a bundle to one of the big credit cards. Visa, I think."

"He did all that from the island?"

"Hell no. He was out in San Francisco or San Jose on the West Coast with the rest of the geeks. After he cashed in, he rode out the mortgage crises with his pile of money. Bought some toys."

"And ended up on the ass end of PEI? Seems ... unlikely."

"Tell me about it. Thorne knows more than me. He's written more than a few pieces on Arnsfeld over the years. If I remember correctly, the story is that his parents brought him up here for vacations when he was a kid."

"Not buying it?"

"Not to speak ill of the dead, but I got the impression that Arnsfeld liked money and attention. I think he saw the cheap land up here and saw an opportunity to be a savior. He'd bring his piles of cash and his geek creds and build a little tech empire on the island."

"Build a legacy."

"A legacy where everyone he saw every day would need to kiss his ring."

"You sound more than a little bitter. I'd think a pile of cash, no matter who it came from, would help this place. Rising tide, et cetera."

"You'd be right, but Arnsfeld is a special breed of asshole. The magnanimous kind that likes to spread the wealth and, don't overlook this sleight of hand, cleverly spread the risk around. You think it's rough around here now? You should have seen it 10 years ago. With the bubble bursting down in the States, tourism was in the toilet. Fish and lobster prices were free falling. Potatoes and farming alone can't carry the economy anymore. It was lean times. And yeah, okay, at first Arnsfeld really did look like a savior, especially when he started a fund and opened it up to the island residents to invest. A lot of them looked at all of Arnsfeld's past successes and just saw dollar signs. They poured money in. Took out loans. Tapped retirement funds."

"What exactly was Arnsfeld selling?"

"Bingo. That's just it. If you really looked and asked some pointed questions, it was all smoke and mirrors. But no one wanted to ask those questions. No one wanted to expose Oz.

But the reality was that there was no product. No real plan beyond getting the money first, figure the rest out later."

"They never figured it out?"

"Not for lack of trying. Or spending. The money disappeared fast. Some people think too fast."

"You think Arnsfeld pocketed it?"

"I just know it was gone. People were wiped out. The town never really recovered."

"But Arnsfeld stayed."

"That might be a bigger mystery than his business plan, but, yeah, he stuck around. Kept a lower profile, started the charity, married a local girl, Stephanie Cote. Maybe she convinced him to stay. Maybe he just chalked it up to business being business. Win some, lose some. He was about the only one that could afford to look at it like that. You were asking about those feet washing up before? More than one person took the high dive option out of debt. It got ugly. Fast."

A half-mile later, they crossed the road. Main Street Hardware and a low-slung white building with a gray and red weather-beaten sign that simply said 'Motel' flanked the entrance to Lee Crane Avenue. Max had spent his first 2 weeks in Prince Creek in room 8. Next to the hardware store facing the street was the Pine Creek Veterinary Clinic. They passed the clinic and the road broke down, cracking and disintegrating at the edges as the fallow fields on either side crept in. They kept walking and kept climbing. The grade grew steep. Some of the less fit townies had stopped to rest. A few had seen the writing on the wall and turned back.

"Who was Lee Crane?" Max asked at one point.

"No idea," Charlie replied between heavy breaths, "but I'm not feeling very charitable toward him or her right now."

"Any idea how much farther?"

Charlie had been looking down at his shoes. He looked up now. "Not far. Never been up here, no reason, but you can see parts of the house from the harbor lighthouse. It's actually higher than the lighthouse, his ego must have loved that, on the crown of the bluff."

Another quarter mile and the grade leveled out and the road bent slightly to the left. The road improved to smooth macadam that arced in a graceful line behind a stand of transplanted trees and shrubbery that shielded the house from view. Two stone pillars with faux old-fashioned lanterns stood sentry at the end of the drive. A capital A in an ornate scripted font was carved into each pillar. An 8-foot, wrought iron fence ran off into the distance.

It all smelled like money. A lot of it.

A police car was parked across the drive between the pillars. Archie leaned against the passenger side door. He was still in his fishing gear but had donned a Prince Creek Police jacket. He gave a wave as he noticed Max and Charlie approach. "You too, huh?"

"Small town," Charlie replied as if that answered it all.

"If any more people show up, we might have to call down to the Mounties in Montague for some help."

Max spotted two more deputies around a knot of official-looking cars parked near the garage.

"I don't think you have to worry. Doesn't look like you have a mob on your hands."

Blocked by the police car from getting closer, the people who had made it to the top had drifted off into the open field opposite the fence which at least gave them a better view of the front door. Max wasn't sure what they were hoping to see. Most of them appeared confused themselves, now that they'd made it to the top but were reluctant to go immediately back down and get on with their lives. They sipped from bottles or cans, he spotted a couple of people with tell-tale brown paper bags so maybe something stronger, and milled about chatting and glancing at the house.

He turned back to Archie. On the boat, he was always unflappable. Now, he looked a little pale. "You okay?"

"Yeah." He blew out a shaky breath and rubbed his face with both hands. "No, not really. I've seen bodies before, but it's always been everyday stuff. Heart attack. Old age. Couple traffic accidents stuck with me, but nothing like this."

"Bad?" Charlie asked.

"Really bad."

"Murder-suicide?" Charlie asked.

Archie looked around. "No. I only looked quickly then got the hell out. Someone attacked them. That's the only word that fits. There's a lot of blood. A lot of ..." He trailed off and didn't finish.

"Here," Max said, remembering the bag of donuts. "You might not feel like eating, but a little sugar might actually help."

"Thanks," Archie said. He looked doubtful but took a bite of a plain glazed. "Let me run these up to the other guys."

Thorne Taylor wandered over from the adjacent field as Archie walked off to share the donuts. He had his notebook in one hand, a small digital recorder in the other. The pencil nub was back behind his ear. "Hear anything good from Archie?"

"Not sure there's anything good to hear," Charlie said.

"Don't be pedantic. You know what I mean," Thorne replied.

"No. Archie looks pretty messed up though," Max said.

"Can't get anyone on record, but I heard the killer used a hammer. It was messy. Topher was tied up."

"Jesus," Charlie said. "You think it was related to his business? The fund?"

Thorne shrugged. "What else would it be?"

"Karma," Charlie said.

"Shit, that's some rough justice," Thorne said.

"I don't see many people crying," Charlie said. They all turned and looked at the crowd, drinking and chatting.

"Charlie said you knew Arnsfeld. Had talked to him. Wrote some pieces."

"Yeah, I did some features. He was always good for a quote," Thorne replied.

"You really think he came here and fleeced the town. Stole the money. Or is that just the story everyone is telling each other?"

Up the driveway, they watched Redd Martin come out of the front door.

"I don't know that it matters, Max, fact or fiction, Topher Arnsfeld is coming out of that house in a body bag because of money. Mark my words."

CHAPTER SIX

Max and Charlie left Thorne searching for a quote and walked back down the hill into town. They didn't talk much, each concentrating on not tripping in the near-dark, lost in their own thoughts. Max was happy to get away from the scene. The sight of people laughing and getting increasingly drunk just steps from a brutal murder scene left him feeling queasy. He said good-night to Charlie at the back door to the bookshop and walked the last mile to his trailer alone. He tried to let the cooling night air clear his head of the beer and the strange hilltop vibe.

Angel Court was quiet. He spotted a few lights on behind curtained windows and could hear a television playing a baseball game. Max guessed more than one resident was up on the hill with a bottle, but maybe that was a harsh judgment on the neighbors he didn't know all that well. Hell, he didn't know more than two by name. If Mose didn't come by or he didn't see the guys at The Rink, he might go days without speaking to anyone but Archie and some crustaceans.

Inside, he tried to distract himself. He felt raw and

scraped out by the day. First, the foot and then the bodies. Going up to the Arnsfeld's house had been a mistake. It shed light on too many dark memories he'd prefer to forget. Too much blood. Too many dead.

He took three steps toward the kitchen and, a split second before his foot came down, he realized he'd forgotten about the damn floorboard. He stepped squarely on it and winced at the ear-splitting cat's-claws-on-a-chalkboard squeal that almost made his ears bleed. The loose flooring had become the annoying itch he couldn't quite scratch. He'd pulled up the carpet and tried to fix it. He'd even asked Mose to look, but they'd both come to the same conclusion. It would be more trouble than it was worth to fix.

"Just don't step on it," Mose had said.

And for the most part, he didn't. Unless he was tired or forgot. Then he contemplated wearing earplugs permanently in the house to avoid ever hearing the sound again.

On the inside, the trailer looked like what you'd expect. Bland and dated, but functional. It was 15 feet wide and 65 feet long. The door opened onto a combo living room-dining room. Archie had helped him haul a couch, coffee table, and lamp from Second Time Around to fill out the space. It still looked empty.

To the right was a compact kitchen with a sink, half stove, refrigerator, and counter space. Max ate most of his meals standing up at the counter or outside in the beach chair. A pocket door off the kitchen led to a utility closet with a stacked washer-dryer set and a toilet. A narrow passage on the other side of the kitchen led to a second bedroom. That room was empty except for a gray patterned carpet with a stain in the corner that Max hoped was only water damage.

The master bedroom was on the other side of the trailer. There was enough room for a queen-sized bed, one nightstand, a closet, two windows, and a dresser. The last room was another bathroom. This one had a shower stall, sink, mirror, and a toilet tucked into the corner.

Bland. Dated. Functional. Max realized that would also have accurately described his one-time prison cell.

He opened the fridge. He felt weary but oddly awake. He considered starting in on the beer again, that was an upgrade over a prison cell, but grabbed a bottle of water instead. He picked up the paperback mystery where it laid splayed on the coffee table. He sat on the lumpy sofa, drank the water, and finished two chapters before his back began barking. The sofa was secondhand for a reason. He stood and tried to stretch his back out. If he was honest, the bed wasn't much better. The mattress wasn't secondhand, but it was cheap.

He turned off the light and headed back to the bedroom. If Lawrence ever saw his current living conditions, he'd be appalled. And pissed. Max could hear his voice. *"Max, you've got money. More than enough. You don't want to live in a house? Fine. You want to work on a stinking fishing boat? Fine. But, God, spend some money on a decent bed."*

And all of that was true. Through various misadventures in the last few years, he had ended up with some cash. Cash that he'd handed over to his friend Lawrence to take care of. And Lawrence had generated more of it. It was what Lawrence was good at. All legal. Or as legal as stock market and real estate investing ever was. But Max was still hesitant to spend it. It might be legal now, but it hadn't started that way. He didn't have to worry about his next meal or keeping a roof over his head, but his bank balance didn't make the ghosts go away either. He still heard from them just about every day. So, he tried to make amends where he could and live a simple life that left him too tired at the end of the day to fight back. Sometimes it worked, but the past always found him and the darkness always returned. The debts he owed weren't to the living.

He lay awake in bed and stared out the bedroom window at the clear bright stars and thought about God. He wasn't sure if he believed in God with a capital G. He'd seen too many things and done too many things himself to sustain that type of faith, but he thought maybe he was coming around to a distinct type of understanding. Call it god with a lowercase G. A belief in the fundamental good of man to override and overcome all the evil that leaked into the world. Evil was something he had no trouble believing in.

He woke up without the alarm and glanced at the clock, 4:30, the usual time he woke up to grab a cup and head down to the harbor, but Archie told him last night they wouldn't be going out today. He offered to kick him 30 bucks from his constable stipend but Max declined. He officially had the day off.

He pulled a pair of clean shorts and socks from the dresser. He left the T-shirt on that he'd slept in. Why get a clean shirt sweaty? He found his running shoes stuck under the couch. He pulled them out and laced them up. Max wasn't a natural runner, he preferred hockey, but he liked having finished a run. He liked pushing himself to empty and the quiet exhaustion that followed.

He drank a glass of water, set the coffeemaker to percolate, and then hit the door. He ran through the gateway of sugar maples, out into the cul-de-sac of Angel Court, then down to Church Avenue and left toward town.

The town of Prince Creek was named after Prince Edward, the long-dead Duke of Kent and Strathearn, and the namesake of the entire island. Prince Edward was the fourth son of King George III and now known to history primarily as the father of Queen Victoria. Founded in the early 1700s by Acadians and first called Red Cliff, Prince Creek was initially a tiny fishing village. The name was officially changed to Prince Creek in 1798 and officially incorporated as part of the province in 1910. In the years since, it had grown little beyond that initial fishing village. The population hovered just above 1000 residents and the economy was still driven by fishing and agriculture and supplemented by tourism. The ferry terminal to Quebec's Magdalen Islands brought in a steady stream of visitors in the warmer months.

Max ran across Main Street/Route 2, the primary business thoroughfare through town, and turned north along the water. Most of the homes and businesses in Prince Creek didn't have the picturesque sea shanty look that appealed to tourists. It was a working town, and the homes and business reflected that work ethic. The properties were small, simple, and practical.

He picked up the pace and ran past the harbor, running down the pier to check on The Miss Ashely in case Archie had changed his mind. Other boats were prepping to head out. Max waved at a few familiar faces, but Archie's truck wasn't around, and The Miss Ashely was dark and deserted.

He jogged out of the harbor and started the slow climb uphill and out of town. He ran past a man on the sidewalk. The man wore an orange construction vest over a black sateen jacket with 'The Undertaker' spelled out on the back in cursive script. Max could see the man was wearing multiple layers of thin T-shirts over his stained navy-blue sweatpants. There was duct tape wrapped around both shoes. He was saying something in a low voice as Max passed.

Max hadn't seen many homeless in or around Prince Creek. Maybe they were drawn to the services and shelters of the larger municipalities like Charlottetown. Or maybe the rural areas had a hidden problem. He leaned into the hill now and thought about that question as his legs and lungs burned with the effort of putting one foot in front of the other. The sun was just coming up when he reached the top of the hill and passed the McLellans' roadside potato stand that marked three miles and his personal turnaround point.

He slowed to a walk and let the wheezing in his lungs ease up. He had been getting better slowly. Even with the oxygen mask and fire-resistant clothes, escaping Carter's basement had taken a toll. He'd had burns on his legs and arms, but they were mostly minor. There was permanent scarring along the shin of his left leg, but his lungs had taken the worst. The searing heat and thick smoke had ravaged the inside of his throat and chest. He'd barely been able to talk for the first week and suffered prolonged coughing fits. Lawrence had wanted to get him to a doctor for an x-ray. Max had refused. An inhaler had helped with the cough. His voice still sounded raw to his ear, but he no longer felt like a boulder was sitting on his chest during his runs.

He looked out over the water and then turned inland and looked at the clipped geometric lines of the farmland. This was the biggest change to the eastern island town in the last 50 years and perhaps a key part of sustaining it during lean times. Starting in the early 1980s, in search of more afford-able farmland, two groups of Amish settlers migrated from Ontario to the island. One group settled in Summerside on the northwest side of the island. The other group settled in Prince Creek. The community in Prince Creek had grown slowly but steadily, both through marriage and children from within, but also from other Amish settlers following them after seeing their success.

Cows and other livestock had already been let out to graze. Max could see three men moving along the edges of a field of maturing corn, occasionally stopping to pull an ear. He took one last deep breath, forcing his lungs to expand, and started the 3 miles back to town.

. . .

Twenty-five minutes later, his shirt sticking to his chest with sweat, he was back on Bishop Avenue. The place was showing signs of life. He said hello to Mrs. Johnson, the octogenarian who liked to keep a lookout on the comings and goings from the first trailer in the lot, as she tottered down to the group of mailboxes by the entrance to get her newspaper. He waved at another man whose name he hadn't yet learned, as the man yawned and climbed into a pickup truck.

He walked down the narrow dirt lane to his trailer and found Archie sitting in a beach chair drinking a large takeout coffee from Robin's Donuts. Given the bags under his eyes, Max figured he'd need more than one to make it through the day.

"There's one in the truck for you," Archie said.

"Sorry, I thought we weren't going out today. Let me just throw on some jeans and a fresh shirt. You been waiting long?"

"No, you got it right. We're not going out." He tipped his head back and looked up through the canopy of trees. "Though I wish we were. Looks like it will be as nice as yesterday. You still need to change, though. Might have time for a shower if you hurry." He checked his watch. "My brother wants to see you down at the station."

"Your brother? The chief?"

"Only brother I got."

"He say why?"

"No, he did not."

As Max went inside to change, it occurred to him that if the time came, they wouldn't come for him with sirens lit up and blaring.

They would come quietly.

They might even send a friend.

CHAPTER SEVEN

The Prince Creek police station was on Main Street, just as Route 2 transitioned to Route 16, at the far eastern end of the business district. It was the first or last thing you'd see in town. It was a low, one-story building painted a uniform government gray. There was a tall flagpole near the entrance, a 200-foot comm tower to the left, and a separate garage and maintenance bay in back.

It was busy this morning. Crammed into the small parking lot, Max counted three official Prince Creek squad cars, the chief's SUV, and four other sedans of various makes and models. Archie pulled his pickup onto the grass and left it next to the garage.

As they walked around the side of the building toward the entrance, Max asked, "How are you doing with all this?"

"Not sure. Not really thinking about it. Or trying not to. I'm just doing the next thing, you know?"

"Going to have to deal with it at some point."

"Yeah?"

"Yup."

Archie shot him a look, but when Max didn't respond, he said, "Or what?"

"Or it will deal with you."

They went through the first set of doors and Archie waved to an older woman with short blonde hair and a bright pink fuzzy sweater who sat in the comm center behind a sheet of glass. She buzzed open the interior door. "Hey, Archie."

"Hi, Marline. You on again?"

"Never went off. Harriet is off visiting her daughter in Quebec. Catelyn was in Charlottetown for her anniversary last night. She's coming in around 9 a.m. to give me a break."

Archie leaned on the counter and made quick introductions. "Prince Creek PD is a small affair. You can count the entire department on almost one hand. Chief, corporal, a full-time constable, and a part-time constable, plus a handful of guys like me that get called in sporadically if needed. There's also Marline here, plus Catelyn and Harriet to run Dispatch. There's a mechanic for the cars and a couple of guys who take care of the computers and other tech. We share the mechanic and the geeks with Town Hall. Most of the time, that's plenty of help. Last night ..." He trailed off and then stood straight. "Right, let me check in quickly with D'arcy and then we'll go back and see Jermane."

He disappeared around the corner and left Max standing at the window opposite Marline.

"So, you're the new guy?" she said. Max caught a whiff of spearmint gum.

"Excuse me?"

"You're the new guy in town." She held out a pen and indicated a book sitting on the counter. "Do me a favor and sign in there, will ya?"

"Archie tell you that?"

She waved a hand. "Nope. Just heard it around." Max

shook his head. "Don't get many good-looking, eligible bache-lors moving to Prince Creek. Word gets out. Fresh meat."

He gave her a longer look. She had to be at least 15 or 20 years older than him, though it was tough to tell in the dim light of the comm center. There was no mistaking the smile she flashed. A lot of teeth. He suddenly felt like a mouse trapped under a cat's paw.

Max picked up the pen and mumbled. "Keep forgetting this is an island."

"Small town, big mouths."

"I'll keep that in mind."

Jermane Roy was on the phone when Archie knocked on the half-open door. He raised a finger but pointed to the two chairs in front of his desk. They sat, and Max took in the room. Jermane didn't become chief for the office space. It was a twelve-by-twelve square in the far corner of the building, so at least it was quiet.

They'd walked down the hall from the comm center, past a small conference room into an open bullpen area. The bullpen had four desks, two each back-to-back. They had partitioned the back corner off with temporary walls. "D'ar-cy's little patch," Archie had whispered. There was a break room on the right just past D'arcy's cube. Max spotted a refrigerator, a round table, and a coffee pot with an inch of oily sludge left sitting on a warmer. Along the hallway, toward the chief's office, were the bathrooms and two closed doors, one on each side of the hallway. "Interrogation," Archie said, pointing to the left. "And supplies, armory, and evidence," he said pointing to the right where the door sported a 5-button Simplex keyless combination lock that Max's brain immedi-ately told him he could get through in less than 30 seconds.

The chief hung up the phone. He looked like he'd aged 5

years since Max had seen him at the harbor yesterday afternoon. Black circles hung under his eyes, and his tan uniform shirt was creased with wrinkles.

"Thanks for coming in. The both of you," he said, settling back in the chair and looking at Max. He paused, appeared to make a decision, gave a brief nod, and sat forward. "Archie tells me you've been here since April?"

You would definitely peg the pair as brothers if you put them together in the same room. They shared the same black-going-gray hair, with wide eyes and a blunt nose but, where Archie was short and blocky, Jermane was tall and lean as if he'd been stretched out like taffy as a child.

Max glanced at his boss, then back at Jermane.

"That's right."

"Where were you before that?"

"South."

"What's that mean? The US? You're American, right?"

"Dual citizenship. My mother was Canadian." A lie that Lawrence had insisted on and one that made paperwork easier.

"That's right. My brother wouldn't do anything fishy with his boat. All on the up and up, right?" He grinned and Max had a feeling this was a long and ongoing conversation that Archie wasn't particularly excited to get into right now.

"Papers all checked out," Archie said.

"Course they did."

Max still wasn't sure where this was all going, but he was starting to relax. Jermane was hinting at something, but Max knew Lawrence's papers and the legacy he'd created for Max were airtight. He bet his life, or at least his freedom, on it every day. He didn't think it was related to his past. Not really. Max was sure he'd run at least a routine background check on his alias before calling him in here. And turned up nothing. Jermane was now, in a ham-handed way, just angling for an edge, a way to control him. He likely figured that a loner showing up out of the blue on a remote island had a past he'd like left behind. He was right, but if he knew who Max really was and what he was capable of, Jermane wouldn't be kicked back in his chair playing 20 questions. This was something else. The question was, what?

Jermane pulled a pile of folders toward himself and started sorting through them. Besides the desk and the visitor chairs, there was a tall wooden bookcase filled with what looked like law or plat map books on one side of the room and two 4-drawer beige file cabinets on the opposite side. Photos of Jermane and various people in typical political glad-handing shots filled the walls. There were no windows. A double strip of fluorescent lights buzzed overhead.

Jermane found what he was looking for and handed a sheet of paper across the desk to Max.

Max took it and read: *When he maketh inquisition for blood, he remembereth them: He forgetteth not the cry of the humble—human five.*

"Psalms 9:12. Except for that last part. Human five. Not sure what that is." He handed the paper back.

"That's right," Jermane said. "You know the Bible?"

"I'm familiar with it."

"Apparently. Not a popular verse. Not according to Father White here in town."

Max shrugged. "I like Psalms."

The Bible was one of the most readily available books in prison, and he'd had a lot of time to kill. He'd read it cover to cover more than once.

"I'll be blunt with you, Max."

Max knew people that said things like that were usually lying. Most people made it to the chief of police by manipulation and usually a fair amount of lying. In polite company, it was called politics. Max wondered which end he'd be receiving, the carrot or the stick.

"I ... we," Jermane continued and extended his arms wide, "need help solving these murders. When word gets out, and it will, no matter how hard I try to keep a lid on it, I don't need people panicking or thinking about any vigilante stuff."

"You think that's likely?" Max didn't see how he'd gotten from two murders to people taking justice into their own hands.

"This is a small, small place. You must realize that by now. Grudges linger. Slights, real or just perceived, fester. This place may look like a quaint seaside town, but it's a tinder box."

Jermane, like his brother, was a talker but where Archie's stories had the joie de vivre of a raconteur entertaining the drinkers at the bar, Jermane's were overlaid with a slickness that might resonate at Town Hall but left a bad taste in Max's mouth.

"Gotta be honest, Chief. I was up there last night and I didn't get that sense. Almost the opposite. People seemed oddly happy that Arnsfeld, at least the husband, was dead."

"Yes, that might be true. Probably is true for a lot of folks. But don't be too hard on them. You weren't here when Arnsfeld went through this town like a hurricane sucking up money and then leaving people high and dry." He shuffled the folders and papers into a pile, squared up the corners. "But I'm not talking about just the Arnsfeld murders."

CHAPTER EIGHT

He pulled the bottom folder out of the stack and placed it on top. Max could see it was thicker than the Arnsfeld file, but not by much.

"Collum Hawkins. Retired lawyer. From what I understand, he was fairly prominent in town back in the 1980s and 1990s but turned into a bit of a recluse. His body was found six days ago off Sinclair Road near Norris Pond. Blunt force trauma to the back of the head with an ax."

"An ax?"

"Yup. One of the small camping-type ones."

"Jesus."

Max knew the spot. Sinclair was a single track, rutted, dirt-packed road off Route 16. He had jogged past it on his runs but never turned down it. Bent trees and thick shrubs crowded up against the edges. It wasn't overly inviting. He hadn't known there was any water nearby.

"What was he doing there?" Max asked.

Jermane shrugged. "No one knows. He had an apartment in town that he'd been renting for over 15 years. We couldn't turn up a reason he'd be out there. There was nothing on his person to indicate a reason. The pond is out of the way and not easy to get to. High school kids sometimes go skinny dipping on a dare. Some locals do a little freshwater fishing there if they're bored, but most of the time it's deserted, other than the flies and mosquitoes."

"What makes you think Hawkins is connected to what happened to the Arnsfelds?"

Jermane had been expecting the question, and Max had the sense that this entire thing was being stage-managed. He just couldn't figure out why. The chief opened the folder, selected a photo off the top, and held it out. Max took it and looked down at a close-up shot of red clay. Part of a shoulder and arm were visible, but most of the photo showed the dirt and vague markings, lines and swirls, that might have been writing next to the body. Max couldn't make anything out.

"More Bible verses?" he guessed.

"That's what we think, yes. Again, to be blunt, Hawkins was found 6 days ago but might have been killed a few days before that. We probably got lucky we found him so soon and recovered anything. As I said, Sinclair is pretty deserted even in the summer. We now think that," he pointed at the photo, "was a message similar to what we found at the Arnsfelds' but there was some overnight rain eight days ago and it washed away most of it." He took another photo out and passed it to Max. "The writing nearest the body is the clearest. The position of the body might have shielded it from the worst of the rain."

This photo was the same as the previous one, but someone had used some image manipulation to increase the contrast to make the marks more legible. It had worked no miracles. The writing, if it was that, was still just faint marks. Max shook his head. "What do you make of it?"

Jermane smiled. "Turn it upside down."

He did, and some letters and numbers became more clear.

He could make out what might be the number nine and the word God, but he wasn't sure if he was just seeing what he wanted to see.

"Okay, maybe a nine? Maybe the word God. Then something that could be 'pay' near the armpit here. You guys find anything?"

"God of vengeance, shine forth! Rise up, O judge of the earth; repay to the proud what they deserve."

"More Psalms."

"Psalms 94. We got hung up on the nine. We thought maybe Hawkins lived long enough to sketch a plate or a phone number in the dirt, but, after last night, we took another look and saw the 'God' and 'pay' you spotted. If you look closely, you can sort of make out 'rise.' The geeks put it through some program that compared it against biblical text and Psalms 94 popped out as the most likely."

"Huh. Okay, I buy that, but I'm still confused about why I'm here and why you're telling me all this. I'm not a cop. Never have been. I'm not sure what you want me to do."

"I wasn't bullshitting you about wanting to solve all this quickly. Solving it quietly went out the window with that scene at the Arnsfelds' last night. We could keep a tight lid on Hawkins because of where he was found and him not seeming to have many friends or ties to the community anymore, but someone will eventually notice he's missing. I want to avoid people getting ... irrational."

"And you think I can help?"

"Archie tells me you're friends with Mose Petersheim."

Max frowned and glanced at Archie. Archie looked embarrassed and studied his fingernails.

"What does this have to do with Mose? I think you're barking up the wrong tree if you think he did this."

"No, no. We don't think Mose is involved." Now Jermane looked embarrassed. "The Prince Creek police department has had some incidents with the Amish community in town. I'm not proud of it and it's getting better, but we are still not on the best terms."

The penny finally dropped. "And you want to use me and my friendship with Mose as a wedge to investigate the Amish."

"Well, that's one way of putting."

"I prefer to be blunt."

Jermane gave a thin smile at that retort, and Max thought he'd finally gotten a glimpse of the man's true face. "Fair enough. Yes, that's what I want."

"Do you have any evidence other than the Bible verses and the Amish's strong faith that one of them might be responsible?"

"No, and, to be fair, they are not the only avenue of investigation we are pursuing. I want to move quickly, and I think parallel inquiries in different directions might be prudent until we get a solid lead and can consolidate our efforts."

"And you think I might have more luck leveraging my friendship with Mose than sending an official department presence?"

"I think if I tried they would just politely stonewall me, and I don't have time for that. Some tough questions might have to be asked. I also don't want to make the relationship worse, if I don't have to. When this is over, we still have to live on this island together. And, to be clear, it would all be official. We'll deputize you and compensate you for your time."

"Thinking ahead to a trial?"

"Thinking like a defense attorney is the best way to beat one."

"What about the RCMP? Surely they have specialists?"

"Yes, they do, and I have informed them. They're sending someone."

"So, you've already decided I'm not responsible then?"

"Best we can tell, the time of death for the Arnsfelds was early evening day before yesterday. Multiple witnesses put you at The Rink."

"That's true. Nothing for Hawkins though."

He gave Max a real smile again. "We don't know exactly when he was killed, but I'm willing to risk it until the evidence points another way."

Max leaned back. If he refused, Jermane could make life difficult for him. And probably for Archie, too. If he was on the inside, he could make sure Jermane or worse, whoever the RMCP sent, didn't get too curious about him. Despite what Jermane just said, it wasn't a stretch to think they'd look hard at a new unknown arrival in town after three people ended up dead. It had happened before.

But there was something else, too. He'd felt a little charge run through his veins listening to the details and sorting through the timeline. He'd felt like he'd been walking in a daze since he'd taken on Carter back in Boston. This was something he could do. This was something he was good at. He was a planner. That was always his signature. What was solving a murder except planning in reverse? Maybe doing this would be another baby step toward making amends for all the terrible decisions he'd made in his past lives. If it quieted one more ghost in his head, it would be worth it.

"I'll help you, but I'm not going to just sell out Mose. I'll talk to him and get you what you need, but I'm not going to just walk away. I'm in for the duration. I want full access. You don't get to pick and choose."

"Done."

CHAPTER NINE

Archie dropped him off in front of the Sugar Maple Cafe on Main Street.

"Sure you don't want me to stick around? I could answer some questions. It's no trouble."

"No. I'm good. You take off. You look like you're about to fall asleep at the wheel. I can read through all this and call you later if I have questions. Probably going to need some time to think."

"A lot to think about."

"Ain't that the truth." Archie pulled away heading east out of town to where he lived in a small apartment on the opposite side of the bay.

Max went inside the Maple and took an empty two-top in the back corner. The Maple was a cozy, homey space that served coffee and pastries in the morning and a light soup and sandwich menu for lunch. Max would have preferred the quieter privacy of The Rink, but it was too early for the bar to be open. He ordered a cinnamon roll and a large coffee at the register and carried them back to his table.

Before they left the station, Marline had made copies of

both murder files for Max. Less than 24 hours old, the Arnsfelds' file was very thin. He flipped through it quickly. It was lacking everything except initial summaries and establishing photographs. He put it aside. He'd need to go look at the scene himself. He'd start at the beginning with Hawkins. He spread the file out on the table, careful to keep any of the photos or more disturbing reports facedown. There was an empty table next to him, but the rest were full. He didn't need anyone losing their breakfast if they got curious.

Max realized he had no notebook or paper to take notes and started collecting names and a timeline on the inside of the folder. Jermane was listed as both the case manager and lead investigator. A man named Burty Leeds was the lead RCMP crime scene investigator who had processed the scene. Bridget Heathers, the third of the three Prince Creek doctors, was the medical examiner of record and the one to make the pronouncement on Hawkins. Alford, Stratton, and Chravette were listed as supporting constables on the scene. Other than the required crime scene tech and Heathers, it had all been kept in-house and very quiet. As quiet as you can keep an ax murder. That all matched up with what Jermane had told him in his office.

Leeds's crime scene report had noted no defensive wounds. The killer had embedded the ax blade over four inches deep, through the skull and into the meat of the brain. It was not a tentative strike and had some strength behind it. Leeds had also noted the angle and height of the blow indicated a person at least 5 feet 9 inches tall and right-handed. Probabilities showed it was a man, Max thought.

The ax itself provided no substantial leads. It was distressingly common. A 12-inch Estwing sportsman's ax with a sanded grip available for about 30 bucks in 75 percent of the hardware or sporting goods stores in the country. The report noted additional signs of wear and use, so it was unlikely the killer bought it recently just to split Collum Hawkins's head open. To his credit, Jermane hadn't just let it go that easily. There was a sheaf of papers showing Estwing sales within 300 kilometers of Prince Creek for the past three years. It wasn't a short list.

The ax itself was common, but Max didn't think it was a common murder weapon. It suggested someone who had these types of tools or equipment handy. A landscaper, an outdoorsman, a craftsman. Something to think about.

He read through the chief's followup report. He'd interviewed people in Hawkins's apartment building and any friends, acquaintances, relatives, or past business associates that he could find. It was a short list. There were 12 people in all. A paltry collection of relationships for someone who had spent 67 years on this earth. Max wondered if his own list would be any longer.

Reading the interview summaries, it was clear that people either didn't know Hawkins, dismissed him as just a small-town eccentric, or were genuinely confused about what had happened to him. Max noted down two people to contact, Aldis Campbell and Safford Lee. Of the twelve, they had the most to say and appeared to have more than just a passing relationship with Hawkins. Or did at one time. They'd both worked with Hawkins in a professional capacity multiple times on contracts and business deals.

Jermane's notes also suggested potential ideas for motives. One was drugs. Hawkins's medicine cabinet contained two bottles of strong painkillers, both legally prescribed by Dick Mulvaney. Maybe he'd been supplementing that with something on the side? But what kind of drug dealer chose Sinclair Lane to do his business? And, maybe more pertinent, what kind of dealer carried around an ax for protection? It seemed like a stretch, more than a stretch, but he noted Mulvaney's name.

The other possibility Jermane noted was a robbery. Hawkins's wallet and credit cards were found on his body, but no cash and no phone. Jermane theorized that maybe the killer had taken the cash and the phone as the things with the most value. Still seemed like a stretch to Max. Why lure someone out there for what amounted to a mugging and then murder them with an ax? And then scribble a Bible notation in the dirt? It didn't make any sense. It was too weird. It was more likely, Max thought, given Hawkins's current mental and physical state, that he had no cash and didn't own a phone. The killer wasn't interested in valuables. Something else was going on.

He looked down at his plate and found he'd eaten the entire cinnamon roll without tasting it and finished his coffee, too. He stood and went to the counter to get a refill on the coffee.

"It'll be a minute or two. A fresh pot is just finishing up," said the woman behind the counter.

"No problem."

As he waited, he drifted over to the wall next to the register where an old survey map of Prince Creek was framed showing the parcels of land divided up. He got his bearings and then traced the line from the cove that bisected the western edge of town, through what was now the town center and then up and out of town to the east until he found the unlabeled and unnamed Norris Pond. It fell within parcel 36 and was owned, at one time, by the McDonald family. He looked at the other large rectangular plots. While the bayside and center of town had changed, not much had changed up on the bluffs. It was farmland on the interior and marshes on the edges that eventually bled into the ocean. Past or present, Norris Pond was miles from anything. What had Hawkins been doing up there? Had he just gone for a walk? None of the people interviewed mentioned walking or hiking as a hobby. They'd mostly described a man who stayed indoors and only walked as far as the liquor store or local takeout restaurants.

"You're Max, right?"

He turned around and found the woman holding out a steaming cup of coffee. She was short and a little wide through the hips, with blue spiky hair and a small silver circle pierced through one nostril. She had an open, smiling face that made you want to smile back. A taller, slimmer woman with a long, braided ponytail worked in the background. As Max watched, she dumped a tray of muffins into a basket. Unlike The Rink, Max hadn't been in here enough to learn anyone's name. But someone knew him.

"That's right. And you are?"

"Ellie Baker." She held out a hand. Max could see flour coating the fine hairs on the back of her hand. They shook. Her hand was small, but she had a firm grip.

"You're kidding."

"Nope. And don't try any jokes. I've heard them all."

"Hadn't crossed my mind."

"Uh-huh." But she smiled as she said it and handed over his change. Max smiled back. He couldn't help it. He was about to return to his table when she continued. "Word is that you're helping Jermane with these murders."

Max was shocked and it must have shown on his face. She kept up the smile, but there was a spark in her eyes that told him she enjoyed hearing the gossip. "You've got excellent sources," he said eventually. "I only learned myself a few hours ago."

"Small town and the best muffin recipe on PEI means I hear it all. Every morning." She plucked one of the warm muffins from the basket by the counter and put it on a plate. "Here. I don't joke about the muffins. Morning Glory. On the house."

"Thanks." Despite already eating the cinnamon roll, the smell of the warm muffin made his stomach rumble.

"So, figure anything out?"

"Not a thing. Not yet. But I'll let you know."

"Not if I hear it first."

Max thought she was probably only half-joking. He was still learning the realities of living in a small town. Essex had been small, but it was a metropolis compared to Prince Creek. Here, he was learning, if you didn't know what you were doing, then someone would tell you soon enough.

He'd just finished reading through the last of the Hawkins file when a woman slid into the seat opposite him. He quickly flipped the folder shut and looked up.

"You're Lindell?" she asked.

He hesitated for a fraction of a second. In the last few years, he'd changed and shed names like a snake molts skin and his brain sometimes fritzed when he was caught off guard. Not a great quality for a fugitive. It was one reason he'd insisted Lawrence give his new alias a name that he could shorten to Max. Lawrence hadn't liked it but had ultimately agreed. He'd gotten used to Max as a first name, but he hadn't mastered his new last name yet.

"That's right. Cormac Lindell. Most people call me Max. Who are you?"

She pushed a pair of black aviators up into her hair. "Imogen Koenig. RCMP inspector. Chief Roy said I'd find you down here."

She didn't offer a nickname. She didn't seem like the type. She was probably close to 40 but could have passed for five years younger. She wore a plain white blouse over a light gray suit. The only splash of color was an aqua and white patterned scarf tied lightly around her neck. Her eyes were a startlingly clear blue offset by high cheekbones and a slightly upturned nose. She had dirty blonde hair piled in a messy clip on top of her head.

"You finished reading the files?"

"Just Hawkins."

"Learn anything?"

"I'm not sure. Maybe a few things. Don't know yet. I didn't see anyone other than Leeds from the RCMP listed in the report. When did Jermane call you?"

"He didn't call me. Not specifically. He called Montague. Montague doesn't have a major crimes squad. They punted to Charlottetown. I was up. I got the files last night. Drove over this morning."

"Did Chief Roy explain my ... involvement?"

"Yes." If she had any hesitation or reservations about his involvement, he didn't see it on her face.

"And?"

"And nothing. Provincial policing is a patchwork solution. We come and help where needed or when asked by municipal forces. If the chief wants you involved, and it's legal, that's fine with me. He said you could help me out with local knowledge."

Max didn't know about that as he'd only been in town six weeks longer than Koenig, but he thought he could see Jermane's play. Get the RCMP involved to cover his own ass, plus use Max as a buffer to keep them off his back. If Jermane could solve it quickly and without help from the RCMP, it would go a long way toward getting his contract renewed when the time came. Even if he didn't solve it himself, he'd still get credit for calling in the experts. Not a bad piece of political jiu-jitsu, but he still needed to solve the murders to make it work. And, based on the Hawkins report and the conversation in his office this morning, Max didn't think

Jermane was all that close to finding a suspect, let alone collaring a killer.

"In other words, you can see through Roy's bullshit just fine, too," Max said.

He thought he saw the corner of her mouth twitch slightly.

"I'm happy with the arrangement as long as we catch a killer."

CHAPTER TEN

Imogen Koenig's RCMP car was an unmarked silver 2016 Ford Explorer. Max climbed in the passenger seat and caught the faint smell of Koenig's perfume, a pleasant lilac scent. He liked it. It was his first time sitting in the front of a police car. He liked that, too.

The car itself had some wear on it, both inside and outside, but, other than a large Tim Horton's coffee cup and a small duffel bag on the back seat, it was spotless inside. As they drove, Max wondered if RCMP kept all their cars this clean or if it was more a reflection of Koenig's personality. Had she just signed it out and gotten lucky or did she use it often and like things tidy? Based on their brief chat and how well she was put together, Max guessed it was closer to the latter. He couldn't see her tolerating fast-food wrappers or other trash accumulating around her feet.

He directed her out of the parking lot behind The Maple and back onto Main Street heading northeast. There wasn't anything to add after that. It was a straight shot out of town until they hit Sinclair. He studied her profile until she felt him looking and turned the reflective aviators on him.

"What?"

"Why do you think Chief Roy waited until the Arnsfelds to call the RCMP? My impression is that murders aren't all that frequent out here."

"They aren't. These three are the first in ten years in Prince Creek."

"All the more reason to get the experts in early."

"Goes back to provincial policing. The RCMP is set up to investigate major crimes, but we need to be asked. Because Prince Creek has its own force, it's at the chief's discretion. Sometimes it's politics. Sometimes it's arrogance or ignorance. Sometimes it's just negligence. I don't really know what the situation out here is yet."

"Maybe a combination of all three."

"Maybe. We haven't been out here much. My chief super doesn't know Roy, but he said the corporal, what's his name?"

"D'arcy Alford."

"Right, Alford. He's been around the block. Super thinks he's got his head on straight. Mostly competent."

They drove on, passing Robin's Donuts and Lee Crane Avenue with the vet clinic and the motel before they left the town behind and drove out into open space and bigger skies. Geometric squares of farmland, ripening with corn and potatoes, rolled away to the left. The dark Atlantic ebbed and swelled to the right.

Six minutes later, by the green digital dashboard clock, Max indicated a break in the line of woods that ran along the side of the road. "Slow up. That's it. On the right. The road is narrow. Not sure how much the Mounties value their paint job—"

"More than you'd think."

"Then it might be best to walk in. I don't think it's far."

"All right."

She eased the SUV onto the thin grassy patch that separated the road from the woods. Max grabbed his copy of the case file and jumped out. He spotted an old rusted pole, canted at an extreme angle, half-hidden in the tangled shrubs and greenery that bordered the entrance. The signpost at the top was missing but showed that at some point the lane had been maintained.

The road was hard-packed red clay that swayed and dipped and would be hell on any car's suspension. The old-growth forest, all kinds of trees, saplings, hardwoods, weeds, roots, and ferns, crowded up against the edges, greedy to reclaim the space. The oldest mature trees arched over the top, creating a dim tunnel that was like looking down the gullet of an ancient beast.

"Not going to learn anything from here," Max said.

"Wait," Koenig said, and Max looked back.

She hustled back to the car. "One of the few times I regret the plainclothes option of an inspector rank. Crime scenes are hell on decent clothes." She pulled a pair of plain white sneakers out of the duffel bag and swapped them for her more elegant but much less practical low heels. "They don't pay me enough to burn a good pair of shoes on this."

They started walking. After 20 yards, the light had dimmed to twilight. After 50 yards, Max noted he'd almost lost his shadow and felt goosebumps prickle his arms as the temperature dropped ten degrees. A half-mile down Sinclair and he felt like he'd walked into a different time and place. The modern world had dropped away. He looked over his shoulder but could no longer see Route 16. Just a few miles from town and he felt isolated and alone.

He reached out and touched the rough bark of an encroaching red pine. It was cold and hard. Somewhere above, the wind blew and rustled the canopy of branches. "Creepy," he said.

She looked at him and then looked around at the thick

forest and gray gloom. "You're only saying that because you know what happened here."

"I don't know. I think some places are just bad. They're marked."

"Didn't peg you as a believer."

"Believer of what?"

"Spirits. Specters. Phantoms. Take your pick."

"I'm not. Not the way you mean, at least. Not with a smirk. But I do believe evil leaves a mark."

"I believe in evil, too. You last as a cop long enough, it's hard to come to any other conclusion. But this is just woods and your imagination." They kept walking another ten yards before she added, "It *is* a good place to kill somebody and get away with it though. There are plenty of places to hide and no one to hear you scream."

Max took out his phone. The signal was weak, but he was able to pull up a map. The Prince Creek PD had left no markings or police tape up after the RCMP tech had cleared the scene, but GPS coordinates marked the location of Hawkins's body on a map in the file. With the additional photos from the file, it wasn't hard to match up exactly where Hawkins had been found.

They didn't need to rely on technology. Max could still see the broken branches and crisscrossing tire tracks that marked the activity around a spot just off the road, to the left, in a small ditch.

They both walked over, and Max held up a photo that showed Hawkins on his stomach, one arm stretched over his head, the other under his body. He looked like he might have tripped and fallen over a root except for the ax half-buried in the back of his head. The rain had washed away any blood by the time the body was discovered and photographed.

Max knelt to look more closely at the ground, but the tire tracks and snapped branches were the only traces left of the grisly event. "And behold, a pale horse, and its rider's name was Death, and Hades followed him."

"What's that?"

"Revelations. Roy told you about the Bible verses?"

"Yes."

"Feels like this will get worse before it gets better."

"Don't say that."

Max stood. "Why was Hawkins even out here? I mean, would you come out here in the middle of the night?"

"We don't know when it happened, unfortunately. It could have been the middle of the afternoon."

"Maybe," Max said, "but I'd bet it was after dark." He walked over to the tire tracks. "Even with the rain, this clay holds an impression, especially in the shade. Look at our footprints through there," Max pointed to a damp patch. "It hasn't rained since Hawkins was found. They took impressions and found nothing that didn't match up to official cars. Whoever did this walked in."

"Or left a car at the top like we did."

"Would you leave your car by a major road when you're on your way to murder someone?"

"Probably not."

"It would be a big risk. Even in the middle of the night, someone might drive past. It's the only road up to East Point."

"But we're not exactly dealing with a rational person when you talk about an ax murderer. Maybe he got lucky."

"Maybe, but I bet he walked and that might tell us something."

"What?"

"First, maybe he doesn't own a car. Second, he's got local knowledge. And third, that he's not just a nut. He's got a certain calculation. But it still doesn't tell us why Hawkins was out here. This wasn't an accidental meeting. What was the killer offering that made Hawkins show up?"

"I'm still not ready to buy a setup. Roy said Hawkins had a reputation of being a recluse or an agoraphobe. Maybe he liked the emptiness and isolation. Maybe being here after dark made it more attractive."

"Maybe." Max didn't mind being alone, but he thought it would take a special kind of mind to enjoy being out here in the dark in a place like this. "What do you make of the ax?"

Koenig blew out a breath. "Well, an ax to the head is obviously a decisive and vicious way to kill someone. It's also very personal. Most murders have very simple reasons. Love or money or anger. Maybe fear."

"So, who felt something so strongly toward an old recluse that they would bury an ax in his head?"

"Maybe we're being too rational. Maybe sanity had nothing to do with it. Maybe it was plain old madness. I've seen that before. You'll never find answers to that. He's just nuts."

"It doesn't feel like that, though, does it? A deranged person might use an ax but would do more damage. Chop him up in a frenzy. That guy wouldn't be able to hide. This feels different. This was deliberate, but not uncontrolled. He wasn't in the grip of a mania. He's punishing them. Getting retribution. He's crazy, but not nuts. A special brand of crazy."

CHAPTER ELEVEN

They wandered around the scene. Koenig asked to look at the copy of the file Max carried and flipped through the photographs and then handed the folder back. They talked for ten more minutes about why Hawkins might have been on the road and why the killer chose an ax, trying to come at it from fresh angles, but didn't get any further.

Koenig looked at something at the base of the tree closest to where the body was found, then stood and brushed off her hands. "Where does this ultimately go?" She asked, pointing farther down the road.

"According to the map, it dead ends at Norris Pond just around that bend."

"You know it?"

"Nope. Roy told me it's a small freshwater pond. Locals sometimes fish it. Sometimes a make-out spot for local teens."

"Should we take a look?"

"Might as well."

It took ten more minutes before the trees and shrubbery

opened up and they saw Norris Pond. It was a small, thin stretch of water 30 feet across and 200 or 300 feet long. An open area laid with rocks was directly in front of them, perhaps used to launch kayaks or canoes. Or just cast from shore. Pockets of algae and thin green rushes grew along the water's edge. The middle of the pond was dark and still. A small wooden building with a dock extending into the water sat on the far side. A skein of that bad mojo that Max had felt in the woods still lingered in the air, but, for the first time, he could also see why someone would come out here. With the sun sparkling off the water, there was a serenity that didn't exist in the bleak woods.

"Who owns this?" Koenig asked.

"No idea. Maybe the town? Roy didn't say. We could check Town Hall."

There was a thin track, maybe a game trail, that looped the lake and they started walking around to the right to get a look at the structure at the far end. They had to push through thickets and brambles that had overrun the path and step around boggy spots, but it was passable.

"Not regretting the sneakers," Koenig said.

"Doesn't look like it gets used regularly."

"If locals are fishing, maybe they stick close to the road."

They approached the building and short dock. The structure was a simple ten-by-ten square with a roof that angled downward from front to back. Each side had a small half-window to let in light. There was a door at the rear and then another off the front that led onto the dock. The dock itself extended 15 feet into the pond. Everything was a warped and weathered gray. The doors hung crookedly in their jambs. A furry carpet of moss covered most of the roof. The window on the left was missing its pane of glass.

Koenig poked her head inside the door. "Looks like someone transplanted an ice fishing cabin from Alberta to

PEI." She stepped inside and Max followed. The floorboards groaned under their combined weight. It smelled of rot and animal droppings. There was nothing inside except a small bench seat attached to one wall and a moldering mattress in one corner. Two rusted beer cans rounded out the decor.

"Maybe it was a changing room at one time," Max said.

"Mattress is probably from the teenagers." She stepped out the far door onto the dock. "Wood feels spongy."

Max stayed in the doorway. Koenig took another step and the dock swayed. "Careful. I don't think that dock has much time left." From this angle, he could see a few missing planks and the entire structure listed to the left. She stepped back into the wooden cabin.

"No point in getting wet. Not sure the pond or the cabin has anything to do with Hawkins."

As they turned to leave, something caught Max's eye. He stopped and swept his gaze over the walls. Nothing. He turned back around and repeated the same movement. He saw it again. A lighter color, something brighter against the old wood, high up, near where the roof met the wall.

Koenig had moved outside and now came back to the door. "What is it?" She asked.

Max kept his eyes on the spot; he didn't want to lose it again in the dim light. "Not sure." He pulled out his phone and turned on the flashlight app, then tested the bench seat with one foot. It felt solid enough. He stood up on it and played the flashlight over the wall. Two sets of letters were carved into the old wood: LR + AB.

"Probably just kids," Koenig said from the floor. "Didn't you ever carve your name into a tree?"

"Sure," Max said. "More than once."

"Loverboy, huh?"

Koenig was probably right. The mattress and the beer cans and the initial conversation with Roy said this was a place where teenagers and their raging hormones sometimes hung out. The odds were that some lovelorn kid had inscribed the letters, but something about it bugged Max. The curves of the R and B were round and well-formed. Max ran a hand over the letters. They were smooth.

He moved the flashlight around the rest of the space. The remaining walls were bare. "Strange that it's the only one though, right? Teenagers are followers. Where you see one, you usually see others."

It didn't feel like a hasty postcoital declaration of everlasting love, either. It looked like someone had taken their time. As if these letters really meant something.

He snapped a photo of the letters and stepped down. Something else to think about.

They retraced their steps to Koenig's car. Max was glad to be back out in the open. He felt lighter. He'd stick by his earlier statement. Some places were spoiled and wrong.

Koenig swapped shoes again and then drove them back toward town. Max was usually comfortable with silence but found himself trying to think of something to say.

"Imogen. You don't hear that name every day. Your parents Shakespeare fans?" She gave him a quick look and one eyebrow arched over the top edge of the aviators. "What? Didn't think an ingrate like me knew Shakespeare?"

"No, it's not that." She tapped her fingers on the wheel and smiled again. "Okay, maybe a little."

Max laughed. "At least you're honest."

"My mother grew up in Australia. It's a little more common there. I didn't learn that Shakespeare invented the name until I got to university."

"Australia? How'd you end up in the great white north?"

"No choice. I was born here. My parents met when my

mother was doing a semester abroad at McGill. That semester turned into a lifetime of love."

It amused Max to see a blush of color rise on her pale cheeks. "So, they're still together?"

"And still disgustingly in love." The smile was still there, but Max could sense a little bewilderment, too. Cops and crooks could get jaded. Sometimes love got elbowed out of the way. A hazard of the job.

"Any siblings?"

"An older brother and a younger sister."

"They cops, too?"

"Oh, no. I'm a classic middle child. Rebelling. They're both in academia. My brother is an economist. My sister is a middle school principal."

They made it back to Prince Creek and Koenig turned right at The Maple. Max thought she was going to pull into the parking lot behind the cafe. It was only a little after 11 a.m., early for lunch, but Koenig kept driving and turned right again onto a short street in the small tangle of residential blocks behind the business district.

The homes and buildings in this enclave were apartments and duplexes. Koenig turned left onto a street with three duplexes on the left and a longer two-story brick apartment building on the right. The second-floor apartments each had a small landing just large enough for a grill and a chair or two. A small playground buttressed the end of the street with two swings and a climbing structure.

She turned the Explorer around so they'd be facing back out and pulled to the curb in front of the entrance to the apartment building.

"This is where Hawkins lived?" Max asked.

"Yeah. Roy gave me a key. Not sure what we're going to find, but Roy says they haven't found any next of kin yet, so no one's touched it since Burty and the other techs finished. Might as well cover all the bases."

"In for a penny, in for a pound," Max said as he opened the door.

They buzzed the building manager from the glass entry vestibule. He came out of a door off the interior lobby and let them in. He was a large man wearing a grease-stained Superman T-shirt and jean shorts; he seemed uninterested in who they were or why they were there.

"Barely knew the guy," he said, chewing and swallowing half a powdered donut in one bite. "Kept to himself. I never had a problem with him. Paid the rent on time. Didn't clog up the toilets or complain. I'm not sure I've even been inside his place in the last 3 years. Frankly, I wish more of the tenants were like him. Makes my job easier."

He directed them down a dim and slightly dingy hallway that smelled of industrial cleaner and cooked onions. Hawkins's apartment was on the first floor, number 5, second from the end, facing the backside of the building.

The apartment was not what Max expected.

"Huh," Koenig said.

"I just had the same thought."

Given all the descriptions of Hawkins as a loner, Max had been expecting to walk into the crowded and perhaps secretive apartment of a hoarder but if the man's mind was disordered, his apartment wasn't. It was plain to the point of being almost empty. Chief Roy's scant report from the apartment made more sense now.

The apartment consisted of two rooms, three if you counted the small bathroom. The front door opened onto the larger of the two rooms, a galley kitchen that flowed into a living room.

The kitchen was carved out of the corner, immediately to the right, inside the door. Refrigerator, two-burner half stove, coffeepot on the counter, and plastic trashcan in the corner.

Max stepped through the kitchen and into the living room. Koenig was looking out the window at a pair of dumpsters, a chain-link fence, and the backside of a similar building on the next street.

"Not much of a view," he said.

She turned back around. "Not much of a life."

He thought of his own spartan trailer. What would she say about his life?

A door to the left led to the bedroom. Max stuck his head in. A mattress and box spring with a particleboard dresser filled most of the rectangular space. The closet door was slightly ajar and Max could see a few well-used shirts and pants hanging from a rod. An interior door led to a bathroom with a shower, sink, and toilet. He stepped back out into the living room.

"You want this room or the bedroom?" he asked.

"Bedroom. Always more interesting."

The living room contained a single reclining chair with a small table and lamp next to it. Each of the walls was lined with rough, maybe homemade, unpainted bookshelves. Hawkins had stuffed the shelves with books, to the point where the wood sagged under the weight.

The room held nothing else. No pictures or art on the walls. No television. No other furniture. Not much of a life. Maybe. But Max didn't think a life filled with books would be all bad. Maybe lonely but not bad. He walked the perimeter of the room, looking at the spines of the books. Hawkins appeared to read widely, almost erratically. He definitely didn't sort and shelve his books according to any logic Max could discern. Fiction and non-fiction were jumbled together. Pulpy mysteries sat next to physics and ancient history texts.

They all appeared to be read. He pulled down a slim book of poetry at random and found more than one page marked with underlined sections or scribbled notes.

He finished his circuit of the room but found only one thing that jumped out at him. A black file box sat on the lowest shelf nearest the reclining chair. Max pulled it out and took off the lid. Labeled file folders filled the box. Max read the handprinted labels. Taxes. Bank. Insurance. Apartment. Will. Bills. He assumed Roy had made copies of the entire box. He could see that the will folder was empty and remembered the notation Roy had made that the will had been copied and passed on to whoever the lawyer handling probate was.

He pulled out the bank folder. He flipped open the folder and riffled through the stack of paper. It was a mix of bank and brokerage statements going back 3 years. The balances surprised Max. Hawkins wasn't rich, but he was in no danger of starving. There was over $200,000.00 in a Vanguard account and $3000.00 in a checking account at a local credit union. Max knew that was more than most people on the island had.

Koenig came back in. "Find anything?" She asked.

He held up the file. "You see his financials?"

"Not yet. Roy said he'd make a copy for me. Anything interesting?"

"He had over $200,000.00 in savings."

"More than I would have guessed, but is that enough to murder him?"

"Depends on who you ask. You find anything in there?"

"No, just the pills we knew about. The man lived like a monk."

"Gotta be something. Monks rarely get murdered."

He went back to the box and pulled out a few more folders. He'd have to see about getting his own copies later and going through them in detail. Koenig went into the kitchen; he could hear her opening and closing cabinets.

"He might have been a reader, but he wasn't a foodie. Canned beans, canned vegetables, some rice, coffee. It looks like a bomb shelter kitchen in here. The only thing missing is military MREs." She came back into the living room. "You know what I find most depressing?"

"No pictures?"

"No, and I did find one photo in the bedroom nightstand. Old photo of a girl. It's the plates and silverware."

"What about it?"

"C'mere."

He dropped the folders on the floor and followed her into the kitchen. She pulled open the drawer next to the sink. There was a plastic silverware organizer. It held one fork, one knife, one spoon. She opened the cabinet above the sink. One plate, one glass, and one coffee cup.

"He knew no one was going to visit. I mean, where do you even buy a single fork?" Koenig said.

CHAPTER TWELVE

They left Hawkins's place with more information, and maybe a better sense of the man, but little that immediately shed any light on why he was dead.

"I need to eat something, and I know I'm not going to feel like eating much after going to the Arnsfeld scene. Any recommendations? Back to that cafe where I found you?" Koenig asked.

"How do you feel about red meat and fries?"

"Two basic food groups."

"All right. Keep an open mind. It doesn't look like much from the outside, but the food is good."

"They always hide the best places behind neon and grease."

They rolled down the hill back toward the center of town. They passed The Sugar Maple, which was doing a brisk lunch business. They crossed Main Street and then took a left where the road dead ended at the water onto Washington Street. One block later, he directed her into the parking lot of The Rink. It looked ragged and forlorn in the bright afternoon sun. The neon sign in the front window glowed a dull and dusty pink.

Despite his earlier assurances, Max could feel Koenig's skepticism as she parked.

"Focus on the neon and grease, Koenig."

"Looks like it's got plenty of both."

As they walked toward the entrance, Max said, "Jerry, the owner and usual bartender, lucked into a local kid with culinary ambitions. He'll probably get bored and move on soon, but he definitely knows his way around a kitchen."

Inside, the televisions were muted. Jerry's personal muse *The Tragically Hip* played from the juke's speakers. Three men were hunched over, drinking separately at the bar. Max didn't recognize them. A couple was eating at a two-top near the pool table. Jerry's head bobbed slightly to the music as he cut up lemons and limes. He nodded at Max and raised an eyebrow at Koenig.

"The kid working today?"

"Yeah, he's back there. Tried to convince me to put coq au vin on the menu."

"You going to do it?"

"If people can't pronounce it, they are not going to order it."

"I don't know. Don't underestimate your clientele, Jerry."

"Trust me, I've been running this place for 25 years. That's almost impossible. Beer, whiskey, and fry oil. It's the Holy Trinity."

"Can we get two cheeseburgers, fries, and iced teas?"

"Proving my point, Max."

Jerry called the order through the swinging kitchen doors and then filled two glasses with ice, slices of lemon, and tea from a pitcher he took from a small refrigerator under the bar. They took their glasses and set them down at a booth halfway down the row and as far from anyone else as they could get.

"C'mere. I want you to meet someone," Max said.

Thorne was in his corner booth near the door. Max and Koenig walked over. A battle-scarred Dell laptop was open on the table. Thorne's notebook and pencil were at his elbow. A few loose sheets of paper were scattered across the table.

"Hi, Max. Or should I call you Constable Max? I heard Jermane has you on the payroll now. How did that happen?"

"He wants me to talk to Mose."

"You gonna do it?"

"We came to an understanding."

Thorne looked at Max for another moment, then shifted his attention to Koenig. "And is this Inspector Koenig from the RCMP?"

"Koenig, meet Thorne Taylor. He's what counts for press around here. Runs the local paper. *The Prince Creek Chronicle*."

"I prefer the title Editor-in-Chief."

They shook.

"You're well informed," Koenig said.

"Small towns leak like a rusty bucket. Nothing stays secret for long," Thorne said.

"We'll see about that."

"Yes, I guess we will. Learn anything interesting this morning?"

"I'll let Chief Roy answer that."

"Ah, you're no fun." He grabbed one of the loose sheets of paper from the table. "Jermane's press release this morning was as bland as Jerry's cooking before the kid arrived. How about you, Constable, anything to add?"

"Are you trying to get me fired before I finish my first shift?"

"We've all got jobs to do."

Max nodded at the pile of papers. "You working on anything?"

Taylor glanced at the computer screen. "Working on the obit for Arnsfeld."

"Figured with the features you already wrote that the obit would mostly write itself."

"It does. I was looking at the last few years. The charity. The initial profiles were all background and focused on his career before he came to PEI."

"The Arnsfeld Association. Charlie started telling me a bit about it the other night after you and Redd left. It runs projects having to do with the environment and sustainability?"

"Bit of a black box but, yes, that's what they claim. I'm digging through their reporting forms."

"You think it wasn't on the level?" Koenig asked.

"No, everything looks okay on the surface. They probably wouldn't get a great grade from the industry watchdogs. Their spend percentage isn't great. They use a lot of money on overhead and expenses, but it all looks legit."

"What's the problem then?" Max asked.

"I don't know. Why such a high burn rate? This isn't New York or even Toronto. The building was a sunk cost from the previous venture. Something just doesn't smell right. Call it instinct. Have either of you ever heard of the Royal Canadian Riders?" They both shook their heads. "It's a local social club. Fraternal organization. Whatever. They've got a place, a clubhouse, off Seven Mile Road near Glenfanning. They're loosely affiliated with the Royal British Legion Riders, who are big around Toronto. Or so I'm told. They've popped up a couple of times in conversations about Arnsfeld."

"He was a biker?"

"No, not as far as I can tell, and these guys aren't the type to attend 500-dollar plate charity dinners. Lots of rumors.

Lots of smoke. But they've never been busted for anything more than drunk and disorderliness, bar brawls, that sort of thing. But their name keeps coming up. It's strange."

"Royal Canadian Riders. I can ask around at the RCMP. See if Intelligence has anything," Koenig said.

"And pass along anything good?"

"We might be able to work something out."

Jerry came around the bar carrying their food and Max nodded him at the table where they'd set their drinks.

"I did have one other question. Does *The Chronicle* have a library of clips?"

"Sure. We've digitized them since 2009, but we store the older ones in the basement."

"Can you set me up with an account for the digital ones? I want to read up more on Arnsfeld."

"Sure, come by the office later. I'll be back with the papers from the printing plant by then. Should be around until 5 p.m. or so."

"Thanks. I'll do that."

They left Thorne to keep digging into the charity's financial forms and retreated to their booth to eat their lunch.

Koenig leaned in. "Is he okay?"

"What do you mean?"

"Can you trust him? Some reporters can see the long game. They'll keep their word, and we can work with them to advance the case. Others just want their names in lights and will burn you for the quick headline."

"I think you can trust Thorne. He's the only game in town, but he also has to keep living and working here. If he burns the police or the RCMP, he knows he'll be stuck for a long time."

She picked up her burger. "I'll ask around on my end. See if anyone else has dealt with him before."

They didn't speak much after that beyond grunts and

requests to pass the ketchup. The kid's food had that effect. When Koenig finished, leaving nothing but a few burnt nibs of fries on her plate, she nudged the plate away and tossed her crumpled napkin on top. "Lake in the woods. Dive bar. Burgers and fries. You really know how to show a girl a good time."

"Never argue with the persuasive powers of grease."

That got a smile, but by the time she drank her iced tea and rattled the remaining ice, the smile had switched off and Inspector Koenig was back. She pushed out of the booth. "Let's go check out the house."

CHAPTER THIRTEEN

They drove past the hardware store, the motel, and the vet clinic then climbed up Lee Crane Avenue. This time, the hill was empty of gawkers. Max felt a mild sense of embarrassment for joining in the previous night.

"Did you know Arnsfeld?" he asked.

"No, not personally. He donated some money to the RCMP. I think he donated to a lot of places. When he first came out here, he spread a lot of money around."

"But you knew the name."

"Sure, it was a big deal. You couldn't avoid hearing about him. He was in all the papers. There was a lot of enthusiasm. A lot of hope on the entire island, even though he would be based out here."

"What did you think about how it ended?"

She shrugged. "I didn't. I guess I was disappointed it had all fallen apart, but it didn't really affect me personally. Success or failure, my job wasn't going to change."

They pulled off the cracked pavement and onto the smooth driveway. A deputy climbed out of a marked Prince

Creek car that sat half on the grass, half on the driveway next to the pillars and driveway gate. He was carrying a clipboard and something else Max couldn't make out. He waved a hand, and Koenig stopped next to him and put the window down.

"Inspector Koenig with the RCMP and Max Lindell with, well, I guess the Prince Creek PD."

The deputy leaned down and looked through the window. The nameplate on his uniform shirt said Chravette. Roy's part-time deputy.

"Heard about you," he said and stood back up. It came out flat, and Max couldn't tell if he resented Max or not. "Chief said you'd probably come by. No one else up here at the moment. Crime scene guys are coming back. They ran back to Charlottetown to get more equipment. You spell Koenig with or without an E, Inspector?"

"With an E." Chravette recorded their presence on his clipboard and then pointed the device in his hand at the pillars and the gate swung open. "Go on up."

Unlike the week-old scene in the woods or the secondary scene of Hawkins's apartment, the Arnsfelds' home was viscerally fresh. You could smell the violence as soon as you walked in the front door. The sickening sweet smell of iron and metal filled Max's nostrils and made him feel like he was chewing on pennies.

"You okay?" Koenig asked. "Here," she held out a small container of mint lip balm, "run it under your nose. It helps. A little."

He took it and dabbed it under his nostrils. "Thanks." He handed the lip balm back and she dropped it in her pocket.

"You'd think after 12 years of crime scenes I'd be more used to it but I'm not. There's just something elemental about that much blood, I think. Deep, deep down in our genes the body knows it's wrong. Fights it."

He wasn't sure if she was just feeding him a line or not, but he appreciated the effort. "Then I'm glad you're still not used to it."

"Yeah, me too." From her other pocket, she took out a pair of purple nitrile gloves and offered them to him. "Best not to piss off the CSI guys."

Sized for her, they were tight on his hands but they would work.

They walked down the hall, careful to avoid the stains marked by yellow numbered evidence markers. The entryway led directly to a large and modern kitchen filled with stainless steel appliances, a rectangular granite island, and blond wood cabinetry. A large farmer's table was to the left. Through another doorway, Max could see sofas, bookshelves, and the edge of a flat screen television.

A chair from the farmer's table was on its side near the sink, one leg cracked. A puddle of dried black blood surrounded the chair. Some drops had splashed up on the counter and surrounding cabinets. Ten feet away, near the large Sub-Zero fridge, was a second area of blood. Even more than the first. Max could see half a footprint and a small handprint smeared across the floor. Someone fighting for their life. And losing.

"Christ," Max said, feeling the kid's burger turn over in his stomach. "Maybe we shouldn't have eaten first."

"Right, you weren't here last night."

"Archie told me it was bad. Roy said it was ugly. But this ... this is something else."

"I read the initial reports at the station this morning." She pointed to the broken chair. "Christopher Arnsfeld, 39, was bound to the chair. Died of a wound to the back of the head, probably from a hammer found on the floor. The wife,

Stephanie, 38, was killed here." She indicated the blood near the fridge. "Also killed by a hammer, most likely, but no official word yet. Her body was in worse shape than the husband's. ME wanted to take a closer look."

"Why do you think he tied up the husband?"

"I don't know. Maybe for convenience? Or torture? Maybe he needed something? Information?"

Max tried to picture the scene. "So, the killer rings the doorbell and the husband answers?"

"It appears that way. We haven't gotten the results back on the blood from the hallway, but that makes sense. Killer whacks him on the head, drags him into the kitchen, ties him to the chair."

"So Arnsfeld probably knew the guy. Or the guy wasn't threatening."

"Why do you say that?"

"You said the hammer wound was to the back of the head. Would you turn your back on a stranger or someone you thought was threatening?"

"Good point," Koenig conceded.

"The wife comes home and what? Interrupts things? Killer jumps her when she walks in the kitchen and beats her to a pulp as she tries to escape?"

"Maybe. Or he beat her because he wanted to write his message."

"What?"

She pointed behind him. He turned to look. On the kitchen wall, written in blood, was the Bible verse that Roy had showed him that morning in his office: *When he maketh inquisition for blood, he remembereth them: He forgetteth not the cry of the humble—human five.* It took up most of the wall and wrapped to two lines. The bloody letters ran down the wall in long streaks, but it was still legible. It looked like it had been written by hand.

"Jesus. Roy told me they'd found the verse at the scene, but not like this."

"All spelled correctly, too," Koenig said. "Takes some steel to stay with the bodies and write a message with their blood."

"A special crazy."

"I really don't have a good feeling about this."

They walked through the rest of the house together. It was modern, and everything seemed to be selected to take advantage of the gigantic windows that lined the side of the house that faced the Strait.

"Office will take some time," Max said as they stepped inside. Papers and folders were stacked up on a large desk.

"Not really my style. We got specialists for that. And for the computer," Koenig said.

Max walked around behind the desk and sat in the chair. The lowest drawer was open and showed a small inlaid safe with a biometric lock. "Safe."

"Roy said they found one in here and one in the bedroom. Should have them open today or tomorrow. He'll let me know."

"What about Arnsfeld's office? Do you know if Roy sealed that off? If this is tied up in the charity or his busted business venture, something might be there and not here."

"We're good there. He had it sealed up last night."

"Nothing was taken here?"

"Nothing obvious. They have no children. A housekeeper came by twice a week. Roy said they would bring her in and see if she spotted anything, but the wife's jewelry is still here. Some pricey pieces, too. There was a roll of money in one of Arnsfeld's shoes in his closet. Robbery doesn't look like a motive."

"Like Hawkins."

They spent another 2 hours going through the house, but didn't find any clues or obvious motives. They'd wait for the official CSI reports and inventory and then come back if necessary.

As they stood outside near the Explorer, Max looked across the road toward the field where the townspeople had gathered last night. "Lots of blood."

"Like the ax, a hammer isn't a subtle instrument."

"Be interesting if the techs pick up anything from the bathrooms. He must have been covered in it. Even if the guy cleaned himself up before leaving, his clothes would have been soaked in blood, right? What was the time of death?"

"Between 5 p.m. and 9 p.m.."

"So, getting dark, or already dark, but not late enough to be sure you wouldn't run into anyone."

"Could have been in a car," Koenig said.

"Even in a car, it's a risk."

"But less of a risk. Maybe he didn't go through town or knew how to avoid people. You're thinking he walked again?"

"Be interesting to look at a map and see what's on the other side of that hill."

CHAPTER FOURTEEN

They walked across the driveway and into the open field. Chravette got out of his car and watched them but said nothing. At first, it was easy going. Directly across from the gates and the Arnsfelds' front yard, the wild grass was matted and trampled down where everyone had stood last night. Once they passed that flattened section, it became more difficult. The field extended a mile or more toward the horizon before giving way to a line of birch and red maples. The thigh-high grass hid ankle-turning hillocks of soil and rock. There was no obvious path. Each of them stumbled more than once.

"We can barely make it through now. If you tried this in the dark, you'd break a leg," Koenig said.

"Agreed. I can't see him going out this way. Not the way we're doing it. We missed a path, or he went back down the road."

They carefully retraced their steps back to the pavement and climbed in the Explorer. They gave Chravette a wave on the way past and drove back down the hill.

"That should be interesting," Koenig said as they passed the motel.

"You staying there?"

"Only game in town that fits the RCMP budget. Will the thread count on the sheets or the daily rate be higher?"

Max was going to say something about his time in room eight but didn't. He saw Randall, the day clerk, had his old Chevy pickup outside the office on the far end. "At least it should be quiet."

She dropped him off outside *The Chronicle's* office. "I'm going to go check in with Roy. See if anything popped during the day. Meet up at The Maple tomorrow morning?"

"Nine?"

"Let's do 8 a.m. I want to go out to the Arnsfeld Association. Hit them early."

"See you then."

She drove off with a wave and Max went inside.

Thorne ran the town's twice-weekly newspaper out of a nondescript two-story building next to Prince Creek's modest Town Hall. Like Charlie Gagnon and his bookstore, Thorne ran the paper from the first floor and lived on the second.

There was a long counter inside the door, bisecting the front room in two. Two desks were behind the counter. In the handful of times Max had been inside, he'd never seen anyone at the desks. A dusty mug from the Vancouver Olympics sat on one desk next to a ream of printer paper and an old Olivetti typewriter with a casing that peculiar shade of turquoise-green that marked it as being made in the 1970s. A disconnected multiline office phone the size of a dinner platter and an answering machine sat on the other desk. Newspapers were stacked on the counter with a small cash box for walk-in sales.

Max walked around the counter. "Hello, anyone home?"

"I'm out back."

Max walked down the hall past the old kitchen that still held the original 1950s era appliances, plus a modern single-serve coffee machine, through another door and into a hoarder's paradise. A snaking path led between stacks of old papers, two trash bins, a rusting 10-speed bicycle, teetering piles of unmarked cardboard boxes, and various other pieces of junk you might find in the typical person's garage. Thorne didn't have a garage. He had a newspaper office.

Max finally made it to the building's back door and found Thorne unloading the most recent edition of *The Chronicle* from his trunk. Thorne was older than Max by at least a decade, and maybe more, but the man's forearms were corded with muscle as he lifted the bundles out. He might spend most of his days pushing words around, but Max wasn't sure he'd want to tangle with him. The one time Max had seen The Rink get rowdy, Thorne had waded in without hesitating and held his own.

Max grabbed two tied bundles from the trunk and hauled them to the door.

"Any luck digging up dirt on Arnsfeld?" Max asked.

"Who says I was looking for dirt?"

"No one, but dirt sells, right?"

"Got that right, especially in this case. But no, no luck beyond what I told you about the connection, if there is one, to that RCR group. How about you?"

"No, nothing yet." Thorne wiped the sweat from his brow and looked at him. Max held up his hands. "I'm serious. We spent most of the day just catching up to Roy. I did put in a good word for you with Koenig."

"You told her I was suave and debonair and hung like a horse?"

"I'm not sure I used those exact words, but I think she's likely to talk to you if you don't hang her out to dry."

Thorne dropped the schtick. "I know how to treat a source and I know how to protect them."

"And that's what I said."

They finished getting the papers out of the trunk and started moving them inside.

"I set up that account for you," Thorne said and handed him a sheet of paper. "Self-explanatory. Log into the site, and there's a search function with filters. If you can Google, you can probably handle this."

"Thanks."

"No problem. Now, anything older than 2009 might come up as a stub. Just a headline and maybe a sentence or two. We had a grant from the Historical Society for a few years that allowed us to go back and digitize the bigger stories in the archive, but the money eventually ran out. Better than nothing, though."

"Do you or the Historical Society have microfiche or copies of things before 2009?"

"Just the boxes of physical clips decomposing in the basement. I can't guarantee it's in any sort of order. Sorry, best I can do."

They finished moving the rest of the papers inside.

"See you at The Rink later?" Thorne asked.

"We'll see. A lot to think about."

"Don't be afraid to share. It's what friends are for."

Max laughed. "Always working, huh?"

"Not always. A man's gotta sleep, too."

He walked the two miles back to his trailer. While not as nice as the previous day, the evening air was still pleasantly warm with a light breeze off the water to counter the humidity. He could smell dinners cooking on barbeques and dodged kids running and biking on the side streets. On Bishop Avenue,

Mrs. Johnson was watering the flowers in the containers by her door. She pointedly ignored him as he walked past. He figured it would take at least a year for her to accept him as a resident.

It all felt rational and normal. Exactly the opposite of how he'd just spent his day. It should have lifted his mood. He tried to smile and made it about halfway before he remembered the scene in the Arnsfelds' kitchen.

As he walked through the tunnel of trees back to his trailer, he could hear the small transistor radio playing the French pop station out of Quebec and could smell the burning meat and charcoal from the little hibachi.

"Goddamn, that smells good. You been waiting long?"

"I don't know. Two beers' worth, I guess. How long is that?"

Max stepped up onto his pallet platform and sat down. "Give me one and let's find out." Mose handed him a cold can from the cooler. "You pissed?"

"What makes you think that?"

He waved a hand at the radio. "You only listen to this stuff when you're upset."

"No. Not pissed. More annoyed. Wished you'd come over straightaway and let me know."

"You're probably right. It pissed me off, tell you the truth. I didn't want him to think I was just his errand boy. I also didn't want you to think that's all I thought of you, either."

"I know you better than that."

"Okay." Max cracked the beer, they clanked cans, and each took a long sip. "How'd you hear?"

"Sharon's sister sells candles down at Marline's cousin's store in St. John's Bay. She must have heard from Marline. Where she got it from, I don't know. Probably Archie or Henry Stratton. I heard she's friendly with both of them."

The way he said 'friendly' was clear. "That right?" Max

thought about Archie and Marline and her mint gum and could only shake his head. He did not want to get near that fly trap. "Small-town grapevine is more efficient than the goddamn Internet."

"I don't know much about the Internet." Mose liked to pretend he was more of a Luddite than he let on. "But, I've found that people still talk to one another in small towns, but, more importantly, they still listen. Funny what you hear when you stop waiting to talk and listen."

"I'll remember that."

"You will if you want to get anything done in this town." Mose leaned forward and flipped the two thick steaks over. "So, go ahead, ask your questions."

"All right. Don't get your hackles up. Say what you want about how he's going about it, but I don't think Roy's wrong to be looking everywhere for possible answers."

"I just hope he's doing that. Looking everywhere, I mean."

"What happened with you and the chief?"

"Nothing with me. And nothing that probably doesn't happen anywhere else with groups of people that fall outside what the majority considers the norm. Some bigotry. Fear of the unknown. A little xenophobia. There wasn't any single incident with us and Roy. Just a lot of petty things. Deputies give us a hard time if they can. Sometimes they make life more difficult than it has to be. And Roy lets it go. Sort of gives it tacit approval. It wears on a man. Eventually, he will push back."

"That happen? Someone push back?"

"No, not yet. Not that I've heard, and everyone would hear if that happened. But it's coming. You can feel it, especially in the younger ones."

"Maybe the chief feels it, too. Maybe that's why he asked me to do this?"

"Maybe. I'm afraid that might be giving him too much credit. Feels more like he's doing what's expedient."

"You think anyone in your community is capable of something like this?"

"Of course. People think we're strange because we dress differently or choose to live our lives differently but, at the root of it, we're still human. Murder? Violence? Give anyone the right motivation and I think they have the capacity for violence. Even extreme violence. I can think of five off the top of my head."

"Okay—"

"I can also think of twice that number from Father White's congregation in town or the Methodists over in Montague. Heck, I wouldn't put it past White himself. You ever get a look at him after a few pops at those interfaith picnics and you'll see him a little differently. There's malice in his eyes."

He pulled a small square of paper from his breast pocket and held it out. Max took it and slipped it into his own pocket.

"The most efficient way to do it might be Sunday after church services. Everyone should be there. Otherwise, you'll be driving all around the 305 to different farms or workshops trying to find those guys."

"Will showing up at the services cause a problem?"

"This week it's at Jacob the Younger's barn. If you wait until after and take it slow, I don't think it will be a problem."

"Okay, I'll do that. I appreciate it."

"I hope not. I hope it's a waste of your time. No offense."

"None taken."

Mose pulled the steaks off the grill and they changed the subject to old car engines, fishing, and what projects Mose was working on in his studio. Friendlier topics. Normal topics.

·   ·   ·

Later, after the steak and more than a few beers, Max found himself lying awake and staring out his small bedroom window thinking about God, or maybe it was god, he still hadn't decided, as wisps of clouds drifted across a waxing moon. If there was a God out there that created everything, how did He create something capable of what he'd seen today? Did you chalk it up to free will? Or did God/god lose track of the rulebook?

He set the big fuzzy ideas aside and thought about Collum Hawkins walking down the red dirt of Sinclair Avenue and never walking back out. He thought about Topher and Stephanie Arnsfeld letting the killer into their house, only to have him paint the walls with their blood. What bound those people together? He had no idea, but it must be something. You might get a spree killer in a sizable metro area. Someone just killing for the fun or random opportunity of it, but he couldn't see it happening in a town the size of Prince Creek. Maybe one random killing, someone passing through, a traveler, but not three. There had to be a link between the victims.

More questions filled his mind. Why Sinclair Avenue? How did the killer get there? How did he get away? Why did Topher Arnsfeld let the killer inside? Did he know him? Did Arnsfeld know Hawkins? Whose picture did Koenig find in Hawkins's apartment?

Why the Bible verses?

Why an ax?

What did Ellie Baker put in those muffins?

What was Koenig doing right now?

CHAPTER FIFTEEN

In Max's experience, prison was terrible in almost all respects. The food, the racism, the overcrowding, the noise, the violence, most of the guards, but perhaps the worst was the drudgery of the daily routine. With few exceptions, every single day was the same. Prison hammered in the daily routine and you had no choice but to take it. Sometimes, those forced changes became permanent, behind bars or not. Max was now a morning person whether he liked it or not.

He showered, lingering a bit until the meager hot water tank ran to ice-cold, then waiting another 30 seconds more before getting out and toweling off. He brushed his teeth and ran his fingers through his short hair, then found a clean T-shirt and pulled on his jeans. He skipped using the coffee maker and was at The Maple with his copied files by 7 a.m. A man in a blue suit with a coffee cup and a paper bag nodded and held the door as he entered. Inside, there were two white-haired women chatting at one of the small tables by the window, otherwise the dining room was empty.

"Early start," Ellie said from her spot behind the register.

She had smudges of flour on both cheeks and the flush of color that said she'd been up and at it for a while. Her tall and silent partner was working in the background, dividing dough and flipping the pieces into a plastic container.

"I think I might enjoy being a cop. I could get used to these hours. With Archie, this is almost lunchtime. What time do you two get started here?"

"Sybil gets here at 4 a.m. most days to get the daily items in the oven. I like more of a lie in. I'll arrive around 5 a.m. or 5:30 a.m. We open the doors at 6 a.m."

"How long have you been open?"

"Well, the shop has been here, gosh, maybe 30 or 40 years in various forms. We bought it from Jackie Shanks ten years ago. It was a bakery then, but more focused on sweets. Birthday cakes, cupcakes, that sort of thing. We'll still do that if you ask, but we revamped it into more of a cafe."

"Ten years ago? Were you around when Topher Arnsfeld first came out here?"

"Sort of. Sybil and I still had a little stand in Montague, a pop-up place, mostly on the weekends, but it was getting some notice. Remember we had the world's greatest muffins. We knew it could work on a larger scale, and we'd started scouting out places. Ended up here."

"No thoughts of investing?"

"With Arnsfeld?" She laughed. "No, we definitely didn't have the type of capital he was looking for. And he wasn't looking to invest in a cafe either. All the spare change either of us could find went into the business."

"His loss."

That brought a smile. "Thanks. I think so."

Max found he wasn't eager to go to a table and dive back into the blood and bodies.

"Did he ever come in here?"

"No, not often. His wife was more of a regular."

"Any impressions of them?"

"I'm probably projecting a bit, but he always struck me as aloof. He definitely didn't want to give off that impression. In fact, he went out of his way to appear more salt of the earth than he was, but he couldn't entirely hide it. If you caught him in an unguarded moment you could see his genuine feelings."

"What about his wife?"

"Stephanie? Oh, she was a local girl and very at ease around here. Even after she moved up five tax brackets. People seemed to like her. She came in with various groups of women. If you're looking to talk to investors, you should talk to Victor Wallace or Brady Stephens. I've gotten to know them a little. They both had money with Arnsfeld. They might be able to tell you something about him."

"They live in town?"

"Sure, Wallace owns and runs the grocery store, Town & Tide, down the street. Stephens is the top dog at the hospital."

"Thanks. I'll check in with them."

"Muffin with the coffee? Today we have corn, blueberry, and pistachio."

He looked down through the glass at the muffins loosely arranged in baskets. "Definitely pistachio."

"Huh. Would have pegged you as a corn man."

Max was forming a followup question to decipher what that meant, was he being profiled based on his pastry choices, when the bell over the door jingled and two guys wearing orange vests and paint-splattered jeans got in line. He took the coffee and pistachio muffin and grabbed the same table in the back corner he'd used yesterday.

He quickly scanned the Hawkins file again and then read his own notes. He realized it wasn't enough. He would go back over the people that Roy had interviewed already, that wouldn't kick up too much dust, but if he was going to find a link from Hawkins to Arnsfeld, he needed more. He was beginning to believe Roy's insistence on keeping it all quiet felt like the wrong move. It was tying their hands. They needed people talking. Someone out there knew something. If he could get them talking, he'd just have to listen.

He added Wallace's and Stephens's names under the Arnsfeld column. He re-read the two Bible verses, though he'd already committed them to memory. A lot of violence and a lot of blood, but not a lot of clues. He had a feeling they were just going in circles until another body turned up. He let that thought rattle around in his head as he picked at the muffin, suddenly not feeling all that hungry.

Five minutes later, Koenig came through the door. She was wearing a navy-blue summer-weight suit and the aviators. She looked rested and ready to kick ass.

She snatched a piece of muffin and popped it in her mouth. "C'mon. Roy wants to talk to us."

"Anything?"

"Don't know but he sounded excited. Damn. That's a good muffin."

He held out the plate. She finished it in three bites.

A constable wearing a Prince Creek uniform was leaning on the counter when Marline buzzed them inside. He had short blond hair clipped close to his scalp, and his uniform fit snugly across his chest and biceps. Max thought it looked uncomfortably tight; he assumed the man preferred it that way. He didn't recognize the constable, but they'd already met the part-timer Chravette at the Arnsfeld scene so this must either be Stratton or Alford. He guessed Stratton, as he didn't look like he had the years or the experience to be a corporal.

"Morning, Max," Marline said with a smile. "Morning, Inspector."

The constable looked at them with flat, gray eyes but made no move to introduce himself.

"Morning, Marline," Max replied and followed Koenig past the two of them and down the hallway.

Koenig gave him a look as they turned the corner and walked through the open area toward Roy's office.

"What?" Max said. "Do I have something in my teeth?"

"Nope. Not that," Koenig said.

They could hear someone talking on the phone in the little cube built into the bullpen's corner. Alford. That confirmed it was Stratton giving them the stink eye out front. Good to know.

"Then what?" Max asked again as they approached the chief's door.

"Hi, Marline," Koenig said in a high voice.

"Oh c'mon. That sounds nothing like me," Max replied.

"Uh-huh." Koenig knocked and poked her head in.

Roy was on the phone but waved them both inside.

He dropped the receiver back in its cradle as they took the two seats opposite his desk. He ran a hand through his limp hair. Max didn't know if Roy was a good cop or not. Or, if he could solve these murders or not, but he looked like he was putting in the effort.

"The mayor," he said. "She was just checking in. She'd prefer I caught this maniac yesterday. I could practically hear the gears turning through the phone. How long before she needs a scapegoat?"

"Try to forget her. All politicians are the same, everywhere I go," Koenig said. "It's not personal. They literally think of themselves and no one else."

"You might be right," Roy said. "But I'd still be out of a job."

"Not if we catch him. You do that, you can write your ticket. Maybe take her job."

Max could tell Roy hadn't thought of that and now that he had, he liked the idea quite a bit.

"So, what did you want to talk to us about?" Koenig continued.

"Right." He sat forward and put his elbows on the desk. "I had a hell of a phone call this morning. A woman called up," Roy searched the paper on his desk and found a yellow Post-it, "name of Kelsey Macias, says she works for Arnsfeld at the Association. She's his executive assistant. And, here's the kicker, she's pregnant with his child. Says she wants to make sure their child is considered in any will."

"Huh," Koenig said. "Did you find a will yet?"

"Not yet. Locksmith is coming in at 9 a.m. If it's in one of the safes at the house, we should know soon. I haven't heard from any lawyers yet."

"Makes you wonder if there are any other little Arnsfelds running around," Max said.

"Interesting question. Dip your wick once you might be more likely to do it again," Roy said. "Not sure how we'd find out unless they called."

"What did you tell her?" Koenig asked.

"Told her to get her own lawyer. What else was I going to say? And do it quick," Roy replied. "Gotta admit it does add an angle I hadn't thought of. You just know money is tied up in this somehow. I didn't think of the inheritance, but I am now."

"Was Macias going to work today?"

"As far as I know."

"We are heading out to the Arnsfeld Association to talk to some people. We'll add her to the list."

"If she's not there, she left an address up in East Point. I'll email it to you."

"Okay."

Max took the slip of paper from his pocket. "Got some names from Mose. Guys he thinks might be a little hinky. Guys with a temper or who wouldn't mind a fight, Amish or not. Wondering if you could get someone to run a quick check on them. Be good to know if any of them have a sheet. I don't want to walk up on this maniac if he's already on someone's radar."

Roy looked at the list. "I know most of these guys. Four of them, anyway. We've never picked any of them up. Not officially."

"Mose mentioned there was some, umm, friction between the department and the Amish."

"Yeah, we've gotten on each other's nerves like I told you yesterday, but there's been no real trouble."

"He was also clear that he could think of twice that number of names outside his community that he'd also put on a list."

"Yeah, me, too. And we have. And we're checking those guys out. Trust me, with no real leads, that's all D'arcy and Stratton are doing, but we need something more. If word gets out, we're just making lists of names, ah God, it would be bad."

"I don't know. It might not be a terrible idea. Ask a bunch of people to make a bunch of lists and see what common names shake out," Max said.

Koenig and Roy looked at him like he was insane. "You want to crowdsource a murder investigation?" Koenig said.

"I'll tell you what, I bet the killer's name would be on more than one person's list. This guy is local. People know him and I bet certain people pick up on a vibe."

"Jesus, let's hope it doesn't come to that," Roy said. He looked at Koenig. "You got anything else going?"

"Not yet," Koenig replied. "We spent yesterday going over

the scenes, reading the background, getting up to speed. Today, we'll go out and talk to the people at Arnsfeld's office. Follow up with a few people from your Hawkins report. See if we can dig out the link between the victims. Gotta be in the details somewhere."

"All right." The chief couldn't quite keep the disappointment from his voice.

"Going to take time, Chief, but we'll get him. Crazy like this doesn't just fade away."

"That's what I'm worried about."

They all stood up.

"You heard of the Royal Canadian Riders?" Max asked.

"The wannabe biker gang up in Glenfanning? Mostly hot air as far as I can tell. Why? Something there?"

"Don't know yet. They keep popping up like a bad penny if you look long enough at Arnsfeld or the Association."

"Well, hell."

"Yeah."

CHAPTER SIXTEEN

The Arnsfeld Association's headquarters was five miles outside of town.

"Who are we talking to?" Max asked.

"Kent Ramsey, head operations guy second in command to Arnsfeld, and Alex Carr, the chief financial officer. And now, maybe this Kelsey Macias. Some details in the file folder there." She motioned toward a folio stuck between the armrests.

He opened the file folder and skimmed the material inside. Christopher Arnsfeld had made his first million, actually $22 million, by the time he was 19. At the start of the Internet age, he and a high school classmate had created online local directories, digital yellow pages for the big US cities, and quickly got contracts with major newspapers. AOL bought them out before graduation. Two years later, Arnsfeld was pushed off the board after disagreeing on the company's growth plan.

The pattern would repeat itself a few years later. Arnsfeld would invest half of his previous windfall in a new financial technology company that made it much easier and more affordable for small businesses to accept credit card payments online. Visa acquired that company. Arnsfeld was the largest shareholder and received $30 million. His prickly personality made his tenure at Visa short-lived, too.

Arnsfeld hit the triple-cherry jackpot with an instant messaging program aimed, not at teens or mobile phone users, but corporate workplaces. It was a huge success when it went public. Arnsfeld still retained a small percentage of stock but had cashed out most of his options for a rumored $100 million.

Max could see why enthusiasm was high when Arnsfeld came on the scene in PEI. Everything he'd touched in the past had turned to gold.

There were brief bios of the other members of the Arnsfeld Association's executive team. Both Ramsey and Carr had been with Arnsfeld on past projects. Ramsey at both the fintech payment company and the business messaging one. Carr had come aboard only since the business messaging one.

There was a large sign in the wedge of grass where Mackimmons Road split off Route 16. Koenig made the turn, but they had to drive another half a mile alongside a crushed gravel walking path, then a large, mostly empty parking lot until they could see the steel and glass Arnsfeld Association building itself. It was four floors of blue-green reflective glass with two wings sprawling to either side of a central entrance atrium.

"Looks a little out of place out here," Koenig said.

"My friend Charlie told me that, once upon a time, Arnsfeld had grand plans. This would be the anchor building for a larger campus. They never made it that far. When the money spigot got turned off, Arnsfeld eventually decided to use the building for the Association."

"Better than letting it rot, I suppose, but it doesn't really give off a charitable vibe, does it?" Koenig said as she swung the Explorer into the looping drive that ran in front of the atrium.

She parked close to the doors, tight to the curb. A security guard, visible through the entry doors, tried to wave her off but she ignored him. He hitched his pants up over his considerable gut and came outside as they were shutting the Explorer's doors.

"Miss, you can't park there. Plenty of parking in the west lot. You passed it on your way in."

She held out her badge but didn't stop walking. Max followed in her wake. "Car stays. RCMP, Inspector Koenig. We have an appointment with Kent Ramsey and Alex Carr."

The guard, the patch over his pocket read Sellers, looked at the Explorer like it was a fly floating in his soup, but then followed Koenig inside. He went back behind his desk and pushed a three-ring binder across the counter. "If you could just sign in, I'll call up. Are you meeting with Mr. Ramsey or Mr. Carr first?"

"I'm not sure. I think we're meeting with both of them." Koenig scribbled her name down as she spoke.

"I see," Sellers responded and picked up a phone. "I'll try Mr. Ramsey's office first." He spoke briefly to someone on the other end and then hung up. "Ms. Holloway, Mr. Ramsey's assistant, will be down shortly to escort you up." He held out two temporary visitor badges. "Please keep these on at all times during your visit."

Two minutes later, a thin, older woman with stiffly-styled blonde hair and a rhinestone brooch in the shape of a wasp pinned to a navy blazer, exited the elevator and approached them. "I'm Jane Holloway, Mr. Ramsey's assistant. I'll show you up to the boardroom." She didn't wait for their names or offer to shake hands, just turned on her heels and headed back toward the elevator.

They rode up to the fourth floor in silence. The elevator doors opened onto a broad lobby. They followed Holloway across the lobby to a conference room.

"Feel free to take any seat. Water and juice are available from the kitchenette just outside. Mr. Ramsey will be down shortly." She then turned and left.

Max raised his eyebrow. "That charity vibe isn't warming up any inside."

"She matches the decor perfectly," Koenig said.

A broad, oval table dominated the room with plush leather seats for 20 or more. Small mics hung from the ceiling and Max saw more mics inlaid through the center of the table. An LCD display screen, at least 80 inches, hung from the far wall. The floor-to-ceiling window panels refracted the outside sunlight and gave a striking view of the Northumberland Strait.

"May be the best conference room view in Canada. Certainly on PEI."

They both turned. Kent Ramsey was a few inches under six feet and a few years north of 50. He still had a full head of wavy grayish-black hair on top of unkempt eyebrows and a fleshy nose. He shook both their hands. His hands were soft, a man who worked behind a desk full-time, Max thought, but his grip was firm. After the introductions, he gestured to two nearby chairs and then walked around to the opposite side and took a seat.

"What can I do for you, Inspectors?" Koenig didn't correct his assumption about Max. "I mean, I assume, you're here about what happened to Topher."

"That's right. RCMP Major Cases is assisting Chief Roy with the investigation."

"How can I help? Do you think what happened to Topher and Steph had something to do with the Association?"

Koenig deflected. "It's only the second day. We've spread a wide net and haven't dismissed anything. Did Mr. Arnsfeld mention anything recently that was bothering him? Work or personally?"

Ramsey leaned back and his gaze shifted over their shoulders to the view outside. "No, nothing comes to mind. I spoke to him that morning; he wasn't feeling well and didn't come into the office, but it was all normal business-related things. Logistics and to-do items for various projects that we have going."

"Can you tell us about those?"

"The projects? Sure, it's not proprietary. Most of what we do is on our website. A lot of it is research-based, looking to create solutions to sustain our natural resources. We have a small footprint here on the island, but we partner with other nonprofits around the world. We're currently working in over 50 countries to address topics like climate change, clean water, sustainable energy, and food density."

Max had the feeling they were hearing Ramsey's standard stump speech.

"And what specifically did you talk to Mr. Arnsfeld about that morning?"

"Let's see. Two things, I think. A water targeting project here locally."

"What's water targeting?"

"We provide guidance on how to better target agricultural conservation on farms to more cost-effectively achieve measurable improvements in the surrounding water supply."

It was clear Ramsey was incapable of speaking in plain English.

"So, keeping all the fertilizer and other cancer-causing crap out of the drinking water?"

Koenig had no such problems. Ramsey gave a thin smile and shifted his weight in his chair. "Yes, something like that."

"Okay, got it. You said two things?"

"Yes, the other was about an ongoing pilot of a zero-carbon district in Toronto. You might say keeping the smog from burning more of a hole in the atmosphere."

"Gotcha. So, partnering and working in over 50 countries, you must have stepped on some toes. Just the way of the world, right? Can you think of anyone that might have wanted to harm Arnsfeld or the charity?"

"Inspector, we are a nonprofit. We weren't doing corporate takeovers or competing for intellectual property."

"Oh, c'mon, there must have been some competition. For grants or government money?"

"Sure, but we also were well-financed on our end. Topher was generous when he set up the endowment. If we missed out on those things, we might have to scale back, but it rarely cost us the entire project."

"Nice situation to be in."

"Absolutely. It allowed us to accomplish a lot in a short amount of time."

"What will happen now?"

"We're still figuring that out. There's a board meeting later this week. Topher was the chairman, but there were no ownership or equity stakes as a nonprofit. Everyone on the board has an equal vote. I expect that things will carry on much as they are. As I said, we are well-funded in the short-term."

"What about personally? The rumor was that Mr. Arnsfeld could sometimes be difficult to work with."

"Ack," Ramsey waved his hands. "That old saw is just left over from his time as a wunderkind and sold his first couple companies. It was a good hook for a story. The journalists loved it, but he'd matured. Yes, he could still be arrogant and irritating, especially when something wasn't going according to plan, but it was all within a business context. I don't think anyone took it personally. Surely not enough to murder both him and his wife."

Koenig closed the small notebook she'd been writing in and glanced at Max.

"Does the Association work with any local groups on the island?" He asked.

"Sure, a whole bunch of small- to mid-sized farms on the water project. Plus a few others on minor things. I don't know how many offhand. We allow our employees to present proposals and, if approved, to run independent projects in the community with small grants."

"How about the Royal Canadian Riders? Ever work with them?"

He frowned and looked genuinely puzzled. "No, that name doesn't ring a bell. I could have Jane check the list. We keep a list of all the partners for reporting purposes."

"We'd appreciate that."

"Thank you for your time, Mr. Ramsey," Koenig said. She stood and handed him a card. "If you think of anything or hear anything, please let us know."

Five minutes later, Jane Holloway escorted Alex Carr into the boardroom. The Arnsfeld Association financial chief was younger than Ramsey by probably a decade, but looked softer and weaker as if he never exercised more than walking from his car to his desk. He had thin brown hair, a pointed nose, and a round chin. He wore khakis and a navy blazer over a blue-checkered shirt. His eyes were rimmed in red. He'd either been staring at spreadsheets all night or crying. Max thought either answer would be interesting.

They shook and did a round of introductions before

taking their seats. Carr stared at them. He didn't appear to be one for small talk. He rubbed his left hand over the blazer's fabric on his right forearm. There was a slight shine to the fabric and Max wondered if Carr had some mild form of autism. He knew many people that dealt with numbers could be on the spectrum. Koenig must have noticed it, too. She let the silence play out until it began to get awkward before she started the interview.

"RCMP Major Cases out of Charlottetown is assisting Chief Roy with the investigation in the Arnsfeld murders." Carr blinked at that but said nothing. Maybe it wasn't autism. Maybe it was drugs, Max thought. It might explain the eyes. Koenig continued, "Do you know anything about what happened the other night?"

That finally punctured whatever bubble Carr had been inside. "What?" he sputtered. "Of course not. I'm not a suspect, am I?"

"No, not right now. We're talking to all of Mr. Arnsfeld's close associates, seeing what they know. So, what do you know?"

"Nothing. I mean, nothing that would make me think Topher would be murdered. This whole situation is crazy."

Koenig took him through the same things they'd discussed with Ramsey. The answers matched up. Max thought she was good at it. She knew when to use flattery and when to bully and when to just let the person talk. She eventually brought it back around to the financials.

"So, the charity is in good shape then? Money-wise?"

"Yes. I don't see any reason for concern. There are ebbs and flows, but that's the nature of nonprofits."

"And Mr. Arnsfeld's death won't hurt that?"

"No. I mean, yes. His death will have an impact. I'm just not sure what it will be. Impossible to tell. His name alone is helpful for fundraising. He isn't great at it, that was more

Connor's thing, but Topher's name still has a cachet to it and some people liked the tech pirate attitude."

"Tech pirate attitude?"

"Oh, it was mostly an act now. Topher could turn it on and off. When he was younger and still in the trenches, he could be a real asshole. Excuse the language. Brash, arrogant, demanding. Got him thrown out of more than one board-room and more than a few parties. But that had mostly waned. I think Stephanie sanded some rough edges off or maybe it was just maturity or the piles of money in his bank account."

This time Koenig asked the question, "What work do you guys do with the Royal Canadian Riders?"

Maybe it was the sudden change in direction, but Carr flinched in his seat and looked like he'd suddenly swallowed a needle. "Royal Canadian Riders? Not sure I know that name."

CHAPTER SEVENTEEN

"He was lying through his teeth."

"And not doing it very well," Koenig said.

They were back in the Explorer heading north again, away from Prince Creek, toward East Point. Kelsey Macias had called in sick that morning. Jane Holloway had provided her phone number. Koenig had called and Macias had agreed to talk.

"The question is why?"

"Why was Carr lying or why would the RCR kill Arnsfeld?"

"Both. Nothing fits so far. I don't see who benefits if Arnsfeld is killed. Despite what they said, the charity has to be on shakier ground without Arnsfeld and, if the RCR were involved, why would they kill him? Why kill the goose the lays the golden egg?"

"Let's step back. I don't think we know yet that Arnsfeld and the RCR were in bed together. The RCR could be legitimately involved with the charity and still be doing something illegal separately. They don't have to be intertwined. I mean, why? How would Arnsfeld benefit from a shady deal with them? It makes almost as much sense as them killing him."

"I don't know, but Carr started looking for the eject button as soon as we mentioned it. Something hinky is going on. Thorne may just run a small paper, but he's not stupid and he's a good reporter. I trust his instincts."

"I honestly thought that was a dry hole until I saw Carr's reaction."

"It's the first tiny splinter in this entire case. We should check them out."

"Oh, they definitely just moved up a few spots on my list."

East Point was a 15-minute drive up Route 16. It became increasingly rural as they passed Lighthouse Road and veered west. They passed large rolling farm plots, through a thick growth of forest surrounding a bay inlet, over a single lane bridge, and then into a small community clustered around a church, a commercial dairy farm, and a ramshackle community center with a swaybacked roof and peeling, jaundiced-looking paint.

Macias's house was two turns, a right then a left, off Route 16 on a small lane within walking distance of the church. It was a single-family home set on a wide plot of grass. Two large flowering bushes flanked the top of the dirt driveway. In the center of the yard, a ring of stones, maybe the cap of an old well, was filled with wildflowers. The home itself was a pale green rectangle with black shutters on the three windows that faced the street. A small elevated wood porch hung off the short side closest to the driveway.

Koenig pulled the Explorer into the driveway behind a dark blue, older model Volkswagen Golf. Local beach permits and parking stickers were stuck to the bumper. As he climbed out, Max could hear waves hitting rocks and smell the slight tang of sea salt in the air, but a screen of evergreen trees hid any views of the nearby water. Maybe when you lived so close you sometimes wanted to forget? They climbed the three steps up to the porch and knocked on the door. Macias must have been watching from a window and opened the door almost immediately.

At first glance, Max had to admit he'd made several wrong assumptions about Macias. He'd assumed, when he'd heard that Arnsfeld had an affair with his assistant, that the woman was young and attractive. He'd believed the cliche, mostly because it was usually true, that Arnsfeld traded in his wife for a younger model. Macias was attractive, but she was likely very close to Stephanie Arnsfeld's age. They looked remarkably similar. Macias was in her late 30s or early 40s, with shoulder-length brown hair shot through with blonde highlights. She had a slim build, but not bony. A woman on the cusp of middle age and comfortable in her own skin. If she was pregnant, she wasn't very far along.

"Hi," she said with a slight rasp. There was no question she'd been crying, and Max realized this was the first person he'd seen that looked affected by any of the deaths. "Please, come in." She held the door open and they entered a small, tidy kitchen decorated in soft grays and whites. New, stainless steel appliances took up most of the space. There was a breakfast nook at the far end nestled next to a bay window. "Coffee? Tea?" They both declined. From this angle, Max could see the trees had been carefully pruned to give a slim view of the water.

Macias walked through a doorway, and they followed her into a living room. She sat down in a cushioned armchair and pulled her feet up under her. A blanket was puddled on the floor next to her chair. A box of tissues sat on a low coffee table in the center of the room. Koenig and Max perched on the matching sofa opposite.

"We understand you called Chief Roy this morning?"

"Yes, that's correct."

"About ..." Koenig trailed off, then started again. "Look, please forgive me, I can see you're upset but the fastest way to do this might be with some blunt questions."

"I understand. Go ahead."

"You told Chief Roy that you're pregnant with Topher Arnsfeld's child?"

"That's right."

"You're sure?"

"Yes. One hundred percent. Topher was my only sexual partner."

"And you're sure about the pregnancy?"

"Yes, very sure about that, too. I had the 12-week checkup last Thursday."

"What did Mr. Arnsfeld think about the baby?"

She looked away, out the window over her shoulder. "He didn't know. Not yet."

"Were you afraid to tell him?"

"No. We might not have stayed together, I'm not naïve, but Topher would have taken care of the baby. I'm sure of that. I was going to tell him soon. I just ..." She looked back at them, "I just hadn't done it yet." Two tears ran down her cheeks.

Koenig gave her a moment and looked down at her notebook, flipped through the pages. Eventually, she asked, "How long have you worked for Mr. Arnsfeld?"

Macias picked up a crumpled tissue from the side table and wiped her nose. "Almost 8 years. I started with him before everything transitioned over to the charity. We were still trying to make the incubator work."

"We've just come from speaking to Kent Ramsey and Alex Carr. They followed Arnsfeld up here from previous ventures. You look more—"

"Native?"

"Yes. How did you get the job?"

"Just because I grew up here doesn't mean I'm some kind of hick. My father had a stroke when I was 12. My mother couldn't handle it. Took up drinking. I was running my family's dairy farm before I could drive, and I kept us afloat for the next 15 years before the locals all sold out to ADL." She waved a hand at the window. "I know my way around operations and the realities of running a business, especially out here. I knew Stephanie from the Prince Creek library board. We'd run into each other occasionally outside of that, at fundraisers, the market, you know. She knew about my time running the farm. One time she mentioned the job. I was getting a little bored and the ADL money wasn't enough to retire on. A day later, Topher called me up. We talked. I started the next day."

"How would you describe Mr. Arnsfeld?"

She gave an abrupt bark of a laugh that got caught in her throat and she almost seemed on the verge of crying again, but pulled back. "It depended on the day. He was always a very demanding boss, but some days he could be affable and understanding. Other days, he could be the exact opposite, just cold and almost demeaning. Anyone who is that successful has a certain meanness, I think. Or calculation. There's a lack of empathy and emotion that allows them to make the cutthroat decisions that often lead to huge success. At least monetary success."

"Doesn't exactly sound like the island vibe."

"No. It doesn't, and I'll tell you we talked about if that was ultimately the reason the incubator failed. If there was something about the makeup of this place that just didn't lend itself to the attitude necessary to compete in today's tech world."

"Why did he stay, do you think? The person you describe

does not seem like he would be satisfied with a quieter life on the island."

"No, you're right. Stephanie was an islander and I think she kept him here initially, but I wonder if their marriage would have lasted." She gave another humorless laugh. "That's probably what all the other women say, right? But I think it might have been the reason we got together in the first place. He was getting restless. He seemed more on edge lately. I think he was getting bored with the charity. I think he missed the rough and tumble of the business world. Topher liked a challenge. I think that's at least part of the reason he started the charity. No one expected it. He enjoyed winning, but he really liked seeing the other side lose. I'm not sure the charity ultimately scratched that competitive itch. It was all too bureaucratic. A little too polite for Topher. There were no stakes."

"When did you and Mr. Arnsfeld start seeing each other?"

"About 6 months ago. We were in Toronto for a series of meetings and, well, dinner, drinks and it just happened. I think it caught us both by surprise. It did for me, at least. There had been no flirting or cues before that trip."

Max spoke up, "You only got to know Mrs. Arnsfeld, Stephanie, later? As an adult? You didn't know her before that?" Koenig looked at him with a raised eyebrow. He knew he'd stepped on her toes a bit, thrown off her rhythm of questions, but that phrase, *Stephanie was the islander,* had sparked something in his head.

"That's right. She was three or four years older than me. We probably were at Prince Creek High at the same time but never crossed paths."

"Okay," Max said.

"If you want to know more about Stephanie from back then, you might talk to Loreen Camille or Diana Goulart. I've seen her having coffee with them in The Maple and she'd mentioned them in conversation before. I got the sense that they were old friends. Either of them would likely know her better than me."

Koenig jotted down the names and then looked at Max. He shook his head, and she continued. "Can you think of anyone that would have wanted to cause Mr. Arnsfeld harm?"

"No. I really can't. I've been thinking about it nonstop since I heard. I could see someone taking a swing at him in the spur of the moment. As I said, he enjoyed winning, and Topher could definitely make people angry, but it was always business. He'd take apart their idea or their plan. It was never personal. A metaphorical bloody nose. Some scraped knuckles if you pissed off the right guy, but it was all boardroom posturing. Nowhere close to murder."

"How about the charity?"

"No, nothing there. It just wasn't that cutthroat. The projects we have going on are helpful but not worth killing over."

"Okay, last thing. Where were you two nights ago?"

"Here. I helped at the community center until 7 p.m., we do a food pantry on Thursdays, then I came home and had dinner."

"Alone?"

"I can give you names of other volunteers from the community center, but after that, yes, I was alone. Topher was supposed to come over, but he said he wasn't feeling well."

She started crying again. Koenig handed her the box of tissues and they let themselves out.

They were both quiet in the car, Macias's grief had dampened their moods. They drove past the community center where two cars sat parked next to a foundation that was sprouting tall weeds. Koenig turned the car left, and they started back toward Prince Creek. Max scribbled down Camille and Goulart's names into his folder of notes.

He put the window back up as they approached the large covered paddocks and milk storage tanks of the dairy farm, but the earthy smell of animals and warm manure had already slipped inside.

"You'd be terrible at poker, Max."

"What's that supposed to mean?"

"It means we've barely known each other two days and I can read you like a book. You're scheming. I can see it on your face. I thought we had a plan. I talk, you listen."

"I was listening. That's why I had to talk."

"Stephanie Arnsfeld."

"Yeah. We've spent the last day assuming this had to do with Topher Arnsfeld, his money, his business, something like that. What if it's something else? I know we don't have an exact time of death, but it's likely Arnsfeld wasn't even supposed to be home. He should have been at work or with Macias if he didn't get sick."

Koenig tapped her finger on the wheel. A tell Max had actually noticed about her, but wasn't going to say anything about. "That's a good point," she said eventually. "We might need some help. Or we'll need to divide and conquer."

"Why don't you take Topher. We'll need official channels to pry some of that open, I bet. Especially when the lawyers get involved from the charity or his will. I can ask around town about Stephanie."

"Okay."

They drove in silence for a mile, Max thinking about the next steps he'd need to take. "You going to check on Macias's alibi?" Max asked as they rounded East Point, the white clapboard hexagon of the lighthouse standing out in the distance,

"Have to."

"You think she did it?"

"Gotta check. She told us she worked on a big farm. Death and blood wouldn't be unusual for her."

"Production animals to humans is a big jump. Besides, what would she gain by killing Arnsfeld?"

"Money."

"Maybe. Need to see what the will says. He didn't even know about the baby yet. Feels like a reach. Laws are pretty strict now. Why go through the risk of killing him when you are guaranteed support at least until the kid is 18? It seems like a risky way of grabbing some of Arnsfeld's money."

"Yeah. That's all true and she almost definitely didn't do it, but that's not good enough. I've seen these situations spiral into some weird places."

"Women be crazy."

"Watch it," but she said it with a smile.

Kelly Macias might have slept with Topher Arnsfeld, an eventual DNA test and a court order would take care of that question, but Max didn't think she was a killer.

As they dropped down off the bluff overlooking Prince Creek and into the business district, Max said, "Listen, I feel like we're boxed in on Hawkins with Roy wanting to keep a lid on his death. He was the first victim and we just don't know enough about him. The man was so isolated that the options to dig out more on our own are limited. Unless you have ideas or RCMP resources we could use?"

"No, I called a contact last night about your Royal Canadian Riders but otherwise we are on our own until something changes."

"You mean more bodies."

"To put it bluntly, yes."

"It feels like we have very little room to maneuver."

She looked over at him. "And you want to create some room?"

"I was thinking about it, yeah. It could break things up. There is nothing in Hawkins's life to grab onto. I've got a few names, but they might not pan out. It will take too long for just the two of us to mine his life and get a hold of something. But if we got people talking ..."

"That would all potentially speed up. You're back to crowdsourcing a suspect?"

"Not a suspect. Just information. And why not? The killer knows all this. We're not spoiling anything. If the public knew what we knew, maybe not all of it, but more of it, in a town this size, it could shake something loose. What do you think?"

"Gonna piss off Roy."

"I don't find that bothering me too much."

"I've been here for two days and I know you're friends with Thorne. Roy must know it, too. How are you going to get it out there?"

"Get in front of it maybe? Go to Roy first. Tell him Thorne got an anonymous tip."

"Preemptive move." She tapped a finger on the wheel again. Max noticed she wore no rings on her slim fingers. "Could work. He'll still be pissed but just maybe not at us. Or not as much. Plus, I'm hungry, I could eat another of the kid's burgers."

CHAPTER EIGHTEEN

Thorne was at his corner table. An empty plate with fry crumbs and a fresh bottle of Molson sat near his elbow. He pecked something into his old laptop with two fingers as Max and Koenig slid into the opposite side of the booth.

"Two questions," Max said, "how did you never learn to type, and what is your cholesterol after eating here every day?"

"Good afternoon, Constables. First, typing while drinking is a time-honored journalistic tradition, so I'm just honoring my forebears. Second, I'm certain my arteries are hard as steel, but if that means giving up these burgers, I don't want to know."

"Gonna be a shame when the kid leaves," Max said.

"Are you two here on official business or just lunch?"

"Both," Koenig said. "Speaking of, give him the pitch, Max, while I put in our orders. Same as yesterday?"

"Why mess with a good thing?"

They both watched her walk to the bar, and she knew it. She flashed a middle finger over her shoulder.

"I like her," Thorne said, taking a swallow of Molson. "She any good as a cop?"

Max shrugged. "How would I know? I've been on the job for all of two days."

"Good point."

"But, yeah, I think so. She seems sharp."

"You guys making any progress?"

"Depends on how you measure progress. I think we're doing a lot of the necessary things, but it's hard to know if we're getting any closer to this guy."

"Ah." Thorne gave a toothy smile and took the pencil from behind his ear, started chewing on the nub of the eraser. "I smell an offer coming."

"We need help. On two fronts. One is mostly just getting the word out about something, see what it stirs up. The second is with research. We need some background that we just might not have time to do with our limited resources."

"And Chief Roy has a different opinion?"

"Yes. He wants to keep everything as quiet as possible in the hopes that it will either go away or we catch the guy quickly. Koenig and I agree that neither is likely at the moment."

"Okay, and what do I get in return?"

Koenig came back with two iced teas and slid into the booth. "We'll answer your questions," she said. "We might not tell you everything, not right away, but we won't lie. When it's over, we give you an exclusive."

"But there's a catch?"

"Until we catch the guy, it can't come from us. We can't go on record confirming things. Gotta leave that to Roy. This all has to come from," she waved her hand, "the air, the ether, God. Take your pick."

"I think I can live with that."

Max glanced at Koenig. She nodded. "What do you know

about Collum Hawkins?" he asked.

Thorne leaned back in the booth. "Not the direction I thought you'd be going. Why are you asking?"

"You first."

He tapped his pencil on his front teeth. "He's the town recluse. Prince Creek's Boo Radley. I'm sure most rural towns have their version. He's quiet, lives alone, keeps to himself. Those three things right there are enough to get the rumor mill churning."

"He's lived here his whole life?"

"Entire adult life, as far as I know. This is where his story might differ from the cliche. He wasn't always the recluse. He was a lawyer. Hell, I guess he still is, and just a normal guy, until about 20 years ago. I wasn't running the paper then. I did some stringer stuff for old Bill Haas, but I was mostly in Charlottetown working at *The Guardian*."

"What happened?"

"Nothing, as far as I know. Nothing that made the papers or made it to Bill Haas, and he had a fine ear for local gossip. Maybe it was mental, or something with his business, or something else, but he up and quit one day. Not just his law practice. Everything. He was never the life of the party, but you'd see him in here or around town. He'd say hi, chew the fat a bit. I was here full-time by the following spring and he had just faded into the background. He'd become the town's wallpaper. He was just a walking ghost."

Jerry swung by and dropped off their burgers and picked up Thorne's empty plate. He raised an eyebrow at the beer bottle, but Thorne waved him off and he left.

"And he never said anything about it to anyone?"

"Nope, or, if he did, they kept their mouths shut. After a while, people stopped asking. He went on living, if that's what you want to call it. And people started making up their own explanations."

"Anyone still around that knew him before he changed so much?"

"I didn't run in the same circles as Hawkins, so no one comes to mind off the top of my head. I could ask Bill. He's over at The Upham House in Montague. Most days his mind is still pretty sharp. He might remember some names," Thorne replied.

"That would be good."

"So, he's dead?"

"Yes. Killed about a week ago. You can probably confirm that with Doc Heathers or the Duncan Brothers, they did the transport," Max said.

"And you think it's tied into the Arnsfelds?"

"Yes. That will be harder to confirm. Roy is nervous about causing a panic."

"Or losing his job. I believe his contract is up in the fall."

"Can't speak to that. To be fair, other than trying to keep it low profile, from what I've seen, he's working it right so far."

"Not sure trying to bury a murder is doing the right thing," Thorne responded. "And I don't think you do either given the conversation we're having."

"I'm not in it for the moral question. I think getting the word out will help. We need people talking. Break up this log jam and get things moving before more people get hurt."

"Or worse," Koenig added.

They walked across the parking lot to the Explorer, simultaneously regretting the fries and wanting to eat even more of them, and about to climb in when Koenig's cell phone rang. She glanced at the screen. "HQ," she said before answering.

Max leaned against the side of the car and waited, feeling pleasantly drowsy with a full stomach in the sun, while

Koenig drifted away, walking in slow circles with the phone to her ear.

The day had started bright and warm, a continuation of the string of good weather on the island for the last week but clouds were building up to the west and Max could feel the increased humidity as his T-shirt stuck to the small of his back. Too early to tell if the clouds would amount to anything, often weather systems would skirt north and out to sea, but Max thought some rain might be okay. The entire area felt like it could use a good drenching.

After five minutes, Koenig slid the phone back into her pocket and walked over to the car.

"Rick Shea, he works in counterintelligence. I called him last night about the RCR. See if they were on anyone's radar."

"And are they?"

"Sort of. They're on a watch list but have done little to warrant any further investigation. In Rick's view, they ended up on the list because they ride motorcycles, some skinheads, some Gulf War vets. Survivalists. Para-military wannabes. He believes they're mostly harmless. Wouldn't want to get into a rumble with them because they're probably a little nutty but probably not into anything to get excited about."

"What would get the Mounties excited?"

"Terrorism, definitely, but not pot or pills unless it was on a big scale."

"But basically they're unknown? Nobody's given them a hard look. Maybe they're not fruitcakes, but just smart enough to stay out of the spotlight."

"Maybe," she conceded, "but how many really smart criminals have you met?"

"Good point."

"He gave me a name. Maddix Arnold."

"Let's go have a chat."

CHAPTER NINETEEN

Koenig punched in the address she'd gotten from Shea into the GPS. "He says it's a clubhouse and we can't miss it. It's got a pirate flag out front."

"You're kidding me?"

"I don't joke about pirates."

They went southwest on Main Street out of town, past Prince Creek Provincial Beach, and over the small bay bridge that served as the town's unofficial boundary. Max glanced right, the first turn after the bridge was the turn to Archie's apartment, then they were past and out of Prince Creek. Main Street became the slightly wider PE-2 West. They drove along in silence, rolling up and down hills, past ripening fields, roadside vegetable stands, and simple whitewashed houses, some in better shape than others. They came up behind an Amish buggy, a man upfront with the reins, and three older girls in the back bracketing a small boy. Max raised a hand as Koenig pulled carefully around and passed. Two of the girls smiled and the small boy waved back.

At the junction near Dingwell Mills, they turned south onto PE-4. They went through the pin-sized townships of

Dundas, Bridgeton, and Primrose before Max noticed a hand-painted sign for Glennfanning tacked to a telephone pole. The town of Glennfanning, in its entirety, consisted of tracts of farmland, thick stands of evergreen trees, and a machinery repair shop.

"Getting close," Koenig said looking at the car's navigation system.

A mile past the machinery shop, the evergreens thinned out, and they drove through a broad swath of green and brown open space. It wasn't being farmed, but maybe it had at one time. There was a small red and white ranch house set back from the road on the left. On the right was a tall pole flying the Canadian flag and, underneath, the familiar skull and crossbones of the Jolly Rodger.

"Jesus Christ," Koenig muttered. "I thought Shea was yanking my chain."

"Slow down, but don't stop," Max said. He took out his phone and snapped a few pictures.

They coasted past the headquarters of the Royal Canadian Riders. There was a circular drive in front of a multi-building cluster. The buildings were set 200 yards from the road and surrounded by acres of fallow pasture. There was a single-story building in the center with two large hexagonal windows on each end. It gave the building's front the appearance of a strange alien face. Three smaller buildings of varying sizes were built around the main building. There was a tall one that was roughly the size and shape of a barn and, to the left and right, like wings or haphazard additions, were two smaller buildings closer in size to big garden sheds or storage units you'd find with upscale homes. Each building looked fairly new and featured a matching aesthetic of bright natural stain on wide wood planks. The steep slanting metal roof of the main building glinted in the sun and appeared clean and undamaged. Three pickup trucks and two motorcycles were parked to the left near the largest building.

Koenig drove another mile before they were screened by the trees and found a driveway to turn around. She pulled back onto the road and then pulled over on the shoulder. "What do you think?"

"I have no idea. I recognize it. I've driven past a few times. The flagpole is new and maybe that building in back. It's different and catches the eye, but so are a lot of places out here. Homegrown construction. Never got a weird vibe off it in the past."

"With all that open land on every side, it will be hard to do any surveillance if it comes to that."

"Maybe that house across the street?" He pulled out his phone and zoomed in. "Looks like it might be a rental. There's a small sign near the mailbox."

"Possible. Not sure we could get approval for that. We don't even know if they're doing anything illegal."

"Is it just me? Feels like something is going on."

"I feel it, too. Let's go rattle their cage a bit and find out."

Koenig pulled into the paved circular drive and took it slow. The macadam was dark, fresh, and buttery smooth. Max would bet it hadn't yet gone through a Canadian winter. They rolled up to the small rectangular patch jutting off the main drive to where the pickups sat. Max could see the grass and weeds around the pad were also matted down. This was a slow time at headquarters. It appeared that more cars and trucks regularly parked on the grass.

Koenig angled the SUV behind the two pickups, blocking them in, and pointed the Explorer toward the road. By the time she killed the engine, a man had come out and stood with his arms crossed, watching them.

You couldn't see it from the road coming south, but the main building's front entrance faced to the side. There was a small two-step porch with two picnic tables framing the front door. Max looked around as they approached. One outbuilding was on the other side and shielded from view, but the big one in back and the other smaller one in view were both closed up tight. No windows, doors shut and locked.

"Who're you?" The man appeared to be in his early 20s with a short buzz of blond hair, acne-pocked cheeks, and the insolent attitude of someone who didn't like official authority.

"Inspector Koenig with the RCMP. Looking for Maddix Arnold."

"You have an appointment?"

"No. Didn't realize one was necessary."

"Well, he's pretty busy. Maybe you should come back some other time."

"So, he's here?"

"And busy like I just said."

"Okay, we can come back. And, when we do, we can bring a truckload of my friends, a warrant, and spend a solid day tearing up your little compound here."

"We ain't done nothing. How you gonna get that warrant?"

"You don't think I can get a judge around here to cut me a warrant if I mention you guys?"

He glared down at her, but Koenig just looked mildly back at him. He cut his gaze in Max's direction but found nothing there, either. "Wait here."

The kid clomped across the porch and pushed through the door. Koenig just rolled her eyes. "So much for coming in with a soft touch."

. . .

Two minutes later, Buzz Cut was back. "Come on in."

"Thank you," Koenig said with a smile. He held the door, but Koenig waved him on. "After you." He shrugged, and they followed him inside.

The inside was brighter than Max expected. There were only two small windows on the side that fronted the street but the entire opposite wall, facing the back of the property, was made of glass and could slide completely open. Half of it was open now and let in a warm breeze that smelled of straw, alfalfa, and damp clay. It almost covered up the scent of sweat, beer, and bleach that the rest of the room carried. Almost, but not quite.

There were five men inside. One was behind the bar that ran the length of the far side of the rectangular room. He was polishing glasses and making a show of not looking at them. Two were playing a game of pool and pretending not to notice them. Max was aware that all three of them were holding weapons, or likely had one within easy reach.

Buzz Cut led them over to the final man. He was sitting alone near the open section of the glass wall at one of the round tables scattered around the room.

He was younger than Max expected, maybe 40, though his full beard and weathered face could push that five years either way. He was heavyset, a gut starting to spill over his belt, with thick arms and shoulders. He wore stained blue jeans, motorcycle boots, and a black vest over a black T-shirt. Max could see three lines of faded blue ink running up his forearm. He was reading a newspaper with small bifocals perched on the end of his nose. Buzz Cut wandered back toward the bar and sat on a stool with his back to them.

"Please, have a seat. Apologies for Brad. He's got an attitude toward authority." Arnold shrugged and slipped his glasses into a pocket of his vest. "Not totally unwarranted given some of his history. But no excuse for bad manners." He folded up the paper and pushed it aside. "So, Inspector Koenig? You have some ID?"

"Sure," Koenig nodded and pulled out her credentials and held them up.

Arnold nodded back. "You related to the Koenigs up in Savage Harbour? Played hockey."

Koenig's eyes widened a fraction. "Actually, yeah. They're cousins."

"Damn. I grew up around St. Peter's Bay. I went up against the pair of them more than once. Whatever happened to Bobby? Heard he got drafted."

"He did. Sixth round by the Blackhawks. He made it as far as Portland in the AHL, but never the big show."

"Fastest hands I've ever seen. I definitely thought he had a chance. Doubt he'll remember me, I was more a puncher on skates than anything, but if you see him say hello for me."

"I'll do that."

"How about your partner here? He got ID?"

"He's here more in an unofficial capacity."

Arnold raised an eyebrow at that and gave Max a second, longer look. "Well, does he at least have a name?"

"Cormac Lindell," Max said. "Friends call me Max."

"All right, Inspector Koenig and Cormac Lindell, what do you want?"

Koenig nodded at the paper. "You probably read about Topher Arnsfeld and his wife getting murdered over in Prince Creek."

"I did," Arnold said. "That was a surprise and a real shame. Topher was a good man. He was trying to get some jobs flowing back onto the island."

"So, you knew him?"

He gave her a disappointed look. "I assume that's why you're here. I wouldn't say I knew him, but I'd met him a few times and the RCR did a few things with the Arnsfeld Association."

"What types of things?"

"Do you know what the RCR is?"

"Not exactly, no."

"The Royal Canadian Riders are a fraternal brotherhood dedicated to helping working-class Canadian citizens find the word of God and live a better life."

"And how do you go about that?"

"Two ways. First, charitable giving is our most important principle. We are a mutual benefit society with a common purpose to help those in need."

"Those Catholics in need?"

"No, we are all God's people. We do use our organization to promote the Catholic views on public issues, but we don't exclude or ignore a hand in need based on their reciprocating views."

"Is that how you got involved with Arnsfeld?"

"Sure, a man with pockets that deep moves in next door, eventually you're going to hit him up. I think it would almost be negligent if we didn't. Let me ask you, how did you hear about us?"

Koenig deflected the question. "The RCR was on a list. What did you do exactly for Arnsfeld?"

"We didn't do anything for him. We worked some security for a few of their events and they gave us some sponsorship for our Spaghetti with Santa and BBQ chicken events." He scratched at his beard, thinking it over, or pretending to. "We had talked about a few other things. Maybe a bigger project. The Association was doing a lot of global projects, but he wanted to stay visible locally, too. I thought the RCR could help with that. Doesn't look like that will happen now."

"Does the name Collum Hawkins mean anything to you?"

Arnold tapped a finger on the table for a moment, thinking, then shook his head. "No, should it?"

"No. No reason." She stood and Max followed suit. Arnold remained sitting.

Sitting across from him, Max had been unable to make out Arnold's tattoo. It was more visible now. He nodded toward it. "For whosoever shall call upon the name of the Lord shall be saved. Is Romans your book?"

Arnold looked down at his arm and then smiled at Max. "Have you been saved, Brother Cormac?"

"I've read the book, but I'll leave my salvation for others to decide."

"A wise man."

They left Arnold at his table and walked unescorted across the room toward the door. Max felt their eyes on his back. As Koenig pushed through the door, he glanced up at the large, rough crucifix that hung above the entrance. A bleeding, perpetually dying Jesus stared back.

As they pulled out of the driveway, Max could see Buzz Cut Brad had come back out on the porch to practice his tough-guy stare and watch them leave.

"Interesting guy," Max said. "Maddix."

"That's one way of putting it."

"Used a lot of big words."

"Too many. I don't like my criminals to be intelligent or interesting. I much prefer them dumb and stupid."

"You already got him pegged as a criminal, huh?"

"I think he's a man who likes gray areas, and I don't think he much minds if he's standing on one side of the law or another. We still don't know if it connects up to what happened to Arnsfeld. Maddix didn't strike me as the ax-wielding type. If he knows Hawkins, he's a good actor. Tell you what, I wouldn't mind getting a look in those other buildings."

"Shiny new locks."

"You noticed, too, huh?"

"Couldn't tell but they looked like heavy-duty Schlages. You're not getting through those without a serious hammer."

"Wonder why a mutual benefit, fraternal charity society needs such security?"

"What are the odds of setting up some surveillance?"

"With what we have now? Still slim and none. I'll give Shea a call and update him, but I don't think we'll be getting any help unless we find out more."

Max was confident that Arnold and the RCR were hiding something. He mulled it over as they drove back past the farm machinery repair shop and through Dundas in silence.

Koenig steered back onto PE-2 and Max asked, "Didn't know you had family nearby."

"You spend long enough on an island and you end up with relations everywhere. Some blood. Some not. But all family."

That felt like a loaded statement, but one look at Koenig's face told Max she wasn't interested in talking about it. He changed directions. "I played some hockey growing up."

She glanced over. "Yeah, you have the look. I would have guessed hockey or soccer."

"Can't tell if that's a compliment or an insult."

CHAPTER TWENTY

They cruised back over the bridge and into Prince Creek in silence. Max could see groups of people walking up and down the thin slip of beach along the inlet, hunting for sea glass. He watched a girl, no more than 10, carry over a piece to her dad, but he shook his head and she dropped it back into the shallow water.

"I'm going to head back to the PC PD building. Roy emailed. The locksmith got both safes open. Business documents, real estate deeds, some rolls of cash, a little jewelry. Nothing unexpected except one thing."

"What's that?"

"No will. In either safe."

"That's a little strange, I guess. Maybe they just haven't found it yet? Or his lawyer is on vacation. There could still be a legitimate reason."

"Sure. Could be. I'll dig through the documents myself."

"Not my specialty but let me know if you find anything. Can you drop me at The Rink? I want to talk to Thorne again. Ask him about Stephanie Arnsfeld. Start digging in that direction."

"I'll put a bug in Roy's ear about Thorne and the anonymous tip. It might be better coming from me. Hook up later and compare notes?"

"Sure. Dinner?"

She hesitated a fraction of a second. "A girl's gotta eat but not another burger."

"Variety is the spice of life. Prince Creek also offers pizza, donuts, fast food burgers, and gas station convenience."

"I hope you're kidding but I'm afraid to ask."

She pulled up outside The Rink.

"There might be one or two other options. Call me when you're clear."

Thorne wasn't at his table. Max hoped he hadn't jumped the gun about the Hawkins story. He went to the bar and ordered a Coke. Jerry raised an eyebrow.

"Just the Coke, Jerry, I'm not Thorne. I'm still working."

Jerry raised his hands in mock surrender, then filled a glass with ice and Coke from the fountain gun and pushed it across. Late afternoon with all the boats back and people clocking off, the place was already half full. He took the Coke back to Thorne's usual corner booth and sat down. He took out his phone. The Rink had good WiFi. Much better than the free router they all shared on Angel Court. With Max's trailer hidden in the trees, the few times he tried to use it had been frustrating.

He pulled out the piece of paper Thorne had given him yesterday with the ID and password for *The Chronicle*'s site. He logged on and navigated to the archives. Thorne was right. It was simple enough. Search box and some filters. He started with Hawkins and got no results. Not a surprise given his recent lifestyle. Thorne had said they'd only digitized the last 15 years. If he appeared in the paper at all, it would be in the earlier physical copies stored in the basement. Or maybe at the Historical Society. He started a new search with Topher Arnsfeld. There were a lot of hits. He filtered the results chronologically and scrolled down the list, clicking on a couple and skimming through the stories. There was the addition of some local angles and some local quotes but much of the information was identical to the file that Koenig had shared in her car.

Max could track the ups and downs of Arnsfeld's venture as he went farther down the page. Thorne's stories remained professional and neutral, but the quotes became increasingly passionate and angry as the business and, more importantly, the money slowly dried up. Max noted a quote from Victor Wallace, the supermarket owner Ellie Baker had mentioned that morning. "I'll tell you what, I'm not a violent or vengeful man but if there is any justice in this world or the next, Topher Arnsfeld will spend a hot eternity in hell for what he's done to the people of this town." Wallace's religious imagery and obvious anger were interesting.

He read a few more stories after the switch over to the charity but the wind had mostly gone out of the story. Or maybe Thorne's interest. They mostly read like reprinted press releases. He tried Stephanie Arnsfeld in the search box. Not as many hits as her husband but more than a few. She'd been active on the library board, as Macias had mentioned, but also several other charitable endeavors. There were a lot of stories about an annual dinner and ceilidh, the local gatherings with traditional folk music and dancing, to raise money for the Prince Creek Food Pantry. Her involvement in that appeared to pre-date her marriage. It was the only mention of her in the paper that wasn't attached to Arnsfeld.

Loreen Camille was now a teacher and the cross-country and track coach at Prince Creek High, and her name appeared frequently in the sports section with local meet results. Diana Goulart's name appeared just once as the caption in a photo for Stephanie Arnsfeld's fundraiser. It showed four women, all of a similar age, with arms linked, standing in front of a stage hung with ruffled bunting. Arnsfeld in the center, Camille, Goulart, and a woman named Kay Proulx flanking her. They looked friendly and comfortable with each other, as if falling into line for a photo like that was a practiced pose.

Max glanced at his watch. Almost 4:30 p.m. He thought he might catch Camille running a practice but then remembered it was August. The school would be closed. He opened up a new tab and searched for Camille's name. He found a Face-book page, but it was marked private. He searched for the main number for the high school. Maybe there were full-time administrators around. He called but it rolled to voicemail after five rings.

He had better luck with Diana Goulart. According to Facebook and Instagram, she was the owner of a gift shop north of Prince Creek, in Red Point, near Singing Sands Beach. Max called the shop.

"Tiny Island Beach Glass. Can I help you?"

"Is Diana Goulart there?"

"Sure, hold on one second, please."

The phone clunked down, and Max could hear the faint sound of music playing through the shop. It sounded heavy on strings, flutes, and ocean sounds.

"This is Diana Goulart." She pronounced her last name Goo-lay.

"Ms. Goulart, my name is Max Lindell. I'm working with the Prince Creek police department on the murders of Topher and Stephanie Arnsfeld. I was hoping I could set up a time to come out and talk to you?"

"Of course. Where are you?"

"I'm in Prince Creek at the moment." He didn't mention The Rink.

"Well, the shop closes at 5 p.m. You could come up here, or I live in Little Harbor, 67 Shetland, it's just opposite the bird sanctuary. We could meet halfway. Say 5:30?"

"That would be fine. I'll see you then."

He checked the address on his phone. It would take less than 15 minutes to drive. If he had a car. He thought about calling Koenig but didn't want to interrupt anything. He called Archie instead.

"Hey, Max. I saw Koenig go into Roy's office. You guys find anything?"

"No, not really. How about you?"

"Maybe Roy or Alford has but not me. Alford has me going through old ax purchase receipts. I think my eyes are bleeding."

"Sorry. It sounds like one of those terrible things that needs to be done."

"Yeah, exactly what Alford said. Days like this, I don't miss the miserly pay, but I do miss the water."

"I hear you. Woke up ready to go at 4:30 this morning."

"Funny how fast it gets into your blood, right? What's up? I'm sure you didn't call to hear me bellyache."

"Need to go out and talk to someone up in Little Harbor. Wondering if I can borrow your truck. Shouldn't take too long."

"Sure, no problem. I've got a couple more hours to go and if I stay past 6 p.m. they order us dinner. Might as well get a free meal for my trouble. Come on over. I'll leave the keys out front."

. . .

It wasn't Marline working at the comm station when Max arrived ten minutes later. It was a different woman. She had blonde shoulder-length hair and wore a light blue cable knit sweater in her air-conditioned dispatch cube. Max remembered Archie telling him that three women worked the comms, but he didn't remember the names of the other two. She was on a call and he mimed starting a car. She smiled, picked up a set of keys with the little buoy keychain that Max recognized, and handed them over.

Diana Goulart's house was only a few turns off the main road and not difficult to find. Max arrived in front of a simple two-story white house with black shutters and a steep dormered roof. It looked pleasantly used and comfortable sitting on a slight rise with a view of the water on the horizon. A silver, rusting Chevy Z71 pickup sat in the short driveway.

The front door was open. Max knocked but didn't get an answer. He cleared his throat and knocked again with a little more force. "Hello? Ms. Goulart?"

"Oh, hi. Come around the side. I'm out back."

He walked through the grass and around to the back of the house. There was a rectangular sitting area made from pre-fab patio stones. There was a single reclining chair with a cushion in one corner and a covered grill in another. Diana Goulart was sitting at a square outdoor table with an umbrella tilted against the sun. A half-full bottle of white wine sat at her elbow.

"I like a glass of wine after work to unwind," Goulart said. She moved her hand to a second empty glass. "Would you like a glass? I didn't know if you were still on duty or ..."

"I wouldn't say no to a glass." Max knew people were more likely to talk if both were drinking. She poured a glass and Max took a chair at a right angle to her so the umbrella pole wasn't between them. Max took a sip. He knew nothing about wine beyond the basic colors, but this white was so tasteless and bland that calling it inoffensive would be giving it too much character. Goulart didn't seem to mind as he watched her take a healthy swallow.

"I'm sorry, what did you say your name was again?" she asked.

"Max Lindell."

"And you're investigating the Arnsfeld murders?"

"That's right."

"How did you get my name?"

Max thought that was sort of an odd question. "Ellie Baker at The Sugar Maple gave me your name as a friend of Stephanie Arnsfeld. Was she wrong?"

"No, no. I'm friends, or was friends, with Stephanie. Did Ellie give you any other names?"

"She also mentioned Loreen Camille. If you had a contact number for Ms. Camille that might be helpful." Goulart nodded and took another sip of wine. Max continued, "I was also going to talk to Kay Proulx." Goulart's forehead creased at that. "No?"

"Why Kay? I can't imagine Ellie mentioned her."

"No, actually, she didn't. I saw her name in a *Chronicle* caption with the rest of you at Stephanie's fundraiser."

"Huh. Must have been an older picture."

"2012, I think."

"Okay, that makes sense. Kay doesn't live on the island. I think she lives outside Toronto now. She came back here after university but didn't stay long. Didn't get tied down. She must have come back one year for the fundraiser but that might be the last time I saw her. She was always the smart one."

She lisped a little on the S in smart and Max realized that it likely wasn't Goulart's first glass of wine. "You're not friends, then?"

"We're not close friends. Not anymore. We're more social

media friends these days. You know, the way people are. You like and comment on the things they post, but you're not really connected to them. You don't know them."

"But you were friends before? When Kay lived here?"

"Sure, the four of us were pretty close back in high school."

"The reason I'm asking is that I'm wondering if what happened to the Arnsfelds was actually something from a long time ago and just now coming back around."

Goulart frowned at that and finished her glass. She refilled it, emptying the bottle. "What do you mean by that? I assumed it had to do with Topher screwing islanders out of their money."

"It might be. It's early and we can't dismiss anything so I'm wondering if you can think of anything from the past, maybe back to high school even, that would be so toxic that it could pop up years later and still have the power to anger someone enough to kill."

"God, like what?"

Was she acting or drunk? It was hard to tell. "Anything. Violence, sex, blackmail, money, power."

Her eyes slid away as she drank another swallow of wine. She looked out over the rolling hills. "You have an awful job."

"Yes," Max agreed. "Awful, but necessary." He waited her out. It looked like she was about to say something, he could see her almost tense in anticipation despite the loosening effects of the wine, but then she pulled back.

"No, nothing like that comes to mind. I mean in high school we raised some hell, but it was the usual kind. Beer, parties, sex, maybe driving drunk. I mean, it sounds bad when I say it like that, but it was all just typical teenage bullshit. God, it was the most fun I had in my entire life." Her eyes had a glassy sheen now.

"No big scandals?"

"No, none of that, and this goddamn place is so small there's no way to keep anything that bad a secret. Gossip, especially scandalous gossip, is like currency in this town. It would have come out. Now it's all just glory days, you know? Things you laugh and reminisce about 20 years later, not find the people and butcher them."

"Did you ever go out to Norris Pond back then?"

She picked up the empty wine bottle and then set it back down. "Off Sinclair? No, we never went out there."

Max watched Diana Goulart keep her voice steady and eyes locked on his as she lied. Maybe she wasn't so drunk.

Before he left, Goulart gave him phone numbers for both Camille and Proulx. He called both numbers as he drove Archie's truck back to Prince Creek but neither answered. He left messages, identifying himself and asking them to call him back. He thought about Diana Goulart's realization at the picnic table. The most fun she'd ever had? Was it better to know you peaked in high school or go your whole life struggling to outlive those days?

CHAPTER TWENTY-ONE

After talking to Goulart, he called Koenig and made plans to return Archie's truck and meet up with her for dinner at 7:30 p.m.

He had 45 minutes. He drove home. Mrs. Johnson was on the bench next to her little garden. He waved and received a frowning stare in return. Max believed that counted as a pleasant mood for her.

He didn't doubt that Koenig could go days without showering and still look great. He was not that kind of person. He could work up a light sweat eating cereal. He showered and found a fresh black T-shirt that looked respectable enough. He sniffed his jeans and put them back on. He didn't want to look like he was trying too hard.

Dressed and prepped, he drove back to the station. The initial frenzy had died down. There was one satellite news truck parked at the curb. The driver gave Max a once over, but didn't budge from his seat. He pulled the pickup around back and parked next to Koenig's Explorer. He left the keys under the driver's side mat and sent Archie a quick text.

Two minutes later, Koenig came out the back door and

indeed still looked shower fresh despite going on at least 12 hours of work. She carried a stack of folders under her arm.

"Dinner reading?" Max asked.

She opened the rear door with one hand and dropped the folders on the seat. She looked fresh, but her smile showed the hours of work. "Maybe just the appetizer."

They climbed into the car. "Head down toward the water," Max said.

"That sounds like the first step toward The Rink."

"It is, but it's not where we're going. I did some research. Turns out, Prince Creek has a couple of restaurants that use cloth napkins."

"Paper or cloth or wet wipes, I don't care. Does it have a decent wine list and something chocolate for dessert?"

Prince Creek wasn't a sizable place, but it had enough seasonal tourist and ferry traffic to support a few decent restaurants. The Breakwater was still casual, but it was seven or eight steps up from The Rink on the culinary ladder, even when the kid was cooking the burgers.

The restaurant was in an old gabled Victorian house on a modest hill overlooking the ferry dock and the town harbor. A wraparound porch held overflow tables from the inside dining room. Max requested a table away from the couples already eating, and the server led them to a back corner. There was no water view, but there was privacy. Max wanted the town talking, but he didn't need them to hear the unedited details. Especially not while they were eating.

They sat down under the white lights strung around the ceiling timbers, a white tablecloth and small votive candle adorned the table. Despite the shower and his own wandering thoughts, Max worried about sending the wrong signal. It felt very romantic and completely out of step with the job of finding the killer. He glanced at Koenig, but she was concentrating on the menu and he couldn't read her. He took a sip from his water glass and then reached for one of the file folders that Koenig had carried from the car. But she beat him to it and put a palm down on top of the stack.

"Let's wait. I need a break. And I really need a drink." She signaled the waitress. "I'll start with an Old Fashioned." She looked up at Max.

"Uh, a draft beer, please. Whatever is local."

"Copper Bottom okay?"

"Perfect."

"Also, we'll have wine with dinner?"

Max wasn't clear if it was a request or a statement. "Sure."

"Then can you bring a bottle of Syrah and open it for dinner?"

The waitress disappeared inside to fill the drinks.

"You're into wine?"

"No, not really. Did I sound like I knew what I was talking about?"

"Absolutely."

"That's the trick. I'm convinced no one else knows about wine either. I've had this one before and liked it."

"Works for me."

She glanced around. "A little better atmosphere than The Rink. You bring all the ladies here?"

"Never eaten here, but I pass it every day and it's almost always crowded. I figured that was a good sign."

"If you can't judge a place by the neon and the grease, then go with the crowd. Not a terrible life lesson."

The waitress returned with their drinks.

"God, I needed that," Koenig said, smacking her lips.

Her words echoed what Max had heard only a few hours ago from Diana Goulart, but this felt more like a cleansing drink than a medicinal one. At least he hoped so. He took another sip of his beer. They looked over the menu deciding on options and then batted some softball questions back and forth. Weather. Past jobs. Outside interests. Max noticed she was just as adept as he was at avoiding answering anything too specifically or too deeply. He wondered if it was a trait of the job. If you spent a lot of time trying to wheedle information out of unwilling suspects did you automatically become more guarded yourself? Eventually, the small talk and the drinks ran low. Koenig took a deep breath and rolled her shoulders.

"Okay, tell me about Goulart?"

Max recapped the conversation.

"How sure are you she's lying?"

"Eh, 70 percent. I don't know if she's lying or just choosing not to answer, but I got a strong sense that she could have told me more."

"The end result is the same for us."

"Right."

"Maybe it gives us an edge with one of the other two women. Proulx and Camille."

The waitress brought their entrees, poached haddock for Koenig and roast pork for Max, and topped off their wineglasses. The Syrah was much better than the wine Goulart had served. Max could feel the alcohol loosening the muscles in his shoulders.

"You think the safes will be a dry hole?" he asked between bites.

"Roy was right. There wasn't a flashing beacon. On the surface, it all looks very typical and boring. Deeds, insurance, legal mumbo jumbo, some financial statements. They cracked the computer, so we have that to dig through, as well. I'm sending it all back to Charlottetown. We've got guys for that."

"You have additional copies?"

"Thought the fine print wasn't your deal?"

Max shrugged. "Can't hurt to look." He wasn't going to tell her he had guys for that, too. Lawrence and his hacker brother might spot something. He'd put the pair of them up against any RCMP specialist.

"Sure. If you need something to help you sleep, I'm sure Roy can get you copies of the stuff."

"Speaking of the chief, did you drop the Thorne tip on him?"

"Yes, he grumbled and made some noise but was surprisingly relaxed about it."

"It was inevitable, even with Hawkins being a recluse, someone would notice eventually."

"We also have an updated report from the CSIs on the Arnsfeld scene. Nothing surprising there, either. The cause of death was blunt force trauma for both, likely a hammer or mallet. The wounds showed Topher was attacked first, maybe up to 3 hours prior to Stephanie. The blood from the message on the wall matched Stephanie."

"So, the killer sat and waited. Or searched the house. Then he killed Stephanie and wrote the verse on the wall. One cool customer."

"Cool and crazy. The housekeeper had cleaned the house the day before so there weren't as many prints or fibers as there might have been. The analysis is still pending on that. Burty said they had at least three partials that didn't match the Arnsfelds or the housekeeper. If we ever get the guy ..." She pushed her plate away. "Roy also said the housekeeper verified that nothing was missing. Nothing big, obvious, or expensive."

"Not surprised. This guy is not interested in valuables or money. He wants to send a message."

"And get revenge."

"Feels that way."

They finished the bottle of wine and shared a slice of chocolate potato cake with a rich chocolate ganache for dessert. They split the check down the center. They walked out to the parking lot. The last slim edge of light was disappearing over the horizon. There was a cool breeze blowing up off the water.

"That was good. Almost as good as the hot grease hit from the kid's burgers. Thanks for the company," Koenig said.

"You're welcome."

"Drop you somewhere?"

"I think I'll walk. It's not far."

"Nothing is around here."

There was a moment, maybe, Max would think later, it was hard to tell in the dark, but it passed. Or Koenig got impatient. She opened the car door and dropped in the files, then turned back around. "If every night was this nice on the island we'd be overrun with people."

He cut across the small harbor park and picked up the Confederation Bike trail that ran through town, the crushed gravel path was quiet at this time of night, and crossed over Bishop Avenue just a few blocks from his trailer. His phone rang after he'd walked less than a mile. He pulled it out, but didn't recognize the number.

"Max Lindell."

"Hi, this is Kay Proulx. I'm returning your call."

There was a lot of background noise. It sounded like she was calling from a restaurant or bar. Was that just convenience or something else?

"Thank you for calling back so quickly." He walked to the side of the path and sat on a bench.

"You said you were an investigator working on Stephanie's murder. It sounded important."

"That's correct, I'm working with Chief Roy and the RCMP on the Arnsfeld case."

If she picked up on his careful tiptoeing language she didn't comment.

"Can I ask who gave you my name?" she asked instead.

That had been one of the first questions Goulart had asked.

"Actually, no one did. I found your picture in the local newspaper with Stephanie and a few other women when I was doing some research into the Arnsfelds. That gave me a few names to contact. I can tell you I already talked to Diana Goulart and left a message for Lindsay Camille. Can you think of anyone else worth talking to?"

"I remember that photo. I'm not in the paper often. From Stephanie's benefit, right?"

"That's right."

She paused and Max wished he could see her face. He could almost hear her thinking through the phone. "Have you talked to Nik?"

"Nik?" Max ran through his mental list of names from the file and came up empty. "Nik who?"

"Steph's brother."

"She didn't have a brother."

"Technically, I guess he was her half-brother. Nik Labat."

"No, we haven't talked to him. Not yet. Nik Labat." He said it again to commit it to memory.

"That's the only name I can think of. Anything else I can help with? I moved away from Prince Creek in 2013 and haven't been back to visit since, oh, the summer of 2017 when my parents moved."

"You were friends with Stephanie Arnsfeld when you were younger, right?"

"Yes, we were friends through high school and stayed in contact after college but drifted apart when I took a job in

Toronto. I'm not sure I'd spoken to her in a couple of years."

"We are casting a wide net at this point. What I'm wondering is if there was something that happened way back, maybe even in high school, that is coming back now? Is there anything that comes to mind?"

"Yes. Maybe," she said it quickly. The question didn't catch her off guard. Max gripped the phone tighter. She'd thought about this before calling. Whatever she knew, she wanted to say it. Had perhaps been waiting for someone to call. She wouldn't volunteer it but if it looked like it would come out ... he kept quiet.

"Prince Creek is barely bigger than a freckle and, in any other place, I'm pretty sure I wouldn't have been friends with Steph Calderot but out there you just don't have that many options. Sometimes there aren't enough people to fill the cliques and cliches. Steph was the popular girl and she made do with what she had. I was the smart girl. Smart for Prince Creek, at least. Diana was the follower. Lindsay was the jock. My parents were always nervous about Steph. She was smart, too. She was in all my classes, but she also liked to challenge things. To push things. She was always in a rush to be five years older than she was. You know?"

"That's not just an island thing," Max said, afraid that anything he said might derail her story.

"No, of course not, but if you didn't grow up in that fishbowl it's hard to explain. It gave her a lot of power, and not just amongst the other kids. I felt like I didn't have much of a choice. It was to be her friend and do what she wanted or go through high school, and maybe longer, on her blacklist. That was not a pleasant place." She was talking faster now. "In retrospect, my mom's resistance probably helped me. She flat out wouldn't let me do everything with Steph. My mom probably paid a price, but I never asked. I knew how this all sounds Mr. Lindell, but Steph liked the power and she was very good at wielding it."

"Was she still like that now?" It sounded extreme, but Max knew plenty of high school bullies grew out of that phase.

"Yes, she was still manipulative and controlling. She'd just gotten more subtle at it. She'd gotten better at it."

"You think someone from her past, your past, got fed up with being under her thumb?"

"It's possible and, trust me, that would be an extensive list."

"So, what? I'll be honest, I suspect you called to give me a name."

"No, that's not true. Not exactly. But there was always this rumor about Steph and parties or gatherings with older men. Men from town. I wasn't involved, but the rumor never really went away and always had at least a slight smell of the truth."

"Men from town?"

"The guys with money."

"And she was in high school."

"Yes."

"And there were parties."

"Something like that, yes. I don't really know much more than that. Steph and Diana would clam up but get these little smiles whenever it came up."

"Where did these parties happen?"

"Do you know where Norris Pond is?"

"Yes." He certainly did.

"Talk to Nik."

CHAPTER TWENTY-TWO

It was after 10 p.m. when he made it back to Angel Court. Mrs. Johnson wasn't outside but plenty of other residents were out in chairs or around small fire pits enjoying the summer night. He waved and kept moving. Back at his trailer, he sat in one of the beach chairs, the one he thought of as his, not Mose's, and replayed the conversation with Proulx in his head. It wasn't definitive. It wasn't direct evidence, but it felt like the first link in a chain. A possible motive. He pulled out his phone to call Koenig and stopped. Was it too late? He didn't think so, but she looked like she needed a break. What did he have? A lurid rumor from an old high school friend and a new name. Nik Labat. Would they be able to do anything with that tonight? Probably not. He'd tell her first thing in the morning.

He tapped another contact instead.

"You know that modern etiquette dictates that it is not polite to call after 8:30 in the evening."

"Lawrence, I know for a fact that you're sitting in your office in front of at least two screens checking the opening of the Asian markets."

"You knowing that does not change the etiquette. You are impinging on my leisure time."

Max had to smile. He didn't realize how much he'd missed Lawrence's voice. They'd met as kids in juvie and bonded over a love of books, a rare thing in the rough and tumble juvenile justice system. The friendship was even more rare as it crossed racial lines, but it had held until they had released Lawrence. They'd lost touch after that until Max found him again the previous year when he'd returned to Boston to deal with Carter. Lawrence had turned out to be an excellent resource. He ran a barbershop in Boston's Dorchester neighborhood and dabbled in other things. Max could never get a straight answer out of Lawrence on what exactly he did, but he knew Lawrence was very skilled at making money. Without Lawrence's help, Max was sure he would have been swept up by the Boston PD or FBI and ended up back in jail.

"Your poor manners aside, I'm bored and by now I know when you call something interesting will happen."

"I'm not sure if that's a compliment or not."

"Me neither, brother, but no matter where you go it seems trouble will find you. Lucky for you, I like trouble because it usually means there's an opportunity to make some money."

"I've got some financial records and computer files. I was wondering if you and your brother could take a look?"

"Whose records and files are we talking about?"

"Christopher Arnsfeld."

"Oh, shit."

"And another man named Collum Hawkins."

"Never heard of him."

Max filled him in on the last three days and Lawrence agreed to take a look. Max said he'd email him what he had in the morning.

. . .

He went inside after that and tried to sleep. It felt like things were moving, slowly, but, like an ice floe breaking, it might suddenly start moving quickly and sleep might become a luxury. He brushed his teeth and laid down, but he couldn't settle. Proulx's call had sent his mind spinning in too many directions.

What had Hawkins and Stephanie Arnsfeld done 20 years ago that led to their murders? What happened at these parties? Drugs? Sex? Did the sex lead to abortion? Max could see something like that festering and eventually exploding. Was someone out there thinking about a child they'd lost 20 years before? Would a man get hung up on something like that or would it affect a woman more? Max didn't know. He assumed the killer was a man. Maybe he was wrong.

If not drugs and sex, what else? Money? Blackmail? Steph didn't have much money 20 years ago but she had it now. That was a possibility.

What did Nik Labat know?

If these killings were about Steph Arnsfeld and something from her past, did that put the RCR in the clear? Or could they still be involved? If the Arnsfelds were being black-mailed, did they try to fight back with the RCR somehow? Seemed like a risky move for the Arnsfelds, but something still didn't smell right about that group. Maddix had his thumb on the scale somehow. That was the one thing Max was sure of.

He picked up his phone again and made one more brief call, thought for a moment about Koenig's smile, and then finally fell fast asleep. The ghosts came, but they were benign. Their visits usually were. They were reminders of past choices and past misdeeds. His wife. His child. Danny. Mary. They didn't need to be malicious. He was hard enough on himself.

CHAPTER TWENTY-THREE

Pretty liked to sleep outside when he could, especially in the warmer summer months. He found his bed and the small bedroom too tight, too constricting. Sometimes he just needed to escape all the people. It wasn't a recent thing or a reaction to the killings. He felt fine about that. He'd just always preferred the stars as his nightlight. He'd sneaked outside to sleep since he was a child. His mother had eventually given up and had taken to leaving a blanket and pillow on the porch.

He lay on his back now and watched a shooting star streak across the sky. He turned his head slightly and studied the faint green and purple ripples of the aurora borealis on the edge of the horizon. Was he crazy?

Maybe, he admitted.

Did it matter?

He didn't think so.

The killings were necessary. He was sure of that, and he'd done the right thing now in seeking out Stephanie Arnsfeld next. He'd wanted her to be last, but Hawkins hadn't been as helpful as he expected. Turned out to be a hard, old guy. He didn't budge an inch and then Pretty couldn't figure out a way forward without killing Stephanie. She hadn't been made of the same stern stuff as Hawkins. She'd provided the other names he needed.

Now he worried that there might be some ... non-essential killings needed. He had an idea that these two new people, the inspector and the local helping out, could get in his way. Koenig and Lindell. They could be a problem. He could already see the ripples of their efforts. People were talking. They weren't waiting for Roy to do something official. People were locking their doors and locking down.

The question then was how to deal with it? Killing one or both would be an escalation. Perhaps necessary, but a definite risk. Potentially a big risk that could bring complications that put the larger project in jeopardy. He wanted to take his time, for his message to be clear, for the guilty to know he was coming, to expect their own deaths, but he knew now he couldn't delay too long. That would put it all in jeopardy.

He stared up at the sky and thought about it. Who to kill? And when to kill them? This was the problem with a small town. Someone was always watching or listening. You could feel it just walking down the street. Curtains twitching, heads turning, people noticing. It was one of the biggest reasons for his rage. How had they escaped punishment last time? Someone knew. Someone should have stepped forward. Someone should have pointed a finger. He could feel the acid boil in his guts. He took a steadying breath. It wouldn't help. Not now. Not for this. He needed to think. He needed a plan.

He had three names: Brown, Harrow, Sykes. Looking back now, as a group they looked obvious. They had been among the richest and most powerful men in the small pond of Prince Creek. They were all older now. Two were retired, but their names still carried some weight. Then two more names: Koenig and Lindell. Up to five total, but in what order?

He didn't think Brown would be difficult. He was the oldest. He was retired and lived with his wife in a large house with a fenced yard up on the hill behind Main Street. Pretty had seen the man in town. He must be over 70, his appetites finally betraying his body. He was bent with age and wouldn't put up much of a fight. The risk of being seen was highest with Brown, but the logistics of the thing weren't difficult.

He had the opposite problem with Harrow. He still lived on his original farm. He'd gotten rich buying up other men's land, but he'd stayed put. Pretty knew the Harrow farm. He'd gone by it in the past, but hadn't been out there in a couple years. He would need to take a fresh look. He knew Harrow still worked part of his land and, unlike Brown, was in good shape for an older guy. Despite his wealth, he still had the makeup of the original island settlers: gristle, muscle and bone. He wouldn't go down easily. Pretty would have to take him fast. Not give him a chance.

Sykes might also be difficult. He lived in a small apartment above his workplace. Pretty had risked going in once, but knew he couldn't do that again. If he was seen, it would be too unusual, too out of place to be easily explained away. He'd have to get Sykes at home, no choice there, and do it late. But how? He'd need to think about Sykes more. Maybe it would make sense to do him last.

And what about the law? If he took Koenig or Lindell first, it would bring a lot more pressure, but would that pressure come right away? Would killing one of them give him a small window to act on the others? Would it sow enough confusion to distract them from finding him? He needed the other three. He'd never rest in this life or the next if he didn't get them. He wasn't sure the order of the three mattered. Once they heard about one, they'd know and it would get harder. Not impossible, but tougher. Might take longer, too. Time he might not have.

And what about Labat? He'd almost forgotten about him. That was six.

He needed to think. Murdering people was complicated.

Maybe he'd let the stars decide.

He was mostly worried about dogs. Not about killing them. Killing them did not differ from killing a man or any other animal. He worried about the noise. Harrow lived far enough out that that any barking was unlikely to raise concerns. Not for a good long time at least. But they would put Harrow on alert. It would just make everything harder.

It was late and thick cloud cover kept the moonlight low. He walked along the side of the road, careful of where he stepped. If he were found out here with a twisted or broken ankle, it would raise uncomfortable questions. Only a single car had passed in the last hour, and he had more than enough time to scramble into the drainage ditch on the side of the road and hide behind a bush. He watched the taillights recede without the hesitation of a brake light. He waited another minute to be safe and then climbed back out and continued walking.

Harrow's farm was on a large rectangle of rolling land divided into grazing pastures. The white farmhouse appeared to glow in the dark and sat at the end of a long, straight paved drive with the cowshed, coops, barn, and grain silo a quarter mile farther back on the left. Pretty stepped around the iron gate at the end of the drive. He felt his shoulders tighten and his guts cramp. That was normal. He kept walking and breathed in the familiar farm smells of dried manure, animal feed, and the chemical tang of fertilizer.

He heard the jingle of the dog's collar before he spotted

him. Then a bark, but just a single tentative one. The old lab came limping around the side of the porch and stopped ten feet away. Pretty waited but no other companions joined the first dog. A single watchdog, not a guard dog. They stood regarding each other. Pretty unwrapped the package of bacon he'd brought and held it out. The dog came forward and took the meat and Pretty walked up onto the porch.

He was about to knock on the front door. It had worked for Arnsfeld, why not Harrow? He liked the symmetry but then stopped and thought about the back door. Knocking on the back door would imply some familiarity. Someone Harrow knew. That might put him at ease. He checked on the dog, still snuffling after the remaining bacon bits, and walked around to the back of the house.

Even when he'd been young and strong and putting in 18-hour days on the farm, Colby Harrow had never slept well. It would exhaust his body, his muscles pleading for sleep, but he could never get his mind to settle down long enough for sleep to take hold. Now that he mostly managed all his property from behind a desk and was suffering from what Doc Mulvaney said was likely stage one of Parkinson's, he barely slept more than four hours in a light doze if he was lucky. Dorothea had long ago moved out and taken to sleeping in the guest room.

Sadie's bark had woken him. It was not unusual. The old dog sometimes got spooked and barked at a passing car or cloud. He heard her moving under the bedroom window toward the front of the house. He rolled over and was just starting to drift off again when he heard the footsteps on the porch.

He sat up. He thought of his kids. His son a lawyer in Toronto. His daughter a teacher in Charlottetown. If something had happened to them? Or the grandkids? He didn't let his mind go there. He swung his legs to the floor. What about a burglar? His shotgun was down in the hall closet. When was the last time he cleaned it? Was it loaded? He heard a light knock on the backdoor's glass. Not a burglar then.

Did good news ever come in the middle of the night? Did it ever knock softly?

He could feel his heart racing. Don't let it be the grandkids.

He walked down the hall to the stairs. He checked Dorothea's door on the way and could hear her snoring softly. She never had a problem sleeping. Should he wake her? No, find out what it's about first. He went down the stairs and turned on the outside lights. He frowned in confusion at the person standing there, facing slightly to the side. Colby Harrow opened the door.

"What do you want?"

The man smiled and Harrow saw the sickness in his eyes. Then he saw the knife. He took a stumbling step back and raised an arm.

Pretty stood over the body, breathing hard but happy. Harrow hadn't been that hard after all. He listened to the rest of the house as he caught his breath. All quiet. Just the groans of the old farmhouse settling in the night. He took one of Harrow's ankles and dragged him out onto the porch and down into the yard. The old man's head banged off the three steps with cracking thuds. Harrow groaned, but Pretty didn't slow down. The dog came back, maybe looking for more bacon or worrying after her master. Pretty kicked out a foot and caught her on the hip. She yipped and scurried back into the hedgerow on the side of the house.

He got Harrow's body across the yard to the barn and

stopped. His chest was heaving. Even an old, worn out bag of bones like Harrow wasn't easy to move. He put his hands on his knees until the blood stopped pounding in his ears and he could hear the cicadas and other night creatures in the dark.

Creatures like him.

Then he took out the knife again.

CHAPTER TWENTY-FOUR

Max was at The Maple first at the same table, blueberry muffin this time, reading Thorne's story on Hawkins in the Friday edition of *The Chronicle*. It was speculative but solid. It would get the job done. He watched Koenig come in, order a coffee from Ellie at the counter, and then carry it over. She still looked good, better than good, but Max could see the stress and maybe the motel's lumpy bed in the lines around her eyes. He kept that observation to himself. She wore a lightweight black blazer over a red-patterned shirt and black pants. Her hair was damp, and he could smell the lightly fragrant soap she'd used. It was definitely not the motel's soap; he was very familiar with their basic soap and shampoo offerings.

"That woman doesn't like me," Koenig said, reaching over and breaking off a piece of Max's muffin.

"Who? Ellie?" Max looked toward the counter where Ellie was laughing at something the next customer had said.

"Is that her name?"

"Yes, and I just watched her smile and pour your coffee."

"It was a smile hiding a razor blade."

Max frowned, truly confused. He couldn't picture Ellie holding anything more dangerous than a butter knife. "You just haven't had your coffee yet."

Koenig took another chunk of muffin. Max tried to change the subject.

"I don't understand why you can't just order your own muffin."

"Why would I do that when you always have a very good muffin waiting for me?"

They both took a sip of coffee and then said, "So ..." at the same time.

"Go ahead," Max said.

"Dinner was nice."

"Yes," Max's tongue suddenly felt three times too big for his mouth and he felt a blush of color rise to his cheeks. He fumbled for something to say and came up blank.

Koenig looked at him and then laughed. "Going to make me do all the hard work, huh?"

"Sorry, I'm way out of practice at ... whatever that was."

He hadn't dated anyone since Sheila back in Essex and, if he was honest, she'd carried most of the water in that relationship. He had still been too broken to contribute much. Before Sheila, there had been Cindy. Before that, no one that mattered. He felt the ghosts start to whisper in his head and tried to focus on what Koenig was saying.

"Listen, I have to run back to Charlottetown tonight to get some fresh clothes and check the mail, but maybe we could do it again?"

"That can be arranged."

She swiped a hand across the table to sweep away the muffin crumbs, and it felt like she was clearing the personal stuff away. She moved onto the case. "I want to check in with Roy this morning, but then I was thinking about going through Hawkins's financials again or taking another crack at

Campbell and Lee. They both seemed to know Hawkins the best back when he was working. What do you think?"

"Before you get to that, let me tell you about my walk home last night."

"What happened?"

"First, more coffee."

He went to the counter and Ellie refilled both their cups. He tried to pay attention to her smile but noticed nothing sinister. He returned to the table and spent the next 10 minutes recapping the phone call with Kay Proulx in as much detail as he could. Then, Koenig took him through it a second time, peppering him with questions.

"You should have called last night," she finished.

"And what would we have done last night?"

"Computers don't sleep. I could have started some searches."

"And been up half the night and maybe miss something today."

She sipped her coffee and nodded. "Okay, fair point. Nik Labat. Name doesn't ring a bell?"

"No, not for me."

"Maybe Roy knows."

"We need talk to Loreen Camille. She might know something."

"We can go back to Goulart, too. If we have something more solid, we could push her. She might crack."

"You think this might be something? It felt right last night, but now, I don't know. Feels like a cheap locker room rumor."

She tapped a finger on the top of her cup. "It's as good as anything else we've got so far." She stood. "Let's go talk to Roy. Maybe he's got something."

. . .

Roy had nothing. "I've got piles of paper and the mayor calling at increasingly shorter intervals but it's all just noise." He picked up a stack of papers with his left hand. "Sales receipts for axes. Nothing." He dropped them back on the desk and picked up another pile. "Statements and alibis from what counts as Prince Creek's criminal and low-life population. Nothing. Turns out almost all of them were at The Rink on Tuesday when the Arnsfelds were killed. Trever Lyle and his band were playing. The few that weren't had decent alibis, though Alford is running them down all the same." He dropped the stack. "We have the financial and legal docs," he gestured at his computer screen, "those are just giving me a headache. And then there's this." He held up the newspaper folded back to the Hawkins story. "Just what I needed."

Max ignored the newspaper story and asked, "You mind getting me a login or setting me up with an electronic copy of the money and legal stuff?"

"You an accountant or lawyer in a past life?"

"Nope, but more eyes can't hurt."

Roy took a beat and then shrugged. "Sure, be my guest. I'll get one of the geeks to set you up with some temporary credentials. That's probably easiest."

"Thanks. Does the name Nik Labat mean anything to you?"

"Vaguely, but I might be getting it confused with a defenseman the Leafs had in the 1980s."

Max went through the Proulx phone call again and could see Roy getting excited at the fresh angle. Any port in a storm.

"She had a half-brother. Shit, how did we not know that?" He picked up the phone and hit a button. "D'arcy, can you pop in here for a second?"

A moment later, Roy's second-in-command appeared in

the doorway. He was a 5-foot 5-inch tall, light-skinned black man shaped like an egg. "Yeah, Chief?"

"Did June Calderot ever remarry after Tom left her?"

Alford scratched at his graying chin beard. "No, she took up with George Labat but I don't think they ever made it official."

"That's it," Roy said and pounded a palm on his desk. "It never popped up in the records because it was a common law thing. George had a boy, right?"

"That's right. Nikolas. Girl, too, but she was older. Moved out, I don't know, ten years ago. Haven't heard from her since."

"There he is. The unofficial half-brother. He still around?"

"Yup, very much around. I'm sure you've all seen him. Well, maybe not the inspector, not yet, but she will if she stays in town for a few more days. You all might know him as The Undertaker."

Max knew the guy. He saw him most days during his morning runs. "The homeless guy down by the harbor?" Max asked.

"That's right," Alford replied.

"That's Nik Labat? How come we've never brought him in?"

"Oh, I'm sure he's been in once or twice, but we mostly take him up to St. Mary's. Father White lets him sleep on a cot in the church basement. He has some mental issues, will go deep into the bottle when he can get his hands on it, but he's mostly harmless. Never seen him get violent."

"Any idea where we can find him?" Max asked.

"In the summer, he usually sleeps in the park behind the monument down by the water. If he's not there, check the church. Someone up there might know."

"Thanks."

"Glad I could help." The corporal nodded and disappeared back to his cubicle.

"Okay, that sounds like something anyway. Keep me up to date. Before you go, any luck with the names from Mose?"

"No, haven't gone out to the community yet. This jumped to the front of the queue."

"I get it, but I'd like to run those down, just to cover all the bases."

And cover your own ass with the voters, Max thought, but said, "Today or tomorrow. Might be easier to catch them at home on a Sunday."

It took the computer geek, named Phil, five minutes to get Max set up with login credentials that gave him access to the Prince Creek municipal government network, more than the average citizen but not as much as a full-time officer. That was fine. Max suspected that Lawrence and Teddy didn't require the credentials, but it would give Max some cover if he ever needed to explain anything they found in the documents. He sent the username and password via the secure, self-destructing text app that Lawrence had set up on his phone. The message would delete itself after Lawrence read it or after 24 hours had elapsed.

They were getting into the Explorer and discussing the best way to approach Labat when Roy came running out the back door heading for his patrol car. He saw them and veered over.

"Got another body," he said breathing hard. "At least I hope it's just one."

"Who?" Max asked.

"Colby Harrow. His wife called it in. She was screaming. Stratton was on patrol. He's a few minutes out. Chravette was east, up by the lighthouse, but he's coming. God, she sounded bad. I know her a bit. She's a tough nut. If she's like this ... we gotta get out there."

"Where's he live?"

"North of town right off 305, Prince Creek Line Road. Just follow me."

Koenig was a good driver. She gave the chief some space.

"He looked a little amped up, I don't want to follow him into a ditch."

They went through town. The chief's lights and sirens cleared the way. Max would get his wish. People would certainly talk now.

Stratton was waiting on the porch. His face was chalky white. The passive aggressiveness from the previous day was gone. He kept trying to spit.

"It's, I mean, uh, the body, is around back. By the barn. You can't miss it and I, uh, threw up. Sorry, Chief."

"That's all right, Henry. Anyone else on the property?"

"No, just Dorothea and a dog. Plus the livestock. They're fenced in. Dog is inside."

"Dorothea inside?"

"Yes, she's pretty shook up. She's in the living room on the couch."

"Okay, that's good. Why don't you go down near the end of the driveway and start a log. More people will be coming, I suspect."

Henry nodded and started toward his cruiser.

"I'll check on Dorothea."

Koenig nodded. "We'll go take a look. I can talk to her later. But give me a quick background on Harrow. Who was he?"

Roy took a moment and gathered his thoughts. "Started like any other farmer. Livestock. Potatoes. But he was smart, had ambition. He bought up the surrounding farms on the cheap when the markets dipped. He was savvy about it. Bided his time. Now, he's probably the biggest private landowner on this half of the island."

"Enemies?"

"I'm sure of it."

"Okay, go see the wife."

Roy suddenly looked like he wanted to be anywhere else, but he straightened his shoulders and climbed the steps. Max followed Koenig around the side of the house. From there, they just had to follow the blood.

Colby Harrow had died hard. He was strung up by his ankles and hung over a low, creeping branch of a yellow birch. His throat had been cut and the blood had leached into the dirt and grass below his head. But not before the killer had painted another message on the side of the white barn.

Koenig walked around the body. Max stayed clear and let her work. He didn't think he'd be all that helpful. He walked over to the barn. There was a brush and a bucket covered with flies laying on its side nearby.

And for your lifeblood I will surely demand an accounting. I will demand an accounting from every animal. And from each human being, too, I will demand an accounting for the life of another human being.

He felt Koenig come up behind him. "A bit literal for our guy," she said. "Recognize it?"

"Genesis. It's God talking to Noah. Blood for blood. A life for a life."

"This guy thinks the people he killed are covering up a murder?"

"I don't think he's picking these quotes at random. They've all been about revenge or retribution. Before this, in the Bible, God let Cain get away with murder. Here he is changing the rules. He's telling Noah that a life intentionally taken will no longer be tolerated. It will be punished by death."

"This guy thinks he's God?"

"I don't know what he thinks other than he believes a reckoning is due."

Ten minutes later, Roy came down to the scene.

"How's the wife doing? She say anything about enemies or rivals or someone that might want to harm Harrow?" Koenig asked.

"She said no one came to mind. Not for something like this. Not going to get much out of her right now. I think she's in shock. She slept through the entire thing and didn't find Colby until she woke up. Even then she thought he was in his office or out in the barn. She sat and had some coffee and a Danish while her husband was swinging dead in the backyard. Colby Harrow was as tough as a twisted old root. Whoever did this to him had to be young and strong. That tells us something."

"Weren't you assuming it was a man?" Koenig asked.

"Yes, but this tells me it's a certain kind of man. I think I can eliminate some names off the list. They just wouldn't have the balls, excuse me, or the strength to try this with Harrow."

"Talk about balls all you want, Chief," Koenig replied. "Interesting thought, though." She looked back at the body. "He might have been tough, but he was old. A woman might put him off guard. Get the jump on him. And a sturdy woman might have been able to drag him out there and do the rest."

"Well, shit, Inspector, I'm trying to narrow the field not expand it."

"I think it's a man, too. I'm just saying."

"It was a man," Max said. "A guy his age wouldn't answer the door for a woman in his bathrobe."

They both looked at him.

"Smarter than he looks," Roy said.

Koenig went over her thoughts on the body with Roy, and then Max repeated what he knew about the Bible verse. After that, there was nothing to do but wait. Redd arrived and pronounced the body and also gave Dorothea a sedative. The crime scene crew arrived. He watched them start to collect samples and put tiny flecks in small bags. He felt like a piece of furniture.

"Let's head back to town," Max said. "Nothing for us to do here until the techs finish."

"What's in town?" Koenig asked.

"Hopefully Labat and some answers. We need to know more about the past. Whatever link or explanation that exists will be back there somewhere. Someone knows or someone wrote it down. That's how we'll get him."

CHAPTER TWENTY-FIVE

They drove back into town and dropped down the hill to the docks, but didn't see Nik Labat. The ferry had arrived, and the road was congested with cars, vans, and people. The ferry departed from Prince Creek twice a day. The crossing to the Magdalen Islands took 5 hours. The small eight-island chain was technically part of Quebec but much closer geographically to the maritime provinces. Max had yet to make the trip, but Charlie and Thorne told him it was full of high cliffs, white sand beaches, and topless, easy women. He believed two of the three.

The weather was still warm but heavy clouds had moved in overnight and promised rain. Koenig grew frustrated with the travelers and tourists walking blindly into the road and turned left down a side street back toward the town's small commercial district. Max's phone chirped and his pulse kicked up a couple beats when he saw the caller ID.

"They're smuggling something through the Canboro library."

No hello. No greeting. No small talk. Kyle kept his

sentences short and precise. No fluff. All business. It's what had made him an elite soldier at one time.

"The library? You're kidding." But while Max had seen Kyle's sly sense of humor a couple of times, he knew it was as rare as a solar eclipse and not on display now. "You're sure?"

"Yes."

"Any ideas what it is?"

Koenig looked over at him with her eyebrows raised. He held up a finger.

"Something small. Probabilities say drugs, pills, or guns."

"How? Break it down for me."

"Library sits on the border. Literally. Half the library is in the US and half is in Canada. They got runners on both sides. One goes into the bathroom with a bag. Another comes out with the same bag. Delivers it to your bikers."

"No border controls?"

"There are. You check in at a centralized station in town if you're crossing. Seems pretty loose compared to the typical crossing."

"They can't be doing huge volume."

"Depends on frequency. I saw three exchanges today. All standard backpacks. Not bulging. Nothing to call attention to it."

"Photos?"

"Not from inside the library, but I have some from the exchanges when the Canadian runner dropped the bag with the bikers. They used a diner and two different gas station bathrooms."

"How many RCR guys were there on the pickup?"

"Just two. One young guy, buzz cut, was the driver. Second, older guy, gray beard, maybe 5-feet 10, bit of a limp." *Brad and the bartender*, Max thought.

"Okay, send me those. Where are you now?"

"Back in the house."

"Did you see what they did with it when they got back?"

"No. But I saw them exiting the new larger structure later."

"Okay. You good to keep watching?"

"Roger that."

"Who was that?" Koenig asked.

"I had a friend watch the RCR clubhouse. We got lucky."

"What friend?"

"Doesn't matter."

"Like hell it doesn't matter. If it comes to court, it will matter."

"We can figure that out later."

Koenig tapped a finger on the wheel, annoyed at being left in the dark, but curious. She finally said, "Well? What did he find out?"

"He thinks they're smuggling something through the library in Canboro. He says it's a town that literally straddles the border. Part is in the US, part is in Canada. Believe it or not, sometimes parts of buildings are in both countries. You're getting coffee in the breakroom in Canada and you're looking at spreadsheets in your cube from the US. That includes the town library. Maddix has set up some mules to bring in bags of something and swap them in the library. One guy goes into the bathroom with a backpack, a different guy walks out with it. That guy leaves the library and meets up with the RCR a couple blocks away and hands it over."

"Your guy didn't see what it was?"

"No, no chance but he watched three swaps in 1 day."

"Huh. I've heard of Canboro. Sort of a quirky tourist spot because of the border thing. You trust your guy?"

"Yes. Absolutely."

They drove past The Rink. It was just past 11 a.m. Two cars were parked near the entrance to Second Time Around, but Jerry's car was the only one on the bar's side of the lot. Koenig continued her crisscrossing pattern around the downtown section of Prince Creek. Five more minutes and they would have covered all the streets in the business district. Still no sign of Nik Labat.

"What do you think it is? If it's anything," Koenig said, taking a left and doubling back.

"C'mon, we both got a vibe off Maddix. It's something. Now it's just a question of what and how much. I'd put money on guns or drugs. Their little fraternal organization combined with the guise of a motorcycle club would give them a fluid distribution network and contacts off-island. Easy to move those things in a saddlebag."

"Your guy sticking around?"

"Yeah. He's around." Max wasn't going to go into details of Kyle being in the house across the street. Illegal entry being a crime in both the US and Canada. Though Max thought of it more as a temporary entry. The house was a rental after all. "I was thinking of running up there tonight. We got lucky to spot this so quickly, but now that we know something is on the property maybe it'll bring in more activity."

"You still think this ties in to Arnsfeld?"

"I'd still put the probability higher that the murders are related to what Kay Proulx said, something in the past, but the probability that it involves the RCR is no longer a long shot. Maddix is up to something and I bet Topher Arnsfeld at least knew about it. If Topher was missing the swashbuckling action of the tech world, maybe a little line crossing or rubbing elbows with a lower class like Maddix gave him the jolt he was looking for. What are the odds that two major crimes happen independently in the same small town?"

"It could happen. Not great, but it could happen. Crime is infectious. Let me make some calls." She shook her head. "Start out with a simple savage murder, end up with a psycho spree killer and a smuggling ring."

CHAPTER TWENTY-SIX

They finished their canvass of the streets and came up empty.

"Check the church?" Koenig asked. "Or get lunch first? Crowds will thin out after the ferry leaves. Might be easier to spot."

"Stop the car."

"What?"

They were rolling down Bella Avenue on the edge of the business district about to hit Main Street again from the opposite end. The simple wooden sign posted beside the brick walk outside the converted residential building listed three tenants. Jules Wood, OD, Optometry. Anders Pennly, Sun Life Financial Advisor. Aldis Campbell, Consumer & Corporate Law. The last space was empty, showing only the sun-faded marking of some prior tenant.

"That office building. The third guy listed is Campbell."

Koenig pulled the Explorer into a small parking lot next to the building. Theirs was the only car in the lot. "Worth a shot."

Despite being listed third on the sign, Aldis Campbell had

the ground floor office. A small gold plaque was affixed to the first door on the left after they walked in. A wooden, banistered staircase led to the upper floors and presumably other offices. A shared kitchen was visible beyond the stairs on the ground floor. A building permit was affixed to the door opposite Campbell's, but they heard no sounds of workers inside.

Koenig knocked on the door. They waited, but there was no response from inside.

"Out to lunch?" Max asked.

Koenig eyed her watch. "Not even 11:30 a.m."

She knocked again and then tried the knob. It was unlocked and opened to a compact waiting room with a padded chair, matching loveseat, and low coffee table with a fanned spread of well-thumbed magazines. An upright water dispenser and small single-serve coffee machine were in the corner. Max could hear classical music coming from behind a closed door to the right.

Koenig approached and knocked. After a moment, the volume of the music lowered and the door opened.

"Hello, can I help you?"

The man was tall, slightly stooped with a long, hooked nose that gave him a bird-like appearance, maybe a raven, if the fringe of hair ringing his ears had been black instead of dusty gray.

"Aldis Campbell?" Koenig asked.

"Yes."

Koenig flashed her badge case. "My name is Inspector Imogen Koenig. This is Max Lindell. We're working with the Prince Creek PD on the Collum Hawkins case."

"Okay." He stepped back and held the door. "Come in, please."

Koenig and Max took seats, they looked to be from the same set as the waiting room, across from Campbell's desk. The inner office was modest and only slightly larger than the waiting room. In addition to the client chairs and Campbell's desk, it held a pair of wooden three-drawer file cabinets, a bookcase with leather-bound law tomes, and the required diplomas and certificates hanging on the wall. Everything was neat and in its place. It gave the impression of stability and efficiency. Max thought Campbell was likely good at his job.

"I spoke to Chief Roy last week," Campbell said as he went around behind his desk and sat.

"Yes, and we reviewed those transcripts. We just have a few followup questions. To be frank, you and another colleague, Safford Lee, appeared to know Mr. Hawkins best."

"Me and Saff? Oh, dear." He pinched his nose. "That's terrible."

"What?"

"That you think we knew him best. I'd hesitate to call him a friend, even back when we were working more closely. I might have said we were business associates. It's just a shame. It makes me feel bad, like I should have done more or tried to reach out when ... he ran into problems."

"What type of corporate law do you practice, Mr. Campbell?"

"Business organization law. How businesses are incorporated and structured and the laws that govern those business types. Hawkins's focus was on contracts. Saff did mostly employment law. Those interlocking pieces led us to work together a lot in the late 1990s. With the boom of the Internet, everyone was forming businesses. It was like a land rush. We handled a lot of incorporations back then."

"And that work eventually trailed off?"

"Well," Campbell picked up a pen and looked out the window. "It has ebbed and flowed over the years with the different booms and busts of the Internet, but Hawkins's involvement certainly did."

"Do you know what happened to Hawkins?"

"No. I don't."

"Do you have any ideas?"

"I'd hate to spread rumors."

Which was an answer in itself, Max thought.

Koenig sensed it, too. "Nothing will go beyond this room. Unless we end up in court, we'll do our best to make sure it doesn't come back to you."

Campbell dropped his pen and pinched his nose again. "None of this is fact. It's all hearsay, you understand, so I doubt I'll end up in court."

"We understand."

"I'm relatively certain Collum lost his license because of drinking. I have an acquittance on the province's disciplinary board and he had gotten in touch at one point, but then I never heard anything else."

"The complaint just went away?"

"I think Hawkins agreed to stop practicing and the board wouldn't continue with the grievance. Any professional misconduct complaint would get filed with the government and be easy to discover on the Internet. It would make getting another job, even one that didn't involve practicing law, more difficult."

"So, he cut a deal."

"That's my guess, but it's just that, a guess. I don't know any specifics."

"Did Hawkins have a problem with alcohol?"

"No. At least not at first. The three of us got along and worked well together. We were all native islanders and shared similar upbringings. I said before I didn't consider Collum a friend, but I might have eventually. Saff and I have become friends, as well as colleagues over the years."

"But it didn't go in that direction with Mr. Hawkins?"

"No, something changed. I remember when I first thought we might be headed toward a problem. We'd just finished a big push, 3 tough weeks to meet an aggressive deadline, but we did it. At that time, my office was down off Church Street and the three of us, plus a couple others on that job, it was a lot of paperwork, were holed up in the conference room. Collum kept stepping out, to the point where a few of us commented on it to each other. More than once I smelled that strong mint flavor you use when you want to cover up alcohol. When we finally finished the job, we had a big blowout dinner at Stone Creek, that was a steakhouse off 355; it's gone now. We all got a little tipsy, you know, blowing off steam, but Hawkins really got lit. I ended up driving him home. He could barely stand. I'd never seen him like that. I had to get him inside. I was a little nervous he might throw up and end up choking. I stayed at his place for an hour or two just to make sure he'd be okay. He said some things that night that made me realize he might be in a dark place."

"Like what?"

"That's just it. That's what's so frustrating. Both then and now. It wasn't specific. It was just drunken rambling. I'm sure it made sense to him, but to me it was largely gibberish. Something bad had happened. That's all I got."

"Bad how?"

"There were no details. If I'd had anything specific, I would have pressed Hawkins on it or gone to the authorities. It was just 'we did something bad, Al. Real bad.' Over and over on repeat."

"He said we? Not I?"

"Definitely 'we.' It was on a loop in his head. It was like he was driven to drink by whatever happened, but the alcohol just brought it all back. A catch-22. I saw him a few more times after that, but we all needed a break after that project. By the time the next set of work came around, he was done. We never worked together on anything again. I saw him at

The Rink once and tried to ask him about it, but he waved me off. The next time he was just ... gone. Here but not here, you know."

Koenig tried to jog something loose by coming at Campbell's story again from a couple of different angles but, other than the confirmation that there was a group involved, they didn't learn anything new.

"You said you were friends with Safford Lee?" Koenig said as they stood to leave.

"Yes, we still see each other a few times a month. Grab dinner or a beer. Talk about the old days. That's what men getting older do."

"Do you think he'd know anything more about Mr. Hawkins?"

Campbell scratched the back of his neck. "I don't know. I doubt it. Believe it or not, I'm the extrovert of the group. We talked about it a few times after it happened. I didn't get the sense he knew any more than I did. I can give you his number, although he's out in Vancouver right now visiting his daughter and grandkids."

"We'll take his number. You never know. Thank you, Mr. Campbell."

They left the man in his doorway pinching his nose. He looked a little more stooped than when they'd first met him, and Max felt a pang of regret for dredging up the past. But only a little.

CHAPTER TWENTY-SEVEN

The ferry had departed, and the small harbor was once again quiet and pedestrian-free. There was a pleasant view if you stopped at sunset, but it was a working harbor for fishing, lobster boats, and the ferry. You might hike up the hill to the small lighthouse, but otherwise there wasn't much of a reason to stick around. And no one had.

Koenig did another drive-by, but they didn't spot Labat.

"For Prince Creek's one indigent homeless man, he's awfully hard to find," she said.

"Worse problems a town could have."

"True. What did you think of Campbell?"

"I think he was telling the truth."

"Not much to lie about."

"No, and it fits with what Kay Proulx told us."

"Something bad in the past."

"Bad enough that Proulx still remembers, Goulart lied, and Hawkins became a drunk."

They each thought about that as Koenig hit the end of Breakwater Avenue and turned left. They drove past the police station. Roy's car and most of the other official vehicles were missing from the lot, likely still up at the Harrow scene. Koenig steered them back into the business district. Max could see Charlie in his bookstore, behind the counter serving coffee and talking to two women. Just past The Maple, Koenig cut down Church Avenue and wound through the small residential neighborhood, then took a left. St. Mary's Catholic Church sat on the corner opposite the cemetery. The large building was constructed with rust-colored sandstone in the traditional Gothic cross style with a tall steeple off center of the narthex and a steep pitched slate roof. Built on a hill near the entrance to Prince Creek proper, it was likely the most prominent and maybe most beautiful building in town.

They parked in the lot across the street and walked up the sidewalk to the church's front entrance. The inside was dim and smelled of dust, wood polish, and incense. It was very large with high ceilings, two rows of pews, and at least a dozen stained glass windows filtering the outside light. The hanging crucifix in the chancel at the opposite end of the building felt half a mile away.

"The entire population of Prince Creek could probably fit in here," Koenig whispered. It was the type of place that made you want to whisper.

"Indeed, it could," a voice answered. They both turned and watched a man approach from a stand of votive candles. He was tall and ruddy with neatly parted salt-and-pepper hair and a gentleman's gut hanging over his belt. "This place can hold 1200, though it's been a long while since we had a crowd that size. Catholicism is still the largest faith group on the island but," he paused, "it's a challenging time for the faith." He held out a hand. "Father White. I'm the pastor. How can

I help you two? You didn't come here to hear me preach. Not right now, at least." He smiled. "Looking to get married? I have to tell you we book up quickly and precedence goes to current parishioners."

Max felt some color rise to his cheeks and was amused to see Koenig just as flustered.

"No, no." She held her hands up as if she could physically ward off the suggestion. "I'm Inspector Koenig from the RCMP. This is Max Lindell. We're helping Chief Roy with the Arnsfeld murders."

"Oh, yes. Terrible, terrible news. Chief Roy asked me about a Bible verse and my opinion on the type of person that might do this through a twisted relationship with God. I have to tell you, I have a hard time seeing that person in my mind. Certainly no current members of this parish come to mind."

"Did you know the Arnsfelds?"

"I knew them. But not well. They weren't part of this parish, but I've been the pastor here since 1992 and you get to know people not just inside these walls. No one deserves that fate. No one."

"Was Collum Hawkins a parishioner?" Max asked.

"Collum? Why, yes, he was. Another tragedy. Are they connected somehow?"

"They might be," Koenig said.

"Did you ever hear Mr. Hawkins's confession?" Max asked.

"Well, that would be a sacred vow and nothing I could disclose."

"Even after he's dead?"

"Dead only on this earth but it's irrelevant. He didn't come to me for absolution. I could tell he was a troubled man and tried to talk to him many times but made no headway. He came to mass fairly regularly and kept his own counsel."

"What about Colby and Dorothea Harrow? Do they attend mass here?"

"No, I believe they're Baptists and attend services in town at the Lighthouse," Father White replied.

Max knew the place. It was on the edge of town near The Motel. It was a simple white structure converted from a failed feed and tack store with a short squat steeple over the entrance doors.

Before White could offer any more on Harrow, Koenig brought the conversation around to their real priority. "Father, we're here looking for Nik Labat. Corporal Alford said you sometimes extend him some hospitality."

"That's true. We run a soup kitchen and shelter out of the basement. Might as well put this big space to some good charitable use. We rarely have lodgers and let Nik sleep in one of the old storage rooms we converted to small bedrooms. He helps when he can with the food intake, moving boxes, that sort of thing."

"Is he here now?"

"I don't know. The doors to the church are open during the day." Father White glanced at his watch. "He might be. During the summer he mostly stays down by the park near the harbor—"

"We've checked. He's not there."

"He doesn't like the crowds from the ferry, and they are the biggest on the weekends. He might have come up here."

"Do you mind if we check?"

"Of course not. I'll come along to make introductions. You know Nik is ... troubled."

They were walking along the back of the church headed for a door in the corner. "What does that mean, Father? Is he dangerous?" Koenig asked.

White flipped a light switch and then paused with his hand on the knob.

"No, I don't think so. In all the time he's been coming here, I've never seen him hurt someone intentionally. He can get agitated and suddenly swing or move his arms erratically. He hit Eleanor Ramp, one of our volunteers, like that, gave her a bloody nose, but it wasn't on purpose. He's hurt himself at times, punching himself or striking walls."

"Do you know what's wrong with him?"

"He's never been formally diagnosed as far as I know. We can't nor do we want to force him into treatment. I don't think he's a danger to anyone. I think he just goes away. Sometimes he's quite lucid, other times he seems to sort of get unmoored in time, drifts backward. He talks as if he's a much younger man. One of our members who helps in the food bank is a therapist and has spent time with him over the years. She thinks he's likely suffering from PTSD or schizoaffective disorder, I think she called it. She believes there was some trauma when he was younger that triggered the sudden change in mood and led to his extreme anxiety. Or, maybe that's all baloney. Maybe it was just bad wiring and he was destined to end up this way. He certainly indulges in drugs and alcohol when he can."

"What about the time slips?" Max asked.

"She thinks those times where he believes he is still in the past are the times when he's re-experiencing the trauma."

"He's having lucid, waking nightmares."

"Yes, that might be a suitable way of putting it."

St. Mary's basement was large, spanning almost the entirety of the church's main footprint. At some point in the past, it had been subdivided into different rooms.

As they walked down the corridor that led away from the bottom of the stairs, White indicated doors and pointed off to different sections.

"These rooms up front are the classrooms for Sunday school. Others are just used for general storage. Vestments, missals, seasonal decorations, that sort of thing. The food pantry and the rooms set aside for the shelter are toward the back. Well, it's technically the front of the church."

White used a key and opened another door. "The food pantry has a separate side entrance."

The left side of the space was large and open. Shelving units cut the space up into aisles. Max could see canned goods lining the front of one aisle and what looked like cereal boxes in the next one. At the end of the aisles were several long tables like you might find in a school cafeteria and on the other side of the tables, along the right-hand wall, were four doors, all closed.

"That side is self-explanatory," White gestured toward the shelves and aisles. "Down the other end, past the last aisle, is a kitchen. This side has three bedrooms. Two for singles, one a little larger in the event we might have a family, and the last one is a shower and toilet. The pantry is not open today, and we aren't expecting volunteers either. Why don't you take a seat? I'll see about Nik."

White went to the second door on the end. There were no windows. He knocked lightly then opened the door a crack and said something before returning to their table.

"He'll be out in a moment. He seemed all right but go easy on him. When he doesn't know something or can't remember, he can get agitated and stubborn. It's a downward spiral from there."

"Thank you for your help, Father."

"You're welcome. You can go out that door when you're done." He indicated a doorway in the corner, across the room. "It should be open from this side and lock behind you. If you need anything else from me, I'll be upstairs or in the rectory."

White left, back through the interior hallway, presumably up into the church. Koenig and Max waited a minute in silence and then the bedroom door opened and Nik Labat emerged. There was little doubt it was the same man Max had seen previously on his daily runs down by the harbor. He wore different sweatpants now, gray instead of navy, but the duct-taped shoes and the Undertaker jacket and orange safety vest were the same. His hair was damp, and his face appeared scrubbed clean. As he sat down across from them, Max caught the potent smell of soap then, underneath that, maybe from the clothes, stale sweat and body odor.

"Father White said you were with the police and have some questions for me? I haven't done anything," Labat said. His face was heavily lined from spending so much time outdoors and living rough, but his eyes were a vivid swirl of green and blue. He stared at them. There was no evasion. He was just stating a fact. At that moment, he seemed far from erratic or mentally unstable.

"That's right," Koenig said. "We wanted to ask you about something that happened back in the 1990s. Probably when you were in high school. That okay?"

"Sure. You can try, at least. Can't promise anything." He pointed a finger at his temple. "My memory can get a little shaky sometimes. Father White might have said something."

"Do the best you can. Your father and Stephanie Arnsfeld's mother got together back then."

"That's right. My old man never made her an honest woman, but they lived together for about ten years."

"How was that?"

Labat shrugged. "It was a little weird at first, Steph and I having some of the same friends and then living under the same roof, but it was mostly okay. Steph and I got along most of the time."

"You didn't find it inconvenient to suddenly have a step-sister underfoot at school? You were older, right?"

"I was a year older, yeah, but Steph practically ran that place from the minute she walked in the door as a freshman. Just who she was, but it didn't bother me too much. I wasn't a social pariah. She was happy to have me bring some of the older guys around."

"You guys ran in the same social circle? Went to the same parties?"

"Sure. Steph was the queen bee, like I said."

"Where were those parties?"

"All over. Maybe someone's house if their parents were away. Out in an abandoned field sometimes." Labat spent five minutes going through all the different ways they would acquire beers and drugs and a party spot. He remembered the girls he took. He remembered the times they had to run from the cops.

"Never did get popped in high school. Neither did Steph as far as I know." He was smiling at the memories. His teeth were yellowed and in dire need of a cleaning.

"Did you know a man name Collum Hawkins back then?"

Labat's eyes faded at the question and he suddenly looked less like a confident party boy and more like a confused little boy. "Hawkins? No, I don't think so. Did he go to PC High?"

"How about Colby Harrow? Ring any bells?"

"Harrow? The farmer?" His eyes had been roving around the room, never settling, and Max noticed his left leg had started thumping up and down under the table.

"Yes," Koenig said.

"Why would I know him? He's gotta be 30 years older than me."

"So, you didn't know him?"

Labat suddenly stood up and started pacing, four steps in one direction, then four back in the other. He pounded a fist against his forehead. He was muttering something under his breath. Koenig glanced at Max. Keep going or pull the plug? Max nodded slightly.

"Are you okay, Nik?" Koenig asked.

He stopped pacing and faced them. Max noticed twin tracks of tears were running down his cheeks. "You're here for the dolls, aren't you?"

"What dolls?"

"Only he can make a soul," Labat continued. "The dolls have no souls, but they exist. The dolls are everywhere. I see them everywhere. They have no eyes, but I know they see me. I hear them whispering about me." He started pacing again, this time banging his head into one of the closed wooden doors.

Max stood. "Hey, stop. We don't want to upset you." Though it was obviously too late for that. Labat was pacing faster and continued to ram his head into the door. Max was afraid he'd soon draw blood or give himself a concussion. He started around the table when the hallway door opened and Father White came in.

"Everything okay? I heard a noise." Labat ran his head into the door again. "Nik, stop!" Father White grabbed him and steered him back toward the bedroom.

"I think we should stop now. He's clearly upset."

"The dolls ... the dolls ..."

"It may take a while to calm him down. I don't think you'll get anything else out of him today."

Labat was now sobbing loudly. Before he disappeared inside the bedroom, he turned and looked back at them. His face was twisted in agony.

"We did bad things. Bad, bad things. All of us. The dolls know."

CHAPTER TWENTY-EIGHT

They left the church and headed back to the Harrow scene. Max's phone chirped after they'd been on the road for only a minute. He checked the display and answered it.

"That was fast."

"Well, we didn't exactly wait for your go ahead." Max could hear the grin in Lawrence's voice. "And you know Eddie doesn't like to sleep. And likes a challenge. But there also wasn't much to find. This a bad time?"

"No, but I've only got a few minutes." He quickly filled Lawrence in on Harrow's murder and the conversations with Campbell and Labat.

"Jesus, Max. You have a way about you. Things are escalating up there. You realize the potential problem, right?"

"Yes." He was conscious of Koenig sitting in the driver's seat listening. The more he got involved, the higher the chance that someone might pay attention to him, but he was determined now to see this thing through. "I'll figure something out."

"Someone else listening?"

"Yes."

"Okay, we'll talk about that later. We searched all the records you sent and then searched some that you didn't. Eddie found them. I read them. I'll send the good stuff back via email."

"But not much there." Max didn't hide his disappointment. He'd hoped Lawrence or his half-brother could find something concrete in the pile of paper that would help bolster his theory of a coverup or blackmail.

"Not much, but I didn't say it was nothing. There were a couple of interesting things that might help. First, Hawkins. We went through all the income and tax statements we could find. He was an average Joe from 1974 until about 2000 when his income falls off a cliff. From what you told me he was too young to retire and not independently wealthy."

"That's right. So, what did he do?"

"Lived on his savings. I know living up there is cheaper, and he was being frugal, but I'm not sure the money would last the rest of his life. His partial pension from the government would have kicked in next year; in the meantime, he was eating into his savings for everyday expenses."

"That all sounds typical. Guy has a mental break, quits his job, and lives off his savings."

"I agree. There are two things worth mentioning. You said he had an apartment?"

"Yes. I've been inside. Two bedrooms. Small, but okay, for the island. Bachelor-type place. Rent probably wasn't super expensive."

"Well, he wasn't paying rent. I couldn't find any payments to any landlord or management place."

"Cash?"

"I don't think so. There were no regular withdrawals that would match up like that."

"Okay, that's odd. What's the other thing?"

"There were regular debits and credits, just not for rent. He has a regular sum of 400 dollars coming in each month to his checking account from Prince Creek Corporate Services Limited."

"Sounds appropriately opaque."

"Yeah, it's a shell domiciled out of Barbados. Eddie took a run at it. He said he can get in, but it won't be easy or fast."

"Forget it for now. Probably would only find another shell."

"That's the game. Here's the next bit. The next day, after the deposit, he withdraws 301 dollars and 70 cents."

"Odd amount. Any ideas?"

"I'd look at money order places. They typically cost about a dollar."

"Huh. Good idea. So, he's living rent-free, or someone is paying his rent, he's getting a monthly booster but then turning around and withdrawing most of it for some unknown purpose." That got a sharp glance from Koenig. "Anything else on Hawkins?"

"No, that's it. Arnsfeld had fresh surprises and, in case you were wondering, I didn't find any money movement from Arnsfeld that matched up with Hawkins. Can't say for sure, rich people have a lot of slippery ways to hide money, but I don't think he was the one paying your other dead guy."

"Good to know."

"Okay, Topher Arnsfeld. The headline here is that he was worth significantly less than what is generally reported. It looks like he took a bath on that for-profit venture up there. He was still rich by most standards, but not by tech or Silicon Valley standards. Not anymore. And it wasn't just the island incubator thing. It looks like he made a bunch of poor bets."

"How bad?"

"Hard to tell exactly, but I'd put his net worth in the 15 to 20 million range."

"Not chump change but—"

"He cashed out of his last venture with about 20 times that."

"Is it some tax dodge? Did he move it into the foundation he set up?"

"No. I thought of that. He funded the foundation at the start, but I had Eddie poke around. The foundation is also bleeding red ink."

Max looked up as Koenig braked and pulled into the Harrow's driveway. Two media vans were parked on the shoulder. Max saw Thorne chatting with a female on-air reporter. The media attention would only grow more intense now. Chravette was still on duty. He lifted the tape and waved them on.

"This is good stuff. Really good. I might have more for you soon. I'm at the Harrow scene. Send me what you have. We'll talk later."

"On its way, man. Stay safe."

He disconnected and could feel Koenig eyeing him. "More friends? You've got quite the list of consultants working this case." But she didn't say it with any real malice.

"Just trying to patch up the holes. I had a guy look at all the financial stuff we've gotten so far."

"Sounds like it worked."

He filled her in on what Lawrence had found on Hawkins and Arnsfeld.

She whistled when he told her about Arnsfeld's recent financial losses. "Not the tune we heard from Ramsey or Carr."

"Maybe they didn't know."

"Maybe Ramsey, he was more the sales guy, but Carr must have known about the foundation's problems. You can't hide that kind of financial trauma from the CFO. Not for long."

"I'll take your word for it."

"Definitely bumps Arnsfeld back up a few notches on my list. Those kinds of losses will stress anyone out. Might lead to some erratic behavior. Might lead you to do something that gets you killed."

They found Roy sitting on a rock outside a ring of crime scene tape watching a tech going over the grass for any trace evidence or DNA. They might find something, but Max doubted it would help them find the killer. He was unlikely to be in any database. It might help eventually convict him, so it had to be done. The body had been cut down and taken to the morgue. Max glanced around. The sightlines were cut off by the house and attached porch. If they were lucky, none of the media had gotten any shots of Harrow's hanging corpse.

Roy looked over his shoulder as he heard them approach. "I'm starting to think running for a third term might be a mistake. I'm not cut out to deal with this type of lunatic." He stood up with the groan that all men over 40 seemed to acquire. "Retirement sounds better and better."

"Hang in there, Chief," Koenig said, then paused as she realized her poor choice of words but she pushed on. "This is likely a once in a career case."

He didn't look all that convinced. Or maybe he did, but once was enough to make a man quit for a simpler life. His skin looked pale and sallow. The grooves that creased his forehead and cheeks made him look ten years older. The case was taking its pound of flesh. "I hear you, Inspector. Not sure how you deal with it on a regular basis." He looked at Max. "I'm thinking about taking your spot on Archie's boat."

"The smell isn't much better. The pay definitely isn't, but it has other benefits."

"That's what he tells me." Roy tried to shake it off. "The media get a shot of you coming in?"

"They saw us, but I don't think they know, other than Thorne, that the RCMP is involved yet. Did you put that in the initial press release?" Koenig asked.

"No."

"Okay, that will give you something to talk about at the press conference."

"You think I should do one?"

"The sooner the better. Today, if you can. Thorne's already linked the first two. Now you got Harrow. Three bodies will make the television people all hot and sweaty. You want to stay out in front of it as best you can."

He rubbed a hand over his face. "Okay. I'll get something set up for 5 p.m."

"Four might be better. Television will appreciate the extra time to get it on the evening broadcasts. You ever done one before?"

"No. Had no reason. Done a couple TV interviews but nothing like this."

She looked at him. "You'll do okay. You got the right look. Don't clean yourself. You want to look a little tired, a little grim."

"Not going to be hard."

"You know what you're going to say?"

"Not really. The truth, I guess."

"Definitely don't do that. They'll crucify us. Give them a story. Give them some gory details. The television people will eat that up. Tell them we're working it, we've got leads, and we should have a lot more in a week."

"Do we?"

"Sort of. It just has to sound good. If we feed them a little bullshit, tell them we think it's a local and we're getting close, maybe it'll flush the guy out. This thing won't last another week."

"You think?"

Koenig glanced at Max.

"Yup," he said. "Crazy fades away or burns out. I don't see this guy fading away."

They all chewed on what the implications of that might be, then Roy asked, "Did you find Labat?"

They spent fifteen minutes bringing Roy up to speed on their conversations with Campbell, White, and Labat.

"Dolls, huh? This thing keeps getting stranger and stranger. What do you think of that? More crazy ramblings?"

"I don't think so," Max replied. "Labat definitely has some issues, that's clear, but they seem rooted in reality, some past trauma. White said one of the parishioners, who was a therapist, believes that. I wouldn't discount the dolls. Not completely. It fits somehow."

Roy nodded and they poked at the theory more, but it was all conjecture.

"I heard back from the researcher at the RCMP on the financials from Arnsfeld and Hawkins. A couple of oddities." Koenig sketched in the details that Max had related in the car. Max was grateful she'd kept his involvement out of it. If they needed it, they could funnel Lawrence's work back through the proper channels. Better not to muddy the waters with more outside 'volunteers.'

"Not sure what to make of that," Roy said. "It does remind me of something though. C'mon up to the house."

CHAPTER TWENTY-NINE

They went up the porch steps. Through the back door, they could see a tech kneeling on the kitchen floor in a white Tyvek suit with the RCMP logo on the chest. She glanced up.

"Leeds still in here?" Roy asked.

"Stay there." She disappeared and they heard her climbing the stairs at the front of the house. She returned a moment later. "He'll be down in a minute. If you want to talk, it might be easier if you meet him at the front door."

"Thanks. We'll do that."

She nodded, then went back to sorting through particles on the floor. It was hot in the house. Without the air conditioning on, Max could feel the heat coming through the screen door in waves. He didn't know how the woman didn't have sweat pouring down her face. They left her and walked around the wraparound porch to the front door and leaned against the painted railing to wait for Leeds.

"How does he get them to open the door?" Max asked.

"What?" Roy said. He'd been looking toward the road. A

third satellite truck had arrived. A knot of people stood on the edge of the property near the Harrows' mailbox.

"I keep coming back to the door. This is just like Arnsfeld. No forced entry. No gunshots or other signs of coercion. Why do they open the door?"

"Given the timing, Arnsfeld was in the afternoon. I don't find it too strange he opened the door, even to a stranger," Koenig replied. "I see your point with Harrow though. It was the middle of the night. He likely would have been suspicious or on guard or something."

"Right. I know what I said before, but maybe it's not a guy? A guy like Harrow or Arnsfeld would feel safe opening the door for a woman."

"No, you convinced me before," Roy said. "Harrow was grizzled and tough, but he had old school manners. Plus, I disagree with the inspector. No woman would be strong enough to string Harrow up like that. Not by herself."

"Multiple people is an idea ..." Max said.

"Let's not go there. Not yet," Koenig said.

"Then it's something else. This guy ..."

Max didn't finish the thought. Burty Leeds, the lead crime scene analyst, came out the door.

He glanced at Max, then Koenig. "Inspector."

She nodded. "Hey, Burty."

Unlike his colleague, Burty Leeds was sweating in his bunny suit. He pulled the hood off and ran a hand over his buzzed black hair. He was a short man with an ascetic's thin build and sunken cheeks pitted with old acne scars.

"What can I do for you?"

"Wondering if we could get a jump on that key? Might make a difference," Roy said.

"Don't see why not? Given where it was found, it's unlikely anyone but Harrow touched it. I'll go grab it." He pulled the hood back on and disappeared back inside.

"They found what appears to be a safety deposit box key taped to the underside of one of Harrow's office drawers. Only two banks in the area. Prince Creek Credit Union and a local branch of CIBC. I called around. Harrow had accounts at the credit union. It'll probably be another three or four hours until we can get into the office and dig through the papers, but I thought you could take a look at the box."

"That's a good idea," Koenig said. "They open on Saturday?"

"No, but I know Cal Newhouse, the president. He'll open the doors for you."

Burty came back and handed a numbered envelope to Roy. "Here you go."

"Thanks, Burty. If I talk to Mrs. Harrow, what should I tell her about the house? When can she come back?"

"We'll keep going as long as we can today but, if she could give us until tomorrow, we should have everything wrapped up by noon. Expect a preliminary report by Tuesday. Wednesday at the latest."

"That all sounds good. I'll tell her."

Burty left, and Roy handed the envelope to Koenig.

"Subpoena to get the box popped?" she asked.

Roy smiled. "In the works. I talked to the magistrate. Should be ready by the time you get back to town. There are some advantages to working in a small town, Inspector."

They ignored the media and drove the 15 minutes back to Main Street and stopped at the Town Hall. They didn't see the magistrate, but a clerk was waiting on the steps. Max thought she looked a little put out for coming in on a Saturday but said nothing. Join the club. Koenig flashed her badge and the woman handed over the paperwork. Koenig skimmed through it to make sure there wouldn't be any snags later. After a minute, she nodded to the woman and slid the paper into her suit jacket pocket. "Thanks."

"Good luck." The woman sniffed before pulling her purse onto her shoulder and walking off down the sidewalk. Koenig raised an eyebrow at Max.

"You ruined her Saturday afternoon."

"Fuck that. The killer ruined her tea and crumpets, not me."

They drove a half-mile down Main. The Prince Creek Credit Union had a plum spot on a corner lot opposite Robin's Donuts. It was an unexpectedly modern building. There was a lot of flat glass, colored accents, and cultivated landscaping. Parking was in the rear. Cal Newhouse was waiting for them, leaning against his black Audi. He was dressed in worn cowboy boots, old jeans, and a pale blue western shirt with white piping on the shoulders. His jaw was starting to sag, and slight wrinkles were etched around his eyes. Max put his age somewhere north of 50.

"Looks less like a bank president and more like a rancher," Max said.

"Just missing the 10-gallon hat," Koenig muttered as she pulled into the reserved vice president spot next to Newhouse.

They got out and shook hands. Koenig handed over the subpoena. Newhouse glanced at it but didn't really read it. "I'm sure it's good. We've had a couple of requests before from Chief Roy. Never had a problem." He refolded it and stuck it in his back pocket. "Shall we?"

They entered through a side door. Newhouse flicked on some lights. "It's back here." He led them down a hallway, away from the teller windows and sales cubicles. "It's not large. As you might imagine, demand isn't that high around here. We knocked out a wall and combined a few closets. In the 20 years we've been offering, I think we've topped out at about 50 percent capacity."

He stopped in front of a plain-looking beige door with a

biometric keypad and lock. He entered a seven-digit code and placed his thumb on the pad. The light on the sensor blinked green and there was the heavy clunk of the lock being disengaged. Newhouse rapped his knuckles on the door. "Wood veneer but steel core."

Inside, gold-plated boxes lined three walls. Smaller, post office-sized boxes on top, larger, more spacious boxes on the bottom. A table sat in the center of the room, and a computer workstation on a movable stand was nestled in a corner.

"Roy said you had a key."

"That's right. A key but no box number."

"For security. We can look up the number here," Newhouse said and went to the computer. "Not hooked up to the Internet." He entered another password and typed and clicked his way through some cascading windows. "Harrow. Box 57."

He led the way to the far side of the room. It was a small box. Max had a disorienting moment where he thought the key wouldn't fit, but it did. Koenig extracted the box and carried it to the table. She glanced at Newhouse who was still lingering over her shoulder.

"Right. Sorry." He looked disappointed not to get a look at what was inside. "I'll be in the lobby when you're done. Just give a shout."

"Thanks," Koenig said.

Harrow had stuffed the box with papers. Koenig took everything out and placed it all on the table. They went through each sheet. Insurance documents, land deeds, bills of sale, mortgages, a will, some old black and white photos. The men and women were not smiling and wore formal attire.

"Maybe his parents?" Max said.

"Maybe." She put the photos in a separate pile.

Underneath the pictures were five stacks of bank-banded money. Koenig riffled the edges of one. "Fifty thousand."

"Rainy day money?"

"Maybe."

The last thing in the box was a slim, unmarked envelope with two more photographs inside. Both were in color and much more recent than the family photos. They definitely did not depict family situations. Neither shot was high quality. Each was pixilated and grainy. Shot in low light.

"They're printouts or reproductions from an original image or a printout from a low-res source," Koenig said.

She handed the first one to Max. It showed a man's legs from the thighs down. Clothes were scattered on the floor around his feet. A naked girl was on the ground. The photo only captured half her body. She was turned away, as if talking to someone off-camera. Probably not even aware of the camera. There was a light source somewhere to the left, but most of the photo was dark and underexposed.

"Can't make out much. It could be from an early digital camera or mobile phone. Given the timeframe we're considering, this was before everyone was walking around with an iPhone or a 12-megapixel camera in their pocket," Max said. "Looks similar in quality to that one photo you found in Hawkins's apartment."

Koenig passed the second one to him. "This one has better lighting but still doesn't tell me very much. You?"

The second photo showed a woman's knees and feet in the foreground. She appeared to be sitting on an examining table. Part of a dressing gown was visible at the top of the frame. An empty chair, small sink, and medical instruments were in the background. A cart with a piece of medical equipment was just poking into the frame on the right. The tip of a black shoe was visible next to the piece of equipment.

"No, beyond the fact that she's at a doctor's office or

hospital. Both pictures look like they were taken without the subjects being aware. The same woman you think?" He handed the photos back.

"Can't tell. Maybe I can get someone to do some measurements or something."

They went out and found Newhouse fiddling with his phone in one of the lobby chairs.

"You mind if we make some copies," Koenig asked, holding up the stack of papers.

"Subpoena lets you take the contents, I believe," Newhouse replied.

"We'll do that, too. But we need to make some copies first. Oh, and there was money in the box. We'll need you to witness that."

"Any clues?" he asked. His eyes brightening a bit, maybe sensing a story he could tell at the bank's next holiday party.

Koenig spotted it, too. "I'll tell you, Cal, everything is a clue until you got the guy in cuffs." She waved the papers again. "These definitely count."

Go forth and tell your neighbors, Max thought.

CHAPTER THIRTY

They stood in the credit union's parking lot. Newhouse had left. The afternoon air was humid but felt good after the indoor air conditioning. Koenig had the money in a bank bag with a receipt, plus a folder of the original documents. Max had added the copies to his notes and file folder. Two days ago, the file had been as thin as a piece of fishing line. Now, it was three inches thick. Max believed the answer was in there somewhere. He just didn't know how to pull it out yet.

"Regroup at The Rink?" Max asked.

Koenig checked her watch. "Roy texted while we were inside. His press conference is in 20 minutes, then I've got to get on the road. I want to get back to Charlottetown while a few places are still open."

"How about a coffee then? Perk you up for the drive? My friend Charlie will fix you up with a cup that will be better than any gas station or drive-thru you hit on your way back. He's part of The Rink crew with Thorne."

"That sounds good." She opened the car door to climb in.

"We can walk. It's right across the street."

. . .

Two patrons were browsing the fiction stacks inside Poor Charlie's Artisan Bookshop and one mousy girl, wearing over-sized headphones, was typing on a laptop at a table in the corner. The shop smelled pleasantly of coffee beans, ink, and paper.

Charlie was behind the counter reading a dog-eared paperback with a lurid painted cover. He held it up when he saw Max come in.

"Hey, Max. Someone dropped off two old boxes of vintage pulp. Donated them. Wouldn't take any money. Said she just wanted them out of the house. Most are too beat up to be worth much, but I should be able to move them pretty easily. I'll let you dig through them before I put them out. I only glanced at them, but spotted some Spillane, Gardner, Stout."

"Thanks, Charlie. Appreciate it. Can we get two coffees? To go."

"Just brewed a fresh pot. Dark roast okay?"

Max glanced at Koenig. She nodded.

Charlie poured the cups and slid them across the counter. "Here you go."

Max made quick introductions and then said, "Wanted to show you something. Get your opinion."

"This have to do with the murders?"

"Maybe. That's what we're trying to figure out." Max glanced at the laptop girl, but she was absorbed in her screen. One patron had taken a book and was reading on the couch. The other had moved upstairs. He took the two photos out of his file and handed them to Charlie.

"Take a look."

His brow furrowed and he studied both photos for almost a minute in silence. He pointed at the one in the doctor's office.

"Can't make heads or tails of this one, but I think this one might be from Mulvaney's office. I was a patient of his before Redd came to town. I think I recognize the office, though I guess most doctor's offices look similar."

"Our best guess is that the photos were taken in the late 1990s. Maybe around 1998 or 1999."

"Well, Mulvaney was around then. Redd and Heathers came later. It was Mulvaney or Cronley back then, though Cronley tended to take the kids. He wasn't a pediatrician by degree, but he had a better rapport with them. Mulvaney can be a little brusque. The division of labor worked out okay for everyone."

"Okay, we'll stop by. We had a couple of other things to talk to him about."

"He might help you out with the other photo."

"Why's that?"

"This birthmark or skin condition on the guy." Charlie tapped a finger near the man's upper leg. Max and Koenig each leaned over and looked. They'd both missed it the first time, but Charlie was right. There appeared to be a distinct discoloration or patterning high on the back of the man's thigh. "Maybe that's why the person took the photo. Your eye goes to the, *mmm*, girl, but I don't see anything distinguishing there. This mark, or whatever, that can't be removed. That's identifiable."

"Very good catch. And a very good point," Koenig said.

They walked back across the street to the Explorer. Max could tell Koenig no longer needed the coffee to feel alert. Max felt the same way. Charlie's suggestion had energized them both.

"I'm really tempted to skip Roy's press conference and go

talk to Mulvaney, but that feels a little like abandoning my post."

"Mulvaney's not going anywhere."

"I know. It just feels like we're finally getting some momentum on this thing." She sighed and tossed her cup in a garbage can on the corner. "C'mon, let's go feed the beast."

The press conference was on the steps of Town Hall. As Koenig predicted, the third murder had stoked a lot of interest. Prince Creek's small town hall didn't have a room big enough to accommodate the print guys, television reporters, cameras, lights, and other equipment, so Chravette had carried a lectern out onto the front steps and then added the Canadian and provincial PEI flags. Against the old brick building, it didn't make a bad backdrop. The bright lights did Roy no favors, but did make him appear steely and forbidding as he peered down at the crowd.

"Glad it's not me up there."

"He's doing alright. He's selling it."

Max had found a spot in the back of the crowd, off to one side. Archie was drinking from a can of Diet Coke and looked only marginally less exhausted than his brother.

"He always did like the shine of attention."

They watched as Roy introduced Koenig. She kept her remarks short and to the point. "As Chief Roy said, we've got some substantive leads and we're working them hard. As part of the provincial policing policy, the RCMP is here to offer expertise and resources, but Chief Roy is running the show."

She looked good, Max thought. Maybe too good. Or too intimidating. There were no followups. She stepped back and the questions picked up again for Roy. It was done in 20 minutes. Ten minutes after that, the sidewalk was empty except for the local rubberneckers.

"You ever get through all those ax receipts?" Max asked Archie.

"Went cross-eyed doing it but yeah it's done. I'm worried now, after Harrow, that Jermane's going to have me chasing down generic hemp rope. You need to solve this thing so we can get back on the water."

"I'm trying."

"I sent Ash out the last two days." Ash Whitaker was a retired local fisherman that occasionally subbed in if a captain was sick or temporarily laid up.

"Split the take?"

"Yeah?"

"How'd he do?" The look on Archie's face told him all he needed. "Better than us, huh?"

He met Koenig in the parking lot by the Explorer.

"He was good," she said.

"I thought so. TV people liked him, especially that blonde woman from Channel Eight."

Koenig's mouth twisted in a frown. "I've had a few run-ins. She's got a rep."

"But she gets the story?" Max smiled.

She didn't rise to the bait. "Let's go. Roy gave me Mulvaney's home address."

"You tell him about the photos?"

"Yes, but I'm not sure he heard me. He had that television afterglow."

"Thinking about Channel Eight."

Mulvaney lived in a simple but elegant natural-shingled house with a steeply slanting roof that made it resemble a traditional A-frame style. A six-foot fence divided the property from its neighbor on the left. The rest of the lot was covered in lush green grass, colorful annual plants, and flowering shrubbery. Someone in the house had a green thumb. Koenig pulled the Explorer into the driveway behind a spotless black Acura RDX.

The doors and windows of the house were closed. Max noticed the shades were also drawn on the lower floor. Koenig rang the bell. They could feel the vibration of someone moving to the door. A moment later, the curtain covering the front door's window twitched. A tall man of 60 with ruddy cheeks and slate gray hair opened the inner door. "Who are you?"

Koenig held up her credentials. "Inspector Koenig with the RCMP. We'd like to talk to you for a few minutes, Dr. Mulvaney."

He studied her identification. "That's Max?"

"That's him," Koenig replied.

"Heard about him," Mulvaney sniffed. He unlatched the screen door. "Better come on in," he said. He limped back down the hallway toward the kitchen. Max could make out the outline of a brace through Mulvaney's tan slacks and remembered Redd said that he'd torn up his knee playing golf. "We rarely batten down the hatches like this but with all the killings it seemed ... prudent."

"Who is it, Dick?" a woman called out.

"Police. RCMP."

They entered what would have been a bright kitchen with views of the side yard and the gardens if the shades hadn't been pulled. What they got instead was a diffused glow that threw soft shadows on countertops and appliances that hadn't been updated in 20 years. But it was all clean, and there was a delicious pastry smell coming from the oven.

"Hello. I'm Dick's wife, Vera. Are you, Max?"

Vera Mulvaney was younger than her husband and almost two feet shorter. A busy vitality radiated off of her.

"Your reputation precedes you," Koenig said with a grin.

"Small towns," Max said. "What smells so good, Vera?"

"I'm baking cookies. I should be out in the garden. A few more days and the weeds will get the upper hand. Dick is driving me crazy keeping me chained up inside."

"Vera!"

"Oh, hush. They know I'm only kidding. Sort of. We're both a little nervous about all these killings."

They sat around the kitchen table, ate warm cookies, and talked about the killings. The Mulvaneys didn't know much.

"I have no idea why it's happening. Just that whoever it is, is killing our friends."

"You knew the Arnsfelds?" Koenig asked.

"Well, no, not really," Mulvaney admitted. "We attended a few fundraisers. I saw them a few times at the office. Routine stuff."

"Did you invest any money with Topher Arnsfeld when he first came to town?"

Mulvaney's eyes shifted sideways. "A little. Lost it all."

Vera jumped in. "The Arnsfelds were acquaintances, but we *were* friends with the Harrows and Collum Hawkins. Col helped us with transferring the practice from Doc Heaney to Dick. That was before, *hmm*, his troubles."

"You prescribed Hawkins oxycodone."

Mulvaney waved away the comment. "Yes, I think he really needed antidepressants, but he patently refused to go to a psychiatrist. He came in a few times and complained about his back. I prescribed oxy. If he became addicted or was self-medicating for other reasons, he was very disciplined about it. Never requested to increase the dosage, never came back early for refills."

Koenig nodded and changed tracks. "We'd like to show you three photographs, Dr. Mulvaney. See what you can tell us about them." Koenig took the photographs out of the envelope and pushed them across the table.

They had added a copy of the photo from the case file that was taken from Hawkins's apartment. It showed a young woman in jean shorts and a halter top, slightly turned away from the camera, with long brown hair that hung below her shoulders and shielded half her face from view.

Both Mulvaneys leaned over to get a closer look. Vera slipped on a pair of glasses.

Max watched Mulvaney's face as he picked up the photo that they suspected was taken in his office. He squinted, and Max saw a glimmer of recognition cross his face. He practically dropped the photo like it was hot and looked at the other two while keeping his hands in his lap.

"Hard to make anything out," Vera said. "Where were they taken?"

"We were hoping your husband could help us with that."

"Me? Why?"

"Is that your office?"

"Maybe. So many general practitioner's offices look the same. Same general instruments. Same setup. I can't say for sure."

He's lying, Max thought. *He knows damn well it's his office. And he remembers more, too.*

Vera picked up the photo and brought it almost up to her nose. "I think this is the office, Dick. It's old, but I remember this print." She tapped the section where a corner of a frame could be seen. "It was before we did the remodel. Yes, look. Remember how that corner of the flooring kept peeling up?

You'd glue it down every Monday morning. I can see it peeling up."

Mulvaney leaned over the picture again but was only pretending to study it. "If you say so. I can't remember. Those early years were a blur of 16-hour days." His eyes drifted to the corner of the room.

"When did you remodel?" Koenig asked.

"In 2001," Vera said.

That fit with the timeline.

"What about the other photos? Do you recognize the girl?"

They both shook their heads. "Can't really see her. You only catch a bit of her profile," Vera said.

Koenig reached over and nudged the other photo from Harrow's box. "What about this, Doctor?" She tapped a fingernail against the man's thigh. "It looks like some kind of skin condition. Can you tell us anything about that?"

He tipped the photo toward the light. "Could be a simple rash or a condition like rosea or eczema. Not enough detail to be sure. Could also be vitiligo or tinea versicolor."

"I've heard of vitiligo, but what's the other one?"

"Spots on the skin that may be lighter or darker than your normal skin color. Sometimes they disappear in cold weather and reappear in the summer."

"Do you treat anybody with those conditions or something like it? Anyone in town?"

He couldn't look at Koenig. "No, I'm sorry."

Lying right to their faces.

Koenig saw it, too. "Okay. If anything comes to mind, please call me or Chief Roy." She took out a business card and handed it to Vera. "Anything at all. We don't want anyone else to die."

Mulvaney tried to pull himself together as he sensed Koenig wrapping it up. "Of course. I'll keep thinking about it.

I can check some records. Maybe there was someone, but I've forgotten. There have been a lot of patients over the years." Now he was trying to paper over the lies with good intentions. Intentions he likely had no plans to do.

"If it turns out you're lying, you can, and will, be held responsible as an accomplice. Spend the rest of your life in jail."

Vera stood up, almost knocking the chair over. "Hey, there's no reason for threats. We're not lying. We want this guy caught just as much as you do."

Koenig kept her eyes on Vera's husband. "Call."

CHAPTER THIRTY-ONE

Koenig's finger was tapping a double rhythm on the steering wheel as they drove over the small inlet bridge and out of Prince Creek. Max could see the vein in her neck pulsing along. "I hate it when they lie."

"Knee jerk reaction."

"He knows something. Maybe he doesn't think it's important or relevant, but that's not his call. If that's his office, and I'm betting it is, Vera seemed plenty sure, then there is a record of that visit. This just slows us down. Worst case, it could get someone killed."

"He might call."

"Only after he shields himself with a lawyer and makes us jump through every hoop possible. We don't have time."

"You could propose some kind of deal. Spill whatever he knows and he gets a pass for obstruction."

"Maybe."

She didn't look to be in the mood to cut Mulvaney any slack. They drove in silence for ten minutes. It was close to 6 p.m. The sun was slowly bending toward the horizon through watery clouds. Occasionally, tiny drops of water coated the windshield but couldn't muster up the energy for a proper shower.

As they passed through the dot of Dingwells Mills and turned southeast onto Seven Mile Road, Koenig asked, "How do you want to do this? Can't exactly pull into the driveway."

He'd come clean about using the rental house. Koenig hadn't been happy, but the discovery of the smuggling had given Max some leeway. "Drive past and let's loop around behind. I'll have to walk in from the back. May have to wait for dark."

"Could be a long walk."

"No reason to rush. Not even sure anything will happen. Rather get a little scraped up or walk a couple of extra miles than blow the cover on that house. Maddix is too smart. It could be a long time before he gives you a second shot."

She drove past the RCR clubhouse without slowing. There were a few more cars than when they'd stopped previously, but it looked quiet.

"You going out to check off the Amish names tomorrow?" she asked.

"That was my plan. You want to come?"

"No. I think Roy's instincts are right on that one. The less official presence, the better. I'm going to spend the day doing laundry and looking at all the paper again. See if I can find something."

"Might take a run at it, too, when I'm done with the interviews. We keep piling up acorns but not looking at 'em. Not closely enough."

They drove another mile and then turned onto Route 321, then a quick left onto an unnamed hard-packed dirt road. According to the SUV's GPS, they were now traveling roughly parallel to Seven Mile Road. Koenig kept her eyes on the odometer and braked to a stop after a mile. They'd agreed to meet up Monday morning at The Maple unless something broke earlier. Max opened the door and jumped out.

Neither one wanted to say it, but any break big enough to bring Koenig back tomorrow would be another body.

He saw nothing but trees and fields for the first mile as he climbed to the top of a slight rise. It was slow going. There was no path, and he had to keep his eyes down and step carefully in order not to turn his ankle or step in a hole. He pushed through thin lines of trees and the unruly shrubs that acted as dividers between the plots of farmland. In New England they might have been knee-high rock walls. You worked with what you had.

When he reached the top of the rise, he could see the low white house that sat across the road from the RCR buildings. There was a chance someone could spot him from the RCR buildings if they were standing just right but the likelihood was slim. He lined himself up with the rental's back porch and started walking again. He took his time. If anything happened, he didn't think it was likely to happen before dark. He was fortunate the surrounding farmland wasn't being actively cultivated. It might have made walking easier, but he'd also be trespassing and have to dodge the odd farmer. Even out in the fields, it felt as if he was being watched. He chalked it up to the paranoia of living in the fishbowl of Prince Creek. It was unsettling that both Dick and Vera had known his name.

It couldn't have been over three miles, but it took him almost an hour to pick his way through the fields and climb the back steps of the rental. He knocked and after a moment Kyle opened the door. Max had called ahead. He didn't want to take chances. Kyle was the shoot first type. And, while guns were much more heavily regulated in Canada than the

US, Max had no doubt Kyle had two, maybe three, within easy reach.

"Anything happening?" Max asked. He'd had Koenig stop for sandwiches and sodas on the way and he placed the plastic bag on the kitchen table along with the now dog-eared file folder he was still carrying around.

Kyle shook his head. "No."

Kyle retreated through an open doorway toward the front of the house. Max followed. The house smelled dusty, with an undertone of mildew and maybe animal droppings. A place that hadn't been used or opened to fresh air in a long time. Kyle had set up in the living room near the window that had the best view across the road. A digital camera, notebook, and a pair of binoculars sat on a table. A sleeping bag, flashlight, and a small backpack were nearby on the floor. Everything a soldier could need.

"Going to look around. Use the head. Plumbing work?"

Kyle grunted something that Max took as an affirmative. Max had gotten used to having mostly one-way conversations with his quiet friend.

The rental was sparsely furnished. Wooden table in the kitchen, four chairs. Old sofa, loveseat, and chipped coffee table in the living room. The dining room held another table but no chairs and had an empty breakfront along one wall. Max walked down the hall. Three bedrooms. One with a double bed. Two with singles. One bathroom with a tub/shower combo along with the toilet.

He relieved himself, washed his hands, and then carried the food back to the living room and set it up on the coffee table. They alternated eating and watching the RCR parking lot fill up as the sun went down. Max filled Kyle in on the Harrow murder, the photos in the bank box, and Mulvaney's shadiness. Kyle asked to look at the photos and studied them for a time but offered no opinions before he handed them back. Tired of the sound of his voice, Max went looking for a distraction and found an old Clifford Simak sci-fi novel in one bedroom and read that until it was too dark to see anymore, then he napped.

Kyle woke him at 1 a.m. He rubbed his eyes and sat up. The old couch had left a deep crick in his back and neck. He stood and tried to stretch it out. "Time to go?" he asked.

"Yes. No new arrivals in the last hour. Four guys just left the main building and headed for the big building in back."

"Maddix?"

"Looked like it. Matched the description you gave me."

"Okay. That's the building I'm interested in. I've been in the main building. Looks like it's just a bar unless there's a basement, but I didn't see anything like that. The two outbuildings are too small to be much more than storage. I guess if it's drugs, they could stash them in there, but it's too small to cook. If anything is going down, it's in the big building."

"You want to go in?"

"Wouldn't mind getting a peek if the opportunity presents itself, but I'd be okay just watching. You see any dogs?"

"No."

"That's good for us."

Kyle took a can out of the backpack and smeared some black paint over his hands and face and then handed it to Max. Kyle checked the pack's pockets then slung it over his shoulders. "Time to go."

No rain yet, but the big boy clouds had rolled in and blotted out the moon and the stars. Fifteen feet from the house's back door and they couldn't see their hands, never mind their feet. Kyle turned on a small penlight and Max did his best to follow in Kyle's footsteps. They walked back to the first line of trees, then cut west until they were out of sight of the RCR's buildings before angling north again to Seven Mile Road. They were half a mile down the road from where they started, screened by a tall line of evergreens. They could faintly hear music, laughing, and conversation spilling out from the bar and catch some residual glow from the overhead lights mounted on poles around the parking area.

"Gonna be tough to get close with those lights," Max said.

If Kyle had any thoughts, he didn't share them. They sprinted across the road in a crouch and then back into the cover of the low, roadside scrub. Kyle turned off the penlight, but his steps didn't falter. Max did his best not to fall on his face. They paused and crouched low as two cars went past, but neither vehicle slowed. They kept walking and eventually cleared the rough line of trees and stood on the edge of the RCR land. An old, maybe abandoned, tractor trailer truck was parked directly in front of them on an unused farm road that bordered a fallow overgrown field of hay. They crawled under the empty bed of the truck. Beyond the field of hay, maybe 200 or 300 yards, were the RCR buildings. The truck gave them an excellent observation spot, shielded from the road and passing cars, and close enough with Kyle's binoculars to monitor any activity in the parking area or near the buildings. But it would be difficult to get closer. If this was all they got, it would have been better to stay in the house.

"That hay isn't high enough to cover us," Max said.

Kyle remained silent and scanned the area back and forth with the binoculars. Max waited. As they watched, the door to the large outbuilding opened and four men exited and stood in the halo of the overhead sodium vapor lights. The last guy out turned and did something at the door. Max thought it was the bartender.

"Punching the lock code," Max said. "You getting this?"

Kyle's binoculars also had a digital camera. It could snap

and store photos of what he was looking at through the glass. They were too far out to get the door code, but they could get decent photos of the four men.

The other RCR guy was Maddix. Max recognized his wide shoulders and thick arms. The final two guys were dressed differently than the biker clothes the RCR preferred but still in uniforms of some kind. Blue jeans and light jackets with a vaguely inspired military feel.

"Got it."

"Is the guy locking the door the one you followed on the smuggling run?"

"Yes. Same beard. Same limp."

As they watched, Maddix hiked up his pants over the swell of his gut and then offered his hand to both of the strangers.

"Shit. We're too late. Something just got done."

The four men walked across the lot and went back inside the bar.

"Maybe not," Kyle replied. "A deal got made but they're not carrying anything."

"Unless they're buying information."

"You don't need a shed that big for information."

"You're right. Not just a handshake deal. A handshake and a drink. Then they load up."

"That's what I think."

The clouds finally got too heavy to hold it all in. The rain picked up; heavy, fat drops that splashed down with a small punch of violence. They stayed mostly dry under the shelter of the truck. The wind picked up and pushed the rain sideways and they got wet.

"Weather helps," Kyle said. "If you want to move, now is the time."

"Let's move."

CHAPTER THIRTY-TWO

They shimmied out from under the truck and tried to stay low, staying in a crouch as they worked their way down the old farming road until the bulk of the largest RCR shed hid them from view of the main building, then they stood up and jogged more quickly, letting the wind and rain cover any additional noise they made. They looped around the field and, ten minutes after they'd pushed out from under the truck bed, they crawled the last five yards until they could touch the back of the shed.

There were two back doors, solid-looking slabs of steel, side by side, that Max thought could swing open wide enough to load freight into the back of a waiting car or truck completely out of sight from the road. Kyle shined the penlight on the door locks. Each looked shiny and new, as if the locks had been installed fresh from their packages last week. And each was formidable.

"Not getting through those without some serious munitions," Kyle said.

"Knew it was a long shot but hoped that making the effort would make some more magic happen." Max wiped the dripping water from his face. "We're already wet. Let's go sit some more and see what happens after those drinks."

They reversed course and crawled away from the shed and took up a new position on their stomachs in the hayfield. They chose a spot that gave them a view of both the front and back of the shed. They would be spotted easily during the day but unlikely to be seen in the dark and rain.

Nothing happened for a half-hour, except the rain let up and cars pulled out and left. Max was wet, cold, and stiff from lying in a puddle. He had to fight to keep his teeth from chattering. He was on the verge of suggesting they pull the plug and head back to the house when the same group of four men exited the main building. One man split off and headed for a cluster of pickups parked on the far end of the drive. The other three walked toward the front of the shed.

"Front or back?" Kyle asked as they heard the truck startup.

"Back. You don't do risky business out front with the lights."

They risked standing and hurried along the edge of the field until they could see the shed's back doors. They slid back into the relative cover of the hay just as the boxy headlights from a pickup washed over them. Max held his breath, but the truck didn't pause or slow. He lifted his head a fraction and watched as the driver lined the truck up close to the double doors.

"Get the plate," Max said.

"Got it."

As they watched, the doors opened and light spilled out from inside. But the angle was wrong. The shed was built on a slight rise that sloped up and away from the hayfield. Max only had a partial view of the shed's ceiling from where he lay.

"Shit, we need to get closer."

"Risky."

"I'll take the chance."

"Go from over there. More shadows from the shed and truck."

"Cover me."

The driver had gotten out and joined the others inside. Max didn't wait. He went for speed over subtlety and sprinted toward the building and slipped into the space between the door and shed. A crack in the hinge gave him a view inside.

It was guns, not drugs.

Most of the inside of the shed was set up as a shooting range. They had set up three lanes with large berms of soil built up to act as bullet traps on one end. The rest of the shed was a dual workroom and showroom. Someone was doing custom design and modifications. Max could see several illegal suppressors on a table along with two cut down shotguns. Ammunition and other handguns were laid out on a table nearby. As he watched, one of the two men in jeans came into view less than three feet away carrying a wooden carton. It was too late to move. Max shifted back into the shadows and tried to remain still.

He heard the man set the carton down, then drop the tailgate before sliding the box into the truck. Max decided he'd seen enough. If Koenig couldn't make something happen now, it was on her. He backed out of his hiding spot, staying against the side of the shed, and, after his eyes readjusted to the dark, picked out the spot he thought they'd been lying, and was about to go for it when the dog barked.

. . .

Jesus Christ, he felt his heart pound his rib cage. Where had the dog come from? Must have been sleeping in the truck and woken up when the guy loaded the carton.

The dog barked again, followed by a deep baritone rumble. The thing sounded enormous and mean. It was muffled by the cab but not enough.

"What was that?" someone said from inside.

"What?"

"Heard Gregor barking."

"Probably spooked by the storm."

"He doesn't get ..."

Max didn't wait to hear more. He ran hard and fast, waiting for a shout or a spotlight or a bullet to hit him between the shoulder blades. He reached the edge of the field and slid into the hay. He kept his face in the dirt and tried to keep the adrenaline from making his entire body shake. He lay there frozen for what felt like an hour but might have been two or three minutes. Nothing happened. He heard the rough scrape of another carton being loaded into the truck followed shortly by two doors opening and closing and then the truck pulling away. A moment later, there was the heavy clang of the steel doors swinging shut. And then silence.

Max waited another minute, then picked up his head.

Kyle was lying next to him. "Fucking dogs," he said.

"You got any extra underwear in that backpack?"

They sat and waited in the dying rain. The adrenaline wore off, and Max felt tired and queasy. After 30 more minutes, close to 3 a.m., the party began to break up and the cars, trucks, and motorcycles began to leave. They retraced their steps around the field, back to the old tractor/trailer, and then quickly across the road. Another long, looping walk through ankle-turning furrows, if anything Kyle went more slowly now, stupid to get hurt or spotted at the very end, and finally back up onto the porch and into the house.

They were lucky that the house still had active power and plumbing. They threw their wet clothes into the dryer and returned to the front room. Max flopped on the couch.

"What now?" Kyle asked.

"Hot shower. Sleep." He glanced at Kyle. The man looked ready for a 10-mile march. "At least for me." He put his head back and looked at the ceiling. "If you could send me the photos you got from the binoculars, I'll let Koenig know in the morning. See what kind of hornet's nest that kicks up. Can you sit on it for another day?"

"Sure."

"I think we're out of it, but I'll let you know." He thought of Dick and Vera Mulvaney. "Might need another favor."

Max felt the fatigue pulling him down. Even the old lumpy rental couch wouldn't keep him up much longer. He traced a crack in the paint along the ceiling with his eyes. It meandered out from the wall, spreading into smaller and smaller tributaries. Hawkins, the Arnsfelds, and Harrow. Four bodies tied to bad, bad things from the past. If you believed Nik Labat and maybe Kay Proulx.

Or not.

He knew Roy wasn't sold. Roy liked the straightforward idea of money as a motive. The news that Arnsfeld's finances weren't in such good shape was only fuel to that fire. But how did Hawkins and Harrow tie into that? Both men had some money, Harrow more than Hawkins, but Lawrence hadn't gotten a whiff of them being tied to Arnsfeld or the Association.

Plus, there were the old photos from Harrow's box. Those were likely taken before Arnsfeld's time on the island. But did they even tie into what was happening? Or, did Harrow keep them hidden for another reason? You could make a strong case they were completely unrelated, except Dick Mulvaney was lying.

Maybe lying and scared.

He woke up to the jarring buzz of the dryer cycle finishing.

CHAPTER THIRTY-THREE

The previous night's storm hadn't washed out the weather system that had been dogging the island. What had started almost a week ago as welcome bright sunshine had turned humid and overcast with occasional downpours. It felt as if they were living under a foggy piece of greenhouse glass. Max glanced out the house's side window as he stretched. The sun was making an effort, but the puffy, fat cumulus clouds promised more rain.

He called Archie first.

"Jesus, Max, what time is it?"

"A little after 6 a.m. I thought all real fishermen never slept past 4 a.m."

"Not on Sundays. I'm not a fisherman on Sundays, I'm a lazy bachelor."

"Duly noted but, since you're up now, I need a ride."

"You're like a pimply 15-year-old without gas money or a car."

"That's a compliment. I've got the sex drive of a 15-year-old."

That got a laugh out of him. Max heard the groaning squeak of the bedframe. "Alright, I'm up and awake but you're buying me a greasy breakfast. Give me 20 minutes and I'll be over."

"Actually, I'm not at the trailer."

"Jesus ..."

He called Koenig next. She groaned into the phone. "Goddammit, Max."

"I thought you were a morning person?"

"Only after at least three cups of coffee."

"I'm sending you some pictures."

"Okay." He could hear the rustle of sheets and blankets and tried not to visualize anything else. Then there was a heavy clunk. "Shit. Knocked over a glass of water on the phone. Shit. Shit. Hold on a second." She went away for a minute. Max could hear faint sounds in the background, then she was back and sounding more alert. "I've got the emails. What am I looking at?"

"It's not drugs. It's guns."

He filled her in on what he and Kyle had seen at the RCR compound.

"Okay, so gun smuggling. Why are you calling me before dawn on a Sunday then?"

"Because I know there are guns in that shed, plus some other dangerous and illegal shit today, but I'm not sure about tomorrow. How far do you want to press our luck on this? We spotted the setup at the library and then we witness a sale last night."

"Okay, let me make some calls."

. . .

She called back in 15 minutes. "I'm not sure how we're going to explain you or your friend."

"I prefer local consultant."

"Not sure I want to see how that holds up in court."

"Let's hope it never gets that far then."

"Maybe a local consultant can say something like that, but not a respected RCMP inspector. We'll cross that bridge later. Your photos hit a nerve up here. So, don't move. Someone from Intelligence will call you."

The guy called two minutes later. His name was Sepp Joris. He spoke in quick clipped sentences and had the gravelly vocal cords of a lifelong smoker. "Tell me what you have. Koenig gave me a quick sketch but I want to hear it from you."

What Max had were photos from the meet last night, Kyle's theory about the library smuggling drop, and some loose theories about the RCR and Arnsfeld. Joris was skeptical about the connection to Arnsfeld. "I've heard of Topher Arnsfeld. Not sure why he'd even shake hands with these guys let alone get in bed with them."

Max didn't blame him. "It does take a little imagination."

"For the past three years, we've seen a slow but steady flow of guns into the eastern part of the country. It wouldn't register as anything but an accounting error down in the States, but it's gotten people's attention up here. Mostly handguns, but some heavier stuff, too. We haven't been able to pinpoint the source. Or how they're moving it. These could be our guys."

"What now?"

"We ran the plates of the truck you sent. We're going to track those guys. Have a chat. See if we can't shore this thing up a little more."

"Koenig told you about the clock on this? Don't wait too long."

"I heard. Sit tight. We're moving. We'll keep Koenig in the loop." The implication being if she wanted to keep Max in the circle, it was up to her.

He disconnected and looked at Kyle. "They're tracking the buyers in the pickup and will try for a warrant on the shed."

"We still in?"

"Not sure."

Kyle's mouth twitched. "Wouldn't mind more action."

Across the street, the RCR was quiet. A few leftover trucks remained in the lot, but nothing and no one was moving. Max took a quick shower, scrubbing off as much of the mud and camo paint as he could, then left Kyle at his window post and walked out the back through the fields. Archie was waiting, leaning against the side of his truck, chewing on a piece of wheat.

"Thought you wanted pancakes for breakfast."

He tossed the grass away. "I do. And not a short stack, either. Get in. I know a place."

They continued west, away from Prince Creek, for five more miles into the town of Montague. Archie filled up on syrup, sausage, and coffee at The Lady Slipper. When he finally pushed back his plate, he said, "Talked to Roy, not that I don't enjoy being your chauffeur and eating on your dime, but he says you can use one of the old unmarkeds they've got at the garage while you're helping on the case. Just swing by and pick up the keys from the comm center."

"Works for me."

. . .

On the drive back to Prince Creek, they talked about the gossip from the docks, The Miss Ashely, the Leafs prospects for next season, and the latest rumors about the price of lobsters. If he closed his eyes, Max almost felt like they were sitting in the pilot's cockpit, making their way out into the Strait. He realized he missed it. Helping on this case plucked at something inside him, something elemental, but he wasn't sure that was a good thing. It stirred up thoughts and actions that frequently led down dark paths. He glanced over at Archie. If Max missed the water, Archie was craving it. He looked like a man being slowly starved of oxygen.

As if reading Max's thoughts, he turned and said, "You gonna get this guy?"

"Yes. I think it will be over in less than a week."

"Really?"

"Town is too small to keep this guy a secret much longer. We're getting closer."

"You got something?"

He told him about the Nik Labat and the photos.

Archie just shook his head. "I'm about ten years older than Nik and Steph and about 15 years younger than Hawkins and Harrow. I sort of fall in the middle, but I heard nothing about invite-only parties or anything like that."

"Maybe I'm wrong. Maybe this town can keep some secrets if they're bad enough."

Archie dropped him off at the police station.

"Where you headed now? Roy give you guys the day off?"

"Hell, no. He did let us off our chains last night to sleep for which I was grateful, at least until some inbred landlubber woke me up."

"I already paid that debt."

Archie belched and rubbed his stomach. "Yes, you did.

I'm headed out to the Harrow scene. CSI cleared it late yesterday. Roy's got most of us searching the place top to bottom today. What about you?"

"Heading over to the 303 to talk to some people."

"Mose's list?"

"That's right."

"Be careful. Don't let their God-fearing ways fool you. Some of those boys will knock you right on your ass if you push them hard enough."

Max wasn't sure why he pushed it. Why he didn't let the little prejudice slide? Maybe it was his friendship with Mose. "That right?"

Archie looked away, out the windshield, embarrassed but not backing down. "That's what I heard."

Marline wasn't working the comms. The woman that buzzed him in was in her late 50s with shoulder-length wavy hair that looked to be natural blonde, now fading to gray. She wore thin, rimless glasses and, with her tan sweater wrapped tight around her in the air-conditioned room, reminded Max more of a librarian than a dispatcher.

"You must be Max?"

This time, he remembered the names. "That's me. And are you Catelyn or Harriet?"

"Harriet."

"Chief Roy said he had a car I could use?"

"That's right. I wouldn't go far and I wouldn't go fast, but Mark says he topped off the oil and fluids and, while the tires wouldn't pass a formal inspection, they won't kill you either. His words, not mine."

"Maybe I'm better off walking."

She shrugged. "Mark's a talented mechanic. If he says it'll run, I think you're okay."

"Alright, I'll take it."

She picked up a set of keys and handed them over. Was it his imagination or did her hand linger on his a beat too long? Maybe they piped something through the vents into that room.

CHAPTER THIRTY-FOUR

The car was white, stodgy and, while unmarked, might as well have had 'police' painted on the side and a lightbar on top. Even a blind man would tag the old Ford as a cop car. The interior smelled vaguely of a fast food restaurant bathroom, but the engine turned over on the first try, the steering felt tight, and the brakes responded. He rolled down the windows as he drove to air it out. It would do.

He needed fresh clothes. He'd dried his clothes at the rental, but there had been no detergent and his clothes smelled ripe and had bits of dried mud and scratchy seed pods stuck in places. Maybe it wasn't the car's interior he was smelling.

He slowed way down as he made the turn into Angel Court. Mrs. Johnson was outside puttering around her extensive container gardens with a pair of scissors. He watched her snip off some dead buds and toss them into a small pail near her feet. She looked up and peered at him as he pulled in. He waved at her and called out the open window, "Morning, Mrs.

Johnson." He was expecting to get a grimace, maybe a slightly more pleasant frown. He did not expect a waving arm and for her to move in his direction.

He braked, and the car rocked to a stop. She ambled slowly across her small patch of yard to the edge of the cracked pavement. Max watched and waited and wondered what she wanted. She got right to the point, which he appreciated.

"You've got mail."

"Okay, thank you for letting me know."

"Mr. James did not deliver it."

Randall James was the deliveryman for the trailer park. Max had met him a few times. Randall usually delivered the mail in the early afternoon, around the time Max returned from the docks.

Max glanced toward the rack of mailboxes next to the wooden motor court sign. FedEx or UPS or DHL dropped the larger deliveries in an open metal box next to the rack. Only if it required a signature would the driver go farther into the park. Max couldn't see all the way into the box, but it didn't look like a package was in there. "A delivery?"

"No. He put it in your box, but it was after dark."

"After dark? You're sure?"

"Yes. And I think he drove by twice. It was unusual, Mr. Lindell, which is why I wanted to mention it. Very unusual."

Max got out and walked over to the mailboxes. Most of the locks were long since broken so there was no problem inserting the mail even if you weren't an official postal worker. Max opened his box and found a slim sealed envelope inside. There was no stamp, address, or writing of any kind on the front. He tore one end open and pulled out a single sheet and unfolded it. *Don't forget about Arnsfeld. Follow the money. Find the crime.* That was it. It was typed, not printed. He could see a slight gap or flaw repeated in the capital F's and could feel the indentations in the paper. Who used a typewriter these days? Someone older. Like all the victims' ages. He carefully slid the sheet back into the envelope. Maybe there would be DNA if the person licked it to seal it.

Mrs. Johnson had made her way back over to her flower-pots, but she was looking at him expectantly.

"You were right, very unusual."

"Does it have to do with these murders?"

"You know about that?"

"Jerry Roy is my godson."

Of course he was. Blood, love, business, or sin bound this entire town together. It's what made the difficulties in figuring out this killer so frustrating in some ways. It should be obvious. Someone should have walked into Roy's office and said I know who is doing this and why.

Now he had this note just when they were picking up speed in another direction. Coincidence? Or was someone trying to steer the case?

"I worked with his mother, may she rest in peace, for 30 years at the hospital. He stops by occasionally," Mrs. Johnson continued, "and watches *Wheel of Fortune* with me. Who do you think suggested he go to you for help with those Amish?"

"Sort of thought it was Archie."

"Ack. A nice boy but he has seawater in his veins. Unless it deals with bait and tackle, he's just not that interested."

Max thought that was a fairly accurate summation of Archie. "What makes you think he drove by twice?"

"It was Saturday, so *Jeopardy* and *Wheel of Fortune* were not on. What was I watching? Must have been the start of the Saturday night movie. They were replaying an old Dalziel and Pascoe movie. I was sitting in my chair by the window, but the lights were off. I can see the television better these days with the lights off. Better contrast. The window was open. It was nice last night before the rain. That's how I heard the car. Never saw it, but I remember hearing a distinctive clicking or tapping sound. It was distracting. It drove past and then came clicking back from the other direction. That time it stopped and I looked out. But the angle to the mailboxes is too tight. Still couldn't see it. The car stopped short and then a moment later it sped away."

"Did you see what it looked like when it drove past the second time?"

"No. It just looked like any old car in the dark."

"A car, though, not a pickup truck or SUV?"

"No, definitely a car. A normal-sized sedan."

He headed back to the truck. "Thank you, Mrs. Johnson, this has been very helpful."

"You're welcome. I'll keep my eyes and ears open and let you know if he comes back."

"Be safe."

"Catch the bastard soon and I'll be safe."

Max did not understand what to think about the note. He texted Koenig. She must have had her phone out. Her reply came back almost immediately. *WTF.* That made Max smile and feel a little better. A real cop had no clue either. He decided he'd drive out to the Harrow scene later and hand it over to Roy before he went to the Amish settlement.

A lot to think about. He took another shower. He always thought better in the shower, but didn't come up with any insights. Dried and dressed, he threw his dirty clothes in the washer and brewed a pot of coffee. He knew last night's activities would catch up with him at some point. While the coffee brewed, he hunted through the kitchen drawers until he found a gallon-sized Ziploc bag. He took the mysterious envelope off the counter and slipped it inside.

As he walked back outside with the thermos, he spotted Mose's toolbox under the old pickup's hood and felt a pang of guilt. He didn't have many friends and he wasn't keeping in touch with those he did have. He promised himself he'd get over to Mose's shop and swing by The Rink today. Maybe a little beer and banality would shake something loose in his head.

He drove straight north out of town on 305 past farms, small isolated houses, fields of potatoes and corn, and then turned left on Prince Creek Line and drove straight until he hit the Harrow farmstead. The media trucks were gone, but Chravette's cruiser was parked on the shoulder, passenger side wheels edging into the muddy start of a cornfield. His arm was hanging out the window and he raised his hand as Max turned in.

He pulled in next to Archie's pickup and a panel van that Max recognized from the crime scene techs. As he got out of his car, the woman he'd seen yesterday working the first floor came out and pulled off her hood as she walked toward the van. She had short black hair that didn't reach her shoulders.

"Hope you haven't been working all night?" Max said.

"No, we cleared everything but the basement. I drew the short straw to come back out."

"Find anything?"

"Nothing beyond mouse droppings and spiderwebs. I don't think the guy stepped more than three feet inside the house."

"But you gotta check."

"But we gotta check or the lawyers will find a way to screw with us."

Max reached back into the car and took out the plastic bag with the envelope and letter. He handed it to her. "Listen, I got this in the mail this morning, well, yesterday, found it today. Hand delivered if you believe my nosy neighbor, and I do. I opened it and read it. It might be related to all these killings. I told Inspector Koenig about it. I was bringing it here for the chief to look at, but I was wondering if you could run it for fingerprints or DNA."

"Looks like a self-sticking envelope so I wouldn't hold my breath on DNA but if Chief Roy and Koenig sign off, I don't see a problem with checking for prints." She handed it back.

"Great. He's inside?"

"He was in Harrow's office last time I saw him."

Max went inside. He could hear people moving around upstairs. Fingerprint dust and evidence markers were scattered around the room. He found Roy in the office. The chief was sitting behind the desk with files and stacks of paper piled up around him.

"Find anything interesting?" Max asked as he walked in and sat in one of the two thick, overstuffed chairs facing the sizable desk.

"No, and, to be honest, I should just leave it. Unless it says, 'Look right here, this is evidence!' I'm not going to see it. I'm more of a people person. But I feel like I need to do something."

"No computer?"

"He had one. Crime scene techs took it." He indicated an empty spot on the corner of the desk. "It's password protected but looks like a basic operating system thing. They said it shouldn't take long to crack. Not sure it matters, looks like Colby mostly used it for email and invoices. He then printed everything out and filed it."

Max thought of Lawrence and his brother. Unlike certain aspects of this investigation, he figured the more information he fed Lawrence and Teddy, the better. "Once they crack the computer, if you let me know, I can take a look."

"Sure thing. I'll let you know when they post it. You should have access with the temp creds."

"Thanks."

He closed the file folder in front of him and put it aside. "What brings you out here? Archie said you were heading up the 303 to check out that list."

"I am. That's my next stop. I wanted to stop by and show you this." He held up the bag with the letter and then explained.

"Sally Johnson is still sharp as a tack. I don't doubt her story." Roy took the bag and looked at the letter through the plastic and frowned. "I wish something about this case would be straightforward. Feels like everything is coming in sideways. You think this is legit?"

"We know the RCMP found some irregularities with Arnsfeld's finances but I'm not sure that's what this is talking about."

"You think it's about the fund Arnsfeld started for the incubator?"

"That was my thought. Someone piggybacking on the murder investigation to get us to look for that missing money."

"Unfortunately, there is no missing money. We looked. Hard. We hired forensic accountants. It's just not there."

"Okay, then it's just a letter. Put it in a file somewhere, but I wanted you to see it."

"Duly noted and seen. I'll have the techs run it for prints. You never know and I don't want anyone coming back saying we didn't do everything." Roy looked down at the typewritten sheet again. "Wonder who uses a typewriter these days?"

Max left Roy to his pile of papers and walked back into the kitchen. He found the door to the basement adjacent to the eat-in area and next to the doorway that led to the living room. He went halfway down, cognizant that this was the one area that hadn't been fully processed yet. "Hello?" he called.

"Yes?" The tech emerged from a back room with her hood up and wearing clear protective glasses.

"We're good to go with the envelope. I left it with Roy."

"Okay."

"Mind if I look around up here?"

"Join the party."

"Find anything down here?"

"Nah. I'm about done."

"You guys find anything at all?" She gave him a sharp look and Max realized that sounded a little accusatory and he held up his hands. "That came out wrong."

"It's alright. We did find one thing. Partial boot prints. Size 10. Harrow wore a size eight."

"Farmhands?"

"Could be. We're checking, but we found a couple right around ... the tree. I'd bet they were from the killer."

"Okay, that could help. Or at least help nail him once we have him. Brand?"

"Not sure. It was a plain tread. Most companies put their logos and brands everywhere these days, and I'm pretty good with shoes. I see a lot of patterns, but I didn't recognize this one. But we got some clean edges from the front and the heel. If you find the boots, placing him at the scene with a match won't be a problem."

"That's something."

Max went back upstairs and wandered through the first floor. Formal dining room, sitting room, and front hallway. He looked at the photos on the walls, knick-knacks stuck on shelves, potted plants. He found nothing on the surface that helped. He moved upstairs. He found Archie searching and documenting the contents of the hallway bathroom. Henry

Stratton was standing on a chair with his head through a hole in the guest room closet, looking in the attic crawl space.

"Anything interesting?" Max asked.

Stratton replaced the board and stepped off the chair. "Just insulation and an old TV antenna."

Max moved down the hall. The last two rooms were bedrooms. It appeared the Harrows slept in different rooms. The smaller bedroom that faced the road had a double bed. The blue quilt and white sheets were pulled down. A chest of drawers and matching nightstand filled the sparse space. This was Colby Harrow's bedroom. A smudged, empty glass and a Bible sat on the table by the bed. Max ran a hand over the side of the chest. It was solid wood and well made. He wondered briefly if it was one of Mose's pieces.

He opened Harrow's closet. Ten or 12 button-down shirts, most of them white or pale blue, hung beside four pairs of plain, durable slacks. A sport coat and a black suit filled out the rack. Three pairs of shoes, two brown, one black, were on the floor next to a pair of white sneakers, caked in the familiar red dirt of the island. Max thought of the rain-slicked clay of Norris Avenue and Collum Hawkins. He picked up one of the shoes. The bottom treads were full of it. He put the shoe back. A bowling bag was tucked into the corner. A veneer of dust was visible on the yellow leather. He hadn't taken Harrow as a bowler. Maybe it was a hobby he'd given up as he got older. He unzipped the bag. There was a blue/black 15-pound ball inside along with a pair of shoes and a patterned shirt. He put it all back and closed the closet. He went into the master bedroom which smelled slightly of stale air, powder, and lilacs. He found nothing of interest in Dorothea's closet beyond a cache of racy romance novels in a cardboard box that was marked 'Baby Clothes.'

He looked out the window over the back forty of the Harrow's homestead and thought about the letter again and the first sentence. Who knew they were moving away from Topher Arnsfeld? People knew about the investigation. They were going out of their way to get people talking, but how many knew the particular twists and turns of the investigation?

CHAPTER THIRTY-FIVE

Max left the Harrow farm and drove south, back toward Prince Creek, and used the long, straight roads and little traffic to think about the case. He was stuck. Yesterday, Harrow's body, Labat, and the photos felt like a break. It felt as if gravity was about to take over and rip the case apart. Now, after he talked to the people on Mose's list, he didn't know what to do. Go back through all the paper like Koenig was doing? Compare notes on any leads they found, if any? Try to talk to Labat again? Track down the photos? Figure out who put that note in his mailbox?

As he hit the northern edge of town, almost in the shadow of St. Mary's steeple, he pulled into a gas station. While he was topping off the tank, two different men in the parking lot waved to him and one called out, "Hey, Max." Max didn't recognize either man, neither looked like a fisherman, so word was definitely getting around. He raised a hand in return and then wondered if the killer had heard about him. Probably. He replaced the nozzle and screwed on the gas cap.

Rather than double back and jump on Route 335 at the small interchange outside of town which would lead him over to 303, he took the long way, going east past the church and some light industrial buildings, before hitting the older residential neighborhood that made up the north side of Prince Creek. He drove by the Mulvaney's house. Everything was quiet and still. No one was out in the garden, shades and curtains still drawn. The Acura was not in the driveway. They could have moved it into the garage. They could be out for Sunday brunch. He took a left at the end of the street out of the neighborhood, drove slowly through the last bits of town, then picked up the speed a bit and eventually took a right onto 335.

When he saw the signs, warning about horses and buggies on the road, he slowed and started looking for the turnoff. Provincial Road 303 was the unofficial boundary for the eastern Amish settlement close to Prince Creek. What had initially started as five families moving from an overcrowded settlement in Ontario in the mid-1990s had now grown, according to Mose, to over 30 families and almost 200 people. It was the largest Amish settlement in Canada outside of the original mother settlement in Ontario. Mose said there was talk of finding more farmland and creating another community elsewhere on the island.

Jacob the Younger was the patriarch of one of the original families to explore Prince Creek as a settlement. His name was a holdover from his time being baptized in the Ontario settlement. He was now close to 80 and, while the Amish religion had no centralized authority, leader, or governing body, age and experience were widely respected, and Jacob the Younger was considered a local community elder.

The Youngers' farm was close to Prince Creek and the

second homestead along Route 303. Max slowed as he came upon a large roadside farm stand selling the Younger farm's produce. It was roped off and closed now and would remain closed for the rest of the day. He turned into the long, winding drive. There was a white, two-story, rectangular farmhouse with a small porch in the front facing the road and a lower, single-story addition that looked to have been added later off to the right. The large barn, also white, loomed over the house from behind. Max drove past the house toward the outbuildings. He could see at least ten buggies neatly lined up next to the barn, with the horses hitched to a long post, eating hay from attached metal baskets. He didn't want to spook the horses, so he pulled to the side in what he hoped was an unobtrusive spot.

With the engine off and the window down, he could hear low, slow melodic singing from the open door of the barn. He couldn't make out the words, but knew that, even if he could, the old German dialect they used for worship would mean nothing to him. He also knew services could last up to three hours. He settled in to wait. The music and the landscape were peaceful. The car was warm.

"Always sleeping on the job."

Max sat up with a start and wiped some drool from his chin. Mose was grinning at him. He could see people leaving the barn and spreading out blankets in the nearby grass. More people were going to the buggies and pulling out baskets and provisions for a community meal.

"If you're done with your beauty sleep, I'll introduce you to Jacob the Younger." Mose dropped the smile. "And we can get this business settled."

Max felt eyes on him as he walked with Mose across the open grassy section between the barn and the back of the

Youngers' house. It didn't feel hostile, but it didn't exactly feel friendly either. It felt ... expectant. As if everyone was waiting to see which way the tree would fall.

"They know why I'm here?"

"Probably, but they didn't hear it from me. I talked to Jacob. That was it. We only have one community phone and no Internet, but we're not immune to gossip. The people here have heard about the murders. And some have at least heard the things you've been spreading around town. Isn't that what you wanted?"

"It was an idea. I never said it was a particularly good one."

They reached the back door and Mose knocked. A thin, young woman appeared at the screen door. She wore a loose-fitting, calf-length pale blue dress with a white apron on top. She had on the traditional white kapp over her long strawberry blonde hair.

"Hello, Bethany. Mr. Lindell is here to have a word with Jacob."

"Please come in, Mr. Lindell." She opened the door wide and Max stepped inside.

Mose remained on the low porch. "I'll be outside. Find me when you're done," he said.

"Jacob is resting before the luncheon. If you'll follow me."

The door opened onto the kitchen. Max followed Bethany past two other women bustling around a wood-burning cookstove, then down a short hallway and into a sitting room.

"If you'll wait here, I'll get Jacob for you."

He nodded and Bethany disappeared. A moment later, he heard her climbing the stairs. The room was furnished with a variety of simple, yet elegant wood furniture in the Shaker style. He walked to a long, narrow table running under the window and ran his hand along the top, admiring the exposed woodgrain. The quality was even more clear with the under-stated design. Two books sat on the table. One appeared to be a German Bible. The cover was cracked and worn. The second book was more modern. The simple letter-pressed cover read, "The Church Directory of Prince Edward Island." Max opened it and started flipping through the pages. It appeared to be a recorded list of all the Amish families who had moved to and lived on PEI. It listed families, children, descendants, births, and deaths. It was a living history of the community's time on the island.

"Every Amish family has at least two books in their home. A Bible and a directory."

Max closed the book, turned, and saw an older man, slightly stooped, with a halo of thinning white hair and a matching beard in the doorway. He wore black pants, black shoes, and a white shirt with gray suspenders. One eye drooped a little lower, maybe from a past stroke, but remained bright and clear.

He stepped forward and offered a hand. "Mr. Lindell. A pleasure to meet you. Mose has told me about you." The old man's callused hand was thick and strong.

"Mose is a good man. I'm lucky to call him a friend. I hope that doesn't cause him any problems here in the community."

Younger smiled and motioned toward two chairs that faced a larger sofa. He sat and moved a pillow to a better position behind his back. "Do you know one of the benefits of having no centralized authority for our worship?"

"Given some of the problems I've seen in other religions, there are probably quite a few."

"Yes, quite right, but I was thinking of one in particular. It allows a certain leeway. Or, more succinctly, an under-standing that, while we place an enormous value on the group norm expressed through the will of God, we also keep some individuality. We do not assert it or display it, but it remains."

"So, as long as Mose doesn't go around bragging about being the fisherman's apprentice friend, he's okay at home?"

"Something like that, but I wasn't just talking about Mose."

Now it was Max's turn to smile. "I gathered that, too."

"Do you know the word *gelassenheit*?"

"No."

"A strict translation might be calmness or composure. I've seen it translated by others as 'submission,' which I don't totally agree with. Perhaps a better understanding of it would be a reluctance to be forward or self-promoting."

"So, you think this list is a wild goose chase? You know the names on the list?"

"Mose and I discussed it for a long time."

"Do you think any of them might be capable of killing?"

Younger turned and glanced out the window as a pack of children ran past, playing a game with sticks. "I've known everyone on that list since they were that size, playing those same games. It is difficult, if not impossible, to imagine any of those men being the person you are looking for."

"Yet, there is still that nasty splinter of individualism you just told me about."

"Yes. I can't claim to see inside their minds. It would be difficult to do what he's done, to assert himself that strongly, and still live amongst the group without us knowing. It would be like living as two distinct people."

"To be blunt, that's not a bad definition of the crazy we might be looking for."

He left Younger staring out the window and showed himself out. Max realized he may have underestimated the waves he would cause through the community by asking Mose to make this list and ask his questions. Murder was just an ugly business all around.

He found Mose talking to another man near the end of the row of standardbred horses the Amish favored for pulling their buggies. Both were dressed in their more formal church clothes: black pants, white shirts, suspenders, straw hats. The day was sweltering despite the cloud cover and both had taken off their matching black jackets. Where Mose was tall and lean, a stalk of summer wheat, the other man was smaller and wiry, a loaded spring, with curly rust-colored hair, a matching beard, and a prominent brow ridge above small black eyes. He was smoking a thin, rolled cigarette.

Mose turned as Max approached and introduced the other man. "Max, this is Isaac. He's a furniture maker like myself, though he favors Shaker while I go more with Mission. Issac, this is my friend Max. He's helping the Prince Creek PD with the recent murders in town."

He caught Mose's look, but didn't need it. He recognized the name. It was on the list.

"That right?" Issac asked.

"Yes."

"What brings you out here then?"

"Need to check everyone. Policing doesn't stop at the community line."

"Stratton send you?"

Max found that interesting but kept his face blank. "No. Just covering all the bases. You got a shop, like Mose, or do you sell from your house?"

"I share a shop with another guy, Jonah Sprauge, out near the intersection with 304."

"You remember where you were last Tuesday?"

"The entire day?"

"Say midafternoon through the evening?"

Isaac scratched his beard and looked away for a second, thinking about it. "I was in the shop until lunch. Then I had a delivery, a table and chairs, then back home for supper."

"Where was the delivery?"

"English family. The Camberts. On Campbell Street, near town."

Near the Arnsfelds, Max thought. If he was a liar, he was a good one. Then, again, Max reminded himself, a total psychopath would have to be a good liar. Still, his alibi would be easy to check. He decided he'd keep the questions short and quick. Get an alibi from each man on the list for the Arnsfeld murders. If they could knock any of them down, Roy would probably bring them in for a more serious chat about Hawkins or Harrow.

Jacob and John Wittmer were brothers and farmers, and wouldn't likely be mistaken for anything else. Both were tall with thick chests, long arms, and the heavy-lidded look that, Amish or not, said violence might lurk close to the surface. Swinging an ax or stringing up a body wouldn't be a problem for either man. Which made the contrast of watching the nine kids running around the two big men on their checkered picnic blankets a little disorienting.

"Jacob is the older brother. He's the one with the scar on his cheek," Mose said. "Wait here."

Mose walked over and spoke a few words to the brothers. Max watched both men's eyes flick to him. They nodded, disentangled the kids, and followed Mose over to where Max stood a discreet distance away from the other families gathered on the side lawn and beginning to eat lunch.

Before Max or Mose could speak a word, Jacob pointed a thick finger at Max and said, "Stratton point you at us?"

Max decided he'd need to have a word with Roy. Wherever Stratton was headed wasn't going to end in a good place. For anyone. Better to head it off sooner rather than later.

"No, we're just throwing out a wide net. Best we can do at this point."

Both brothers looked unconvinced, but they didn't walk away.

"You talking to everyone in the community?" Jacob asked.

"More or less," Max answered and pushed on quickly. "Just wanted to ask if you remember where you and your brother were last Tuesday afternoon."

"It's August, so we were in the fields harvesting. It's where we spend 18 hours a day in late July through early September."

"All day?"

"You ever tried to harvest 70 acres by yourself?"

"No."

"Didn't think so or you wouldn't have asked."

"Anyone else see you or vouch for you?"

"Me and John work adjoining fields, so I guess we could vouch for each other." John nodded along with his brother in agreement. "The older children also worked. You could question them or our wives. At one point or another, they were all in the fields with us until it was suppertime."

"Thank you. That won't be necessary."

"What's up with Stratton?" Max asked as they walked through the crowd, looking to spot the last two people on the list. "You ever have a run-in with him?"

"Just in passing. Nothing like those boys."

"What does he do?"

"Whatever he can get away with."

"And all the deputies are like that?"

"Stratton is the worst offender."

"Any specific reason?"

"No. I don't think so. You know as well as I do that there are a lot of reasons a person decides to become a police officer. Not all of them are charitable."

They passed a long table full of plates loaded with porkchops, ham, and roast beef. Other plates held vegetables. Max spotted peas, corn, zucchini, beets, and sauerkraut. At the end of the table was a spread of breads, cookies, pies, and cakes. Even after his diner breakfast with Archie, Max found his stomach rumbling at the smell of the butter and molasses from the shoofly pie.

A young woman offered him a plate as they walked past. She had light gray eyes that sparked against her dark braided hair. "Care for something sweet?" she asked.

"Not right now," Max said, returning her smile.

"Careful," Mose whispered as they continued toward the barn. "She's married."

"I was more interested in the pie," Max said.

"Uh-huh."

The last two men had solid alibis on the surface. Neither alibi would cover the men for the entire time, but it would make the timeline very difficult.

Samuel Petersheim was the community farrier. He wore round, gold-rimmed glasses and had a full bowl of brown hair that fell over his ears. Despite his age, which Max judged to be around his own 35 years, a patchy beard hadn't completely filled in along his jawline.

"Mose," he said as the pair approached.

"Samuel." Mose made the introductions.

"Last Tuesday?" He took a small notebook out of his shirt pocket and flipped through it before closing it and putting it away. "I spent most of the day at the Swarey's farm. Examined, trimmed, and re-shoed all of their draft and standardbred horses. On the way back, I made a stop at the Renno's place. One of their horses was lame, but it wasn't the shoeing. I told them to call the animal doc. After that, I was at home. I mostly make house calls, but my workshop and supplies are in a shed behind the house."

All logical and easily checked.

The last man on the list, Abram Marks, was a farmer with 50 acres just a mile or so from Mose's furniture shop on 335. He was a heavyset man with a weathered face from being outdoors and dirt-crusted nails, even after cleaning up for church. He also was able to quickly supply an alibi for the Arnsfeld murders.

"One of the horses spooked in the field after lunch and threw my oldest. He broke his ankle." He pointed over his shoulder, and Max saw a boy of about 12 or 13, looking miserable, on a nearby blanket with a white cast on his leg and wooden crutches at his side. "Spent the rest of the day down in town at the clinic seeing Doc Stephens and getting it set."

And that was it. Mose spent a few more minutes making small talk with Abram and asking about the crops and a common neighbor, then he and Max went through the line and got plates of food. The shoofly pie tasted as sweet and good as it looked. By 2 p.m., he'd said goodbye to Mose and was back in the car. He pulled over on the shoulder after he was a few miles clear of the Youngers' farm and made some quick notes on the five men. He planned to spend the rest of the day at the trailer going through all his notes and files. The devil was in the details. He just had to dig him out.

CHAPTER THIRTY-SIX

He drove past the Mulvaney's house again on his way back. Nothing had changed since his first trip past. House quiet, shades drawn. He pulled to the curb and got out. The rest of the neighborhood was more alive. He could hear kids playing on a nearby swing set, and a man was hand watering tomato plants on the lot next door.

Max walked up the driveway and peered into the small detached garage. It was empty. Probably too small to fit the Acura in. He peeked over the back fence and saw nothing but dragonflies and bees drunkenly flying between all of Vera's flowers. He went to the back door and knocked, but no one answered. He leaned on the doorbell. Same result.

"Hello there! Mr. Lindell?" someone called.

Max turned and saw that the tomato man had turned off the hose and was standing by the five-foot high wooden fence that divided his property from the Mulvaneys'. He was about 60, with a ring of gray hair around a sun-spotted bald pate. He was wearing a light pink golf shirt with the collar turned up against his neck.

"That's right, I'm Max Lindell."

"I'm Thomas Parks. You looking for the Mulvaneys?"

"Checking in, yes."

"I saw you over there yesterday with the female officer. Everyone in town knows you two are working on catching this maniac. About an hour after you left, I saw Dick loading up the car with two suitcases. I was out watering the yard. I waved a few times, but he never acknowledged me. I mean, we're not friends, they are a little older, but we're friendly enough, been neighbors for almost twelve years. He didn't even give a cursory wave. A few minutes later, Vera comes out, the same thing, and they just take off."

"What do you mean by 'take off'?"

"They backed out and were gone. Like they were really anxious to get going. And, just to double down on that theory, I noticed their timer lights were on. You know the ones you set up when you're going away on vacation? They have one in the living room. Clicks on about 7:30 p.m. Clicks off at 9 p.m., and then another one clicks on upstairs for another hour. My wife and I joke about it being a neon sign blinking: 'The Mulvaneys are away.'"

Goddammit, Max thought. He took his phone out and called Koenig.

"That little prick."

"I thought that's how you might feel. Were we too nice yesterday?"

"I always prefer nice and cooperative, but that's out the window now. Time to bring in some official heat. He knows something and now he really needs to tell us."

"I saw photos of two kids in the hallway. They might have run there."

"I'll get a records search going."

"I didn't get a close look, but I think they were both girls. If they married could be a little harder."

"Then we do an informal records search. Is that neighbor still standing on his lawn?"

Max looked out the passenger window. "Yup. Still pretending to water his plants, but keeping an eye on me."

"Go ask him. I bet he knows."

And he did. Tracy and Nicole. Fifteen minutes later, Koenig had an address for Nicole.

"She's younger than her sister by three years. Lives just outside Toronto."

"I doubt they drove through the night to Toronto."

"I'll get someone in the office to track down Tracy. If we can't find her by morning, I'll get someone from Toronto to lean on Nicole."

Max gave a last wave to Thomas Parks and then drove back to Angel Court. Mrs. Johnson was in her chair in her front yard working on a puzzle book. She didn't smile as Max drove past, but she waved which Max took as a sign he was doing something right.

Inside the trailer, it was warm and stuffy. He opened all the small sliding windows and the door, but it made little difference. He carried his file folder outside and sat in his porch chair. It wasn't much cooler outside. The air had become hot and stagnant. Max could see a line of thunderheads moving in from the west. Maybe that would help.

Before he went through the file, or maybe to put it off a little longer, he called the Prince Creek PD and got patched through to Roy. He filled Roy in on the Mulvaneys doing a runner and then on his time out at the Youngers' farm.

"Not much I can do about the Mulvaneys unless they change their mind and turn around. I can have a patrol swing by a few times tonight to check if they come back, but it sounds like they've made up their minds."

"That would be good. You never know."

"What do you think about the Amish guys?"

"If you could shake someone free, it shouldn't take long to verify the alibis. Most of them appeared tight but maybe not airtight."

"I can do that. Send me your notes, and I'll get D'arcy on it first thing tomorrow. You get a feeling from any of them? A vibe?"

"None of them were wearing a psycho nametag but there are a couple, the older brother John and Isaac maybe, that you might be careful with. It didn't feel so much like violence as much as frustration. Which reminds me ..."

Max told him about Stratton, and Roy said he would talk to the deputy. They agreed to check in again in the morning when Koenig was back and then disconnected.

He opened the folder and started reading. Something had been rolling around in his head for the last two days, like a tiny pebble in a shoe. Two hours later, it was still there. He couldn't find it and was left with a headache from staring at the photocopied text of all the reports and his own scribbled notes. When the raindrops started, he gathered it all up and went back inside.

They needed to know what Mulvaney knew. Why was he running? Was there another way he could come at it? He could try Labat again. Maybe the man had come down and was more lucid again. He knew something, but it would be trickier pulling it out of Labat than it would be from Mulvaney. Maybe they could get a psychiatrist involved? Would that make it better or worse? He listened to the raindrops ping off the trailer's metal roof. The poor weather might make Labat head for the church. He took out his phone and looked up the rectory number for St. Mary's. It rang five times and rolled to voicemail. Sunday evening. Not unexpected. He called Roy back and asked him to see if they could find Labat tomorrow or find Father White and see if the man was lucid enough to talk. Roy said he'd relay it to Patrol and add it to D'arcy's list.

He stood up. The used couch was giving off a smell in the heat that had him second-guessing the purchase. He paced the tiny room and thought about the other messages he'd left. Why hadn't Loreen Camille called him back? Your friend is killed and the police called looking for help in finding the killer, you'd think you would call them back. Kay Proulx had, but it was going on three days now with no word from Camille. He looked up her number in his notes and punched it into his phone. Still no answer. He called the police station and identified himself, then asked, "Do you have any contact information available for a Loreen Camille?"

He heard keys clacking and then the dispatcher said, "I have a landline number for an H. Camille at 37 Rue Spring Street."

"That's it?"

"Mobile phones are only voluntarily listed in the directory. A search on that would take longer."

"Okay, give me that one for now. I'll let you know if we need to do the other search."

He dialed the number for H. Camille and was surprised when a human answered.

"Hello?" The voice had the fragility and slight waver that told Max it was an older woman.

"Hello, my name is Max Lindell and I work for the Prince Creek Police Department. I'm looking for Loreen Camille. Does she live there?"

"No, I'm sorry. I'm Helen Camille." Max felt a slight tinge of disappointment. He'd just have to keep trying the mobile number he had. Maybe Koenig could work some government magic and track Loreen down. But then the woman continued, "Loreen is my daughter, but she's long since moved out. She has a place over the bridge outside of town off 306."

"I've been trying to reach her. It's important. I've left her several messages. Is she on vacation or out of touch for any reason that you know of?"

"Yes, she's in South Africa. She's the track coach and teaches health at Prince Creek High. She takes a group of students down there each year for a retreat and a training camp with a local school."

At least now Max knew why she wasn't returning his calls. "Do you know when she's due to return?"

"Let's see, what day is today? When you get to be my age, they all run together."

"It's Sunday."

"The trip was ten days, so next Thursday, I think."

Whatever was happening would be over by then.

Max thought about mothers and daughters and those fraught teenage years. Would Helen have known what her daughter was up to? Definitely not all of it, but maybe some of it. Parents, at least a certain type, made it their business to know, bruised feelings or not. Was Helen that type of parent? He would not get any further tonight sitting in his trailer.

"Miss Camille, do you mind if I come by and have a quick chat with you?"

CHAPTER THIRTY-SEVEN

If her daughter was in the same class as Stephanie Arnsfeld, then Helen Camille must have become a mother late in life. The woman who opened the door of the small shared duplex house was over 70, maybe closer to 80. She was a hair over 5 feet, but if she lived a few more years, she'd probably dip back under. She wore a purple tracksuit with pink piping and was in the middle of setting her plume of white hair with hot rollers.

"Come in, come in, young man," she said holding open the door. "Don't let the heat out. Your phone call caught me just as I started my hair. I play bridge on Monday at the senior center. The club provides a free lunch."

The house was as hot as a kiln, and Max immediately wanted to open three windows. He stepped into a narrow living room that fed directly into a dining room. The house was cluttered, but clean, with shiny plastic covering the chairs and sofa in the living room. He followed Camille through the living room, the dining room, and past a wooden hutch filled with framed photographs of a younger Camille with a girl, who slowly became a woman as the photos moved from left to right, who Max presumed was Loreen. She shared her mother's trim build with a slightly pinched face and close-set eyes.

They entered the kitchen and sat at a chipped Formica table. A set of orange rollers sat warming in a setting tray at one place. Max sat and Camille pushed a blue tin of Danish butter cookies toward him. "Would you like some coffee or tea?"

He glanced around the kitchen and found a lot of evidence of a solitary life. One placemat set out on the table. Single-serve coffee maker. One mug drying on the sideboard. Max thought, despite her claims of interrupting her hair routine, she was happy to have a visitor.

He wasn't particularly hungry or thirsty, but took a cookie and said, "Maybe a glass of water." He could feel the sweat already dripping down his back. If he sat here longer than ten minutes, he was risking dehydration.

"Water and cookies? Blah. How about a glass of cold milk?"

"That would be good."

As she fussed in the cupboards for a glass, Max asked, "Has Loreen always been a runner?"

"Yes, ever since she was a child. That girl would just take off. Wind her up and she was gone. She'd run around the neighborhood, you know, playing tag and other games. It started to get more serious when she was maybe 11 or 12. She started winning more organized races. Even beating most of the boys. That didn't make everyone happy, but she didn't care. And neither did I." She came over to the table and placed the glass of milk in front of Max. He took a sip and smiled. She sat and continued. "She was no dummy. I worked as a cashier at the Town & Tide grocery store for 40 years. Not a bad job most of the time. I'm not complaining. But you aren't going anywhere as a cashier. You're making do, treading water. I wanted more for Loreen. She wanted more. She ran her way to a scholarship at the university. Ran all over Canada. Got her teaching degree. She makes twice what I ever made. Smart girl. The world will always need teachers."

"Like I said when I first called, I'm working with the Prince Creek PD on the recent murders in town."

"Awful, terrible things. Never had anything happen like that in town since I've lived here." Max saw that she said it with a certain light in her eyes. She might think it was awful, but it was also exciting. It would likely be a big topic of conversation at bridge tomorrow. Max thought back to the first day when he climbed the hill to the Arnsfelds' with Charlie and didn't blame her. It was human nature to be fascinated and repulsed by murder.

"She was friends with Diana Goulart, Stephanie Arnsfeld, and Kay Proulx in school?"

He thought he caught a slight jolt in her posture at the mention of the names, like she'd received a small electrical shock. She reached for a curler and started expertly rolling it up into her hair. "Yes, she had other friends on the track team, but those are the girls she hung out with the most." She said it with a certain tone.

"You didn't approve?"

"Does a mother ever approve of all her daughter's friends?"

"I don't know, to be honest."

"The simple answer is no."

"What's the more complicated answer?"

"That every mother was also a daughter at one time."

"So, you let her know, but let her decide."

"That was the idea." She finished with another roller and folded her hands in front of her. Her eyes focused on the table, but Max could see she was looking much further. He waited. He had to let her tell it. After a moment, she looked at him and said, "But teenagers do a lot of stupid things. Things that they regret. Things that seem harmless at the time but could end up ruining their lives."

She stopped. A secret held for so long can build up its own resistance. Max knew this better than anyone. He nudged her. "Is this about Stephanie Arnsfeld's parties?"

"God, I bet she loved that last name. Arnsfeld. She was always trying to be someone else. Someone new. She was just as poor as the rest of us, but she never met anyone in town that she couldn't look down on. I probably sound like a horrible person, but that woman was a snake even at 16. She knew how to disguise it, too. She could be sweetness and light right until she put the knife in your back. I could never understand what Loreen saw in her."

"Maybe protection. Better to be under the umbrella than out in the rain."

"Maybe, but that didn't always spare you. That girl left a path of destruction in her wake. It didn't matter if you were a friend, an enemy, or just a bystander."

"Is that what happened with the parties?"

Her eyes went around the room. She folded and unfolded her hands as if vacillating between prayer and protest before making up her mind. "You're too old to be afraid of ghosts, Helen," she said to herself and then looked up at him. "I only heard about all this later, months later, right before Loreen went off to college on that track scholarship. I think it has haunted both of us ever since. I know it's haunted me, but we've never talked about it directly since that night. You might judge me for it, and you'd be right, but I wanted her to get out. I wanted her to have a genuine chance. I didn't want to look up in five or ten years and find her working at the next register. Isn't that what any mother wants? It just didn't seem right to pull her life apart over something that was done and dusted. What would you have done? Ask yourself that when you're judging me. We didn't even know all the details. We didn't know ..."

She was spinning off the rails. "Miss Camille ... Helen, what happened?"

"Stephanie was always desperate for money. Desperate for it. Desperate not to let you know it, of course. She wasn't a beggar, nothing so pedestrian, but that girl would scratch and claw for every nickel, dime, and penny. She was always good at getting others to do what she wanted. It didn't matter if you were four years old or 44. She could sell, what's that saying, ice to an Eskimo. The parties started innocently enough. Kids are gonna drink or try to. Stephanie set up these parties. Made it sort of like a game, a scavenger hunt to find the place. You'd pay ten bucks and get the first clue. That would lead to more clues and eventually you'd get the location for the party. She'd get her older brother to buy the alcohol. No big deal. I wouldn't be surprised if the police knew about it and sort of turned a blind eye. Better to know where they are and what they're doing, right? I'm sure she was making decent money. I mean, how much money does a teenager need? Especially a teenager stuck in this place.

"But Stephanie was never satisfied. Never. I don't know if someone approached her or if she approached them but the parties ... evolved. They turned into something more private and exclusive. I think she kept up the beach and woods parties for her classmates, but she also started a new high-end sideline, with a different clientele."

A horrifying picture started to form in Max's mind. "What kind of clientele?"

Helen gave him a look that said he was being intentionally naïve. "Who do you think?"

"Older men."

"Older men with money. Stephanie wasn't interested in dock workers or fishermen."

"You're telling me Stephanie was running a brothel in high school?"

"I guess that's what you'd call it if you had to put a label on it."

"There can't be many men in Prince Creek willing to risk that."

"You'd be surprised at the appetites around town. There were enough."

"And your daughter was involved in this?"

She physically jerked back from the table. "No! She went to the beach parties at first, everyone did, but once Stephanie started with the older men Loreen got uncomfortable with the whole idea and stopped going. Stephanie pressured her to keep her mouth shut about it, but she didn't make her attend the parties either. She didn't need her to attend the parties. She had plenty of girls at that point."

"What girls? Do you know any of their names?"

"I know Linda Goulart and Nik, Stephanie's older half-brother, were involved, but I didn't know any of the Amish girls."

"Amish girls?"

"Yes, that was the particular heinous genius of Stephanie's plan. The Amish girls were on, what do you call it? There's a word for it. The time when they cut loose and be normal kids, like spring break, before they join the church or whatever."

"Rumspringa?"

"Yes, that's it. She got the Amish girls on rumspringa to be her party favors."

"Jesus," Max said, feeling slightly dizzy as he tried to wrap his head around Helen's story. "I didn't think the community out here did that. Rumspringa."

"They don't. Not anymore."

. . .

He sat in the front seat of the old police car at the curb outside Helen Camille's house, but found he couldn't turn the key. He still felt slightly unhinged as he sorted through all the past pieces of the case with this new information. He played back the last bits of conversation as they stood at the door. Helen didn't know anything else, and she swore that Loreen didn't either.

"I've always known when she was lying ever since she was a little girl. I bled her dry that night. I know what she knew and now you know it, too." She stood up from the table, looking almost as stunned as Max. Maybe it was a story she never expected to tell.

"I know it stopped suddenly and Stephanie was nervous for a long time. She pushed the girls really hard to keep their mouths shut about all of it. Maybe Linda Goulart knows more. She was always the tightest with Stephanie. Or the most under her thumb. She was the poorest of all of us. Her dad worked the docks. Her mother ran off with a school administrator when she was in grade school. She never had two nickels to rub together, Mr. Lindell. I always wondered where the money came from for that gift shop?"

A good question. Where indeed?

Max took out his phone and called Koenig. He needed to talk this through with someone.

"Max! Good timing. I was just going to call you."

She sounded out of breath.

"What are you doing?"

"Running for my car. Turns out the other Mulvaney daughter, Tracy, she lives in Charlottesville. I'm taking a couple of guys and heading to her address."

"Take it easy on them. They're old. Don't give them heart attacks with the SWAT team."

"These guys aren't the SWAT team. They will make an

impression, though. Don't forget Mulvaney is about a hair's breadth away from being a fugitive. And he lied to us."

"Okay, okay. I hear you. Just take it easy."

"Don't worry. I'll push them but I don't plan on killing them. What did you want?"

"Can you stop for a second? I'm not sure you should be driving when you hear this story."

"Will it keep? I really want to nail down Mulvaney."

He knew she was feeling the rush and it might be better to let her run with it. "It'll keep. Call me back when you nail his ass."

"Will do." And then she was gone.

Max didn't want to go home and wait in his half-empty trailer. That only left one option.

CHAPTER THIRTY-EIGHT

The rain was coming down in sheets and showed no signs of slacking as he hustled from the car to The Rink's side door. A flash of lightning lit up the sky, followed by a crack of thunder. Inside, patrons filled more than half the dining room. It was a good crowd for a Sunday night. Maybe the heat and the humidity from the past week had made people leery of turning on their ovens. A waitress, whose name Max didn't yet know, was working the floor. Jerry was behind the bar. Max waved and Jerry gave him a distracted nod in return. Drinkers lined the rail and he was hustling to pull drafts. Another rumble of thunder boomed overhead, close enough to rattle the framed photos on the wall and make people glance around.

Max found Thorne in his corner booth with Redd. Charlie was absent.

"Hey, guys."

"The prodigal son returns," Thorne said.

"Hi, Max," Redd said.

"You left me high and dry on Harrow," Thorne said.

"Don't whine, Thorne," Redd said. "He's not a mole planted inside the police to feed you information."

"No? Pretty sure that was close to the deal," Thorne said, giving Max a look.

"Not exactly, and I had nothing to give that you didn't get later at the press conference."

Thorne sniffed. "Maybe you can redeem yourself. Anything happen today?"

"Went out and talked to some folks on the 303."

Max ordered a beer when the waitress swung by and then filled the pair in on his interviews with the five Amish men. Thorne thought he might have interviewed Samuel Petersheim for a feature about interesting jobs, but didn't recognize any of the other names.

Redd didn't think any of them were patients either and could offer no insights. "When they need any medical help, they tend to go to the clinic. You might stop in there and talk to some people."

"Not a bad idea. I've been meaning to swing by and talk to Dr. Stephens. You know him?"

"Sure," Redd replied. "He's been the primary doctor there for a while now. Does a good job, I think. Why did you want to talk to him?"

"Ellie Baker at The Maple thought he might have invested some money with Arnsfeld for the incubator. The case appears to have veered off in another direction, but I thought it might be worthwhile to get his feelings on how that all went down. Maybe see if he knew someone angry enough or ruined enough to go after Topher."

"So that angle's been dropped completely?" Thorne asked.

"Maybe not completely, but it's fallen far down the list. Listen, did you guys ever hear any rumors or stories about some wild high school parties going on around here back in the late 1990s?"

Max didn't want to get into the specifics of what Helen Camille had just told him, not yet, but they still needed some facts. It felt like Nik Labat's cryptic warnings, Mulvaney running, and Camille's confession had brought them right to the door, but it remained frustratingly locked. If there were some town gossip or old rumors that could get him through that door it was worth asking the question.

Both men looked at him with confused and quizzical expressions.

"High school parties?" Thorne said.

"I wasn't much out of high school myself then. I was doing my residency in Toronto. Moved here in 2006 so I'm no help," Redd said.

"These would have gone beyond the usual Friday night keggers," Max said. "They would have stood out and perhaps reached the ears of the town, not just the kids in high school."

They both shrugged.

"That was right around the time I was moving out here," Thorne said, "but I don't remember hearing anything like that. I still owe you a visit to Bill Haas to ask about Collum Hawkins. I can ask him about that, too, if you want?"

"Can't hurt. When do you think you'll make it out there?"

"Tomorrow's edition is just about done. I should be able to get up there by lunch."

"Thanks."

"You might ask Jerry. After Bill, he might be the most likely person to know. He hears just about everything that happens in this town."

They all glanced over toward the bar which was still doing a brisk business. Jerry didn't appear to have time to chat. Just then, Max felt his phone vibrate. He pulled it out expecting Koenig with word on the Mulvaneys but it wasn't a number he recognized.

"Lindell."

"This is Sepp Joris." The intelligence guy looking into the brushfire that he and Kyle had kicked up with the RCR. "Koenig with you? Her phone is off."

"No, she's supposed to be chasing down two elderly fugitives."

"What?"

"You don't want to know. It's not related to the RCR but might be related to the murders we're working here in Prince Creek. You get a warrant for that shed yet?"

Joris hesitated. He knew Max was a local and barely law enforcement, but Max had provided the tip on the guns. Eventually, he said, "It's Sunday, so the warrant is taking a while, probably won't have the paper until tomorrow, but we might have something better."

"You got the buyers?"

"We got the buyers and we leaned on them."

"The government is good at that."

"It can bring some serious weight when it wants to. They both cracked right down the middle. They know little about how the RCR operates or moves the guns, but one of them heard the RCR guys bitching about quote 'making the Monday run.'"

"That sounds promising."

"Very promising. We did a drive-by. Koenig said you got eyes in that rental house across the street?"

"Yeah, there's a guy in there."

"Okay, tell him he'll have company tonight."

"You going to let us tag along if things start moving tomorrow?"

"I'll leave that up to Koenig. You're her problem."

"Been a pretty good problem so far."

Max thought he might have heard Joris laugh just a little as he disconnected.

"What was that about?" Thorne asked.

"One second. Let me make a call. If I forget, there's a genuine chance someone gets shot." He called Kyle and told him to expect some Mounties at the back door after dark.

"Don't shoot them, please."

"I'll try not to."

Fifteen seconds after he hung up with Kyle, as he started to explain to Thorne, his phone buzzed again. Koenig this time. "Hold on," he answered. "Let me move somewhere quieter." He slid out of the booth and headed for the short hallway where the bathrooms were located, along with an old pull tab cigarette vending machine. There was an alcove at the end of the hallway that used to hold a payphone that had been removed sometime before Max arrived in town. Now there was just a rectangle of plywood nailed up over a hole. Still, the compact space offered the only place in The Rink, save maybe a bathroom stall or going back outside, with any privacy. Max could hear the rain pounding on the roof. He wasn't going outside. And, as a rule, he tried not to spend any more time than necessary in The Rink's restrooms.

He put his back to the wall so he could see anyone coming.

"You find them?"

"I'm looking at them."

"You get anything useful?"

"Not yet, but I was just telling Dr. Mulvaney that he was covering up for the murders of at least four people and by keeping his mouth shut, or worse, lying to us, the other day and then running with his wife to his daughter's house, he's got the whole family involved in what I would call a criminal conspiracy."

"They're all sitting right there, aren't they? Am I just a prop? You putting a little more fear of God in them?"

"That's right, but I was leaving the big man out of it. I was talking more about a retirement in Shepton. I don't think Dick would last all that long in prison."

Max thought he heard someone crying. It wasn't pleasant. "He call for a lawyer yet?" Max thought a man who would openly weep wouldn't likely hold out long before calling in help.

"We did just discuss the potential of representation. That's an option. I did also have to explain that we would then be heading back to the station where I would be booking all three of them for obstruction of justice. Maybe a few other things if I was feeling creative. I was then wondering which property the good doctor would mortgage to make bail. His house or his office?"

Max could hear another voice, he thought it was Vera. "Jesus, Dick, just tell them what you know."

"Hold on, Max, let me put this on speaker so we don't have to repeat ourselves."

There was a clunk as the phone was set down and then Dick Mulvaney started talking.

"I never trusted that girl. Never."

"Who?" Koenig asked. "Just so we're all on the same page."

"Stephanie Arnsfeld, though her last name was Cote back then. She showed up late, practically after hours, one night. There were no other patients left, I remember that, just Carol helping me finish up the day's charts. Carol was our nurse back then."

"When are we talking?"

"I don't know exactly. It was in the fall. Stephanie was still in high school, still young. Ninety-eight? Ninety-nine? Something like that."

"Okay, go ahead."

"She came in with another girl, about the same age. I didn't recognize her. She barely spoke the whole time. Steph told me her name was Leah and that she was a friend. She was hurt. Or, Steph said she was. She barely let the girl talk. Any injuries Leah had would have been internal. Other than her ribs, her body was unmarked. She complained about pain when she breathed and occasional sharp pains in her abdomen. She had some bruising along her ribs, but it was light. Looked old. Almost healed. I asked her about it. Steph said she'd fallen out of bed, which we all knew was complete horse shit. The bruises were all the same. God, I can still seem them. I've seen some similar ones since then, mostly after bad domestic disputes or bar fights. Long and skinny and uniform. Looked more like someone had hit her with a broom handle or a bat. I told her she probably had some cracked or broken ribs. She said her urine was clear, but I still told her she should go to the clinic and get checked out more thoroughly. I didn't have an x-ray machine or any diagnostic equipment beyond my stethoscope."

"Did she?"

"I don't know. I never saw her again. I gave her some bandages if she wanted to tape up her ribs, you know, keep them a little more secure. Plus, I gave her a few days of Tylenol No. 3. That's the most I could do."

"Did you follow up? Do you still have the chart?"

"That's the thing. I couldn't follow up. I guess I could have called down to the clinic, but the chart disappeared. I had a bad feeling about it at the time. I remember going in the next day to look at the chart again, maybe add some notes, get Carol on the record, you know, in case we got sued or something, and I couldn't find it. Never did. I think Stephanie took it."

"Did you report it?"

"No. What would I report? There was no break-in. What was the crime? That'd I'd lost a chart?"

"You were afraid of Stephanie Cote?"

"No ... yes ... I know it sounds ridiculous. To be so kowtowed by a high school girl, but I was relatively new in town. I had just bought the business. Any accusations would have caused a lot of trouble for me."

"Did she ever say anything to that effect?"

"Not directly. But she had a certain reputation."

"Is that all?"

"There was one other thing. She asked if I could give Leah a pregnancy test."

"Was she?"

"I don't know. I didn't do it. I told her they could probably do it at the clinic if they didn't want to buy an OTC test at the drugstore."

"Dick, why'd you hold out on us? You royally screwed this up."

"I didn't know anything. Not for sure. I knew that Stephanie had brought a girl into my office for an examination 20 years ago."

Max felt that he and Koenig were holding opposite ends of the same stick. "But you knew Stephanie's reputation and you heard rumors," he said.

Koenig was smart enough not to jump in with her own questions.

"You hear things over the years. Bits and pieces at parties or fundraisers, but I never heard from anyone directly. It was always obliquely, always after a few drinks. I'm not sure anyone knows the truth anymore. What I'm telling you could be a total fabrication. You can see why I didn't want to bring it up. It could be all wrong."

"Dick, just tell us what you heard. We'll take it from there," Koenig said.

"Steph ran these parties. There were girls available. If you had enough money and knew the right people, you could get an invitation."

"Parties for adults?"

"Yes."

"Did you ever go?"

"Jesus, no! I wouldn't have gone even if I got an invite."

"But you knew people who had?"

"No, I don't even know that much."

"But you could make up a list for us. People you think might have gone. I don't imagine there were that many people in town that would make the grade."

A pause. "I could do that," Mulvaney finally said.

"Do it. Right now," Koenig said. "You do that and, if it helps us avoid someone else getting murdered, maybe you avoid jail time."

Koenig took him off speaker. "You knew about the parties?"

"It's why I was calling when you were headed out after the Mulvaneys." He told her about Helen Camille.

"Jesus, what a mess."

"We're getting closer. I'll take this unpleasant mess over the absolutely nothing we had before. It was just random bodies. Now we know the connection. The town is not that big. We will find the right person soon. We find out who else was at these parties and we have a potential victim list. Self-preservation will kick in."

"They kept it all a secret for a very long time," Koenig said.

"That's when they all had something to hide and protect. People are dying. It's all going to come out now."

"You think one of the guys from the parties is doing this? That he grew a conscience all these years later?"

"Doubtful, don't you think? Feels more like someone connected to the girl, Leah."

He filled her in on his morning at the Youngers' farm.

"It's horrifying, but it makes sense in some ways. It's how so much of this stayed under wraps for so long. If you brought in escorts or some pros from off-island they would stick out like sore thumbs. If you tried to use local high school girls, someone would have spilled the beans a long time ago. That community is already self-isolated. If Steph and the men kept their mouths shut, it might stay secret. None of the men set off your radar this morning?"

"Nothing dramatic. A couple of them looked capable of pushing back."

"We'll have to take a much closer look now. Maybe expand the list."

"I know. I'm not looking forward to that. There's already a tense relationship between the town and the settlement."

"We could ask Roy about bringing in outside people."

"Might be worth talking about. I don't think Roy is keen on digging into it further, either. You find anything in all that paper today?"

"Not much before we got word on Mulvaney's daughter. Nothing that really pointed in this direction. Might be worth another pass now that we know about the parties."

"What's next?"

"First, I get this list from Mulvaney then I head back to Prince Creek and then we catch this guy."

"Look, you sound a little wound up. Take it easy on them. Put a little more fear into the Mulvaneys to keep them in line, we don't need Dick or Vera chatting with anyone he puts on his list, but not so much that Dick might have a stroke."

"A stroke might be letting him off easy." She was hardcore. He heard Koenig blow out a long breath. "I hear you. I do. It might be a good idea if they stay with the daughter for a few days. Feels like we're running downhill now. I don't need the killer hearing about Mulvaney and deciding he needs to go, too."

CHAPTER THIRTY-NINE

He disconnected and walked back to the table. Charlie was now sitting with the other two men. The tables and stools were also full, but it was a mellow crowd mostly interested in one last drink or two to fortify themselves before facing the workweek. The Tragically Hip's *Phantom Power* was playing on the jukebox. The place smelled, not totally unpleasantly, of rain, beer, and the collective funk of humanity.

Thorne pinned him with his eyes as he slid in next to Charlie. He smelled a story. Max picked up his warm beer and clinked it lightly against Charlie's. "Charles."

"Maxwell."

"I thought you might have fallen in love and eloped in that hallway," Thorne said, not asking the question he really wanted to ask.

"Don't The Hip's have a song about that?" Redd said trying to keep the mood light.

Max knew that Thorne wouldn't be put off so easily, not with an edition set to go out tomorrow. "That was Koenig. She's back in Charlottetown. She was taking care of some personal stuff before coming back tomorrow, but it turns out she was in the right place at the right time. Thorne, you can't write about any of this tomorrow. No one else is going to have it so you won't be missing out. I'll make sure Koenig gives you something good for Thursday's edition. Deal?"

Thorne rolled his empty glass of beer between his palms, maybe considering if he should ferret out the story himself. Then a crack of thunder pealed somewhere over the Strait and someone opened the door and shook the rain off their shoulders. Charlottetown would be a solid two-hour drive in this weather.

"Deal," Thorne said.

"Okay, it turns out one of Mulvaney's daughters now lives in the area ..."

He recapped the Mulvaney situation, keeping the details of Steph's after hour's office visit to himself, but telling them the rest of it. He was glad to see each man's face reflected the same nauseous, thunderstruck look he felt. Even Thorne, who was the most jaded of the group.

"So, I think our best shot at the killer is backtracking him through Mulvaney's list." *Or using one of them as bait*, Max thought but didn't say out loud. "This doesn't feel finished, not yet. I'm wondering if the three of you might come up with a list of your own that we might compare to Mulvaney's. I know each of you didn't live here at that time, or were new in town, but it might be worth trying. The men we're talking about were wealthy and probably in positions of some power. It's unlikely many of them moved on, especially with this shared secret. They'd want to stick close and keep their finger in the dam, so to speak."

"I don't know," Redd said. "That makes me feel a little squeamish. Putting names down on paper. Feels like we're putting a target on people's backs."

"I understand, though someone has already put a target

on their backs. What we're trying to do is see it and get them out of the line of fire. Obviously, we won't tell them how we got their names."

"I'll do it," Thorne said and pulled the pencil from behind his ear and rooted in his computer bag for a notebook.

They ordered another round of drinks, turned out the waitress's name was Mindy, and started creating a list. After an hour, they had whittled down 22 names to 12. He tried to call Koenig to compare the list of names to what Mulvaney had come up with, but it went to voicemail. He declined another round. He wanted to get home and look at all the case notes himself through this new lens. See if any of the names they'd collected jogged anything loose. There was still something he could feel just out of reach. He should probably also get some sleep. He was getting too old to pull 20-hour days, but he felt so wired he wasn't sure that would happen anytime soon. He left some money on the table, said goodbye to his friends, and headed for Angel Court.

It was that goddam squeaky board that saved him.

He drove past Mrs. Johnson's trailer. The lights were off, but he could see the blue glow of her television flickering through the open window and he wondered what old movie she was watching. He hoped it was something that made her smile. She didn't show it often, but he decided it was a nice smile.

He parked his bland sedan on the red dirt path just as it narrowed between the two sugar maples. It might fit through, then again it might not. The rain had tapered off and he could walk the last 50 yards without risking the town's paint job, even if a few scratches might add a little personality to the car.

He found himself half hoping to find Mose waiting in the

clearing like a perverse Mary Poppins to cheer him up and talk through the case. He knew it was a false hope. Mose wouldn't be out in this weather and rarely stayed up past 9 p.m. Indeed, when he made it to the trailer, the clearing was empty. The rusted pickup, porch chairs, and prefab trailer just looked sad, wet, and lonely. He tried not to see that as a larger metaphor. The energy he'd felt at the bar had dissipated, and the beers and lack of a proper dinner had left him feeling low. He tried to shake it off and get inside before any more metaphors for his life occurred to him.

He only had a single light next to the couch and moved in the dark to put the notes down on the coffee table. His plan was to spread out the notes on the floor, when he heard the ear-splitting screech of the loose board.

For a split second, he thought Mose really was there. Then he dismissed it. Mose would never do that. Another, deeper part of his brain told him it wasn't Mose. He didn't move like Mose. He was quicker and lighter and probably younger.

That split second cost him. Max ducked but still caught a heavy blow across the back of his neck and shoulders. He grunted and went down. He knew if he stayed on the floor, he was done. He quickly scrambled forward, using his knowledge of the trailer to his advantage. He grabbed the edge of the cheap coffee table and flipped it up behind him. He didn't think it would do any damage. He just wanted it to slow the attacker down. He heard a quick gasp and a stumbling step.

Max's eyes adjusted to the dark interior of the trailer. He grabbed the skinny lamp from beside the couch and swung it around in a vicious arc. He hit something soft and solid. The other man cried out but recovered quickly.

He came in low and his shoulder hit Max in the stomach, knocking the wind out of him. Max staggered back and threw out one arm for balance. He hit the far wall and felt a sharp pain as one hand went through the cheap window screen over the couch. He tried to swing the lamp again, but the man was too close, and his grip felt slick and loose. The man wrapped him up and tried to get him on the ground.

Max dropped the lamp and hammered the man on his back with his fists. The man released his grip, ducked back, and when Max took a step to follow, the man quickly came forward again and connected a solid punch to Max's jaw. The room lit up with stars and Max suddenly felt very dizzy. He stepped back and tripped over the lamp he'd dropped. He quickly tried to scoop it up. It took two tries, but he finally got a hold of it. His left hand felt awkward and bulky. Something wrong with it. He gripped the lamp tighter with his right and swung out blindly, going low, aiming for the knees. The effort made his vision go dark at the edges, but he missed. The room was empty. The trailer door hung open. The attacker, in all likelihood the killer, was gone.

Max lurched to his front door and looked out but couldn't see anything. He thought he heard something moving in the trees. He stood in the open door and tried to pinpoint the direction, but it had stopped. Everything was silent, save for the dripping of water on leaves.

He made it to one of the beach chairs and collapsed into it. He dropped the lamp. In the scant moonlight, he could see that his left wrist and palm had deep cuts that were bleeding freely. He thought he should take care of that. But he was also suddenly and deeply exhausted. His head swam. He'd just close his eyes for a moment, then clean himself up.

CHAPTER FORTY

He woke up tied down. There was a moment of panic when the fight in the trailer came flooding back to him and he flailed his arms, desperate to move. He felt firm hands on both arms pushing him back down. A noise, a shrill beeping went off. He forced his eyes open and saw Koenig's face inches from his own.

"Easy," she said. "Just take it easy, Max. Relax."

He let himself sink back and look around the room as two nurses in blue scrubs burst through the door. There were no restraints. He was in a hospital room. Multiple tubes, IV lines, and monitors ran to his right arm. One nurse checked that he hadn't ripped them out when he woke up. The second nurse checked his vital signs and made notes on a clipboard. He closed his eyes and drifted off again.

The second time he woke up, he remembered where he was and didn't panic. He also found he remembered something else. Something important.

The lights were off. The room was dark other than the

blinking medical equipment. He tried to sit up but then thought better of it when spots of bright light danced in his vision. He listened. Not much noise inside or outside the room. He tried to spot a clock but couldn't see one. He glanced toward the windows. The blinds were drawn but he could see blackness at the edges. Still sometime during the night.

He stared up at the ceiling and thought about all the facts he had piled into his head in the last five days. It had taken literally getting hit on the head to rearrange them into something that might prove to be an answer. There was a beep and then a buzz from the IV machine to his right and then he felt a warm sensation where the needle was stuck in his arm. A timed dose of some medication.

There was a phone on the wall, just above the bedside table, within reach, behind the IV stand. He carefully rolled over and lifted the receiver. He paused to let the wave of nausea pass. His back and neck were aching. When he was sure he wouldn't throw up, he dialed a number from memory. One good thing about having few friends was that you had fewer phone numbers to remember.

"This is Max Lindell for Mose Burkholder." He left his message and lay back on the bed. The soft darkness came on like a warm enveloping wave. *Strong drugs*, he thought, as the wave lifted him up and carried him away.

The third time he woke up, the room was brighter, and he felt a little sharper. He took a quick inventory of his injuries. His left hand was heavily bandaged and secured in a wrist splint. He did a quick check. His shoulders were sore, but he could feel the pain meds softening that. That would likely get worse. He wiggled his fingers. His right hand was fine. Legs and feet were also okay. He noticed he was wearing only a hospital gown underneath the bed's heavily starched sheet.

Koenig was back in a chair next to the bed, watching him. She was wearing a lightweight gray suit with a white pinstripe and white blouse.

"What happened?" Max managed. His mouth was pasty; his throat was so dry it ached.

Koenig reached for the plastic pitcher on the table and poured a small amount of water into a cup with a pink straw before holding it out to him. He took a sip and would have drunk it dry if the nurse hadn't walked in and piped up. She was tall with broad shoulders and a flat nose that looked like it had been broken and re-set more than once.

"Not too much. The mix they have you on will make you nauseous if you drink it too fast." She picked up his chart, made a note, dropped it back in a holder at the end of the bed and left.

"That's Barb. I think she's taken a shine to you."

"Huh?"

"You better watch yourself. Barb really likes to take your temperature ... rectally."

He couldn't suppress a laugh. "Jesus, that hurts. Don't make me laugh."

Koenig smiled. "I think she likes to sneak a peek, too. You know, under the johnny." She leaned forward and flicked a hand against the sheets. "Check that the equipment is all working."

"Stop! Laughing feels like someone is pounding nails into my ears. Besides, I'm pretty sure Barb plays for the other team."

Koenig sat back. "You might be right about that." She dropped the jocularity. "The docs said it did look like someone tried to pound nails into your head. You've got a large contusion on your neck and some impressive bruising along your shoulders to go with your sliced and diced hand."

"Got jumped at my trailer. Got lucky or I'd look even worse. There's this squeaky floorboard that I can't seem to fix. The guy stepped on it and it gave me the split second I needed to duck."

"Not fast enough."

"No, but enough. If I hadn't moved, he would have taken off my head. He clipped me, but I think I got a few shots of my own in. He took off. Unfortunately, I was in no shape to chase him."

"Why not just shoot you? Or stab you? Or hit you with another ax? It's not like he's hesitated to use violence with the other victims."

Max shrugged. "I don't know. Trying to scare me more than kill me? Warn me off? Killing a cop, even a newly deputized one would probably bring a lot of attention. Maybe the plan was to hit me, then kill me?"

"Maybe."

"You sound disappointed."

"No, just trying to figure out what that might say about the killer?"

"I've got too many drugs in my system to string that many thoughts together. What time is it?"

Koenig glanced at the wall above his head. "A little after 9 a.m. Monday morning. I think they had you sedated for a bit when they were setting your hand."

He'd been out for over 12 hours. The Arnsfeld case was still less than a week old. It felt like months. "How did I end up here? I don't remember much after the guy ran off."

"I found you slumped over in one of those ugly chairs in front of your trailer."

"You found me?"

"Yes, after Mulvaney, I packed up and decided it would be

better to get back here ASAP. I tried calling you multiple times on the way and couldn't reach you. I ended up calling Roy and getting your address. I'm sure he now thinks we're sleeping together."

"We're sleeping together and you had to ask for my address?"

"If you haven't noticed, the chief tends to jump to the easiest conclusion. Anyway, I found you unconscious and bleeding in your chair. I called Roy and got you in an ambulance."

"Thanks, Koenig."

She waved him off. "Docs said it's all mostly superficial. Some simple R and R will take care of your head. Just a mild concussion. You were luckier with the hand. You'll probably have a gnarly scar but the cuts missed any nerves or major arteries. Even if I didn't show up, you probably would have been fine. You were doing a slow drip bleed."

Max knew she was selling herself short, but he let it go. "Thanks just the same. I was in no condition to walk or drive even if I did get out of that chair. And if Mrs. Johnson had taken me, I have a feeling we'd still be on our way."

"Is that the old woman in the first trailer?"

"Yeah," Max said, surprised. "Sort of the local neighborhood watch. She's the woman who told me about the guy that put the letter in my mailbox. Did you meet her?"

"Yes, she flagged me down after the ambulance left. She was sweet. She seemed very concerned. I told her I'd let her know how you were doing."

Sweet and Mrs. Johnson were not two words he'd put together before. Severe, maybe. Before he could ask Koenig any more questions, she stood up.

"Now that you're awake. I can do that, and I can check in with Roy. He'll want to get an official statement from you for the record."

Before he could respond, her phone buzzed in the clip on her belt. She looked at the display, frowned, then answered. A chirping sound started from the drawer next to the bed. Max gingerly turned on his side and opened the drawer. A clear plastic bag with his meager belongings, including his phone, were inside. He managed to pull it out and answer.

"We're moving," Kyle said.

"You invited along?"

"Sort of."

"You're following. At a discreet distance."

"Yes."

"Headed to the library, you think?"

"Going in that direction."

"Okay. Koenig is here. I'm guessing she's talking to Joris and getting the same information. There have been some developments on my end." He briefly sketched in the attack and his current location.

Kyle stayed silent for a moment. Max thought maybe he'd lost him in one of the island's many dead zones but then he said, "Anything I can do?"

"Not right now. Stay with the Mounties. Let's see this through. If anything changes on my end, I'll let you know."

"Okay."

He hung up and turned to see Koenig watching him from the foot of the bed.

"RCR's on the move. Joris thinks they will do a pick up or a buy."

The Monday run. "That right? You going along?"

"I was invited."

He pushed the blanket back, swung his feet over the side, fought off a brief surge of dizziness, and said, "Then let's go."

CHAPTER FORTY-ONE

It took Max a half-hour to sign his name in triplicate enough times to convince the doctors he wouldn't come back and sue them. He'd felt all right in the hospital, but the cocktail of drugs was wearing off and his head, neck, and shoulders felt as if they'd been tenderized by a hammer. His left hand and wrist mostly felt numb, but he didn't think that would last. It had taken 30 stitches to close the wound. On the way out, one of the doctors had taken pity on him and given him some Tylenol No. 3. Max thought he'd need them sooner rather than later, but knew any pills now would make him slow and sleepy. Two things he didn't want to feel right now.

It was Monday morning and, while the traffic never got that heavy on the island, there were cars on the road. Max was not sure Koenig saw them. She was pushing the speed limit. He thought about closing his eyes but didn't want to give her any more evidence that he should be back in bed. He might have wiggled his way out of the hospital, but he was still trying to convince Koenig he would be okay as he sat in the passenger seat of the Explorer.

"Still don't think this is a great idea," she said.

"Never said I was a smart guy."

"No, you didn't."

During the drive, Koenig called Roy and filled him in on Mulvaney and the party rumors. Something neither of them had done yet with all the drama at Max's trailer. Roy was dumbfounded and kept repeating, "I just can't believe it." She read him the list Mulvaney had provided. There hadn't been time to stop at Max's trailer and get his notes and the list the guys had come up with at The Rink. Roy was skeptical, he knew most of the names on the list, but agreed to start some background checks. He stopped short of outright warning anyone. "Just no cause yet. It's one man's opinion. I don't want to send people into a panic." Max disagreed but kept that opinion to himself. It wasn't his neck on the line. Roy also agreed to keep working on checking the Amish alibis and keep an eye out for Nik Labat. They agreed to stay in touch throughout the day and then disconnected.

They didn't talk much after that. Max let her concentrate on driving. Once they cleared Charlottetown and made it over Confederation Bridge, the roads improved and opened up to multiple lanes. With Koenig's heavy foot and occasional emergency lights, and with just one stop for gas, sugar, and coffee, they passed St. John and then into Canboro in just over four hours.

Koenig called Joris, and they agreed to meet up at the Canboro police station.

"We made up time on the road. They got here 20 minutes ago. Joris will fill in the locals, give them a heads up."

"Where did the RCR go?"

"He's got two cars still on them. He says they pulled into a Tim Horton's about a mile away from the station. There are two of them, both in a booth drinking coffee and eating donuts."

They followed the car's navigation system and ten minutes later pulled into the police station. They parked next to a blue Mustang. A man in jeans and a T-shirt was leaning against the passenger door smoking.

"You with Joris?" Koenig asked.

"Yeah, I'm Martens. You Koenig and Lindell?"

"That's us."

The man was short, five-feet six, with kinky black hair, three-day stubble, and a face you'd forget 2 minutes after seeing him. Max thought he was probably a very good undercover cop.

The guy eyed Max's hand. "What happened?"

"Baking accident. Shouldn't have gone for that third layer."

The guy smirked, then shrugged. "As long as you're not watching my six."

"Let's hope this is just mop up duty," Koenig said

The guy shrugged again. "Maybe. Don't know much about this RCR. Maybe they fold. Maybe they think they're outlaws and want to go down in a blaze of glory."

"The head guy, Maddix, is pretty bright. Not your average imbecile criminal. I'd expect he told them to lie down and start screaming for a lawyer if anything went wrong," Max added.

"Never can tell until the chips are down."

"Joris still inside?" Koenig looked toward the door.

The man flicked the cigarette butt away. "Yeah. Been inside about 15 minutes."

"Going to be a problem?"

"I doubt it. If he's smart, the chief will want this to go away quickly. Tourism is a big deal for the town. They'll frown on anything that dents that reputation. Better to deal with it quickly. Even better if he has some outsiders he can use as scapegoats if anything goes wrong."

"They going to be part of the op?"

"They're not a large force, from what I understand, but I think Joris will use them as backup to keep them invested and out of the way. Maybe put some cars on the main exits out of town as a backstop."

"Works for me."

At that moment, the back door opened and a man came down the steps. He was dressed similarly to Martens in jeans, broken in boots, and a black T-shirt. He was taller and thicker through the chest than Martens. As he approached, he slipped on a pair of sunglasses that partially covered the long, thin scar that stretched from his left eyebrow down to his chin.

They did a quick round of introductions and then Koenig asked, "We good to go?"

"Yup. No problems with the Canboro PD." Joris handed her a portable radio. "This should keep us off the public airwaves. Chief seems excited to help. I think I made his day. It will make an excellent story for the office Christmas party this year," Joris replied.

"As long as he's not too excited," Koenig said.

"He seems to have his head screwed on right. We should be fine. He's redirecting three cars to the outer edges of town to help if we need it."

"Okay. What's next?"

"I just checked in with Liam and Jacob, they make up the rest of my team with Martens here. Liam said the two RCR guys are still at Tim Horton's. Looks like they're pretty settled in. Jacob is up at the library."

"Is he inside?"

"No, we don't want to spook anyone. He's watching the door. If they follow the pattern you described last time, the person will be on foot. We don't care so much about the runners. We want the RCR guys. As long as we tag the runner on the way to the drop and get that on tape, the library swap itself doesn't matter as much. We can ID and pick up the runner later if we want."

"No risk in missing them leaving the library?" Koenig asked.

"It's a Monday afternoon at a public library, not a train station."

"Okay, good point."

"Are we staying here or getting closer?"

"You got a vest?"

"Yeah."

"I always prefer to be near the action."

"Good. Me too."

The main business district of Canboro was laid out in tidy blocks like a mini metropolis. Easy for tourists to navigate and easy to tail two degenerate suspects. Not as easy, however, to sit and watch those same suspects sip coffee.

The Tim Horton's chain coffee shop sat on a corner block opposite a law office, a pharmacy, a Subway sandwich shop, and an A&W burger joint that Max was sure had gone bankrupt but apparently not in Canada. The traffic was light on a Monday afternoon. Many of the tourist attractions were five blocks farther south, closer to the St. Croix river. The library was in the middle, two blocks south and a block west.

Joris and Martens pulled to the curb half a block past Tim Horton's. Liam, driving a red Mazda 3, left the bank's parking lot across the street and circled around to find a new spot farther up the street and out of direct sightlines.

Koenig drove past the coffee shop and then Joris and Martens. A third car moving around might be too much. Two blocks south, Koenig turned right and double backed. The block behind the principal street was light residential with some scattered smaller commercial properties. She pulled the Explorer into the parking lot of a sprawling, two-story brick apartment house. There was an open field and a small playground next to the building, and they could just make out the top of the red Tim Horton's sign peeking over the fencing separating the properties. They lacked direct sightlines but were close enough to jump in when things started. There were enough cars and traffic in the apartment lot that they could sit undisturbed for a while. Still, Koenig called in their location to Joris, who relayed it to the Canboro PD. If someone reported them, the last thing they needed was a local squad car pulling up to check them out.

They sat for 20 minutes. Max called Kyle and checked in. "You still out there?"

"Across the street. At the diner. Fish and chips. Not bad."

"I'll post your review on TripAdvisor."

Kyle ignored him. "Taking too long."

"Thought the same thing. Maybe the runner got held up? I wouldn't want to sit there that long if I were those guys."

"Want me to check? Head up to the library?"

"Give it ten more minutes."

Everyone was getting antsy. Koenig hopped out and grabbed her ballistic vest from the trunk and threw it in the back seat. Joris and Liam swapped again. Martens got out and walked a couple blocks on foot. The initial rush had worn off, and Max could feel frustration creeping in.

"How long have they been in there?" Max asked. He'd been watching two boys throw sand at each other on the playground.

Koenig glanced at her watch. "Coming up on an hour."

"Let's move up. Unless something's gone wrong, I don't think it will be much longer. They wouldn't want to sit in there longer than necessary. They can fake an hour, but even that's pushing it. The employees will take notice. You don't really want to be regulars when you're trying to smuggle guns over the border."

She started the car just as Jacob came over the radio. "Got one leaving the library. Male, mid-20s. Green buttoned shirt, short sleeves, khaki pants, loafers. He has a blue backpack. Heading in your direction."

"Roger that," Joris came back. "Okay, Jacob, you stay on the library to see if you can spot anyone else but, if this is our guy, we take them after this. Let this guy do the drop and then let them get outside. Do not let them get in the car. Koenig move up in the back. Liam loop around and give me a visual on the guy and then pull into the A&W lot across the street. Don't move until the suspects have the backpack and are clear of the store. We don't want a hostage situation. We all come in at once from three directions. Pin them in."

They all confirmed the plan and got into position. Koenig took a minute to swap her suit coat for the vest and then drove slowly up the side street and approached the Tim Horton's coffee shop from the rear. She idled at the curb, half a block back. A curious neighbor was cutting his lawn and gave them a look. Koenig held her creds up to the window, the man nodded and went back to his mower.

"There he is," Max said. They watched the man approach from the south. He looked like a student or possibly one of those people that knock on your door around dinner trying to drum up support for Greenpeace or The Red Cross. Clean-cut, earnest-looking, and utterly not suspicious. The back-pack looked full but wasn't bulging or straining. He didn't hesitate. He walked up the sidewalk, into Tim Horton's, and disappeared from their sight.

There was a side entrance to the parking lot off the cross street that allowed cars to get into the drive thru lane without clogging up the main drag. Koenig inched up the side street, trying to time it just right, and turned into the lot.

"He's at the counter and ordering," Joris said over the radio. "Okay, he's got his drink. He's left the drink on a table and he's heading for the rear of the building. Must be the bathroom. One of the RCR guys is up now. He's following. He's also carrying a bag. Looks like they're doing the library swap in reverse. They're out of sight." There was a pause as the transaction went down behind closed doors. "Okay, the kid is out. Still has a bag. Here comes RCR. The bags look identical. Gotta assume they swapped. The kid's got his drink again and he's heading out. Let him go. I've got a Canboro patrol inbound to grab him. Okay, both RCR guys are up and heading for the exit. Be ready, we are a go."

Koenig accelerated and maneuvered the Explorer around a parked car so they had a view of the side and the rear of the building yet still blocked the drive thru exit. The RCR's Chevy Silverado pickup was toward the front of the lot directly opposite the door. A line of sickly, waist-high evergreen shrubs ran along the edge of the lot separating it from the sidewalk.

Koenig took her gun out of the storage compartment that sat in-between the front seats.

"Stay in the car," she said. Max heard her click off the safety.

After that, everything sped up.

CHAPTER FORTY-TWO

Pretty thought he could solve two problems with one visit. Instead, he might have ended up with some broken ribs and a lacerated shin. Pretty knew it could have been worse. He didn't require a doctor and both injuries could be covered. He would have had a harder time explaining any injuries to his face. He'd scraped up his knuckles with the punch but that could be explained with his job. He felt no shame in running away. It was the expedient thing to do. His ultimate mission was still to get Brown and Sykes. He was so close now he could almost taste it.

It had become clear that morning that he had a Max Lindell problem. He considered it more of a business problem. It was unrelated to the mission, but it could jeopardize it. Who the hell was this guy? Pretty hadn't even heard of the man until a week ago. If he didn't already believe he was on the side of angels, he might question Lindell's sudden arrival as God's will. But Pretty knew it couldn't be that.

Lindell wasn't a regular member of the Prince Creek PD. Pretty had enough experience with them to know that for certain. He didn't act like a typical cop either. He sort of ambled around, asked questions, hung out at the coffee shop and the bar. Even so, somehow, it was working. Instead of waiting for Roy or one of his dipshit deputies to do something, people were talking and they were looking around. Soon they might start asking questions.

He had to finish the mission before that happened.

So, he had decided he needed a gun. A gun would take the uncertainty out of things and it would allow him to move more quickly. It occurred to him that a member of the police would likely have a gun so he thought he would pay a visit to Lindell's home. He might find a gun and he might take care of his business problem.

He breathed in and winced at the stabbing pain in his side. Only, it hadn't worked out that way. It hadn't been difficult to find out where Lindell lived, and Pretty had been both surprised and pleased to see that Lindell wasn't at home. Getting the gun was more important and safer for the mission than another killing. If he had the gun, he could always come back and take care of Lindell later.

Better yet, Lindell lived in a tiny, crappy trailer. He would be in and out in no time. The door was open, which gave him pause. Would someone with a gun inside leave the door open? Maybe it was locked up separately? That could be a problem.

He slipped inside. He left the lights off and began to search the handful of compact rooms. He'd been inside five minutes when he heard a car approaching. He'd brought no weapon of his own. He didn't want to risk being stopped or spotted with it. He rushed to the kitchen, but couldn't find any knives in the dark. He fumbled around but felt time running out and eventually grabbed a pan off the stove.

Things didn't get any better after that.

The fireflies flitted around his head in the hot August night.

The night sky was blotted with clouds, but occasionally he could spot the stars blinking through. The Little Dipper, the host of the north star, gleamed brightest. He watched it glide by and felt a certain kinship.

He shifted to find a position that didn't make his ribs ache. He'd have to sleep inside tonight. He could feel the water seeping through the blanket he'd put down. His shin had improved throughout the day and he no longer had to try to hide a limp, but his ribs still hurt badly. Each breath brought a tiny flicker of fire along his left side. That was the only thing he'd taken from the trailer. He still had a Max Lindell problem and he still needed a gun. He couldn't think of a better way to get one than the police. Surely, some farmers around here had shotguns in their closets for vermin and some other neighbors might have permits for hunting, but how would he find out? He didn't know any personally and asking those questions right now could be dangerous. He had no time. He kept coming back to the police. He couldn't walk into the station and take one. Even Roy's department wasn't that stupid. Ignorant, sure, but not stupid. He needed another way.

As he stared up into the heavens, he felt the touch of God's divine smile as a new plan formed in his mind. He didn't want to make the same mistakes he made with Lindell. He didn't want to rush into it without thinking it all the way through, but an hour later he still thought it would work. Better yet, this time he really could take care of two problems with just one risk.

There might be just enough time to still do this right.

CHAPTER FORTY-THREE

Max and Koenig watched the two men exit Tim Horton's. Max quickly confirmed it was young Brad and the bartender from their visit to the RCR clubhouse. They were talking as they stepped off the curb and headed for the Chevy. The bartender laughed and pulled at his beard.

Out of the corner of his eye, Max saw a shop employee come out of the building's back door carrying a bag of trash and heading for a rusted dumpster.

Koenig opened the driver's side door and stepped out. Joris's blue Mustang roared into the lot, he was out and yelling at the pair almost before the car had come to a complete stop. Martens was out the other side, gun up.

Brad and the bartender froze halfway between the door and their pickup truck.

Max spotted Liam's Mazda hung up in traffic halfway across the street.

Joris was screaming, "Police! On the ground! Get on the ground!"

Koenig was clear of the car door and moving up on the pair. Max saw the bartender glance back and spot her.

The employee swung the leaking bag of trash into the dumpster and then dropped the lid. It hit with a sharp, staccato clang of metal on metal. Everyone flinched and froze in the sudden silence.

Brad reached for something under his shirt and ran for the pickup. The bartender hesitated then followed.

"Gun!" Joris yelled.

Max heard three sharp cracks.

Koenig hit the pavement then scrambled up and ran for the car. Martens and Joris ducked behind their doors. Koenig and the intelligence guys were directly opposite each other and no one wanted to risk hitting the other in the crossfire. They had the RCR guys pinched but couldn't finish it. If they made it to the pickup, they'd have a chance.

Liam was still stuck in the street but must have reached the same conclusion. He jumped out of the Mazda. He had a better angle and risked a shot. Max thought he saw the bartender stumble, maybe Liam clipped him, but then they were both in the truck and it was moving. Brad was behind the wheel. He cranked the engine, jumped the parking chock block, slewed right, ripped through the meager shrubs, and then bumped off the sidewalk onto the side street. Max watched the brake lights flare and then saw the big black hole aimed in their direction.

"Shotgun!" he screamed.

The ear-splitting boom of the gun cracked the air and Max heard the pellets scrape the hood and windshield of the Explorer.

"Fuckers!" Koenig yelled as she jumped in and started the car, reversed quickly, and then went in pursuit.

. . .

The RCR pickup was headed north and stretching out the gap, weaving in and out of traffic, unafraid to clip any unlucky bystanders. Max watched two banks, a school, an auto parts store, and a small hotel flash by as they left the commercial district and then sped past more apartments and subdivisions.

Joris was directly behind them in the Mustang, then Koenig, presumably Liam was back there somewhere, too. Max kept his eyes forward.

"You okay?" Koenig asked.

He patted himself down. Didn't find any new holes. "I'm good. You?"

"Five by five."

Max realized they were both jacked up and yelling. He took a deep breath and tried to steady his hands. He reached down and grabbed the handset radio from where it had fallen into the footwell. The frequency was a mess of crosscutting voices. Much of the conversation was about Koenig's silence after the shotgun blast in their direction. Max jumped in and let them know that he and Koenig were not hit and were in pursuit.

Koenig was doing 60, but Brad was pushing the pickup faster. It bounced and shimmied over the road.

Brad had the advantage now, but the longer it continued the more the odds tilted in favor of the police. He left the driving to Koenig and grabbed his phone. He brought up the navigation app and tried to figure out where they were going. He studied the map. He thought Brad would soon have to make a choice: jump on the highway and try to outrun them or stick to smaller roads and make the police back off.

"If they stay on this road it's about five miles until they hit Route 1."

"That wouldn't be bad," Koenig replied. "Gives us more space. We could block the roads. Put down some strips."

Max hit the number for Kyle with his thumb and tucked the police radio into the space between the armrest and the seat. He could hear the high RPMs of the engine when Kyle picked up.

"You behind us?"

"No. Same direction but heading parallel. If they hit the highway or county road, I should be out in front."

"Stay in touch."

"I got the police band."

"Right." Max had passed him the Canboro emergency frequency earlier.

They were coming up fast on the highway interchange. Other traffic had thinned out. Everyone was piled up in a straight line now: RCR, Joris, Koenig, and Liam. Behind Liam, Max could see more emergency lights, presumably the local Canboro PD getting in on the chase. A minute later, they were on a straight stretch, past any houses now, with just trees on either side of the two-lane road. Max spotted a flashing lightbar coming at them from the opposite direction.

Koenig saw it, too. "Shit," she said. "He's going to block him from the highway."

Max wasn't sure. The pickup wasn't slowing down. In fact, as he watched, it surged forward, and Max wondered if Brad would make a suicide run and try to ram his way through any blockade, but just as he was about to tell Koenig to slow down to avoid any pile-ups, the Chevy braked hard and swerved right, almost rolling onto a dirt side road. The truck didn't roll. It scraped against some trees, then straightened and disappeared down the dirt road. They all followed.

Joris's Mustang was no good on the dirt track. He and Martens were getting bounced all over the place, and the Chevy quickly pulled farther ahead and disappeared around the curves.

"Where's he going?" Koenig asked.

"No clue, he's off the map. It looks like some kind of fire or access road. The map shows a set of train tracks farther east."

They went over a rise and then around a curve and just caught the Chevy's taillights disappearing over another hill ahead. They were all backed up behind the Mustang and losing ground. The road widened slightly at the bottom of the rise near what might have been a trailhead. Joris pulled the Mustang to the side and waved them forward.

Koenig hit the gas. The Explorer was more nimble and handled the dirt and divots better than the Mustang, but that didn't mean it was a smooth ride. They were both thrown around the cabin, but they quickly closed the gap on Brad to just over 100 yards. They were kicking up a thick cloud of dirt in their wake, and Max couldn't see if the others were keeping up.

Brad must have felt the pressure. He tried to increase his own speed to match but, while the truck had the horsepower, it didn't have the maneuverability. Around the next curve, he veered left and caught his wheels in a natural drainage ditch along the roadside. He then overcorrected and went off the road on the other side and into the trees.

"Oh, shit," Max said.

Koenig slowed and stayed on the road. They climbed out.

The Chevy was still going fast, but it was out of control. It was all gravity now as it went down a hill, cutting a path through the undergrowth and small saplings. But it was only a matter of time.

Max and Koenig could do nothing but watch. Max heard the other cars pull up.

Two hundred yards into the trees, Brad's luck ran out and the Chevy hit an old oak head-on and came to a sudden stop with a crunch of metal and a shattering of glass. Then everything went quiet.

"Everyone okay?" Joris asked.

There were nods and murmurs of agreement all around. They all heard the screech of metal on metal and looked back at the now smoking truck. The driver's side door was open, and Brad stumbled out. He looked up the hill at them, put his hands on his knees and threw up. Then he started running downhill.

"Of course he's a runner," Joris sighed. "Let's go get him but be careful, he might still be armed." He turned to the two local Canboro cops. "You guys stay up here and coordinate. What's through these woods?"

"You'll hit some CSX freight tracks and then a small airport."

"Okay, see if you can get some of your guys around on that side. I don't think he'll make it that far, but I didn't think he'd make it this far either." The older of the two cops nodded, and they headed back toward their patrol car. "Let's go."

They spread out and started jogging downhill through the woods, following the path of the Chevy. Max felt his scarred lungs burn with the effort, but his neck and shoulders hurt more. He tried not to look left or right. The tree trunks wavered in front of him and he felt his legs protest. He slowed down and tried to suck in a few deep breaths. The vertigo passed.

He joined Joris at the wrecked pickup. The bartender was dead. He hadn't been wearing a seatbelt and had gone halfway through the windshield. His neck and right arm were bent at extreme angles. Blood was dripping onto the truck's hood. Joris double-checked for a pulse and then they kept moving.

It was slower going once they were past the truck. The hill flattened out, but the woods thickened up with waist-high brush and low branches that slapped at them as they passed.

Max felt one branch whip at his face as he passed and a moment later felt blood running down his neck. *Just put it on my tab*, he thought.

Brad was also slowing. There was no subtly or stealth about the chase. He watched Martens trip and fall to his right, Joris was swearing in French to his left. They watched Brad go down and then pop back up. He limped through a wall of brush and disappeared. Max heard a train whistle and then felt the low rumble through his feet. "You hear that?" he shouted.

"Can't let him get to the tracks. Those trains are miles long," Joris called back.

Max ignored the pain and pushed harder. He brought his arms up to protect his face as he went through another patch of briars. Then he was out in the open. A large swath had been chopped down and maintained on either side of the tracks to keep debris and animals off the tracks. The train was coming. They could see it as well as feel it approaching from the south.

Brad had reached his limit. Max was only 25 yards behind and closing when Brad suddenly turned and brought up a gun. Max hit the ground and kept his head down. He couldn't hear any shots over the deep rumble and noise of the approaching train. The engineer must have spotted them. He was leaning on the train's whistle.

When he risked a look, Brad was running again, the limp getting worse. He had to throw his left leg out in an awkward movement to keep moving. Koenig came up on his left. Max spotted Joris and Marten farther off to his right.

"He's not going to make it," Koenig said.

"No."

Brad seemed to realize it at the same time. He looked over his shoulder, slowed to a stumbling walk, then turned around. He still had the gun, but he had it down at his side. The train crept closer.

"Put the gun down," Joris yelled.

Brad swiped at a line of blood that ran down his face from a cut somewhere on his head. His clothes were torn and ripped. The big blue and yellow diesel engine chugged closer.

"C'mon, just put it down," Joris repeated.

"Why'd you shoot first?" Brad yelled back.

"What?" Joris repeated. The train was on top of them. Max could feel the engine's power thrum through his chest.

"Guess it doesn't matter." Brad tossed the gun aside. They all stood up and relaxed a fraction. This would not end in a shootout. Max watched Brad drop his head. He said something, then he turned and started scrambling up the track embankment.

Max turned away. He didn't need to re-live this in his dreams.

Brad didn't make it.

CHAPTER FORTY-FOUR

"I thought that was supposed to be easy," Max said.

It had taken almost six hours to take everyone's statements, get the bodies moved, and the train rolling again. They were now back at the Canboro PD tying up the last loose ends with the town's prosecutor before they could head back to Prince Creek. Max was in the men's room with Joris. A small first-aid kit sat out on the sink between them. They'd both gotten scratched up chasing Brad through the woods. Max smeared ointment on the cuts that slashed across his cheeks. He stuck a Band-Aid on the largest one below his jaw. If it was possible, he felt worse than he looked. The emergency pills from the doctor were long gone and so were the analgesic effects. He felt held together by string and gauze.

"You can never tell. Makes this job exciting."

"Why did they run in the first place? And why did he keep running?"

"Panicked would be my guess."

"I'll be interested to learn the rest of Brad's history.

Maddix hinted that he had some issues in his past. I wonder if that's the reason he jumped."

"You sure he jumped? Don't think he was trying to make it across?"

"Pretty sure. He was timing it."

"Truth? I'll take that rather than him trying to shoot it out with us. He easily could have hit one of us."

The entire thing just left Max feeling empty. He did not doubt that Brad was a bad guy and probably would have caused someone more misery down the road but ... seeing a six-ton train flatten someone will give you second thoughts. "What's going to happen to Maddix?"

"I talked to the rep from the New Brunswick's CAO. She's going to have to coordinate with the guys from PEI, but she was confident they'd get him on something. Having those two around as witnesses would have helped, but we still have the runner and the two buyers from the other night. I don't think he'll wiggle all the way free."

Max washed his hands and wiped them on a rough paper towel from the dispenser. "Well, good luck with that. I told Martens, he's not your typical dirtbag so don't count your convictions too soon."

They shook and Max hobbled out of the bathroom with a bandaged wrist, stiff neck, cuts across his face, a torn-up shirt, and a serious headache. As he wandered down the hall in search of Koenig and a ride home, he had to wonder if it was worth it or all a waste of time.

He ducked into an empty conference room, called Kyle, and told him to take off. Earlier, he'd filled him in on the details from the scene.

"You're sure?"

"No, but I'm sure this part of it's over."

"The guns?"

"The RCMP thinks they have enough with the buyers and the strawman making the exchanges to, if not takedown the RCR, then put a serious dent in their plans."

"You going to follow up on that?"

Max knew what he was really asking. "I'll keep an eye on it, but I'm not planning anything."

"So, we're done?"

Max knew that Kyle lived relatively close, within a day's travel, but didn't know anything more specific. He had a contact number and that was it. Safer for both of them.

"Yeah, we're done. I'm going back to Prince Creek and plan to find this other nutcase we got running around."

"Okay." And he was gone.

They all congregated in the Canboro PD lobby. There was a final round of handshakes and some cautious backslapping. The op hadn't been clean, but all the good guys were still walking around and some convictions would come out of it. If you were to weigh things up, it might be a little messy, but Joris thought it would tilt in their favor.

The media had gotten a sniff and a few satellite trucks were parked out front. Joris and Liam were sticking around overnight to do a press conference with the Canboro chief in the morning. Max wanted no part of the media and neither did Koenig.

"The boss wants my face on TV but fuck that. This was a clusterfuck. It might smell okay now but, trust me, there's going to be some stink coming off it when people take a closer look. Safer to get back to Prince Creek and our psycho killer."

Max didn't disagree. They slipped out the back and, five

minutes later, they were on Route 1 heading north with Koenig pinning the speedometer at 90.

They stopped after an hour for drive thru burgers and to fill up the gas tank. Max was happy to find some packets of Aleve at the gas station counter. He took six. It was like pricking an elephant with a safety pin. It might have dulled the sharpest edges of the pain but that might have been wishful thinking. He didn't hurt as much as just ache all over. He tried to move as little as possible in the passenger seat. They drove across the bridge and then across the island on the increasingly narrow and rural roads in silence. But a companionable one.

He tried to use the time to think about the case. He went back to square one, the Hawkins killing. No, that wasn't right. If Helen Camille was telling the truth, then all the blood started spilling years earlier. He let the details wash over him, but nothing popped. His thoughts felt slow and sludgy. He needed sleep. There were too many breadcrumbs, too many details to track. He couldn't make sense of it all. It just remained scattered.

e woke up to a hand gently prodding his arm. Koenig had pulled the Explorer through the trees and up close to the trailer.

"Sorry," he said.

"Christ, don't apologize. I don't know how you even made it this far."

Despite the infusion of Aleve, the lengthy drive back had done nothing to loosen or heal his sore muscles. He opened the door and stiffly swung his legs out like an elderly man. "You want to come in? I know I at least have beer."

"How can I resist that offer? I'd better, just to make sure you don't decide to sit in that beach chair again and get stuck."

He made it up the short steps. Barely. He might need to fill the prescription for painkillers in the morning just to function. As he opened the door, he realized he had no idea what the place looked like since the fight.

"Umm ..." he said, as he stepped inside. But everything was neat and back in its place. There was even a piece of wood nailed neatly over the broken window screen.

Mose, Max thought.

"Bathroom?" Koenig asked.

"Down the hall."

Max looked around, but there wasn't much left for him to do. The case notes were stacked on the coffee table next to the materials that Max had called Mose about from the hospital. He grabbed everything and moved it all to the kitchen counter. Work could wait a few hours. He went into the kitchen and opened the fridge. Mose again. He found a fresh six-pack of Copper Bottom with a short note taped to the carrier: *"Figured this might be the best medicine."*

He took two cans back to the couch. Koenig came back down the hall. He handed her a beer.

"Helluva day," she said.

They touched cans lightly and each took a long drink.

"Did you hear what he said? Right at the end?" Koenig asked.

"This will stop the pain. At least, I think that's what he said. The train was loud." *Or maybe that's what I would have said*, Max thought.

"Can't stop thinking about it. Tough way to go. Oddly courageous."

"Or desperate. Clearly, the kid had bigger issues than a potential gun bust. You don't end up under someone like Maddix if you're well adjusted."

"Don't make it out like he had no choice. There are always choices. Maybe not pleasant ones and maybe not a lot, but Brad wasn't forced into anything."

"I know. You're right. Someone out there cared at some point." Max paused and finished the rest of the can. "Just not enough."

He got two more beers and chased his first swallow with

more Aleve. He could feel a little buzz. They'd skipped lunch and the drive thru burger and fries on the way home weren't cutting it. He searched the cabinets but there was little to eat beyond canned soup and crackers. He was drinking too fast, but he just wanted to forget everything for a few hours. He didn't want to think about bodies, or trains, or killers, or secrets. He went back to the couch.

Koenig's eyes had gone soft. "You pissed about Brad?"

"No, not really. It's nobody's fault but Brad's and he paid the price for it. I'm just disappointed, I guess. In who or what, I have no idea."

She put her beer on the coffee table and touched his chest. "That's okay. I don't want to figure it out. Maybe tomorrow, but not tonight." She traced the cut along his jaw with her finger. "I could help you get out of these clothes. Maybe wash your back. That's not going to be an easy job."

"How can I resist that offer?"

He woke up later and she was gone. He got out of bed and went to the bathroom. He flicked the light switch on, and hot lances of pain shot through his head. He turned it back off. It was probably optimistic to think even a minor concussion would heal in a day. Especially with the day he'd had yesterday. He cautiously moved his head and neck and arms. There was a dull throbbing, but the pain felt less prickly and sharp. He looked at the dirty, gauze-wrapped splint. He took four Aleve and went back to bed. He thought about the list of names they were compiling, then the one photograph from Hawkins apartment, then the initials carved into the dock. Then sleep pulled him back under.

The next time he woke up it was light outside. He rolled out of bed and started the coffee maker. He thought about break-fast but couldn't get beyond the effort level of toast. He went back to the bathroom, brushed his teeth, and carefully unwrapped the splint. The zigzagging black thread of the stitches stood out like splashes of paint on a white wall. He cautiously rotated his wrist. It was stiff and tight, but it moved. He stood in a hot shower until the tank ran out. He toweled off, dressed, re-wrapped his wrist, and thought about the case as he drank two cups of coffee. His body was bruised but his mind felt clearer. He didn't know if it was the sex or the sleep, but more pieces fell into place.

First, Topher Arnsfeld and his charity. The case had been off the rails almost from the start because of Arnsfeld's money and history with the town. A lot of people had a lot of reasons to see Arnsfeld, maybe not killed, but taken down a peg or two. So, plenty of motive but little means or opportu-nity. They'd uncovered an affair and a potential heir, more motive, but Max did not see Kelsey Macias butchering her lover and putting her child's custody at risk. She didn't give off that vibe. Intentional or not, Arnsfeld's wealth had been a smokescreen.

Topher and the Association had also led them to the RCR and, despite the odds of having two major crimes going on at the same time on a small island like PEI, that appears to be what happened. Maybe Arnsfeld was involved? Maybe he got bored of just running a charity? Maybe money was getting tight after a series of bad investments? Carr's reaction in the interview told him something hinky was going on. But maybe not. Maybe there was no connection beyond Maddix trying to drip some cash out of him. Max wasn't sure they'd ever get the whole truth. Topher Arnsfeld had caught a cold and had been home when he should have been at the office. More smoke.

His wife, however, had been in the thick of it. According

to Helen Camille, Stephanie Arnsfeld had run a high-end brothel for select town clientele using the local teenage Amish girls on rumspringa as her lures. Max was still having trouble wrapping his head around the concept. Not that it was possible, he was well aware of the ongoing depravities of human sex trafficking, but that a girl in high school would be the ringleader and have the means and will to keep everyone quiet for so many years.

But quiet about what? That was still the big question left unanswered. And, who else had she kept under her thumb other than Hawkins and Harrow? Max was sure this wasn't over. This guy wasn't just going to kill and walk away. It would end with a bang. So, who else? They had Mulvaney's story about Stephanie bringing another girl in for a surreptitious after-hours exam but that looked to be a dead end with the stolen record unless they could get someone to identify the people in the photos from Harrow's box.

He pulled the case file over and made more notes on the inside cover. They needed to talk to Diana Goulart again. This time not on her porch with a bottle of wine. He knew that Koenig could play the bad cop if needed. If not her, they'd have to find Nik Labat.

More thoughts: Why had the killer waited so long? Who had left that note in his mailbox?

CHAPTER FORTY-SIX

All the questions left him feeling restless and brooding. The thought of eating dry toast for breakfast made his throat ache, so he tossed the dregs of his lukewarm coffee in the sink, swallowed two more Aleve, apologizing silently to his liver, then dumped a few extra pills into his pants pocket. He took the case file and Mose's materials out to the car and drove the old police sedan into town to the Sugar Maple.

It was early, but not for a baker. Ellie was flour-dusted and smiling, which Max believed was likely her default mood most of the time. She was one of those people.

"How are you feeling? How's the head?"

"Finally, the Prince Creek party line has something wrong. It isn't my head, not exactly, it's my neck and shoulders." He held up his wrist. "And my wrist, but this was mostly self-inflicted."

"I will make that correction. How's the neck and shoulders then?"

"I feel a bit like the Tin Man in the Wizard of Oz. Stiff

and sore and creaky. I need to turn my whole body to look behind me, but I'll live."

"Let's hope nobody sneaks up on you then. What can I get you?"

"Large coffee and one of those chocolate chip muffins, please." Caffeine, sugar, and fat. "To go." He knew if he sat down, he'd eventually eat another muffin and he was sure one pastry had enough calories to get him through to lunch. He was already abusing his liver with the Aleve, no need to open a second front with his gut.

Ellie poured his large coffee and put two muffins in the bag. She smiled. "Give one to that Mountie partner of yours. I know she likes them."

Now it was Max's turn to smile. The woman didn't miss much. "I think this place will be a success."

"Thanks, Max. Can I ask you something before you run off?"

"Is this for the party line?"

She glanced around. "Sort of."

"Go ahead, ask."

"These murders? Should I be worried? Maybe take off for a while?"

So, people were worried. That could be a useful thing. People would be wary and on guard. That might notice something. "You should be careful, but I don't think you need to close the shop. This is happening for a very specific reason."

"And what's that?"

He hesitated, but he didn't think that was a detail he could share yet. "If only you'd opened The Maple 20 years ago, I'm sure you could tell me and solve this thing in one shot."

Max dodged past the comm center where Marline was on the

phone and found Koenig at an empty desk in the bullpen area. She looked clean and fresh and smiled at him. He glanced at the small photo on the corner of the desk, Chravette and a blonde woman with a deep tan on a boat somewhere. The deputy was nowhere to be seen so he took a seat opposite her.

"How was the motel?" he asked.

"Not as good as this dumpy trailer I visited."

He looked around. He could hear keyboard keys clacking behind D'arcy's cube walls, but the rest of the place was empty. "You could have stayed."

"I know but this town has enough to talk about already."

He left it at that and handed her the grease-spotted bag. "Ellie sends her regards. Or at least a muffin."

She snatched it up and took three big bites. He wasn't sure she even chewed. She took a sip from her coffee mug. "Didn't I tell you I liked that woman? Even makes this black breakroom swill taste passable."

She finished the muffin and then said, "Let's go see Roy. Figure out how to end this."

Roy was on the phone, but motioned them into the chairs and finished up the call quickly.

"Mayor?" Koenig asked.

"You guessed it. She's called twice and it's not even 9 a.m. Pretty sure the only reason I still have a job is that there are no suitable alternatives. The press conference bought me a little time, but even that is running low now."

"You find anything from those names Mulvaney gave us?"

He pulled a pile of paper closer. "Sure, he gave us, uh, eight names, right? Two are deceased. Natural causes. Two no longer live on the island. Four are still around and they're all wealthy, or well off, retired, and puttering around trying to fill up their days."

"You talked to all of them? The remaining four in town?"

"We talked to three of them. One guy, let's see, LaVerne, was off golfing in Summerside. We'll get to him today just to cross his name off the list. But I don't expect much. They all did business with, or knew of, Hawkins and they knew Harrow, at least socially, given their wealth and status in town."

"What did you tell them?"

"Just that we were looking into Hawkins's and Harrow's past. They didn't blink, but I'm not sure this is getting us any closer to finding this fruitcake."

"The names are about trying to find out who he might target. We're holding both ends of the stick and trying to work toward the middle. Faster than he is," Koenig replied.

"I get it. It just makes me uncomfortable."

"What we need, I think, is more names. I've got another list, but that's not enough. We need to get more," Max added.

"I don't know. It seems like a potential waste of resources."

"We're looking for the names that appear more than once. We get enough names those will start to pop. That's who we look at."

"I don't know."

Max could see Roy was feeling the public and political pressure and wasn't going to be convinced. Anything he did would be safe and careful. Max dropped it and instead asked, "How about the other end. Did you trace down the alibis for the Amish men?"

He perked up a little at that, happy to be on more solid footing. "We did run most of those down. We're still checking on the guy that did the delivery in town, but the rest check out. It gives us a timeline to work off if we bring any of them in."

"I haven't seen those interviews yet. I'd like to get a look at them," Koenig said.

"Not a problem," Roy replied. "D'arcy has all the paper."

"Anything on Labat? We might need to talk to him again."

Roy scratched at his day-old stubble. "That might be a problem. No one's seen him since you guys talked to him on Saturday. We've got a bulletin out to the RCMP and the surrounding towns, plus Father White and some of the church people are checking their contacts but so far everyone's come up empty."

They all thought about what that might mean.

"Then I think we need to bring in Diana Goulart. Push her hard on the identities of the girls that Steph used."

"We can definitely do that," Roy said. "I'm coming. I need to get out of here before the mayor calls back."

CHAPTER FORTY-SEVEN

They might have come on too strong. It might have been Roy insisting on going in with his lights lit up. Or maybe Diana could just sense the net tightening around her, but by the time they'd all parked and made it inside Tiny Island Beach Glass, empty on an early Tuesday morning, she already had the phone in her hand. She held it out toward Roy as they all filled up the space around the cash register.

"My solicitor," she said.

Roy glanced over at Koenig, clearly not expecting her to pull the trigger on a lawyer so soon. She stepped in, "Ms. Goulart, my name is Inspector Imogen Koenig with Major Crimes out of Charlotteville. Talking to a solicitor is well within your rights and we will respect that. We can go down to the Prince Creek PD and have your solicitor meet us there and do that whole dance. However, things are moving quickly, and we are trying to catch a murderer before he kills anyone else. We are not trying to cut corners, but we are also trying not to waste time. You are not a suspect, but we believe you may have vital information that could help us. Vital information you may not even know that you know."

Max could hear tiny squawking from the speaker of the mobile phone and assumed that the solicitor was having a small coronary at Koenig's posturing but, until he or she was there in person, they were powerless to stop it.

Koenig continued, "If we could just ask you a few questions now, we could be out of your way quickly and let you get on with minding your store. If we take you down for a formal interview, it will take time. There is also the chance that if something were to happen in the interim, you could end up charged with obstruction or as an accessory if the information you withhold now could have helped prevent a crime."

Goulart's face hardened at the threat. She did not resemble the worn-down woman with perhaps a bit too much fondness for wine that Max had spoken to in her backyard the previous week. There was a reason this conspiracy had stayed in the shadows for 20 years. Whatever had happened back then, whatever information she held in her head, it was locked up tight. She wouldn't be broken so easily.

She lifted the phone a little higher. "My solicitor," she repeated.

They drove Goulart back to the station. She opted to sit in the back of Roy's official SUV. At the station, Roy led her to one of the empty interview rooms and then it was a waiting game. They didn't try to talk to her, and she didn't say a word to them other than to ask for the restroom once and for a glass of water another time.

Goulart's solicitor was no rinky-dink local lawyer. Felicity Clarkson specialized in high-profile criminal cases with offices off-island in Moncton. Three hours after they'd first heard her tinny voice screaming over the mobile phone, she breezed into the police station wearing a bright red jacket and matching skirt, looking like she was ready to rain down hell on all of them.

"Which room?" she asked.

Koenig pointed to the first door; they'd left it open. Clarkson entered and shut the door.

"Not what I was expecting," Koenig said. They'd spent much of their waiting time reading over the reports the deputies had filed when they'd checked the Amish men's alibis along with the more skeletal notes D'arcy had put together on the men from Mulvaney's list. Two of the men on Mulvaney's list were also on Thorne's list. The rest of the time they'd spent arguing about where to go for lunch. "I wonder how she affords her. She seemed to get her on the phone pretty quickly this morning."

"Part of the payoff?" Max suggested. "Like seed capital for the shop?"

"That would be my guess. From what we learned of Stephanie Arnsfeld, she wouldn't leave anything to chance. If the cops come calling, keep your mouth shut and call this number."

"She talked to me the first time."

Koenig shrugged. "Maybe that was a way of finding out what we wanted. Knee jerk reaction call to a lawyer doesn't look great for just a background interview."

They went back to arguing about lunch. Max pushed for one of the kid's burgers and Koenig stumped for one of the food trucks down near the beach. Another 30 minutes passed before Clarkson opened the door again.

"We're ready."

Koenig and Roy went inside. They all agreed they shouldn't put Max near anything official. He watched from the observation room and was happy to have the glass separating himself from Clarkson. She went on a blistering rant about their treatment of Goulart that morning and the implicit threats Koenig had made. Koenig countered that they were not threats but only suggestions. And they weren't lies. There was a clock ticking on this. That brought a withering look, but Max thought Koenig held her own. Roy stayed quiet and out of the fray. The initial opening salvos set the tone and they spent much of the next hour in trench warfare that brought no fresh information.

Finally, Clarkson threw up her hands. "I think we're done. My client has been more than cooperative. We request that you either formally bring charges or release her."

Roy wanted no part of Clarkson and Max didn't blame him. All they had were rumors and high school memories that Goulart and Stephanie had been best friends. If they wanted another shot at Goulart, it was clear they'd need to gather more hard information.

"Worth a shot," Max said as they watched Goulart climb into Clarkson's Mercedes and pull out of the lot.

"Waste of time. We just burned through more than half the day," Roy said.

"Not entirely. No one who is completely innocent reacts like that. Clarkson was over the top. Any competent lawyer in town could have stonewalled us. It was like weeding your garden with a flamethrower."

CHAPTER FORTY-EIGHT

Koenig said she'd lost her appetite and went back to the deputies' notes. Max decided grease and cheese would make a good antidote for his foul mood. And maybe a walk back and forth to The Rink wouldn't hurt either. He could feel his muscles stiffening up the more he sat in the rickety bullpen chair. He called in his order, confirmed that the kid was working the grill, and got a grunting '10 minutes' from Jerry. He grabbed the thin book Mose had dropped off at the trailer and slipped out of the station by the back door.

Marline was smoking just outside. "Hey, stud," she said, with a smile that suggested she was contemplating certain acts that might be illegal in Canada.

"Hi, Marline. Can I ask you a question?"

"Sure."

He knew most of her randy tomcat persona was an act, but he still found it unsettling. He decided the radio array behind the station was extremely interesting and integral to the conversation. "How long have you been one of the dispatchers for Prince Creek?"

"Is this a roundabout way of asking me my age?"

"No, no. It's about the case."

"Oh, that might be even better." And Max realized he might have found her kryptonite. She had that small-town thirst for gossip. "Let's see, Jermane is my third chief, so that goes back to right around the millennium. I think I started in May 2000."

So, not before this entire thing started, Max thought, *but maybe close enough*. "What did you do before the dispatcher job? You lived in town?"

"Oh, sure. Was born in Cardigan but moved to the big city after high school. I worked part-time as a cashier at Town 'n Tide. Sometimes helped at my sister's shop up on 335."

"I wonder if you could do me a favor? Could you come up with a list ..."

He explained what he wanted and, after stamping out her second cigarette, she agreed. Maybe a bit too eagerly, Max thought, but he was also sure he'd have more names by the time he finished lunch.

While it was on his mind, he went back inside.

"Change your mind on the burger?" Koenig asked when he sat down.

"No, the kid is probably flipping it right now. I ran into Marline outside and asked her about coming up with a list of names."

"Might get more than you bargained for there."

"Maybe, but I don't mind more right now. I thought I might also call those two lawyers that knew Hawkins back in the day, Campbell and Lee."

He could read the skepticism on her face. She wasn't buying his big data approach. Even if his big data only amounted to half a dozen lists and maybe 50 names. "Anything in the interviews?"

"Not really. Still some time gaps someone could wiggle through but nothing else is jumping out."

"What do we have to lose? Goulart is stonewalling us. Labat is in the wind. The Amish guys all have decent alibis. What else can we do?"

She shrugged. "Your call."

Something was eating at her, but he wasn't sure what. He let it go and took out his phone. Aldis Campbell picked up on the second ring and Max re-introduced himself and explained the reason for his call.

"Huh?" Campbell said when Max finished. "I have no idea how the courts might look at it, but I sort of like the idea. And now you got my brain spinning. Give me your email address and I'll shoot over some names soon."

He called Campbell's colleague, Safford Lee, next. He knew Lee was across the continent in Vancouver visiting his grandkids, but finally, after a pregnant pause, there were a few canned rings and Lee picked up. He had a deeper, phlegmatic voice than Campbell, and Max pictured a portly man in a colorful sweater vest.

Without the benefit of a prior face-to-face, it took longer to explain the reason for his call to Lee. Max wasn't sure if it made him a better lawyer than his friend, but Lee asked a lot more questions. Eventually, Lee agreed to talk to Campbell to vet Max and, if his friend signed off, he would send a list of names to Max.

As he walked out the back door for the second time, Max thought he'd at least accomplished something in exchange for a cold burger.

Twenty minutes later, he was sitting on a bench in the dockside park with a white takeout container on his knees watching the last fishing boats coming back and a few tourist boats cruise around. The fries were hot and made up for the lukewarm burger. He'd grabbed a Diet Coke out of the cooler from the little bait and tackle shop on the corner. He stopped thinking about the case for ten minutes and just ate his food and watched the scene.

Despite Felicity Clarkson putting a damper on their morning, he was feeling okay by the time he finished the burger. He threw the food container in a nearby garbage can. He'd been right. Cheese and grease and a little sunshine weren't a bad cure. They were cracking this thing, Max was sure. It was just taking longer than he expected. They had time ... maybe. He worried that the killer was cracking. Talking up the case had given them fresh leads, but maybe it had amped up the pressure on the killer as well.

He took a slow loop around the park. It didn't take long. It was a pocket park squeezed onto some otherwise unusable land, bordered on one side by the water, on the right by the marina, and hemmed in by the road and accompanying seawall. It looked nice; it *was* nice but was in an awkward spot and often empty. Max knew it was one of Nik Labat's preferred spots, but he didn't see the troubled man today. Where was he?

He returned to the bench and checked his email on his phone. Marline and Aldis Campbell had already sent their lists. Marline added a note that she would keep thinking about it and would it be all right to ask her sister. Max responded that would be fine. Campbell mentioned he'd spoken to Safford Lee and told him to stop being a stick in the mud and give Max some names. The list was growing. He would go back to the station, check in with Koenig, and then build a master list and cross-reference the names. With any luck, the lists would show some consensus and they could warn potential victims or, if Roy didn't want to do that, maybe circulate more patrols by their houses.

Big nimbus clouds were pushing in again from the west but, if the pattern of the last few days held, the rain would hold off until evening. Or miss them entirely. Sitting on the bench, stomach full, the warm humid air mixed with the briny ocean breeze felt good on his skin. He grudgingly stood and started back toward the station but took a circuitous route. He told himself he was looking for Labat but, in reality, he just wasn't eager to return to the recirculated air and burnt coffee perfume of the police station, even with the prospect of Koenig sitting across from him.

CHAPTER FORTY-NINE

Max worked his way away from the water, walking down a few cross streets, eventually ending up back on Main Street a block south of Town Hall and *The Chronicle's* office. He recalled that Thorne had planned to talk to the paper's old editor, Bill Haas, yesterday about Collum Hawkins. Maybe Haas could also gin up a list to add to the mix? From what Thorne said, the man had had a keen ear for gossip.

Away from the sea breeze, the air was thick and hot, and he was sweating again as he stepped inside the office. The front room was empty. Thorne hadn't been in his usual booth at The Rink when Max picked up his food. Maybe he was out reporting a story. Max went around the front counter and sat at the desk with the typewriter and the Olympic mug. The Vancouver games were in 2010, only a decade earlier, but it felt like a lifetime. Max had been another person. It was right before his life exploded.

He remembered watching the gold medal hockey game with Danny. USA versus Canada. The US had tied it late by pulling the goalie. He and Danny had gone nuts when Parise scored. Cindy had been so mad because it had woken up Kylie from her nap. The celebration was short-lived. Sidney Crosby had won it for Canada in overtime. He nudged the mug with his knuckle. So much dust. All of them gone now. Dust to dust. He had a different life. He was no one. He had no one.

He slipped a sheet of printer paper out of the package that sat unused on the desk. He'd leave a note and stick it under the door leading up to Thorne's apartment. He was searching through the pens in the mug for one that would write when he heard a noise, a muffled crash and grunt, from somewhere deeper in the building.

"Thorne?" He walked back through the kitchen into the crowded storage area in back. He followed another thud to a half-open door next to a teetering stack of yellowing newspapers in the corner.

"Dammit," a voice said from below. *Definitely Thorne*, Max thought.

"Thorne, you down there?"

"Max, is that you?"

"Yeah."

"Ask and it shall be given. Seek and you will find."

A Bible quote, interesting, thought Max.

"Knock and it shall be opened to you," he responded. "I was just leaving you a note."

Max descended the stairs into an area somehow more chaotic and disorderly than the room above. The ceilings were low and bare, showing the joists and floorboards above. A mismatched mélange of old filing cabinets, shelving units, and stacked cardboard boxes filled the space, sometimes forming tight aisles, other times petering out into dead ends. Occasional lightbulbs with pull strings hung around the space.

"Over here," Thorne called out. Max carefully walked, turning sideways when necessary to avoid knocking over any stacks, following the lightbulbs like breadcrumbs to a makeshift aisle where he found Thorne kneeling by an open box. Max spotted a few fallen and cratered boxes farther down that were likely the source of Thorne's shouts.

"Welcome to *The Chronicle's* morgue." He flung one arm out, almost knocking over another box. "All the news that was fit to print about Prince Creek since 1908."

"That far back?"

"No, not really. The paper started publishing in 1908, but that grant I mentioned took all the ancient stuff out for preservation. There are still some disintegrating boxes down here from at least the 1940s though."

Max glanced down at the particular box Thorne was searching in. It was full of photos, but not from the 1940s. "But you're not going that far back."

"No, but you are the reason I'm down here stuffing my sinuses with dust and old newsprint and other things I don't care to think about. I drove over to Montague and talked to Bill Hass on Monday. We got lucky. He was having a lucid day, for the most part, he kept calling me Jimmy, that was his son, but his memories were sharp. I asked about Hawkins. He remembered the man and described him to a T. He wasn't mixed up on that."

"Did he have any idea what made Hawkins quit and become the town recluse?"

"No, nothing more than the same rumors you heard about drinking and possible censure from the Bar Association. He remembered something else I found interesting. I mentioned Colby Harrow also being killed recently and he said maybe he should watch his own back as someone was knocking off old bowlers."

"Bowlers?" Something pricked at Max's memory.

"Apparently, Bill Haas was an avid bowler. Prince Creek used to have its own 10-lane, 10-pin setup off Route 2 where

Carquest Auto Parts is now. The town had an active and competitive league. Haas said Harrow and Hawkins were on a team called The Holy Rollers. He thought it was strange two members had been murdered so close together."

Max remembered now. The old bowling bag he'd seen in Harrow's bedroom closet. "That is a little strange, I guess. Did he remember any other members of The Holy Rollers?"

"No, he sort of faded out at that point, but he said they won the league a couple times and he was always a little piqued that he had to put their picture along with a brief story in his paper. So, I'm down here looking for that picture."

"Why not look for the paper if he was complaining about putting it in?"

"Ah," Thorne said, pointing a finger. "Excellent question. Let's just say Bill's writing and reporting were far superior to his organizational skills. Now, Emily Jean, his long-suffering wife, gave up on trying to help him years before, but she was also the unofficial town photographer and was much better with her management of the photos and negatives."

"And?" Max knew from Thorne's bar stories that he liked to gild the lily if possible with drama.

Thorne pulled out a faded 4x6 photo. "And I found it." He held it out and Max took it.

He tilted it toward the light and immediately recognized the bar and photo-covered walls. "Taken at The Rink, huh?"

"Yup, they must have gone there for a post-victory cele-bration."

In a way it was another list, just a visual one. The photo showed four middle-aged men, each holding a glass of beer, their arms around each other, sweating and disheveled, smiling at the camera. He could see Jerry, slightly out of focus, behind the bar, but also looking up toward the camera. Each man wore matching white and red bowling shirts with

what appeared to be their first names stenciled on the pockets. It was hard to make out in the photo. Max recognized
Hawkins on one end. Harrow was standing on the opposite
side. "You recognize the two in the middle?"

"No, before my time."

"But someone around here will."

"Definitely. Just need to ask the right person."

"Isn't that always the trick?"

CHAPTER FIFTY

Koenig was walking across the parking lot toward the Explorer when Max made it back to the station.

"Was just going to find you."

"Got something?"

"D'arcy talked to the woman that Issac Riehl delivered the furniture to last Tuesday. He arrived around 2:30 p.m. she says, brought the pieces in, set them up, and was finished by 3 or 3:15 p.m. at the latest."

"If I remember, that's what he told me on Saturday. He dropped off the furniture, went back home and had supper with his family."

"I'm not saying it's not true, but it's the only alibi from the Amish guys that leaves enough wiggle room. We've tightened up the rest to the point where I think it's very unlikely that any of them are involved."

Max pictured Issac Riehl with his coiled intensity, reddish beard, smoking his hand-rolled cigarettes, standing next to the taller Mose at the end of the line of horses during the community picnic. "He's about the right height, I think. And he's a woodworker so he'd have easy access to tools. What do you want to do?"

"Let's go talk to him. Maybe talk to the wife."

"You find Labat?" Koenig asked as they drove Route 304 in search of Riehl's furniture shop.

"No, he's still AWOL, but I found this." He held up the photo that Thorne had given him. Koenig glanced over at it for a moment. "Always had a thing for men in bowling shirts."

"That right?"

"Maybe it's just men in uniform."

"That sounds like something for your therapist, not your partner."

"We're partners now? You give yourself a promotion?"

"We are for a few more days at least."

"As long as you keep bringing me muffins. I don't think she'll poison me if she thinks there's a chance you might eat them, too." She glanced over at the photo again. "Where did this come from? I recognize Hawkins and Harrow. Who are the other two?"

"It came from *The Chronicle's* old files. Thorne dug it up after talking to Bill Haas. We don't know the names of the other two. Not yet."

"But you think it's relevant?"

"You don't? It's the only connection we've found between Hawkins and Harrow."

"But we already knew they ran in the same circles."

"I think we assumed that was the case, but we haven't been able to confirm who else was in that circle and who might have received invites to Stephanie Arnsfeld's parties."

"And you think his bowling team might be in the circle?"

"It shows a certain closeness. You don't spend that much time with people you don't like. Got any other ideas?"

"Don't get your panties in a wad. I didn't say it was a terrible idea. After we talk to Riehl, we'll start on that. Maybe they'll be on your lists."

"Very funny."

As they drove through the surrounding countryside, Max took out the thin book he'd asked Mose if he could borrow and began flipping through the pages.

"What's that? Where you'd get it?" Her tone was sharper than usual, and Max glanced up.

"Mose lent it to me. While I was lying in the hospital, it occurred to me that we had another list available to us." He held up the book. "It's the church directory of Prince Edward Island. It lists Amish families, children, descendants, births, and deaths on the island. Think of it like the Amish Internet. Or maybe the old Yellow Pages. Mose tells me every community around the country has a version. Sort of a cross-reference and a living history."

He flipped to the R's and found Riehl and read down the rows of names. "This is strange," he said.

"What?"

"Isaac Riehl is listed. The Riehls were early settlers here from Ontario. He was born here on the island. He's married to Sarah, nee Raber, and has four children, at least at the time they printed this."

"What's curious about that? He's young, but large families are the norm with the Amish, right?"

"Sure, but he's the only Riehl left on PEI. It appears the rest left for a different settlement."

"Huh. That is a little strange."

They found Riehl's shop near the intersection with 305, as

he'd said. It was close to the road, with a small dirt parking lot and was surrounded by potato farms. There was no signage. Max figured if you knew what you were looking for you'd find it. Or maybe the Amish viewed advertising as pride and an affront to God. He'd have to ask Mose.

The shop was a single-story white rectangle with a low-pitched roof and wide barn doors opened on the short side of the building facing the parking lot. They could hear the clang of tools as they parked and climbed out, the smell of fresh-cut wood and sawdust mixed with the turned earth and fertilizer of the nearby farms. There were a few finished pieces set outside near the open doors, but this wasn't a showroom. This was a working woodshop.

A man stepped outside as they approached. He must have seen them park. Koenig glanced at him. Max shook his head. It wasn't Issac Riehl. This man was Amish, however. He had the identifiable chinstrap beard framing a pair of thin, gold-rimmed glasses balanced on a thin, knife-like nose. A tangle of curling brown hair receded from his forehead. He'd rolled his blue shirt sleeves above his elbows, sawdust flecked his beard and forearms.

"Help you, folks?" He said it pleasantly, but there was a guardedness about his eyes. The deputies had been out here before. He knew they weren't customers. He brushed absently at his arms and wiped his brow with a handkerchief.

Koenig held out her creds and introduced herself. He just nodded at what he knew all along.

"I'm Jonah. I'm Pretty's partner. Pretty's not here right now. He's out on a delivery and then likely headed home."

"Sorry," Koenig said, "Pretty? Is that Mr. Riehl?"

"Isaac, yes. As you can imagine, we've got quite a few Isaacs in the community. Can't throw a rock without hitting a John, Aaron, Daniel, or Isaac so most have picked up nicknames over the years. Half of them make little sense and we've forgotten the origin but the nicknames stick." He shrugged as if that's all there was to say.

"Okay, makes sense. So, Isaac is gone for the day?" Koenig said.

"Given the time, I expect so, yes."

"An officer was out earlier this week to talk to you?"

"That's right. Corporal Alford stopped by. He talked to me and Isaac."

"You remember anything else since then?"

Jonah wiped at his brow again. "Can't say that I do. They didn't have much to ask me."

"How long have you worked with Isaac?"

"Oh, a long time now, I guess. We opened the shop maybe 10 years ago."

"It's a little unusual for two men to open a business together, isn't it?" Max asked.

"You mean two Amish men? Yes, I suppose, but we found we complimented one another. Pretty is good at the finishing work. I'm a little better at the initial cuts. We were young, unmarried, and just starting out and the community thought it made sense."

"So, you get along all right?"

"We've lasted this long, so I suppose so. We have our disagreements from time to time." He paused as if debating something. "Pretty can sometimes be a little stubborn, maybe heated, about how certain things are done. I'm a little more easygoing, so it usually works out."

"Hmm," Koenig said and then moved on. "Mind if we take a quick look in your shop?"

"Sure, no problem," Jonah said and waved a hand toward the open doors.

There was a sense of organization inside, but Max wouldn't call it neat or tidy. Everything had a place, but you needed to know where to look. Long tables and benches were laid out around the space and supplies, sheets of raw wood and smaller tools were scattered like satellites along the walls and among the benches. There were no modern table saws or drill presses, but as Max wandered around the room he spotted a dizzying array of hand planes, spokeshaves, chisels, mallets, files, cabinet scrapers, and more hand tools that he couldn't identify.

He was about to step back outside, Koenig was asking Jonah a few more followup questions, when he stopped next to a simple table that was upside down on a bench being stained. Something had caught his attention. He stopped and let his eyes drift back over the Shaker table. It was a simple design with clean lines that were rounded at the edges. It had a small skirt that ran around the length just under the tabletop, otherwise the piece was empty of ornamentation. What had caught his eye? He leaned over and looked closely at the underside of the table. Another tumbler clicked into place.

In the corner was a small carving of four letters, only an inch or two high, but carefully carved and legible. IRJS. The initials of the creators, Issac Riehl and Jonah Sprauge. He'd seen this before. Not the letters themselves, but the carving style. At Norris Pond, in the moldering little changing room at the end of the crumbling dock. LR + AB. He glanced over at Jonah and Koenig. Jonah's back was to him. He took out his phone and snapped a few quick photos of the letters and then walked back outside.

Max waited until they were back in the car.

"I think he's our guy. Riehl."

Koenig looked at him. "Because Sprauge said he sometimes gets intense? Seems a little thin."

"No, not just that." He pulled out his phone and showed

her the pics. "Someone carved this into the underside of one of the tables. Recognize it?"

The long, straight road was empty. She glanced over and then put her eyes back on the road. Max kept silent. He wanted to see if she came to the same conclusion or if he was jumping at shadows. She tapped a fingernail on the steering wheel. "The pond."

"Exactly."

He scrolled back through his photos to the one he took at Norris Pond. "The letters carved on that beam were LR + AB. The R is almost identical." He took out the church directory again and found the page with the Riehls. "He also has a sister named Leah."

Issac Riehl's wife was a thin woman with a sharp angular face and straight thin hair streaked prematurely with gray. She might come across as severe on looks alone if she had been able to meet anyone's eye. Max's aunt would have called her a shrinking violet. She answered the door but quickly put her eyes on their shoes. Max could see three children, ranging in age from a toddler up to six or seven, gathered around a doorway in the background. The middle child was a girl; she was clutching a simple burlap doll to her chest while sucking the thumb of her other hand.

They had stopped at Jacob the Younger's house on their way. Bethany had told them where to find the Riehls' homestead. It hadn't been far, just a few miles farther north on 305. Like most of the homes in the community, it was a simple two-story box painted white with a small porch running along the front. A separate smaller outbuilding, maybe a workshop or storage shed, was partially visible in the back. Smoke drifted from a metal stovepipe jutting from the corner of the roof.

"Yes?" Sarah Riehl said in a soft voice.

"Mrs. Riehl, my name is Inspector Imogen Koenig with the RCMP. We were hoping to have a few quick words with your husband."

She stepped out and let the door ease shut behind her. "He's not home."

"Do you expect him back soon?"

Max watched her eyes drift off behind them. "He is usually home for supper."

Not exactly an answer, Max thought.

"And that's soon?" Koenig prodded.

"Yes, but he also has a delivery today, I believe."

"That's correct. We just spoke with Mr. Sprauge at the shop. He thought Isaac might be back."

"No, not yet."

Max had a sense they wouldn't learn much from Sarah Riehl. The woman either didn't know her husband or didn't want to know. He glanced at Koenig and could see she had come to the same conclusion. "Is that your husband's shed out back?" Max asked.

"Yes."

"Mind if we take a quick look?"

"He keeps it locked."

"Oh," Max said. He knew, again from talks with Mose, that most Amish had locks on their doors for when they were away from their property or for use at night, but many didn't use them and preferred to leave the doors open in case anyone who needed help could enter. To have a lock on a shed was a little peculiar. "Do you have a key?"

For the first time since they arrived, she raised her eyes and looked them in the eye. "No."

"You saw the girl's doll?" Max asked.

"No face."

"*We are all alike in God's eyes.*" Those Amish dolls are in all the souvenir shops on the island. Should have thought of it earlier when Labat was talking about dolls and souls, but I didn't make the connection. We should have been out here sooner."

"Neither of us have kids. No reason to connect his ramblings about dolls to the community."

"We were looking for clues. We knew he was involved. We should have picked apart anything he said."

"I was there, too, remember. He went loopy. He was rambling and I'm still not convinced Labat freaking out about dolls has nothing to do with Riehl's sister. He's a sick man."

The sun hung low on the horizon as they drove back toward town. It lit up the undersides of the approaching storm clouds in dark, vivid hues of orange, red, and purple.

"Wouldn't have minded a quick poke around that shed," Max said.

"I wouldn't have minded a quick poke around in that woman's head."

"You think we should try to talk to her again. Maybe make it a little more formal?"

"Because that worked out so well with Goulart?"

"I can ask Mose about her. Maybe get a little more of the story."

"If Isaac is our guy, we'll need her for the trial, but I don't know if we need her right now."

"He's the guy."

"Says you."

"It's not just me anymore." He ticked reasons off on his fingers. "It's the carving, the initials, the leaky alibi, familiarity with tools, right height according to Burty, and the locked shed."

"All circumstantial. We need something solid so he can't wiggle free and we can get a warrant for DNA. If he's our guy, we'll find something to put him at one scene."

"He's our guy."

CHAPTER FIFTY-ONE

Pretty rinsed the razor in the small bucket and looked at himself in the mirror. It had been 15 years since he'd seen his clean-shaven cheeks. *Not bad*, he thought. He tried a smile, but it felt wrong. It had never felt right. And other people knew it. His eyes always gave him away.

He dumped the water out and tossed the bucket and razor back into the buggy. It was still too early. He was more comfortable in the dark. He could wait. He was safe for now. There was little risk of anyone finding him down here. No one visited here anymore. Just like his smile, they had defiled it in a way that most people could sense and avoid.

He sat by the edge of the pond. Pretty realized he'd turned a corner. That after this was over, he'd have to go away. But hadn't he always known that? Why else had he bought the razor, the phone, the clothes, and other supplies back in the spring when he'd bought the ax? He smiled at the memory of the ax. No, he'd known this was a one-way trip. He'd have to leave his wife, his children, and the community. He didn't have a problem with that. He felt no emotion over it. If anything, he felt a certain joy in finally being free. Hadn't the community abandoned him and his sister years ago? Hadn't his family? Hadn't the entire town? Why should he show them any loyalty now? It was right there in the Bible: *"The righteous will rejoice when he sees the vengeance; he will bathe his feet in the blood of the wicked."*

Two more killings. It was a matter of honor that had been put off for too long. The wicked were getting old and frail and, if Pretty didn't act soon, they might escape. He could not let that happen. Once they had repaid their debts, Pretty would go away. Then maybe he could find some peace, some rest.

Or maybe not. He thought back to his meeting with Hawkins and to the Arnsfelds' kitchen. There was that satisfying thunk of the ax and the crunch of the hammer. He enjoyed the memories. Maybe he would keep going after he moved on. Maybe he'd continue to be God's sword.

The first stars had appeared over the bay. It was time to go to work. He stood and brushed the bits of dirt and grass from his pants. The clothes felt stiff and foreign on his body, but he figured it was like breaking in a new tool. It would take time to adjust. God would provide. He unhitched the horse from the buggy, grabbed his small bag of supplies, and walked back up the path toward the road. He took out the mobile phone and punched in the number. He'd called earlier when he was in town to make sure the deputy was on duty. It connected and he told the woman his problem. She told him help was on the way.

He smiled. If you couldn't get a gun, make the gun come to you.

The thing Pretty had learned about racism, or xenophobia, or maybe just humanity, was that it was often predictable and stupid. It wasn't difficult to make bigots do what you wanted.

Deputy Stratton pulled up in his squad car ten minutes later, lights flashing but no siren. Pretty checked the road; it was empty in both directions. No cars had passed since he called. It was one reason, one of many, that he had picked this spot.

Stratton had given him some token harassment in the two years they had employed him at the Prince Creek PD, but Pretty was far from his favorite target. He didn't think the racist cop would recognize him, at least not right away, and maybe not at all with his shaved beard. He was counting on the momentary confusion.

Stratton climbed out of the patrol car.

"Hi, Officer, thanks for getting here so quick," Pretty called. He stood just outside the reach of the headlights holding his small carry all.

"Call said an Amish man was having trouble with his buggy." Pretty knew Stratton would jump on any call involving the Amish.

"That's right. Horse got spooked just down the lane here," Pretty started slowly walking backward, "and one of the wheels got wedged up in an old rotted stump. Just plain bad luck, but I think with both of us pushing we should be able to get her out." He kept walking, but Stratton stayed where he was.

"You don't look like anyone from the 305."

Pretty looked down at himself. "Oh, the clothes. Yes, we're trying something new for those of us who regularly go into town for deliveries or the produce markets. Help others feel more at ease."

Stratton finally started moving down the shallow hill toward Pretty and the entrance to Sinclair Road. "That sounds like a real good idea. Never understood why you had to keep yourselves separate and dress differently. Like you were better than the rest of us."

"Not at all, Officer. We try to stay humble." Pretty reached the entrance to the narrow, overgrown road. While there was enough light to see up on Route 16, it was a deeper, darker blackness down here on the edge of the wooded path. He slipped the woodworking chisel out of the front pocket of his jeans. It might be mistaken for a screwdriver. It had the same basic shape: a handle grip and a slim metallic end. But the chisel had a sturdy and very sharp tip. He'd used this very tool in the past to carve through hickory like softened butter. He didn't think he'd have any problem with Deputy Stratton.

"Hmmph. Could have fooled me."

He heard Stratton pause, maybe regretting not grabbing his flashlight. "In there? What were you doing down there at this time of day?"

Pretty ignored the second part of the question and kept walking. "Yup, just around the bend there. Not far. I've got a battery-powered lantern."

After a moment, he heard the man's footsteps follow. He wouldn't want to be considered a coward. Not by an uppity Amish man. Stupid, racist, and predictable. He should have listened to whatever had made him stop on the threshold of the road, Isaac thought.

Too late now.

He'd paced it off earlier. He didn't think the odds of a car passing at the exact moment he struck were high, but why take the chance? After 20 steps, they were fully concealed from the road. He slowed and let Stratton get closer, and then he tripped. Or pretended to. He felt Stratton instinctively reach out to steady him.

"Easy there," he said.

Pretty dropped the bag, pivoted back, and drove the steel chisel up and into the deputy's stomach. There was a sudden gasp and Stratton looked down in surprise. He pushed Pretty backward and, this time, Pretty did trip. He hadn't been expecting that, but he recovered quickly. Stratton was backpedaling, trying to unsnap the holster on his belt while keeping a hand over the bleeding wound. Pretty ran at him. He was smaller than the deputy, but he was determined. And he had God on his side.

There was more blood than he expected. Both his hands and forearms were slick with it and he could feel some on his face. He should have thought to bring another shirt, but maybe Stratton had extra clothes in his patrol car. Or he could take something from Brown's house. He still needed to be out in public tonight, so he took the time to jog back to the pond and rinse as much blood as he could from his skin. He could just make out the dimmer shadow of his nearby horse as she ripped and chewed at the waterside reeds and rushes. He scrubbed his face, still finding the soft smoothness of his cheeks alien, but thankfully easier to clean, and then jogged back up the path.

Stratton was dead. He dragged the man into the brush on the side of the road and removed the gun from his holster. He'd never handled a gun before in his life. It was lighter than he expected and felt slick and dangerous in his hand. He put it in his gear bag and then patted down the rest of Stratton's body for the car keys but didn't find them. He must have left them in the vehicle. He unclipped the handcuffs and dropped those in the bag, too. He was about to step away when he looked at the chisel. He'd embedded the blade up to the wooden hilt in the left side of Stratton's chest. One of Stratton's hands was wrapped loosely around it as if he made one last effort to pull it out. Should he take it? It was a good sharp tool and might come in handy later in the night, but he ultimately decided to leave it as a calling card or perhaps a warning for the rest of the racist trash in the department.

The keys were in the ignition. Taking the time to wash up had been smart, but he felt like he was pushing his luck staying here any longer. He got behind the wheel and figured out how to adjust the seat forward and turn off the emergency lights. The car was large and bulky, and the dashboard was filled with knobs and buttons and dials. Just like the gun, he'd only had a few instances in his life to be inside a car, never mind try to drive one but he understood the basic concepts and figured if an oaf like Stratton could do it, so could he. He would only need to drive for a brief distance.

After a few halting, jerking attempts, he managed to turn the car around and proceed back to town. He took it slow. He didn't think that would be suspicious. Cops cruised slowly all the time. He turned right before passing the police station. He'd heard the dispatcher calling to check in with Stratton twice already. He tried to turn off the radio but kept hitting the wrong switch. He eventually gave up and the dispatcher's increasingly calls put him on edge. He turned into Main Street Hardware and pulled around back. He had one last thing to do before he paid Goodwin Brown a visit. He hopped out of the car and grabbed the length of tubing from his bag.

As he drove down Brown's street, he worried about leaving the patrol car on the street. Even at night, without the sirens, a police car makes people sit up and take notice. Maybe get too curious. The timing was crucial here if he was going to pull this off. He slowed as he approached Brown's blue and black Victorian and exhaled. He shouldn't have worried. God, as always, looked out for his flock. The driveway wrapped around to a separate freestanding garage. The car wouldn't be visible from the street. There was a light on in the back and one on up on the second floor. He followed the driveway and stopped as close as he could to the back door.

He grabbed the gun, handcuffs, and plastic milk jug from where he'd placed them in the passenger footwell and then climbed out. The back door had a large glass pane and Pretty was about to knock when he saw a man walking down the hall toward the door, a look of puzzlement on his fat face. His face wasn't the only fat thing about him. It defined him. It ran down in a solid mass from the thick folds of his neck to the rolling skin around his ankles.

Pretty worried for a moment that if Brown wasn't intimidated by the gun that he could overpower him. He must outweigh Pretty by 200 pounds. He decided that if it came to it, he'd shoot first, damn the noise.

Pretty watched, keeping a smile on his face, as Brown set a glass down on the kitchen counter and wiped a hand on the blue and yellow patterned pajamas that were draped over his sizable frame and then opened the door.

"Can I help you?"

Pretty brought the gun up, stepped forward, and pressed it right up against Brown's fleshy breast.

There was no fight in him. He'd been successful and comfortable for too long. He took a stumbling step back and almost went down but grabbed the counter.

"Good, who is it?" a female voice called from upstairs.

"Tell her to come down. Tell her it's the police," Pretty said.

"Barb, can you come down here for a minute?"

"What?"

"Come downstairs."

They heard movement above their heads and then feet on

the stairs. Barbara Brown was as thin and lean as her husband was wide and stout. A bizarro version of Jack Sprat and his wife. She wore a pink-quilted housecoat, despite the heat, and white slippers. Her white hair was pinned back, and she had a pair of reading glasses on a chain looped around her neck.

She didn't see the gun at his side. She looked at Pretty and asked, "Who are you?"

He raised the gun and he saw her eyes open wide. "Do you want to tell her, Good, or should I?"

"How can I? I don't even know who you are!"

"For a long time, people said I looked like my sister, but I haven't heard that in a while. There are probably only a few people left with clear memories of her."

Goodwin Brown's face again assumed that expression of puzzled bewilderment and Pretty wondered if that was his default facial expression and, if so, how he got so far in life.

"You might not have met me, but you met Stephanie Arnsfeld and at one point you definitely met my sister." Pretty was happy to see Goodwin's face go slack and his shoulders slump.

"You."

"Time to pay your debt." Pretty placed the handcuffs on the table. "It's long overdue."

"Good? What's he talking about? Good? Good!"

CHAPTER FIFTY-TWO

Koenig had steered the Explorer through the last curve of 305, past the looming spire of St. Mary's church, when they saw the smoke. It was thick and dark, a twisting shadow twining its way into the twilight sky toward the black storm clouds above.

At the next intersection, a ladder truck and ambulance with full lights and sirens, coming from the opposite direction, slowed slightly, then turned right.

Max glanced at Koenig. "You think?"

"I don't have a good feeling." She turned and followed the emergency vehicles. "Call Roy, see what's up."

Max took out his phone. The chief answered and spoke before Max could say anything. He was driving and Max could hear the stress in his voice. "Fire at Goodwin Brown's house. A big one."

"Who's Goodwin Brown?"

"Retired car dealer. Owned a bunch of dealerships in the area. Was on the town council for 20 years."

"So, another rich guy."

"I guess. I gotta go." He disconnected.

"What's the deal?"

"Could be our guy. Goodwin Brown." While he had his phone out, he went to his email and quickly scanned the lists that Marline and Campbell had sent. "Wealthy. Had some juice. His name is on both lists I got from Marline and Campbell. Not sure about the guys from The Rink, but I wouldn't bet against it."

They followed the emergency vehicles to the correct street. The fire was loud and hot. Stepping out of the car, Max could feel the heat from half a block away. Neighbors were out on their lawns but most were keeping their distance. Max spotted Roy trying to direct traffic and set up a perimeter at the opposite end. It surprised Max not to see another deputy's car. The fire trucks, a second had joined the ladder truck, had pulled up directly opposite the burning house and the firefighters were hooking up hoses to the closest hydrants, but Max could tell they wouldn't be able to save the house. The flames had engulfed both floors and jumped to one of the big maples in the yard. Any fight would be about stopping the spread and saving the other houses on the block.

There was something else.

"Is that?" Max asked.

"Yeah, I think so."

When a human body burns, it has a very distinct smell, like gamy and greasy barbecue. "I've come across it when I was on patrol a few times. Not something you easily forget."

"Ah, God." Max felt his stomach knot, and he wished he'd skipped lunch like Koenig.

While the firefighters went about their business, they walked down the street and spoke with Roy.

"Where's your help?" Koenig asked.

"I called in Chravette and my brother. They're on their way. Stratton is on duty, but no one can get him on the radio."

More people were showing up to watch the spectacle, and it reminded Max of the first night at the Arnsfeld scene.

"Hey, buddy. Stay back," Roy shouted to one guy with a beer can in his hand who was wandering down the sidewalk, hypnotized by the conflagration.

"Jesus, it's like moths to a flame. You'd think these people had never seen a fire before."

"You mind if we talk to a few people? The neighbors? See if anyone saw anything?"

"You think this might be deliberate?"

"You will definitely find bodies in there—"

"Yeah, I can smell them."

"Given what else is going on, it would be a big coincidence."

Max took his phone out of his pocket and brought up the bowling team photo and held it out to Roy. "You recognize any of these people?"

Roy wiped the sweat from his eyes and took the phone. He squinted at it and then used his fingers to pinch and zoom. "That's definitely Harrow on the right. Not sure about the other guys. How old is this? Where you'd get it?"

"Got it from *The Chronicle's* morgue files. It's about 20 years old. The guy on the left is Hawkins."

"Really?" Roy adjusted the photo and looked again. "Okay, yeah. I can see that. He's about 20 pounds heavier and smiling, but I see it."

"We were wondering if one of the other two guys was Brown?"

Roy looked again but shook his head. "I don't know. I didn't know Brown very well. He was off the council by the time I got the job. I recognized him enough to nod and say hello, but that was it." He handed the phone back. "You think this guy is targeting a bowling team?"

"No, not necessarily, but we think he's targeting a group, and this is the first link we've found between two of the victims."

He emailed the photo to Koenig and they started canvassing the street. They avoided the lookie-loos that were congregating behind the barriers at the ends of the street and stuck to the residents and neighbors who were standing or milling about on their lawns.

Max hit on the third try. It was a man and his wife, both comfortably in their 60s. The man was wearing faded blue jeans and eating spaghetti from a bowl. The smell didn't seem to bother him. Maybe he didn't know what it was. His wife, small and plump, tutted around him like a mother bird, her hands never quite still.

Max explained who he was and what he wanted.

"Sure, we heard about you. The new guy helping the police." Max just nodded, no longer surprised by the breadth or width of the town's informal news network. Max held out his phone, but the man had a plate in one hand and a pasta-entwined fork in the other. "Shelly, can you take the phone?"

"Yes, yes," she said and hopped forward to take it. She stepped back and her husband looked over her shoulder at the same time.

"We're most interested in the two men in the middle."

The man squinted and Max had an idea there was probably a pair of neglected glasses in the house. "Can you make it a little bigger, Shel, zoom in on their faces?" She manipulated the phone with her fingers and then her husband nodded and pointed with his fork. "Yup, that's Good in the middle. The shorter one. He was crazy about bowling for a while there until the arthritis got too bad. He tried to get me to join up, but it's just not my thing. I liked the beer and social aspect, but the actual bowling I just never got the hang of."

"Any idea about the other man?"

The wife spoke up. Her voice was surprisingly rough and deep for her small stature. Maybe she'd been a heavy smoker in a past life. "I think that's Thomas Starling. I think he had boys the same age as Good. What do you think, Marty?"

"Could be. Yes, I could see that."

"Any idea where we could find him?"

"Sure, just across the road from St. Mary's."

"Marty!" His wife swatted at his arm and the remaining spaghetti sloshed to one side. "He passed six years ago. Pancreatic cancer."

"If you need more specifics," Marty chimed in, "Jerry would know. They were pretty good friends, if I recall."

"Sorry, Jerry?"

Shelly handed the phone back. "Sure, Jerry Sykes, runs The Rink." She nodded at the phone. "The other guy in the photo. Everyone knows Jerry. He's been around forever."

"And he was a bowling nut, too," Marty chimed in. "He might have been the captain of The Holy Rollers. He might have even had a stake in those lanes, come to think of it. He was always a good businessman."

Max felt his stomach knot even tighter. He'd only thought of Jerry as being in the background, an artifact of the photo, not part of it. He scanned the street but didn't see Koenig. Big fat drops of rain started to fall and hit the street with an audible splat. He started jogging as a crack of thunder split the air. Everyone had been so focused on the fire that they had missed the dangerous thunderheads creeping up on them.

Max had a feeling that was the whole point.

CHAPTER FIFTY-THREE

The rain pounded the windshield like machine-gun fire as Koenig drove as fast as she dared through the tangle of residential streets. The sudden deluge had doused people's curiosity and left them fleeing for cover. People ran into the street without looking and Koenig liberally used her horn along with her emergency lights as she tried to break free.

"Gonna have another murder if you don't slow down," Max said, gripping the overhead handle.

She growled something in response but kept her eyes on the road. The adrenaline had them both on edge. They were right behind Riehl now. They could feel it. And they were determined he wouldn't get another chance to leave a bloody message.

Koenig bottomed out the Explorer crossing Main Street and then goosed the accelerator again as they finally dropped the crowds and headed down toward the harbor. Thirty seconds later, she slammed on the brakes and the Explorer skidded to a stop in front of The Rink. Max opened the door, but she put a hand on his arm. "Glovebox."

He opened it and found a short stubby Taser made of heavy black plastic, plus a small slim can of pepper spray. "Better than nothing," Koenig said as she grabbed her service Glock from the storage compartment. "Same idea," she said, nodding at the Taser. "Just point and shoot."

He grabbed both, stuffing the pepper spray into his pocket, and got out of the car. They were both soaked in seconds.

The sign on the door was flipped to 'Closed.'

"Not good."

Max tried to look in the high casement window to the left of the door, but it was impenetrable with dust and years of grime. He strained to hear something, anything over the rain, but it was impossible. He pulled gently on the handle and felt it move slightly. Riehl hadn't thrown the deadbolt. He'd probably been in a rush or distracted. It was an old door with an old lock. It would keep out the curious or the drunks wandering by, but it wouldn't keep out Max.

He put his mouth next to Koenig's ear. "You have a credit card? I can pop the lock." She went back to the SUV and returned after a moment and handed him a Petro-Canada card. He slipped it in at an angle, wedging the corner of the card between the door and the strike plate, then straightened the card out so it was perpendicular to the lock. He then carefully slid the card in farther, hoping the sound of the rain was now enough to cover any noise he might be making. He wiggled and bent the card until he felt it compress the latch.

Koenig raised an eyebrow. He ignored her and pointed toward the end of the building and then at himself and mouthed "Side door. Two minutes." Koenig nodded. He jogged around the building and repeated the lock pick card process with the back door and slipped inside.

He was in the hallway near the bathrooms.

There were four people inside.

Three were standing near the bar. Jerry, Isaac, and Thorne.

One was bleeding on the floor.

Isaac held a gun, now pointed at Max. He'd shaved off the beard and wore a Leafs cap, T-shirt, and jeans.

"Was hoping for a few more minutes," Isaac said.

"Out of time, I'm afraid."

"One more body won't make much of a difference."

Koenig stepped in and Isaac swiveled the gun in her direction. "Whoa, right there is good."

He pulled Thorne back against his chest, putting the gun against Thorne's temple.

Jerry was behind the bar, but Max could see a thin line of blood running from his hairline down across his cheek before dripping onto the floor. His jaw was tight and his eyes were wide, but he didn't look scared. He looked like he had a plan and that worried Max. This wasn't a bar fight to break up.

Max took a moment to glance down at the body on the floor. The kid's eyes were closed and his chest was moving, but a pool of blood was spreading out from under him. He was still alive. For now.

"You okay, Thorne?" Max asked.

"I'm okay. We were just having a chat when you and the inspector arrived."

"We know about your sister, Isaac. We know about Steph's parties."

"You don't know anything."

"They'll finally be held responsible for what they did."

"Who? Who will be held responsible?"

"Jerry, for one."

"He's the only one left. I waited years, decades, and nothing happened. The only reason anyone is being held responsible is because of me. Me!"

"I can't make up for the past, but I can help now," Max

said. He could see Koenig slowly shifting to the side, trying to create an angle that wouldn't put more people in the crossfire.

"*The sluggard craves and gets nothing, but the desires of the diligent are fully satisfied,*" Isaac said.

"*Never avenge yourselves, but leave it to the wrath of God, for it is written, 'Vengeance is mine, I will repay, says the Lord.'*"

Isaac smiled at that, but it never reached his eyes which burned with bright insanity. "It figures the devil would send someone who could memorize verse but I've seen past that now. My faith is about more than certainty, scripture, or power or having something to prove. It's about trust. I am where I'm supposed to be. I'm doing what I'm supposed to do. He will guide my hand. I'm in the arms of the angels now."

"That's not the God I know."

"Then you'll soon lea—"

Music suddenly blasted out of the old jukebox at an ear-splitting volume.

Everyone froze and then the shooting started.

Max hit the ground next to the kid. "Koenig!" he shouted, but he could barely hear his own voice over the music and the gunfire. The smell of burnt sulfur and charcoal from the shots mixed with the sweat and beer that coated the rubber floor. He crawled to the end of the bar and peeked through the stool's legs. Koenig was writhing on the ground, hurt, but alive. He couldn't see around the other end to where Thorne and Isaac had been standing. He quickly put a hand to the kid's neck. Still alive. He stood slowly. They were gone. The door to the kitchen was swinging slowly. He needed to check on Koenig and Jerry, but he didn't want to get shot in the back either. He moved to the side door and opened it a crack just as a Prince Creek police cruiser flashed past and out onto the road.

He went back into the bar and ran to Koenig.

"Hurts," she whispered through her teeth.

"Where?"

"Fuckin' everywhere. I think my side."

He rolled her slightly and pulled back her jacket. Blood had soaked through her blouse. He peeled it up gently. She hissed. A two-inch chunk of flesh was missing just above her hip. It looked ugly and would leave a big scar but, if they could get the bleeding under control, it shouldn't be life-threatening.

"Stop whining. You just got grazed."

She lifted her head and tried to see. "Feels like I got stabbed with a rusty pitchfork." She let her head fall back and stared at the ceiling. "Never got shot before. Only got off one shot. A goddam reporter was in the way."

He took out his phone and got the ambulances and EMTs moving. Then he went back behind the bar. Jerry was on his back, half of his head was missing. A nicked-up baseball bat lay next to his body. That had been Jerry's big plan? Hit the music and then take a swing?

Max reached over and hit the switch under the bar that turned off the jukebox, then he grabbed a handful of clean bar towels and went back to Koenig.

She was still looking up at the ceiling. "Suit is ruined. Should have changed clothes before we came inside." Her eyes were shiny. He didn't like that look. She was going into shock.

The puddle of blood was growing. He pushed the towels against the wound and then moved her hand over them.

"You need to keep the pressure on. The ambulance is on its way."

But her hand slipped off. He stripped off his belt and looped it quickly around her waist along with a wad of towels and then pulled it tight. She blinked up at him. Her eyes looked a little clearer for the moment. She pushed the car keys and her gun toward him. "Go."

CHAPTER FIFTY-FOUR

What the hell had happened? He'd been talking to Lindell, thinking about who to shoot first and had decided on Jerry, he was the mission, if he didn't kill Jerry it was all for naught, and then his head had exploded, punched by a sonic boom.

He'd flinched and then started pulling the trigger. He'd been right. Operating a gun was no more difficult than driving a car. Push the pedal and go. Point the gun and kill. By luck or skill or divine intervention, he'd hit that fucking, miserable bastard right above the eye and watched him fall straight into hell.

Then he'd felt an angry bee buzz past his ear. That bitch inspector was trying to kill him! And she'd come damn close. Too close. After that, he just wanted to escape. Jerry was dead. Mission accomplished.

He tightened his grip on Thorne, who was writhing and squirming, and shot at the cop. She dove behind some tables. He wasn't sure if he hit her or not. Didn't matter. Not right now. Maybe he'd come back for her later, but right now he needed to get out. He hit Thorne in the back of the head with the butt of the gun to get him under control. Maybe too hard. The old man sagged but stayed on his feet.

Lindell was somewhere near the side door and the bitch cop had the front covered, so he backed up with Thorne into the kitchen and then pushed the older man past the refrigerator and flattop and out the service door into the parking lot. He used the handcuffs he'd intended to use on Jerry; he had a pang of regret that he wouldn't be able to make the man suffer more on this earth, eternal damnation would have to do, and locked Thorne's hands behind his back and pushed him into the cruiser's trunk.

Now he was driving away through the slanting rain. Running with no destination in mind and trying to keep the unfamiliar lump of panic in his chest from bubbling up. Panic was not part of the plan. His hands were slick on the wheel. He gripped it tighter and just managed to keep the car on the road. Hold on. A thump came from somewhere in the back. He needed to get rid of the car. And Thorne. Almost done.

Max jumped in the Explorer, started the engine and ... sat there. The streets were empty. The rainwater sluiced down the hill, overcoming the sewers. And it was still coming down. Big, old maples and oaks bowed in the wind.

Where would he go? Max wondered. He only had to think for a moment, then threw the Explorer into drive and took off. Only one place he could think of. If he was wrong, Thorne was likely dead. Even if Max was right, they both might wind up dead.

Isaac took the turns without thinking. It felt like he was almost in a trance. He turned on the radio at one point. He thought maybe he could listen to the cops and figure out what they were up to, hide that way, but it was all gibberish and he quickly turned the radio back off. He trusted the voice in his head more. He just had to listen.

He kept driving. Dirt, mud, trees all passed in a flash. If it hadn't been for his buggy blocking the road, he might have driven straight into the pond. Maybe that was the way to go, but he didn't have the guts. Not right now. He hit the brakes and the cruiser slewed to a stop.

Max hadn't been wrong. He could see the fresh tire tracks sliding across the mud-slicked Sinclair Road. He found the police car by the little canoe launch next to an Amish buggy. The driver's door was open, along with the trunk.

It was dark. The rain and clouds blotted out any moonlight. Max got out slowly and stayed crouched by the steel and aluminum bulk of the Explorer. He was aware of the encroaching woods and the fact that Riehl still had a gun. There were a lot of places to lie in wait and ambush someone.

He heard snapping twigs to his right. Whatever was coming was big. He leveled his gun over the roof and just avoided shooting the horse. It must belong to the buggy. The animal paused at the edge of the clearing, appeared to give him a disapproving look, then continued down to the water and took a long slurping drink.

Isaac pushed Thorne ahead of him and then stumbled on a root, went to a knee, and almost lost the gun. Thorne didn't appear to notice. The man was in his own trance. Riehl forced himself to slow down. He stood, got himself under control, and kept walking.

He'd almost gotten away clean. He'd been so close. He'd

taken care of Brown easily enough. His fat carcass was slowly roasting in hell now. He wasn't sure where the wife had ended up and he didn't care. Collateral damage.

So close. If only Lindell and that cop had been five minutes later, he would have been gone. Maybe he should have let Thorne go, but he'd spotted the old man leaving as he'd walked up and it seemed like providence. He knew who he was. The old bastard had interviewed Jonah and him once for a story about Amish woodworking. And now God had put him right there in his path. How could he refuse? He'd forced him back inside the bar. If things went sideways with Jerry, at least he could tell the reporter the full story. It had seemed like a good backup plan. Now he wasn't so sure. But it provided him a hostage and maybe a way out. He had to think. God worked in mysterious ways.

He heard an engine approaching. He glanced back across the pond and could see headlights through the trees.

So dark. Max could barely see his hands. But that went both ways, he reminded himself. Harder to spot him, too. He stepped away from the car. He remembered the thin path around the pond. He and Koenig had gone right last time. It was a little wider, appeared a little more used. He guessed Riehl would go that way. He went left, down to the water, then crept along the edge until he found the thin path. He took his time. His eyes slowly adjusted to the deep blackness. The rain downshifted to a steady drizzle. There was a crack of thunder, but the storm had moved out over the Strait.

He slipped inside the old changing cabin's front door and wiped the water from his face. He could see the two men standing out on the old dock. It sounded like Riehl was talking. He inched forward and his foot kicked a crumpled beer can. It sounded as loud as the jukebox had in The Rink.

"No need to be shy, Lindell. Come on out and join us. The water's nice." Riehl laughed, a high-pitched giggle that made Max think he might be too far gone.

He stepped carefully onto the dock. The rotting structure swayed and groaned under the three men's combined weight. Riehl was 15 feet away. He could just make out his face over Thorne's shoulder.

"Toss the gun in the lake."

Max hesitated. Riehl ground his gun into Thorne's temple. Thorne grimaced and instinctively raised his arms.

"Okay, okay." Max tossed the gun into the water.

"That's better. I was just telling Thorne here that this is where they held the parties. Some of them, at least. They didn't have to go far to find their depravity. Just down the road from town."

"Who was AB?" Max asked.

"You found that, huh? Truth is, I don't know. We'll never know. We never got to meet him or her. AB. A baby. Best I could do."

"Your sister was pregnant." Max thought about Labat and the dolls that haunted him.

"Yes."

"And they killed her."

"Yes. She was naïve enough to get herself involved with Steph and the parties, but she would have never given up or gotten rid of a child. So, they got rid of her instead."

"Who?"

"Does it matter? All of them. They all covered it up. They were all guilty."

"I'm sorry."

"Far too late and, if you were actually sorry, you wouldn't be here."

Riehl moved the gun from Thorne to Max. Max felt the

black eye of the barrel push into his chest like a physical pressure.

Then Thorne moved his hands and Riehl screamed. Thorne dove sideways into the water. Max pulled the Taser from his pocket, took three steps, felt himself start to fall as the dock broke under his feet, and pulled the trigger. The prongs hit Riehl in the chest and he screamed louder, a keening wail, as all his muscles contracted. He took a convulsive step backward and fell off the dock. The Taser was yanked out of Max's hand.

Thorne surfaced ten feet away, eyes wide and arms flailing. He went under again. Max hung from the dock up to his waist. He pulled himself free from the broken wood and then jumped back in. The water was cold and clotted with weeds and plants. He started swimming toward where he'd seen Thorne go under. His friend surfaced again, sputtering, and started to slip back under. Max wasn't sure there would be another chance. He stroked hard and grabbed him by the back of the shirt. Thorne swung an elbow and clipped Max on the side of the head. Max held on and flipped him over. "Stop fighting, you bastard. It's me, Max." He took a few strokes toward the edge of the pond and then his hands scraped the bottom. He stood up. The water rose to his waist. He pulled Thorne to his feet.

"You okay?"

"No. Not even close. Where is he?"

They both turned and looked back at the dock.

"I don't know. I hit him with a police Taser and he went into the water."

"Electrocuted?"

"No, I don't think so. They don't work that way. What did you do? Why did he scream?"

Thorne managed a grim smile. "Stabbed him in the face

with my pencil." They were both silent after that, studying the water. It remained undisturbed other than the soft whisper of the rain.

"He could still be out there."

CHAPTER FIFTY-FIVE

Riehl was out there. It took another day, but they found him. Roy had to call in divers. Norris Pond formed on a glacial shelf that dropped off quickly from the marshy shore. It was 40 feet deep in the middle and teeming with hornwort, water lilies, and other underwater plant growth.

Isaac Riehl's body wasn't the only one they found. The divers brought up a set of bones. It would take time for an official identification, but a preliminary examination showed the remains were from a teenage female. Max had little doubt that the eventual identification would show Isaac, his sister Leah, and his unborn niece or nephew had all died in the same pond.

Roy put the autopsy report down. "Redd says there was water in his lungs but that Riehl's heart also showed some abnormalities. He may have suffered from something called Brugada syndrome, a genetic disorder where the electrical activity within the heart is abnormal. The Taser may have amplified that and sent him into a cardiac event in the water."

Max remained silent at this piece of news, and Roy may have taken the silence as guilt or worry.

"Even if you had pulled him out almost immediately, he might not have survived."

Max wasn't feeling guilty about his role in Riehl's death. Riehl had ended up where he deserved, and Max was sure it wasn't with God in heaven. If Riehl had slipped away, Max was sure he would have killed again. Max did regret not being able to ask Riehl one last question.

Roy was still talking. "You'll have to complete a formal statement and go over some paperwork with the town's attorneys, but I've talked to the mayor, finally a call I was happy to make, last night and we're all on the same side. It might take a couple weeks of red tape, but nothing is going to stick to you."

Max didn't know if Isaac Riehl would be another of his ghosts, but he didn't doubt Roy about the politics. He stood. "I'd hand in my badge and gun, but I never had one to begin with."

He stuck out his hand. They shook across the desk, and then Roy surprised him. "Any chance I could talk you into sticking around? I'm down a man and you make a pretty good detective. That list idea was unorthodox, but it worked."

Stratton's body had been recovered the next morning. Max didn't know if the lists would have spared Stratton's life, but he thought they might have saved the Browns or Jerry if they'd started earlier. Each man was on all the lists.

"I'm not sure there's enough crime to keep me busy."

"You'd be surprised."

He moved toward the door. "I think it's time your brother and I got back on the water."

"You lobstermen are all stubbornly the same. I know where to find you at least."

· · ·

He sat on his beach chair, closed the slim book, and then tossed it on Mose's chair. "You can take your book back."

Mose looked up from the engine block. "What's that?"

"I said, you can take your directory back."

"Find what you wanted?"

"Not exactly."

He watched his friend work on the dilapidated truck. Would it ever run again? Or was that beside the point? Was putting in the effort what mattered?

"How are you feeling?" Mose asked a few minutes later.

"Getting better." And that was true. A couple more full nights of sleep and he would be back to normal. The bruises across his back and neck looked horrible, a dizzying array of purple and yellow, but they didn't hurt much anymore, just a dull ache when he thought about it. His wrist was stiff and sore and itched like hell, but he could move all his fingers. "Beer is helping."

"It always does."

"Is Riehl's family coming back for the bodies?"

"Yes, that's my understanding."

"Why did they leave in the first place?"

"I didn't live here then, but I doubt it's a simple answer. Everyone deals with grief in their own way."

Max knew that was true and was in no position to judge. He drank more beer instead.

"You want to do the honors?"

Max glanced over. "What do you mean?"

Mose dangled a key from one finger. "Technically, I'm not supposed to start it."

"But you can work on it?"

"It's a gray area."

"That's what makes life interesting." He stood and walked over to his friend. "Is it really going to start?"

"Let's find out."

. . .

Two days later, Max was indeed feeling better. The sun was back, but the kiln-like humidity of the past week was gone. Summers were late and brief on the island. He'd gone for a slow run, more of a walking jog really, his lungs burned and his muscles ached but in a pleasant way. If Roy thought fishermen were stubborn, he should be thankful his brother wasn't also a runner.

After he showered and changed, he stopped by Mrs. Johnson's trailer and said hello. Helping to catch a deranged killer and solve an old mystery appeared to have some side benefits. She was still prickly, but Max knew she was just keeping up appearances. Everyone has a part to play in a small town.

Charlie's shop wasn't open yet and there were no lights on in the apartment above. He was a night owl. No matter, he'd see him tonight. As he crossed the street toward The Sugar Maple, he spotted Nik Labat as he turned the corner toward the docks. They never found out where he went but Max was glad Riehl hadn't either. No one was interested in punishing Labat. He did enough of that on his own. People had different feelings about Goulart, but she was stonewalling with Clarkson and, with everyone else involved dead, any case against her was likely dead as well.

It wasn't Max's problem anymore.

The Maple was bustling and smelled like sugar, butter, and dark coffee.

"Nice to see you up and about. I was starting to think you didn't like the muffins after all," Ellie said with a smile.

"Nothing could be further from the truth. I'll take two, actually." He glanced down at the case. "One blueberry and one sour cherry chocolate. And a large coffee."

"That's more like it. Coming right up."

"What's the Greek chorus saying?"

"I think most people are just trying to wrap their heads around it still," she said and handed over the bag and coffee. "Going to take some time."

"Death always leaves a shadow."

He walked over to *The Chronicle's* office. Thorne poked his head out of the first-floor kitchen. "Hey. One second." He disappeared again and Max heard the hiss of the Keurig one-cup machine kick into gear. Max went around the counter and sat at the desk with his favorite Olympic mug. He was two bites into the sour cherry muffin when Thorne came out and took the opposite desk.

"What's up?" Thorne asked. "How're you feeling?"

"I'm doing all right. Got a run in this morning."

"Ugh." Thorne grimaced. "Running. Probably did more harm than good."

"How about you?"

"Not sleeping great, but the doc gave me some pills. He thinks it will fade. If it doesn't ... I'll figure it out."

"Don't let it get on top of you. Sometimes just telling the story to someone else is enough. Sort of like bleeding the pressure off an old radiator."

"I'm the old radiator in this analogy?"

"Goes without saying."

They sipped their coffees.

"The kid going to be okay?" Max asked.

"Yeah, last I heard. Going to have a long road of rehab, but better than the alternative."

"Any idea what will happen to The Rink?" Max asked.

"Too early to tell. Jerry didn't have any kids. Maybe they'll dig up a distant relative. Redd talked about pooling our money and buying it."

"Not a terrible idea."

"If I had any money."

"How much did you lose with Arnsfeld?"

Thorne tried on a confused look, but it was forced. "What do you mean?"

"It's the only reason I can figure you sent me that note." Max reached out and tapped the spacebar on the old Olivetti typewriter.

Thorne's shoulders slumped. "Enough that I'm not going to be buying a bar, even a podunk affair like The Rink, and retiring soon. I thought if there was a chance that Arnsfeld had involved himself or the Association in a crime that it might open the door back up for a civil suit or past creditors to recoup some of the missing money. When you and Koenig started looking at Stephanie, I thought maybe nudging you back in the other direction might ..." Thorne shrugged and looked embarrassed, but not exactly apologetic. "Everyone in town got screwed. That money is out there somewhere."

CHAPTER FIFTY-SIX

His last stop was the small Prince Creek hospital. Max nodded at the woman at the reception desk and then again at the charge nurse farther down the hall.

"All good, Mary?" Max asked.

"As good as she will get staying here."

"Moving day, huh?"

She glanced at the wall. "Doc should be around to discharge her in an hour or so."

Koenig had a single room at the end of the hall. He knocked softly.

"Come in."

He went in, closing the door behind him.

She was in bed, in a sitting position with a blanket pulled up to her waist, watching a TV mounted in the corner. She still looked pale, her cheeks sunken, but the spark was back in her eyes. That was an improvement over the blissed-out stares from the IV drips of the first few days.

She hit the remote to turn off the television. "Less than a

week and not even a followup mention. We are old news, partner."

"Sort of the way I prefer it."

"Yeah, me too, I guess."

"They got you off the hard stuff, I see."

"Yeah, it was time to kick the habit."

"Here." He held out the muffin bag. "Might be harder to kick this habit. Ellie was afraid you might be getting too skinny."

The way she ate the muffin was the surest sign yet that she was getting better.

Max tried to find a more comfortable position in the hospital chair. He'd concluded over the last few days that comfort had not been a consideration in their design. He kept trying anyway.

"How are you feeling about all this?" Koenig asked. They hadn't talked about it while she was on the drugs. They'd mostly watched TV and made stupid jokes.

"Feel fine. I do feel bad about Topher and Brown's wife. And what happened to Thorne and the kid. Going to be awhile before they're all right. If they're ever all right again. You?"

"I'm just thankful it's over and I'm still here."

"Yeah," he said.

"You sure you're okay? You seem ... distracted."

"There's one thing I can't figure out in this whole mess."

"What's that?"

"They had all kept it a secret for so long it was about to die out. Literally. Most of the men would have been dead on their own in another five years or so. How did Riehl get onto Steph Arnsfeld after so long? Why did Riehl wait so long? Why now? It doesn't make sense."

"Who knows? No case ties off every lose end. There will always be questions."

Max nodded but continued. "Riehl had no real means of investigating himself. He was too young to remember much when it happened. He would have needed help. Or a little push. Had to be someone with a hard grudge against Arnsfeld."

He paused. She just stared at him.

He kept going. "When people start over, they will often change their last names but keep their first names or something close to it. Trust me, I have some experience."

"It was the book right? The directory?"

"It was a few things over the last week, but Imogen is not a common name. Not by a long shot."

"My mother's curse."

"Did you leave the community because of what happened to Leah?"

"Yes and no." She looked out the window. "It was the final straw. My mother was not Amish. She gave it a real honest effort but, if you are not brought up in that culture, it's really difficult to live like that when you know what else is out there. So we left. We were shunned but we survived.

"I was on the periphery. I was friends with Leah but a couple years older. Too old for Stephanie's purposes, but I caught wind of some of it. It was awful and infuriating and nauseating. After we moved, the farther away I got, the more insane it all felt. I kept waiting for it to fall apart. For someone to be held responsible. I checked the news all the time, but nothing happened. The community covered it up. The town covered it up. They were getting away with it. Leah had ceased to exist."

"Why not get the RCMP to do an official investigation?"

"An investigation of what? There was no body. No report. No evidence of a crime. There was no official way to do anything."

"So you pointed Isaac Riehl toward Hawkins and Stephanie."

"For a long time, I didn't know what to do. But recently it felt like time was running out and I felt like I owed it to her to try. Hawkins was the one name I had from Leah. I thought if I could get Isaac Riehl to kick up a fuss then something might happen. Maybe he could get Roy to look into it. I hadn't been back since we left. I didn't know about the tensions between the community and the police. I definitely did not know Riehl was crazy. He was a 10-year-old kid when I left."

"But you let the genie out of the bottle. You should have said something."

"Like what? I didn't know the other men involved."

"You knew it was Riehl. Koenig, you sorta killed Topher Arnsfeld and Barbara Brown."

"Bullshit. Steph, Jerry, Goodwin, Collum, and Colby killed them. They spent years, and who knows how many dollars, covering up the murder of Leah and her baby. Isaac Riehl was the result. Reap what you sow."

"Jesus."

"One of the few people not involved."

They each lapsed into silence after that.

"What are you going to do, partner?" she finally asked.

"I'm not a cop as of this morning. Even if I was, I'm not sure I could prove you committed a crime. I don't think it was right but there's not much I can do about it."

Max thought the town might be poisoned. Thorne trying to get his money. Koenig trying to get her revenge. The police department's xenophobia. The Amish turning their backs on their own. Prince Creek had become a salted field.

She reached out a hand, but he shifted away.

Maybe it was time to move on.

Get more free books, crime fiction news and other exclusive material.

I'm a crime fiction fan. I love reading it. I love writing it. And I love connecting with other fans about it. Talking with readers is one of the best things about writing.

Once a month I email a newsletter with crime fiction news, what I've been reading, special offers, and other bits of news on me and my writing. There might also be the occasional story or picture about my dog, Dashiell Hammett.

If you sign up for the mailing list I'll send you some free stuff:

1. A copy of the Max Strong prequel novella SLEEPING DOGS.
2. A copy of the short story collection OCTOBER DAYS, which includes the award-nominated short HOW TO BUY A SHOVEL.

You can get both books, **for free**, by signing up at mikedonohuebooks.com/starterlibrary/

Did you enjoy this book? You can make a big difference.

Reviews are the *most* powerful tools that I have as an indie author to bring attention to my books. Honest reviews of my books help bring them to the attention of other readers.

If you've enjoyed this book, I would be very grateful if you could spend a few minutes leaving a review on the book's product page. It can be as short as you like.

Each review really makes a difference.

Thank you very much.

ABOUT THE AUTHOR

Mike Donohue lives with his wife and family outside Boston. He doesn't think reading during meals is particularly rude. Quite the opposite.

You can find him online at mikedonohuebooks.com.